Grimmbell
Riders of the Black Spirit Horses

R. R. Duneman

ISBN: 979-8-9915120-1-5 (Paperback)
ISBN: 979-8-9915120-0-8 (eBook)

Table of Contents

Chapter 1: The Penetrator

Ella watched from her garden as a large dark figure dismounted from the sunken-backed, worn-out horse, surreptitiously moving toward the front door of her herbal hut.

She entered the back door of the apothecary shop, resting her waistline against the counter as the dark form now moved itself into a new position, standing inside the frame of the front door.

I have a bad feeling about this one.

Leaning over so as not to hit the top of the doorframe, the figure finally made its way inside, its ominous black trench coat concealing all of its form other than a pair of boots and a large-brimmed hat.

That dark form could be a man of some kind, but I'm not sure. And much larger than any person, isn't he? Can't see any facial features to distinguish yet, Ella thought.

'He' walked up to the counter, and Ella stepped back. Sure enough, the figure was a huge man, broad-framed, towering over her.

"What can I help you with?" she asked.

The figure said nothing at first, pulling the brim of his hat down. "I'm in need of a blood brick and possibly some earther food balls."

Ella bit her lip hard.

Did he really ask for a blood brick? Why would this thing think I have a blood brick here? Blood bricks are super rare and safely stored and guarded inside the walls of Grimmbell Cemetery.

"I do have earther food balls if those might interest you, but they're still curing down in the root cellar," she said, shaking her head. "As for blood bricks; well, I don't have any of them here. As you likely know, they're not kept—"

She was about to say they were not kept here. But he didn't allow her to finish, appearing in a rush. "How long have the food balls been aging?"

"Um. The ones I have, they've been curing for at least twenty-six to thirty months."

The brim of the black hat nodded. "That's a decent length of time. For me, it would have to be at least two years, so that sounds adequate."

"You do realize that the earther food ball is powerful in its own way, right?"

The figure nodded but didn't look up. "I have been told that you can survive for years with one and even though I don't doubt it, I have never tried."

"Well, yes you can. An earther food ball can provide an individual with lifesaving nutrients lasting up to twenty years. Whichever way you look at it, it's an incredible food source."

"That's amazing. What was the natural age of the earther before it died?"

"This earther cured to the age of 210 years."

"That sounds delicious."

"Well indeed. It's the highest quality, but I must warn you not everyone has a taste for it. When you age an earther so long, it takes on a flavor all its own. I can't really describe it. Some like it, some not."

"Have you tested the product?" said the dark figure.

"You're not from these parts, are you?"

The figure bobbed his head back and forth. "Sort of."

"Yes," said Ella with a visible cringe. "I have tasted the product. And I consider it the finest in all the valley because I make it here myself with these very hands." Ella raised her hands to the figure.

"That's in accord with the information I received."

"What kind of information did you receive, exactly?"

Turning his head, he poked at a bag on a nearby shelf. "That you make *good stuff*."

"Thank you, I guess I do," said Ella. "The earther ball growth chart, if you don't know, tests the quality of an earther food ball according to how many feet a plant will grow in roughly eight hours. My product achieves an average of three feet five inches in just a little over two hours. And as I say, that's merely the average achieved across a large number of balls, so I also produce individuals that far outstrip this. Thus, I can safely proclaim mine to be the best. That may sound boastful, but I assure you, ask anyone who has used them, and they will say—"

"Right." He cut her off again, something that appeared to be a habit. "Could I examine the product?"

"Yes, you can." Ella retrieved the plant from the back room, setting it on the counter. By now, she had seen that the less she talked and the more she demonstrated, the happier the visitor would be.

"This product here and the cured earther food ball I have down in the root cellar grew three feet ten inches in just a little over one hour. Sixty-eight minutes to be exact. As I said, they differ."

The stranger tilted his head back and sniffed the air. "That would make the food ball a quality product. In that case, I would like to purchase twenty food balls."

"Twenty food balls? I'm sorry, but I don't have that many. And the fact is that I can sell only a certain quantity each year."

The visitor huffed and puffed as if most displeased and vexed. As if she had said something quite preposterous. "Very well. Then how much to buy your store? Maybe I could make my own."

"It's not for sale. The—the store. It's not on the market."

"I see, but everything has a price you know. How much for a blood brick? I can smell the aroma of one. I definitely need one of those." The figure continued inhaling deeply.

"I don't have the privilege of owning a blood brick, or even being able to touch one. Wait here, please. I will get you a sample of the earther food ball to taste."

The visitor exhaled hard. "And what would the point of that be? Since you will not sell me the store and cannot sell me twenty earther food balls, then there would seem to be little point in sampling one. Or do you have more information to which I am not yet privy?"

"I—I just thought if you tasted one, it may convince you to buy the few earther food balls I do have available for you, and to return next year for a fresh supply. In fact, if you order now, perhaps I could set some aside."

The visitor continued sniffing the air. "That would be delightful. As are you."

Ella pushed through the curtain entering the back room. There, she kneeled, unlocking a half door used for fires and emergency exits if needed.

This one is definitely stranger than any customer I have had in the past.

And I still don't know if he or it has any eyes or even a face. Could be a faceless daytime spirit troll.

They have been known to wander out of Grimmbell Cemetery, but not this size and not so black in color.

Ella returned with a pie-sized piece of the earther food ball, setting it on the counter. "Check this out. It's very good."

"Don't mind if I do." The stranger slammed his face on top of the counter, devouring the sample in one bite. "This is excellent! How much did you say for the store?"

Now, it was Ella's turn to heave an exasperated sigh.

"It's not for sale. Why do you keep asking? Look, I'm rather busy, so I think you should leave. We clearly are unable to strike any sort of a deal."

"I would be willing to give you a generous price." He now began squirming and swinging his hips, howling like a wolf, digging his hands deep inside his trench coat. A horrifying sight!

Ella stepped back, but not too far to grip the dagger from under the counter, concealing it behind her back. "I don't own the store. I can't sell it to you! Please, just go!"

The dark figure piled a handful of coins on the counter. "Is this enough?"

With her free hand, Ella sifted through the pile of coins, slipping one upward into her cuff and then down into her apron pocket. "These coins can't be for real. Where did you get these?"

"Why, what's wrong with them?"

"There's nothing wrong with them," said Ella pushing the coins away. "It's just…"

"It's just what?" said the stranger, shrugging.

"Those particular coins are extremely hard to get."

"As are your earther food balls," he remonstrated. "Yet I do not recall saying to you that your food balls cannot be real, simply as they are in short supply. Did I say that?"

That was a fair argument. Or an unfair one. She was unsure.

Ella had insufficient time to think it all through and come up with a response. "No," she answered. "You did not say that. I apologize. You are correct," she said, unwilling to argue.

The stranger seemed satisfied.

"I won the coins in a *deal of the death* card game. Not a problem, right?"

"These coins are life coins though! How could you have won them in a card game?"

"What do you know about life coins?" asked the stranger.

"Look here," said Ella. Finally, her patience had snapped. And now, if she had to, she *was* willing to argue because this shady character was proving obnoxious and argumentative himself.

"I know that a life coin is presented to each individual upon being born or created inside the Darkan Territory. In some ways, it can be used for the identification of species. But not always. And I know that life coins have been called dimensional coins, along with the fact that they can only be given away willingly to another by the owner of the coin. And in the case of sudden death, then you must follow through the very detailed steps of a procedure called the Exit of the Unknown Soul."

Grabbing the coins, the dark stranger pushed against the counter. "Who owns your store? I demand to know!"

Ella glared back at the unknown figure.

"Kula. *Queen* Kula. Queen of the Dragoons. You need to talk to her."

"Dragoons? You mean dragons, surely."

"No. I mean dragoons," insisted Ella. "Kula and her clan of dragoons are different than your ordinary dragons. For one thing, they're a whole twenty-five percent bigger—like, massive—with special sea battle-hardened turtle shell armor and an internal napalm combustion and holding chamber.

"Then, they also have interchangeable wings with a

precision cut two-track rail system allowing the wings to fold down, adjust for variable elevations. They can even lay them flat for optimum battle tactics and precise dive-bombing maneuverability. Quite a nifty toolkit, as you can imagine."

"Quite, and I…"

The stranger's observation was cut off; Ella's description still wasn't finished. She sucked in a humongous breath, ready to carry on.

The stranger stared, wide eyed. Maybe slightly irritated. Or more than slightly.

"Custom eye shield protection with enhanced low light silhouette tracking. And let's not forget about the enlarged eight-chambered double heart-pumping system, enabling a mix of two types of blood. One being of dragoon blood with a high intensity for quick clotting if needed, and then there's the inherited incarnation blood, the supply that is alive inside the veins of the dragoon. These blood fluids, due to the two hearts, can pump blood forward or backwards at a rate of twenty-one barrels per minute."

"Is that it?" asked the stranger. Ella pondered for a moment.

"Yes, that's it," she said. Then, "Ah! No. I forgot something. Did I mention they can sing?" The stranger huffed an impatient sigh.

"I never even realized all that about Kula and her… her, umm, *dragoons*. Kula never told me this."

"You know the Queen?" Ella inquired.

"Our paths could have crossed. Anyway, what about that blood brick I asked you about?"

"I don't have any blood bricks. I also told you that," remonstrated Ella.

The stranger began tapping a coin hard on the counter.

"You are lying. I can smell the aroma of a blood brick. And I smell one here, close to this store."

"Okay, Mr. No-Face Piece of Shit, you can buy an earther food ball, then you need to leave." The *no-face* stranger reached across the counter, grabbing Ella by her hair.

Ella cried out in pain. "What are you doing? Release

me now." Striking at his hands, trying to pull herself free, Ella added, "You will answer for this!"

"Where is the blood brick?"

"I do not have any blood bricks!"

The stranger leaped over the counter, pulling Ella to the ground.

"Get off of me," Ella shouted, spitting in the intruder's face. "You piece of garbage. I knew you were trouble the first time I saw you."

Tipping his hat back, the dark creature cried out, "I am nothing you have ever seen before! I am Arune, the Penetrator of Darkness!"

"I don't know what a Penetrator is, but whatever it might be, you're still an asshole." The Penetrator grunted, driving Ella's cheek into the dirt floor.

Ella pushed herself up on one elbow. "Kula is going to kill you for this."

The Penetrator ripped off a chunk of skirt, exposing Ella's underwear, stuffing the torn garment into Ella's mouth. "Now I don't have to listen to you cry in pain when I filter myself into you with the power of the blood brick."

Ella spit the piece of clothing out and screamed, "Kula! Help me!"

"She is not going to hear you. *Nobody* will hear you. Now where's the blood brick?" Ella caught a tiny glimpse of orange hair out the corner of her eye.

What in hell's name is that? This is only getting worse.

Suddenly arching his spine, and grabbing for the back of his neck, the Penetrator cried out, "Son of a bitch!"

Brown gooey liquid was dripping from around his neck onto Ella's chest. Something had cut the Dark Penetrator deep.

The unknown stranger released the iron grip on Ella long enough for her to kick the stranger in the chest and crawl behind the nearby food storage barrels.

"You're not going anywhere, Kula girl. I'm not through with you yet."

Ella scanned the room, looking for the best possible path to the escape door. That's when she saw a smaller figure with partial orange and gray fur lurking behind the gallon jars of dried spider legs.

The creature commenced tapping loudly on the jar lids.

I can't believe this! That looks like Blackjack, the royal magicjack messenger for Queen Kula. And it has metal claws. Wow! What is it doing in my store?

Ella bobbed her head around to get a better look at this furry creature. Blackjack continued tapping on the jar lids, *ping, ping, ping,* as if daring the Penetrator to come his way.

Ella got a full view of Blackjack.

I can't quite believe it, but it fits the description of the Rarebrook Blackjack. Kula's messenger and bodyguard.

Four colors covered its body in the arrangement of a calico cat, orange, black, gray, and white. But this was no cat. It resembled more a muscular jackrabbit weighing close to ninety pounds, with vicious titanium claws. It was four feet high with blue-gray eyes that seemed to slice through steel with a glance.

Ella caught movement from the Penetrator as it shook off the painful cut and advanced toward her. "Not this time." She bolted through the curtain doorway, ripping it down as she made her escape through the half door, locking it behind her. She looked left and right.

Where to hide? Where to hide?

Her eyes caught the foot trail leading up to the nearby butte where the prepping center for the reincarnation of the earther food ball was shaped.

Wrapping the curtain around her, she ran up the trail, retreating behind one of the many large, petrified rocks circling the reincarnation cemetery.

I don't think that entity can enter here. At least, I hope not.

Chapter 2: Broken Circle Axe Symbol

From the petrified rocks, Ella could see the front and the back of her medicine shack, waiting in anticipation for this thing called the Penetrator to come out of one of the doors.

Maybe I should start running now and hide higher up in the hills?

Ella heard a howl and a huge crash inside the store.

Who's winning the battle inside my house? That sounded like someone is hurt.

Abruptly, the wooden wall of the store facing Ella cracked open with another wolf-type yowl.

I think I need to make a run for it. I could hide in one of the tombs in the cemetery.

Suddenly, the back door tore from its doorframe, sailing into the air and crashing to the ground. The Penetrator exited the doorway with the furry creature clutched in its hand, dangling by the ears.

"Dammit! The dark figure has transformed, and now, it has red glowing eyes and human-looking hands. I didn't want this to happen. That thing can't defeat a Blackjack, can it?" Ella mumbled to herself, searching for a rock or something big enough to throw at the Penetrator. Then she noticed she still had the dagger in her hand from using it to cut the curtain into a makeshift dress. She peeked over the rock, watching the Penetrator round the corner of the shop. *I'm getting out of here.*

"I'm coming for you next, Kula girl," the figure shouted, pointing up at the rock orchard. Before bolting, Ella noticed Blackjack smile and blow her a kiss.

"Really? That crazy-eyed magicjack blew me a kiss. Where did that come from? What the hell is he thinking?"

She watched Blackjack spin his body 180 degrees, cutting the Penetrator's arm off at the elbow with one quick swipe of his orange-colored titanium claws. Kneeling, the Penetrator howled, trying to pick up the severed dark body part.

Blackjack sprinted up the hill, before stopping in front of Ella. "Are you okay?"

"You can talk?" asked Ella.

"Last time I checked," Blackjack answered, tilting his head. "Yes, I can talk."

"Your fur… it's so sleek and shiny."

"Why, thank you. I use Prediction Number Five."

"What?"

"Never mind. Can you run?"

"Yes, I can run. Wait a minute, look over there," said Ella, pointing. "Blue sage smoke. It's rising up into the sky really fast."

"It's supposed to," said Blackjack. "You started the fire?"

"I had it set to go off at a particular time."

"Then you obviously know that's the emergency signal for Kula, Queen of the Dragoons."

"I certainly do."

"Oh, my God," said Ella. "Look at me. I'm wrapped in a curtain. I can't be seen like this in front of the queen."

"I wouldn't worry about that right now."

"Easy for you to say. Your hair is shiny like gold."

"Ella," said Blackjack. "Your tall, dark, and handsome creature is coming up the hill rather quickly."

"Oh shit! Really?"

"Ella, listen to me." Grabbing of her shoulders, Blackjack continued, "You start running for that blue sage that's on fire. Don't stop. Don't look back. Keep running toward the flames."

"What are you going to do?" Ella asked.

"I thought I'd have a little chat with your friend."

"Are you serious?"

"Yes, I'm serious." Pointing, Blackjack said, "See that fire there?"

"Yes."

"Run to it."

"You're kind of bossy."

"Go now!"

Without looking back, Ella ran toward the fire. Blackjack leaned against the petrified rock, grinning and licking his titanium, unbreakable orange claws. "I can take this molded form of troll shit any day of the week," Blackjack said, jumping to his feet. "Saying that, it's pretty fast for an unknown molded entity."

The Penetrator moved up the hill toward Blackjack, getting closer to striking distance.

Blackjack crouched down, hands in front, claws extended full length. "I'm going to rip his head off and shit in his lungs. That's if it has any lungs." Blackjack stepped out from behind the rock, yelling, "Come on moose breath. I don't have all day."

Just as the Penetrator closed in within five feet, the sunshine dimmed, a huge flying fortress blotting out the sun.

Ella stood motionless, looking toward the sky with her mouth open.

"Oh, my God. She is beautiful, graceful, and very big. I hope I never make her mad."

Blackjack chuckled and looking at the Penetrator, he pointed up at Kula. "You said you wanted to buy the Medicine Shoppe. The owners just arrived. Be my guest, and good luck."

The Penetrator growled, swinging his sword for Blackjack's head. "I'm going to use your skull as a candle holder."

Blackjack dropped low as the enemy blade swished through the air. "You are faster than you look. But not fast enough, chicken lips."

Blackjack jumped three feet into the air and sliced deep as if aiming for the Penetrator's heart. The Penetrator clutched his chest, kneeling to one knee but there was no howl or grunting.

Landing back on his feet, Blackjack crouched for another attack when suddenly, the lengthy cut in the Penetrator's chest exploded with a tonnage of what looked like black sticky chimney soot, knocking Blackjack unconscious to the ground and rolling him over and over like a leaf in the wind.

The Penetrator walked toward Blackjack, directing his open discharge of blackness and burying him in a pile of mushy paste. Walking up to the black mound, he tapped on the top with a loud thud. "Perfect," said the Penetrator. "Cocooned in a hardened glass case, so much easier for transportation."

"Not so fast," said Ella and with dagger in hand, she charged the dark figure. Barely covering two steps, she immediately kissed the dirt as a crushing wave of hot air blasted from her toes to the top of her hair. Lifting her head and spitting dirt, she saw Kula soar into the sky with the tail end of the Penetrator's black trench coat flailing between her claws.

With a big grin, Ella watched Kula.

"I think that's going to be a big no on selling the shop." She watched Kula bank to the left, lowering her altitude as she made her approach to land in front of the shop. Kula slowed, then flared her wings before setting down with the Penetrator clutched tight in her powerful claws.

Kula stood motionless as her eighty-foot-high frame scanned the area with precision. The blue dragoon armor plating covering her entire body made her look almost statuesque.

Turning her head, she exposed a golden yellow armor plating beginning at her throat, running down across her chest into the bottom of her belly. The golden yellow lined the edges of her wings and covered the back of her head, all the way down to the tip of her tail.

Ella dropped to her knees, looking up at her. "Y-you are Kula, the Queen of the Dragoons, Keeper of the Darkan Territory in the Valley of the Tomb Sleepers?"

Kula looked down. "Yes, I am."

"My Queen. You are beautiful. My name is—"

"I know who you are."

"Of course, you do," said Ella.

"What do you know of blood bricks?"

Ella looked down. "I know of the blood bricks only by legend."

"Are you the one who set the blue sage on fire?"

"No, my Queen, I am not."

Kula studied her surrounds. "Is there someone in the shack?"

"No, my Queen."

"Then who demanded my presence?"

Ella pointed to the other side of the cottage. "That… furry thing. It looked like a royal messenger."

Kula leaned to her right, looking around the building. "I don't see anything except a large shiny black rock."

"That's the one."

Kula looked at the black rock again, then glanced down at Ella. "Are you trying to trick me?" Arching her chest, wings flared, she exhaled through her nose, scorching Ella's eyebrows.

Covering her face with her hands, Ella cried out, "Please don't burn me. I would never seek to trick you."

"Then who sent for me?"

"Trapped inside that black glass of a rock is a furry looking rabbit creature, at least four feet high and weighing eighty pounds. Orange-tipped ears and long metal claws. He can talk. I talked to him. I have never seen one before. He even blew me a kiss."

Kula raised her head high. "Slow down! Slow down! You're telling me that in that sphere-shaped black rock is my royal messenger?"

"Yes, my Queen. He fought against that thing you have in your talons."

Kula looked at her catch. "So *that's* why he called me. He has something here that needs my attention."

"Yes, my Queen. That thing in your grasp"—Ella nodded toward the figure— "came into my shop. It was acting strange, and it wanted twenty earther food balls and a blood brick."

"It wanted a *blood brick*?" asked Kula, her eyes narrowing. "And my messenger fought this wad of darkness I have in my talons?"

"That is the truth, my Queen. And that's not all."

"Why, what else did it want?"

"It acted as though it knew your name. Wanted to have contact with you. It—or he—continued asking to buy my shop even though I advised it's not for sale."

Holding up her fist of black trench coat, Kula said. "This thing here said it wanted a blood brick?"

"That's what it said, and other not so nice things."

"Pray, tell me, what else did it say? It sounds

somewhat opinionated if you ask me."

Ella held up the coin she took from the counter. "Opinionated and demanding, my Queen. And it had a bag full of these in its possession."

Kula tilted her head.

"Really? A life coin? We need to figure that out later. Right now, we must break that rock open."

"Oh, my goodness," said Ella, running to the spot where the pile of soot had hardened to a chunk of black glass lying on the ground. Kneeling, she placed both hands on the shiny black rock.

"Can you sense Blackjack inside that thing?" asked Kula.

"Not at this moment." Placing her ear against the glassy exterior of the rock, she listened, making a motion that implied, *hush, while I listen.* She added, "What kind of magic is this?"

"I don't know," said Kula. "Is Blackjack still alive?"

"Quiet please. Sorry, my Queen, I'm trying to hear whether—" Then Ella fell silent, hugging the rock as if it were her dearest friend, listening for a sign of life. "Oh yeah, he's still alive."

"Well, can you speak to him in some way?"

"No, I can't, but he did speak to me."

"He spoke to you? How can he speak to you?"

"He said to stand back because he was going to break this hex into little pieces."

Kula lifted her wing to shield them from the blast. "Stand behind my wing. Quickly!"

"What about that thing in your claws though? I thought I saw him move. He was going to kill me fifteen minutes ago."

"Don't worry about Mr. Dark and Depressing. I have a hunch we are going to barbecue him later." Ella pushed her shoulder against Kula's wing. "Is anything happening yet?"

Kula peaked over her shoulder. "Something is starting to happen. Looks as if it's vibrating and… the top of the rock is starting to glow green and yellow."

"Green and yellow?" said Ella. "That's interesting."

"And *why* is that of interest?" asked Kula.

"I don't know if it applies here, but when I mix some of my herbal bags for health and healing, I use a combination of yellow and green ingredients. It reflects my strength and abilities."

"Oh," said Kula. "The black sphere is spinning counterclockwise. Now it's glowing red. I think it's going to blow." Kula hid her face behind her wing.

"I swear I can hear a hissing noise," said Ella.

Suddenly, a loud explosion thrusting chunks of the black rock pelted Kula's wing.

Ella removed her hands from her ears. "My ears are ringing, and I can't hear anything."

Kula lowered her wings. "Whatever that cocoon of black rock is made of, it's stuck to my armor with a slow burn. Are you okay?" Kula asked.

"What?" Ella replied.

Kula stepped forward. When the smoke and dirt faded, she could see Blackjack sitting on the ground, shaking his head, and picking at his ears.

She approached him, grabbing his hand and pulling him upright. "Are you okay?"

"Wow! That was a hell of a ride."

"Do I want to know what happened inside that shell?" said Kula.

"When I was inside that shell, I had thousands of hands poking and grabbing at me. Each time it jabbed at me; it was as though they were trying to pull something out if that makes any sense."

Kula rolled her claw upwards. "It makes sense. Depending on what type of magic I have here in my hand."

"I see you got my smoke message," said Blackjack. "Thank you, my Queen."

"Yes, I did. I was in the immediate area when I saw it, and I had a clue it was coming from you because of the orange tint in the smoke."

"Yeah, I thought I would throw that in for more color clarification. But right now, we need to gather all the pieces of the rock."

"Sure, we can do that," said Kula. "Some of those pieces were actually burning my armor."

"I saw a symbol when I was inside that spell rock,"

said Blackjack.

"What kind of a symbol?"

"I'm not sure, because it only appeared when it got hot. Then boom!" Blackjack said.

"When it got hot?" said Kula.

"I can heat it up again. Do we have to have the exact piece?" asked Blackjack.

"Yes, we do."

"We need all the pieces together," commented Blackjack.

"Okay," said Kula. "Ella is already collecting them together."

"Did that thing ever touch her for a long period of time?" Blackjack wanted to know.

"I don't know," Kula replied. "We would need to ask her."

"You have what's left of it in your claw," he replied.

"I thought I would wait till I got you out of the rock prison and we could look at this thing together."

"Is it dead?" Blackjack inquired.

"The human side of it might be dead but not the magic side."

"*Human?* Did it have a human side?" said Blackjack.

"It had a human form somewhat," Kula advised.

"Yes, I suppose you're right."

Kula then asked, "Did it move like a human force when you fought it inside the shack?"

"For the most part, it did. But it was the smell that really made my hairs stand up."

"How did you know it was at Ella's?" Kula questioned.

"I was on the other side of Five Buttes when Brazel notified me that I should check on the young lady at the herbal hut."

"Brazel?" Kula said, her eyes wide. "You're going to have to explain to me sometime how this Brazel works with you."

"Sometimes, I don't even know, but it's like having a superpowered subconscious mind."

Kula said, "Sounds to me as though this subconscious counterpart gives you insight into danger.

Quite an asset. What I wouldn't give to be in possession of such a talent."

"True," said Blackjack. "It has helped me in the past. The inner voice usually informs me about good things as well as bad. Not always, and sometimes, it gives me very little information to go on. But in this case, it hinted to me to check out Ella. I never know if the experience will work in my favor or not."

"How did you break the holding spell?" she asked.

"I utilized the three most powerful energy forces within my mental grasp."

"Could you explain that in more detail?" asked Kula.

"I employed the power of you, Ella, and the Penetrator, combining all three energies to work in a linear fashion."

"How though?"

"I used Ella's energy as a soothing sleeping pill," Blackjack commented. "Then I combined your strength with the aggressive exploding power of the Penetrator."

"That's amazing," said Kula.

"You put it to sleep. Then with my strength to push against the shell with the exploding dark energy of the Penetrator, you caused an explosion."

"Well said, my Queen. I don't know if I could've explained it any better."

"You are truly an amazing individual."

"I would have been unable to do it without your strength or Ella, so I would say it was a team effort."

"Modesty," said Kula. "Great power with modesty. To me, that combination would serve for the makings of a great warrior, groundbreaker or even a king."

"Queen Kula," Ella said, suddenly returning and setting a basket at her own feet. "I have gathered all the pieces of the evil rock that I can find."

"Very good. Thank you, Ella."

"You are very welcome, my Queen. May I be excused?"

"You may. Is there something wrong?"

"I am standing in front of royalty," Ella answered, pulling on a torn edge of her dress, "wrapped in this ragged curtain. I would like to change into more appropriate attire."

"You may be excused. We can talk later." Ella bowed, walking quickly to her herbal hut.

Blackjack kneeled next to the basket inside Ella's medicine shop, poking at the pieces. "Do we have the piece that had the symbol on it?" Kula asked.

Scanning the basket, Blackjack replied, "I believe we do."

"The symbol," said Kula. "We need that piece."

Blackjack sat down next to the basket, picking out each piece. "Ouch! This has to be it," he said, quickly throwing it to the ground. "It's the only one that burns me."

"Leave it right there," said Kula. "I'm going to make it glow. Then we're going to be able to see that symbol again."

Blackjack threw his hands in the air. "Kula's fire coming your way," he said, kicking at the dark bundle in Kula's claw. "Heat that baby up. Oh yeah."

"Do we have a piece of wood close?" Kula asked.

"I have the perfect piece," said Blackjack. "The wooden club I used when I knocked the Penetrator on the head."

Kula inhaled, her chest coming alive with a bright red-orange glow, then she spit the sticky napalm lava onto the piece of rock. It smoldered for several minutes before bursting into flames.

"Wait till it burns out," said Kula, "then press the wood against the rock. That will be the brand. The symbol we are looking for."

Blackjack nodded his head yes. "I'm ready. Let's find out who this asshole is working for," he said, kicking at the smoldering pieces.

"Press the wood. Get the brand," said Kula.

"Here! Got it! It's the same symbol I saw on the inside of the glassed black cocoon."

"Let me see it."

Blackjack held the branded board high over his head for Kula to view.

She studied the symbol closely. "I have seen parts of this symbol before. Like the All-Verse Circle and, of course, the axe… but not in this type of design. This All-Verse

Circle was broken by a violent act, thus penetrated by an axe with all the essence of the circle draining out."

Blackjack lowered his arms to view the symbol himself. "What does it mean?"

Kula stared down at Blackjack. "I don't know the origin of the symbol but the grains of life that flow out of the circle mean the power arrangement of the Darkan Territory, mainly Grimmbell, will be altered or destroyed."

"How can one... destroy Grimmbell? Is that even possible?" asked Blackjack.

"Getting inside a superior power source, like Grimmbell, and using an object of penetration, the nature of which we don't know yet. Yes, it's possible. It's like using something old and symbolic, like an elder blood brick against something new and totally unpredictable... like this Penetrator entity."

Blackjack threw the branded symbol to the ground. "So, in other words, what we are faced with is an unknown force trying to stab us in the heart."

"I'm not sure of the totality of this Penetrator force," said Kula. "But I'm certain it's not done here today. The worst is yet to come."

Chapter 3: Penetrator Attacks… Again

Kula picked at the outside wrapping of the black unknown trench coat entity, which tried to conceal its form by transforming itself into human clothes. But in reality, it looked like a seven-foot-tall, 250-pound Tootsie Roll with attuite. Some type of penetrator of life.

"A Penetrator," said Blackjack. "I don't know if I would've thought of that name. I would say that's pretty accurate though."

"Blackjack, you can read my mind," Kula voiced. "I didn't even know you could do that. And to be honest, I'm not sure if I *like* you doing that."

"I'm sorry, my Queen. I didn't do it intentionally. But if I'm within twenty or thirty feet of an individual, I can usually read what they are thinking."

"You are truly full of surprises."

"I'm sorry," Blackjack said. "Then I will shut that power off for now."

"Is that your subconscious Brazel thing?"

"No, it's merely a Blackjack thing."

Kula spun herself around, facing him. "You definitely turned it off because the next thing I was going to ask, for the sake of Ella, was if you can turn into Bradicus for now?"

"I am truly not sure what you're asking me for."

"Ella's been watching us from the window of the shop. If I'm not mistaken, she's had quite a day. A Penetrator attack, and I believe seeing you—a Blackjack— for the first time scared the shit out of her."

"Well, if she sees me change from Blackjack to Bradicus, she'll freak out even more."

"That's why I was thinking if you can go out behind the herbal shop and make the change over, we can say that Blackjack had to leave."

"I can understand what you are saying, but I want you to know I have to be in my animal form to fight the

Penetrator."

"I know that" said Kula.

"Okay, then I'll go out back and see you in about two minutes."

"Sounds good," Kula affirmed.

"I knew you were going to say that." Grinning, Blackjack gave a quick wave and disappeared behind the herb shop.

Kula re-directed her attention to the seven-foot Tootsie Roll lying on the ground, rubbing her fingers into the burned symbol branded into the piece of wood.

Bradicus appeared from behind Ella's shop. "My Queen," he said, bowing his head, "may I be of service to you?"

Kula looked over her shoulder. "Bradicus. Wow, that was fast."

"I do my best. Seriously, what are your thoughts of that symbol?"

"I think if I burn the dark messenger, and another symbol of the same design appears on this lump of garbage, then that would indicate to me it's this one brand of symbol that made the Penetrator attack Ella."

"So, what are we waiting for? Let's burn it."

Kula's chest came alive with a bright yellow glow. "I won't use the sticky stuff at this time. This special blend is not as aggressive as the really hot napalm."

"Sounds logical to me," said Bradicus. "But first, let me shield my eyes before you light him up."

Kula spun the Penetrator package to where the head position was pointing toward her feet and blew the yellow fire mix over the Penetrator. It quickly caught on fire and Kula took a step back.

"Bradicus, look at that."

Bradicus nodded in agreement. "It's starting to spin."

"Yes, it is," said Kula. "It's spinning and spinning counterclockwise, exactly the way it did when you were encased in that cocooned prison of obsidian-looking glass."

"That's interesting," said Bradicus. "Because I don't remember spinning when I was trapped inside.

Oh hell, look at that. It's bouncing as if it's going to take off."

Kula looked on. "Whatever's inside that black log of evil, it's trying to escape."

"*Can* it escape?"

Kula stepped forward. "Bradicus, give me your sword."

Sword in hand, she harpooned the center of the package, plunging through the Penetrator and into the ground, stopped only by the cross guard of the sword.

"Now, it can't escape!"

Bradicus looked wide-eyed at Kula. "Yes ma'am, it's not going to escape and it's not moving anymore. Stay out of her way because Kula means business."

Suddenly, the Penetrator started to bounce higher. "Okay, so I was wrong," said Bradicus.

"Something is trying to get out," said Kula. "Protect yourself."

A long yellow and black striped serpent snake pushed its head out of the charred log. Swaying, the unknown creature blinked its one V-shaped eye.

"Holy one-eyed-striped snaky shit balls," said Bradicus. "I haven't seen one of those before."

"Bradicus, can you read its mind?"

"I can try."

"Be careful," said Kula. "I think that snake spirit animal was the mechanism that was poking you when you were trapped inside the black cocoon."

Bradicus sat on the ground, legs crossed, focusing on the snake.

Kula watched Bradicus in curiosity as his breathing slowed, to almost no sign of breath. "I hope that's part of the process to reading this snake thing?"

Kula coughed up a fire ball, holding it in her mouth. "I will burn it to the ground before it tries to attack you again," she said to Bradicus.

Kula continued to referee the staring match while napalm dripped from the corners of her mouth.

Suddenly, from the neck down, the snake's body spun clockwise, producing a merry-go-round of yellow and black light.

Studying the snake, Kula curled the tip of her tail to look like an upright snake, positioning it close to the yellow and black serpent. She wiggled her tail, but the penetrator snake didn't change its position and continued its laser vision on Bradicus.

"It's locked on Bradicus. It could be a trap." Kula spit a rope-thin line of fire across the top of the snake's head. The snake spun around, turning its attention away from Bradicus and focusing instead on Kula.

Ella shot out of the front door of the medicine shack before stopping behind Bradicus.

"Be careful," said Ella. "It's the Penetrator wanting to attack again. It's using a different form in the shape of a snake. I don't know which one of you it could penetrate. Just don't let it in."

"I'm not letting anything in," said Kula. "It hasn't moved. And what did you do with the shape of your eyes?"

"Oh, it's looking at me now, my Queen. Ooh! It's a gnarly looking thing. That eye," Ella said.

"Ella, what is wrong with your eyes?"

"There is nothing wrong with my eyes. Well, I modified them to resemble snake eyes. Cool, huh?"

"What are you talking about?" asked Kula.

"To make a long story short, I merged the magic eyes from my pet snake Asylum. I'm looking through its eyes with different colored filters. But in any case, I see what the penetrator snake sees."

"You can see *exactly* what it sees?" asked Kula.

"Not exactly, but I can see what it's doing. The Penetrator thing has arms."

"Arms?" Kula asked.

"Arms like a caterpillar," said Ella. "It's drawing a portrait of you."

"A portrait? Of me?"

"That's what it looks like to me," Ella answered. "And in great detail."

"Did it do a portrait of Bradicus?"

"I don't think so. I don't see one."

"Well, what is it using to draw on?"

"It's drawing in thin air. The shape appears for five seconds and then it disappears," Ella confirmed. "Is it still drawing me?"

"No. It's moved back to Bradicus. It's talking to

someone."

"Who is it talking to?" asked Kula.

Bradicus waved his hand. "It's looking for the blood brick. *Your* blood brick?"

"My brick?" whispered Kula.

Kula perked up. Lifting her wings head high, she blew a sticky lava-napalm mix of fire on the top of her wings. "Keep your heads low. I'm going to kill the snake."

Kula flung her wings at the snake as though they were her hands. Left right. Left right. Another left and right.

Stepping back, she inhaled, increasing her chest capacity five times. She ripped a wave of hot lava-napalm at the snake more intensely than the last discharge.

Ella waved her hands at Kula. "Kula. My medicine shack. It's smoking."

"The snake is still alive," said Bradicus. "Ella, bring me the axe hanging on the side of your shop."

"The axe?" asked Ella.

"Yes," said Bradicus, pointing. "Bring me that axe. I have a hunch about it."

Ella sprinted to her shop, reaching for the axe. "Damn it's hot." She plunged her hands into the rain barrel. Removing the axe, she hauled it back to Bradicus. "What are you going to do with the axe?"

Clutching the axe from Ella, he called out, "Kula, my Queen, I need your help."

Kula spun around, lowering her head to their level. "That's one tough snake. If we can't kill it, how do we capture it?"

"The club I used to hit the Penetrator. Get it hot."

"Here it is," said Ella.

"Perfect," said Bradicus. "I need Ella for this to work."

"For what to work?" said Ella.

"Kula, my Queen, when you heat the axe, we are going to draw the symbol of the broken circle with the axe on the axe head and this is where Ella comes in. We need your blood."

"You need my blood? I don't think so."

"Yes, I do. Here is my knife. We don't have much

time. Do it quickly."

"Then what?" said Ella.

"We coat the axe blade with your blood because you were the person the Penetrator was programed to penetrate first. But I think your blood should work for us. Well, I hope so, anyway."

"You hope?"

"Do as he says," ordered Kula. "Where do we cut her?"

"We need to cut her just below the belly button."

"Ella, lift your shirt. Do it now," barked Kula.

Ella exposed her belly button. "This is going to hurt."

"Only for a minute," said Kula. "Bite down hard on this bone."

"Ready?" Bradicus held the axe with two hands as he sliced into Ella's soft spot. Breathing heavily through her nose, Ella cringed, her eyes watering.

"I'm sorry, Ella, it's the only way."

"Kula, I need you to send another of those tidal waves of fire at the snake. I will follow your wave while I transform into Blackjack, and resort to cutting the head off the snake."

"I hope you know what you're doing."

With a huge breath, Kula inflated her chest. "I'm ready when you are."

Bradicus crouched down, nodding to Kula who ripped the wave of fire at the snake.

Transforming into Blackjack in mid-stride gave Bradicus super speed and when the fire had burned down, Kula and Ella looked for Blackjack.

"Oh shit," said Ella, pointing. "Look out there. The shiny furry one's down on the ground."

"That's five hundred yards away," said Kula. "How did he get out there so fast?"

"I don't know," said Ella, leaning on one knee.

"Ella, my dear," said Kula. "I'm so sorry, let me help you to your shop. I can fix that cut."

"Thank you, my Queen. Get me to the shop, I know what to do from there. Go help Blackjack."

"As you wish, *Queen Ella*."

"That's funny," said Ella. "Don't try to make me laugh."

Kula helped Ella through the door and with one whip of her wings, she straddled Blackjack, rolling him onto his back. "Are you still breathing, or do I have to start mouth-to-mouth resuscitation?"

Blackjack lifted his arm. "I'm still breathing. I cut its head off, but that sumbitch bit me."

"We need Ella to take a look at the bite. She can fix you up."

"I hope so, because it burns like a thousand red fire ants crawled up my bung hole. Is Ella, okay?"

"She is fine. Still calls you the weird shiny rabbit with scary eyes."

"That's okay, I've been called worse."

Chapter 4: Snakebite

Kula escorted Blackjack to the front door of the herbal shop. "Ella, open the door. It's me." There was no answer. "Ella, open the door. It's me."

A small patch of a head and one eye could be seen looking out the window. Suddenly, the door flew open. "I'm sorry. I was in the back room. What happened to his arm?"

"It's a bite from some form of the Dark Penetrator," said Kula. "You can heal him, right?"

"A snake bite from the dark figure?" said Ella. "You know the dark figure called himself Arune."

"Wait a minute," said Kula. "Arune?" Sorting out a small cloud of smoke, she added, "Why didn't you tell me that before? *Arune?*"

Ella folded her hands together on her chest. "I'm sorry, my Queen, it just popped into my head. I'm almost positive that's what it said when it came into my shop. Why did Blackjack need my blood?"

"I'm not sure at this moment, but right now, I need your wisdom in healing his arm."

Ella hooked her arm under Blackjack's armpit, sitting him on a chair. "You two really tore up my store. Look at it! It will take me all day to sort this mess."

"I'm sorry about that," said Blackjack.

"It's not your fault; you saved my life. Anyway, why did you blow me a kiss back at the shop?" With an uneasy grin, Blackjack shrugged. "I don't know. I guess I didn't want you to panic." Sitting next to Blackjack, Ella rolled up his shirt sleeve and looked closer at the bite.

"What are you thinking?" asked Blackjack.

"I'm thinking what a beautiful animal-human you are. I thought you would have turned back into Bradicus."

Blackjack looked into Ella's eyes, pausing before he spoke. "I tried, but I think this nasty bite has messed with my head."

"Hang on a minute," said Ella, reaching for a small leather wrap.

"What is that for?"

"My tools," said Ella. Untying the leather string, she opened the wrap, waving the palm of her hand a few inches above the bite. "There's something under the skin."

"What sort of something?" said Blackjack.

Slowly moving the palm of her hand back and forth over the bite, she said, "Yeah, I can feel a force pushing back."

"A force?" said Blackjack.

"What kind of force?"

"I'm not sure yet. How do you feel?"

"My arm burns like it's on fire."

Touching his forehead, she asked, "Do you feel sick?"

"No."

"Well, you don't have a fever. Any weird thoughts or hallucinations?"

"No. Not yet anyway."

She dipped her finger at the wound then touched her tongue. "I don't taste any type of poison."

"That's a good thing," said Blackjack.

"Yes, as far as poisons go, which leads me back to the unusual force pushing out from the bite."

"Okay," said Blackjack. "How do we get this *unusual force* out of my arm?"

"Can you go into an unconscious or comatose type of mindset?"

"Yes, I can."

"I figured you probably could. I've been told by travelers that you have specific powers."

"Really?" said Blackjack. "Do you remember who told you that?"

"I do, but I don't want you to get the wrong idea."

"What would that be?"

"In my line of work, I meet a lot of creatures, human and otherwise. At times, we get into lengthy conversations about all types of magics and such. But before you say anything, let me remind you that whatever information I gather stays here."

"I would be interested in who shared info about me. Do I have to protect myself?"

"No, nothing like that," said Ella, pushing and probing her fingers around the wound.

"But right now, I need to heal your arm. There seems to be some piece of metal under your skin. Again, I can feel energy pushing against my hand, like some sort of filtering device. We need to get it out, right now."

"A filtering device?" Blackjack asked. "Like some sort of transmutation maneuver?"

Ella twisted her head, rubbing the bite. "Yes, something like that. Whatever it is, it's not good for your longevity."

Blackjack nodded in agreement. "Let's get this thing out of me. Although, what is really interesting is the fact that the Penetrator was going after Ella before I came along. Was the device to be used on Ella?"

Ella fluffed the pillow. "When you're ready, lie down here."

"Okay Ella. Once I go into this hypnotic state, what are you going to do?"

"I am not going to be able to use my conventional tools. I'm going to have to get *creative*."

"In what way *creative?*" Blackjack looked perturbed.

"I'm going to have to enlist the help of Asylum," Ella said.

"Asylum? You mean your pet snake?"

"Yes, that's what I mean." She said it as if it was obvious.

"How are you going to have your snake remove the device?" Blackjack wanted to know. "I have a plan, but I'm not going to tell you what it is."

"Why not?"

"I have my trade secrets too," Ella said. "I am entitled to them, don't you think?"

"Okay, that's fair. Let's get the show on the road."

"How long will it take you to get into the alternative mindset?" Ella asked Blackjack.

"Blackjack, this is Brazel. It will take two minutes."

"Thank you," said Blackjack.

"For what," said Ella. "I haven't done anything yet."

"Never mind. Then it will take me two minutes to go

to dream state."

"Wow, that's fast. Okay, let's get started."

"Wait a minute," said Blackjack. "How long will this take?"

Ella shrugged her shoulders. "I'm figuring around three hours."

"Three hours?" said Blackjack, eyes wide. "I will tell myself to sleep for three hours." Closing his eyes, Blackjack relaxed his body. "See you on the other side."

Ella counted to 120 and pinched Blackjack on the side of the neck.

No response. "That's good." She quickly went to the cage where she kept Asylum, picking up the snake, she walked to the front door. Opening it, she went through and stopped in front of Kula.

"Kula, this is going to sound weird," Ella said, pointing, "but I need to go over by that rock there. You were listening, correct?"

"Of course, if that's what it takes to heal the bite."

"That's what it takes. For some reason, at that area by the rock, I feel that same type of force pushing against me. I'm going to put my snake on that specific piece of ground. From there, I will be able to transform Asylum into an altered dimension to retrieve whatever bad magic is inside Blackjack's arm."

Kula produced a soft smile. "Do you use that area by the rock often?"

"Actually, I've dug up some of the dirt. I keep a bag inside my shop, but for this particular challenge, I need to be closer to that source."

Kula nodded. "How long before Asylum is ready to go?"

"I figure fifteen minutes."

"Kula, my Queen," said Ella, rubbing her forehead. "I really don't understand why Bradicus—or Blackjack—couldn't just fix himself. I've been told he has great powers."

"I don't know for sure, but maybe he's testing your abilities."

"Testing my abilities for what?"

"Maybe that's what both of us are trying to find out."

Chapter 5: Asylum Backfires

Ella sat at a wooden table next to the big rock adjacent to the herbal shop.

"Don't know what it is about this rock, but when I'm near it, I feel so good. I've created powerful herbal magic at these times; it's a voice in my head that tells me how to make all these wonderful creations. Did you know the earthers came to me to help them create the Earther Survival Ball?"

Kula leaned down, sniffing the rock and the immediate area around its base. "I know that aroma. This is where my blood brick plummeted into the ground when I dropped it many years ago."

Ella somehow connected with the brick. I'm going to have to tell her about it sooner or later.

"The earther food ball," said Kula. "That's the first item my warriors pack whenever they go into battle. It's an amazing creation. A life saver."

"I sure hope I have saved lives with it."

"Oh, you have," said Kula. "Did you know that the ESBs—that's what my fighter dragoons call them—can be used for more than food? And that they have been used for more than that?"

"Why, what else have they been used for?"

"The ESB has been used for administrating healing herbs into wounded fighters and warriors, along with anybody else who happens to be sick. It has been used for growing crops of tobacco too, our number one crop here in the earther valley. On the other side of the coin, the food balls have come in useful for the destruction of our enemies."

"To destroy our enemies, you say."

"That is correct."

"But I'm not sure how I feel about that; I didn't intentionally make the food ball to kill others."

"I know that," said Kula. "I just need to warn you

though."

"What? *Warn* me?" said Ella. "Did I do something wrong?"

"No, you didn't do anything wrong."

"I helped Roko make the survival ball. We made it together. He came to me."

"Ella, I know that. *I* sent him to you. Roko is the architect of the Bloodtobacco mixer, a combination of blood spilled on the Grimmbell battlefield and the essence of all those spirits and souls, mixed with tobacco, herbs, and spices among many other things I don't know about. It's an end product he uses to talk to the many realities of the dead. Or maybe it's even better phrased as being able to understand some aspect of the All Universe. What I am trying to tell you is that you are not responsible for the Earther Survival Ball. I am."

"I didn't mean any disrespect, my Queen."

"I know that."

"Kula, my Queen," Ella said, touching Kula's hand. "Sometimes, I get very confused about what I'm supposed to do with my abilities."

"You have been doing a great service," said Kula. "From what I observe, you know precisely what to do with them. You use them very well and—"

"Many different characters," said Ella, "human and otherwise, come into the shop requesting herbs and potions of all kinds and I have this ability to make what they want, and they pay me for it. I have a bag of money. I don't know if I'm supposed to spend it or not."

"You can spend it," said Kula. "I mean, what else do you suppose you would do with it? What use is money if not for spending?"

"Yes but..." She appeared momentarily flustered. "You see, I have these life coins. I don't know if I'm even supposed to have this type of wealth. I haven't touched the life coins. I can show you where I hid them, in the root cellar, concealed in a jar of Ten-Berry Dark Moon Jam."

"I would like to see the life coins that Arune had with him. They could tell us where he has been lately."

"Yes, my Queen, of course." Standing up, she added, "Anything to help."

Kula blocked her path with her wing. "But first, it has been fifteen minutes. Asylum should be ready for the task by now, right?"

"Yes, Asylum is ready," said Ella. "The first thing we need to do is cut her up into an odd number of pieces. Nine or thirteen is usually the best."

"Okay," said Kula.

"The second thing we need to do is to make sure the cuts are precise and clean. We cannot do it by an ordinary knife or sword."

"So, what do we use?"

"I would like to be able to use your talons."

"My talons? You want *me* to cut Asylum?"

"It would be the perfect choice for slicing her up. The dark side of the penetrator snake would never expect the Queen of the Dragoons to actually make the cuts."

"And that would give us the advantage," said Kula, flexing her talons.

"It would be added power, strength, and agility. Quite frankly," Ella said, smiling, "it's going to kick the dark side of their ass. Are you ready, my Queen?"

"I am ready. What do I have to do exactly?"

"That will be step number three. I'm going to pick Asylum up, and I'm then going to throw her right at your face and just the same as if an intruder gets too close to you, you will protect yourself."

"How do I know to cut her into nine or thirteen pieces?"

"Don't worry about that. Just act naturally and make the kill, that's the important trick. Slice her as if you were in actual battle. Ready?"

Ella presented the snake in front of Kula. Kula nodded.

Ella leaned over and with a two-handed grip, threw the snake right at Kula's eyes. Asylum twisted in the air, sprouting small bat-like wings.

"Shit," said Ella. "I didn't know that was going to happen. Something is seriously wrong." Asylum zigged and zagged in front of Kula's face.

"Kula, kill the snake! Kill the snake! Do it now, before it starts to grow."

Kula made a right-hand sweep at Asylum but missed. "Um, what did you mean by *before it starts to grow?*"

"Just kill it," said Ella. *Did I give it too much power? Too much time on the special dirt?*

Kula adjusted her feet to a wider stance and hunched down. "Come on, flying snake, let's dance."

Hovering in front of Kula, Asylum grew to the dimensions of a purple milk cow. In other words, she was huge.

Ella jumped around on the ground like a cricket in a frying pan, screaming at Kula, "You have to kill it before it gets to the same size as you."

Still growing, Asylum circled Kula.

"What happens when it becomes the same size as me?"

"I'm not one hundred percent sure, but I think it will mirror your strength."

Asylum, tripling in size, slammed into the side of Kula, pushing her three feet along the dirt surface before peeling off, circling around for another attack.

Kula spit fire into the air, breathing on her talons that glowed red hot. "This little charade has gone on long enough. No one pushes me around and gets to talk about it," Kula muttered.

Meanwhile, in front of the shop, Ella had engineered a five-pointed studded death coin on the tip of an arrow shaft, snugging the bow line to the side of her face. Taking aim, she was ready to shoot.

Kula had taken to the air, racing past Ella.

"Don't even think about it. This thing's going to die." Flying straight for Asylum, Kula's chest glowed bright orange and red as Asylum charged head-on toward Kula.

Kula smothered Asylum with a wave of fire, then came the cherry on top in the form of a heavy coat of sticky, hot, napalm. Blinded by the intense heat and weight of it, Asylum faltered in mid-air, falling to the ground with a huge thud. Now, Kula was on top of Asylum like a fat kid on a cupcake.

She began slicing her into eleven pieces.

And seeing the outcome, Ella pointed her arrow into

the dirt.

"That was close. Kula might be pissed at me," she said to herself, running to Kula's side and looking at the ground. "Eleven pieces; that's even better."

Kula spit what napalm she had left in her mouth over the top of Asylum. She stared at Ella. "Did you forget to tell me a few things?"

"I'm sorry, my Queen, I didn't know that was going to happen. I was ready to kill it with my bow and arrow, but then saw you'd overpowered it."

"Yes, I see that. I noticed your tip on that arrow shaft. A deaf-death stone made into an arrowhead.

Where did you learn a skill like that?"

"Like I said, my Queen, a lot of times, the voice in my head shows me how to make things. This was one of those things, so I'm not sure how. Are you mad at me?"

"No, I can't be mad at you, can I, because I'm the one who put you here in the first place. You are my secret weapon. You just don't know it yet."

"I don't know what you mean. How can somebody as great as you want me as a secret weapon?"

"Because of that rock over there." Kula pointed. "But it's not the rock, it's what's under the rock.

That's where you get your power. That's why we're here today. Me, Blackjack, Bradicus, and the Penetrator. It's a long story, but... right at this minute, we need to help Bradicus remove that filter device in his forearm."

Ella had already begun picking up the eleven pieces of her snake, putting the portions into a basket. "I need to destroy the internal filtering spell."

"Follow me," said Ella. "You can watch through the window."

Ella went to the shelves with the jars, shuffling some from the front to the back and vice versa. "Whoa! At first, I thought I didn't have any. We would've been in deep shit if that were the case."

Picking a jar off the shelf and unscrewing the lid, she retrieved a two-finger wad of a red waxy substance, scraping the wax into the center of a copper bowl. Emptying the eleven-piece basketful into the bowl, she carried the copper pot to the window.

"Kula, I need you to heat this, but not too hot that it boils. Just enough that it melts."

"I can do that."

Ella sat the copper bowl on the window ledge. "Remember, just enough heat to melt it." Kula exhaled through one nostril, heating the bowl to perfection.

"Perfect," said Ella. "Now, I'll pour the melted sun wax mix into the bite. Then I need you to burn the bite closed so it's sealed. Okay?"

"I'm ready," said Kula.

Ella poured the waxy substance onto the snakebite, smoothing the wax evenly with a wooden spoon. "Okay Kula, seal the wound."

Kula breathed a soft breath of fire through the window, singeing the hair on Blackjack's arm while sealing the wax bond.

"Oh shoot," said Ella. "I need to tie his hands and feet to the chair. Could get a little froggy here.

Okay, that's done. Now, we sit back and wait."

"Internal filtering spell," said Kula. "Is that what it's called?"

"It's what I call it."

"How does it work?"

"It works off of energy and vibration," responded Ella.

"That makes sense," said Kula. "I know that Bradicus gives off high-energy, and because of his internal powers, that high energy; well, it's going to bounce off everything he's around, amplifying his internal energy. He is a walking transmutation of power."

"That's pretty much how it works," said Ella. "Sending the waves of energy into the atmosphere.

Someone or something knew what they were doing."

"There is no doubt that someone does have a plan," said Kula. "That's not all, my Queen."

"What do you mean?" Kula asked.

"Not only would Bradicus with his high internal powers give off a high-energy signal but also, when he is close to a larger in size energy source… such as you, my Queen, then… all hell breaks loose."

"Are you saying I'm fat?"

"No, I'm saying you are large and in charge."

"Of course," said Kula. "Together, including you too Miss Ella, we three would be one of the Earthers Valley's highest output of filtering plants, broadcasting, Come and get us. Here we are."

"That's what I think could happen, but I can't prove it."

"You don't have to prove anything right now. You were attacked by an unknown entity. This unknown thing had knowledge that the blood brick is here."

"Do you think it was going to kill me?" said Ella. "I don't think it wanted to hurt you."

"My Queen. It ripped my underwear off and stuffed it in my mouth."

"Again," said Kula, "I don't think it wanted to hurt you or even assault you."

"I find that hard to believe," said Ella, looking away.

"An entity like the Dark Penetrator wanted to use your body to find the blood brick and then try to blend you and the brick together. The easiest human portal to get inside you would be your womanhood."

"Why would it want to do that?"

"It wants to rule."

"Rule what?"

"As much as I don't want to think about it, to rule the Darkan Territory," voiced Kula.

"Wait a minute, my Queen," Ella interrupted, running to Bradicus and pushing down on the back of the cot. "We got action. Asylum has entered the broken axe circle. His body is going to shake, twitch, tremble, lurch, and hopefully, blow lunch."

Kula cringed. "You want him to puke?"

"Yes, I do. The wound is closed, so there are only two ways for it to come out of his body: the mouth or the pooper. Naturally, I would prefer the mouth."

"Yeah, I would too. Do we know what this blood filtering device looks like?"

"No, we don't," said Ella.

"Then how do we know if we get it out of his body?"

"We'll know, because it will pull all types of blood metal to it. That's why I have this copper bowl.

When he pukes, I need to catch the gunk in this bowl."

"Then what?"

"Then the copper bowl will either levitate or collapse upon itself."

"How do you know about this type of stuff?" said Kula.

"I think you answered that yourself not too long ago." Softly nodding, Kula said, "The blood brick."

"Here we go! Here we go!" said Ella, positioning the bowl just under his chin. "He's lurching forward; he's going to blow chunks."

"Raaalph."

"I don't get paid enough to do this," Kula said, turning her nose away.

"Raaalph."

"What the hell has this guy been eating? Roadkill?"

Suddenly, Blackjack was slammed onto his back, crushing the cot into small pieces.

"Wow!" said Ella. "A last-ditch effort by the dark side to keep the metal blood magic inside him."

"Did you get it?" asked Kula.

"The bowl is getting hot and starting to pull away from me. We got it. Kula, can you flick the notch open on that iron trunk there? I can't reach through this window opening. Can you use the tip of your tail?"

"I can. It's open."

"Good, cause this thing wants to take off."

"How is that wood chest going to hold it?"

"That's no ordinary wood chest. That's a Darkan Territory blood-soaked wooden chest."

Bradicus sat up, clutching his throat. "Hello! What the hell is going on? My mouth tastes like I gave birth to a rotten egg mud toad."

"Well, hello Bradicus. You are back. You have transformed. Yeah, well, that's what it smelt like too," said Ella, latching the lock on the chest.

"Bradicus," said Kula. "How are you feeling, and can you travel today?"

Bradicus stood up and brushed the puke off. "I can travel today, my Queen."

"Bradicus, Brazel here. Your friendly subconscious mind. You need to burn what's left of the entity to make sure you have all of the Dark Penetrator out of you. I believe the filtering spell bite is a distraction from the real objective of this so-called unknown black entity."

"What happens after we burn it?"

"When the broken circle axe symbol appeared on this much larger portion, you need to cover the remaining burned package with the sun burst wax left over and then bind it with Kula's dragoon rope. If it can pull away from the larger mass and transform into another form, it could attack again. You have to keep it sealed. Airtight."

"Brazel, do you know what this thing is?"

"I have a heavy hunch it could be a Darksidian Portal Penetrator."

"Bradicus, are you listening to me?" barked Kula.

"Yes, I am. I can travel today."

"Good. It would be in our best interest to deliver the remaining portion of this dark messenger to Grimmbell. I want it isolated in the same holding hollows as the Tri-Eight. I have enclosed my seal on this leather wrap containing the instructions to make this happen. I have also banded our friend here with my personal dragoon rope. It will levitate behind you, wherever you go. Don't let go of the rope. Make sure you talk to Luxen for the proper placement in the Tri-Eight holding chambers."

"Kula, I have been talking with Brazel. He has suggested that you burn the dark messenger to see if the broken circle axe symbol will appear again. That will prove it is that specific entity and we need to cover it with Ella's wax, then tie it with your rope. You already were going to tie the black bundle with your dragoon rope, but we need double the security on this package."

"Has your Brazel encountered this symbol before?" asked Kula.

"I don't know if he has encountered this thing before. He wanted us to make sure it doesn't escape.

He said it could be some type of power driven by a portal."

"Powered by a portal? Wow," said Ella, gripping her hands tight. "To my knowledge, the power of the portal is uncontrollable. I don't know of anyone who has mastered the supremacy of any single gateway, but I need to melt down a bigger batch of the sun burst wax if I'm going to cover the rest of this thing."

"Yes, I figured that," said Kula. "Is that all you had in the jar?"

"No, I have five twenty-pound blocks. Plenty."

"Okay," said Kula. "But right at this moment, I need to burn the creature to make sure it is what Brazel said it is. Everyone, please step back."

Kula inhaled a quarter of a breath and covered the creature with the red-yellow sticky paste. The creature twisted back and forth numerous times and then nothing.

Only smoke and a hissing sizzling sound could be heard.

"Don't breathe the smoke. Stay upwind," said Ella. "It will plug your lungs. It appears to have the consistency of coal dust but a thousand times thicker."

When the smoke cleared, a linear six-foot-long, 250-pound red lump of evil lay on the ground with a waffle iron imprint.

Bradicus was the first to speak out. "Look. Right there. It's the broken circle axe symbol. Now, we know that whoever owns this symbol owns this creature."

Kula leaned down, sniffing the object.

With the flick of her wrist, she rolled the package over. "I don't see any other symbols, but I do sense vibration. So, the sooner we get it covered with wax, the better."

"I will get the wax. Can you drag the package close to the door?"

Kula looked at the package on the ground. With a flick of a talon, the smoldering 250-pound Tootsie Roll hit the front door.

Ella exited. Holding three five-pound blocks of wax, she placed them two feet apart along the length of the black roll. "Give it a couple minutes to melt and dry and you'll be ready to transport."

"Good," said Kula. "Very good." Turning her attention to Bradicus, she added, "I gave you my leather wrap with the Queen's seal."

Bradicus patted his chest pocket. "I have it right here."

"When you get to Grimmbell, give it to the earther that controls the iron gate bell. Someone will take you to Luxen."

Bradicus finished tying Kula's dragoon rope around his waist. "I'm ready to go."

"What path are you going to use?" said Kula.

Bradicus pulled his hat down. "With this special package, I will have to use the sunken single track."

Kula nodded yes. "I was thinking you would take that route. This is going to be a dangerous journey.

You do realize that you could encounter scorpion moles in the single tracks?"

"Yes, I do," said Bradicus.

"Plus, at least going off what I have witnessed here, this unknown entity appears to be giving off high energy vibrations to lure creatures to it, filtering them to transmute itself into, well, anything it wants. Fricking scary. If you successfully make it to Grimmbell, I will give you a life coin. Is that fair?"

Bradicus bowed his head. "That is more than fair, my Queen. I do not need a life coin to accomplish this task but will accept the reward if I succeed. One more thing, my Queen."

"What is that?"

"I will have to pick up an extra bag of Brown Leaf Barrel Number Five tobacco."

"Of course," said Kula. "Leave now."

She turned to Ella. "Now that I have Bradicus on his way, it's time to talk about you."

Chapter 6: Scorpion Mole Tunnel

Bradicus looked back at Ella's sugar shack. That was what he called it.

If you had a sweet tooth for jellies and—more importantly—for magical herbs, you would go see Ella. Bradicus watched Kula with her hand gestures, trying to explain something to Ella.

Tugging at the rope tied around his waist, he focused on the landscape in front of him. "I do hope Kula's rope can keep this nasty bundle secured till I get to Grimmbell."

He started down the slope off the butte from Ella's hut. He could see where he had to go. One point of entry to the scorpion tunnels—or the sunken tracks as Kula called them—would be located on the valley floor two miles along the present trail.

Bradicus stopped at the entrance of the mole tunnel, a large granite rock rested near the underground opening which had a warning carved in the side: *Enter this tunnel, and you are governed by Serpentine, the King and largest of the scorpion moles.*

The moles traditionally had fed on earthers—their favorite food—in battles of years gone by.

In the earlier battles between the moles and the earthers, it had all been about who owned the underground. Both species lived beneath the earth, but the earthers could and did live above ground too. Scorpion moles, on the other hand, could only function underground.

"Well, let's hope I have a good aura with Serpentine."

He pulled at the rope to make sure the dark package was secure around his waist.

"I want to have both hands free in case I have to fight my way through the tunnel," Bradicus said, transforming into his advanced animal form, Blackjack.

Blackjack was an unusual and rare animal that Kula had rescued from a tribe of Grokers; they had been using him at an infant age, hoping to locate and harness the understanding of Persalamite.

The Grokers, on the other hand, were a small nomad race, mostly identified as ground rovers. Kula found the Grokers had imprisoned the young Blackjack in a flat ground energy gravity ball. The tribe would kick the energy ball in front of them when they wandered the Valley of the Tomb Sleepers, to identify any magical sinkholes with unknown pockets of static magic the tribe would harness for themselves. Because of the extraordinary and mysterious power of this Blackjack, the gravity ball would stop and levitate three feet above the ground when a magical sinkhole was found.

Even more astonishing was that Blackjack would absorb that magical force.

Eventually, according to earther folklore history, the tribe came upon a deeper than normal magical sinkhole containing a violent vortex of energy, causing the gravity ball to rupture, and killing the members of the tribe. Blackjack absorbed all the energy inside the flat ground energy ball in which he was imprisoned, allowing him to escape his harsh environment of the gravity ball prison.

Thus, an unknown entity in its own right was created.

During a scheduled flyby, Kula and a handful of fighter dragoons spotted Blackjack wandering the valley floor. Injured, Kula brought him back to her rock castle in the Maroot mountains and there, they became close friends. To this day, the true strength of his power was still unknown.

Blackjack quickly blinked three times to activate his infrared vision before entering the tunnel, all his other senses also intensifying one hundred-fold.

"I hear earthworms moving in the walls near me. I smell the scent of mole already and feel vibration on the tunnel floor."

Blackjack had traveled five hundred yards when he came across a bone protruding from the tunnel wall. Grabbing the bone, he pulled on it. Suddenly, the cave wall dissolved in front of him.

Jumping back, a pile of bones dumped onto the tunnel floor. *Is this a trap?*

Looking down the tunnel, he could see a thousand yards before the tunnel made a sharp left turn; he didn't see any scorpion mole heat images.

Looking back at the entrance of the tunnel, he thought, *Maybe I should go back, but I can't now. I need to find out who or what these bones belong to. They're probably earther bones. The record keepers of Grimmbell will want to know if they belong in the cemetery.* Setting his external border alarm marker at fifty yards, the sensor would alarm him if anything got closer than the fifty yards.

Kneeling, Blackjack started the task of digging through the pile of bones. All the images of them would be recorded to his subconscious entity Brazel for storage and transfer at a later date.

A quarter of the way through the pile, it appeared to consist mostly of bones from earthers, but then the bones grew, beginning to take on a shape resembling scorpion mole tail sections and human bones.

"This is a rather surprising mix of bones. All in one place, and especially all three types of bones located in a scorpion mole tunnel." He continued to dig, uncovering a leather bag. He opened the bag, and to his surprise, he could make out the shape of two human skulls.

Could these be the missing skulls of the two kings? Oh, the earthers will want to take a closer look at these. He continued burrowing in the leather bag.

To his surprise, he found three scorpion stinger tail bones.

Wow. Stinger tails are a hunted item.

The stingers were extremely strong, having the same durability as molten steel. They could be worked into tools of death, and it was never necessary to sharpen the resultant weapons.

Someone or something went hunting for this variety of bones, or they stole the bones from a sacred battle site or from Grimmbell Cemetery.

He continued digging into the bag, revealing the last remaining bone.

Grabbing the creamy colored artifact, it sent a chill slashing through his claws, down his legs, and stinging each one of his toes. Stomping his feet until the bee sting went away, he backed up against the tunnel wall with deep breaths. "Everything is going to be all right." Covering his hand over his chest, he said, "Okay, Mr. Heartrate, slow down. Inhale. Exhale. It can't be what I think it is. No way."

He held the bone with both hands, studying the width of it like an archaeologist.

"About eight inches wide. And six holes evenly spaced throughout the bone's length." He knew what he had, but still didn't want to believe it.

"The bone appears to be that of a Blackjack, but that couldn't be true, could it? There are only two Blackjacks, Brazel and I. But Brazel is a spirit energizer now residing inside my subconscious. Never knew of a third one. And I very much doubt there can be one."

Why today of all days?

I had to fight off the attack of a Penetrator, set fire to the blue sage to signal Kula, cut the head off a snake, puke in a copper bowl and now, transport the Penetrator through a mole tunnel... and now this!

His concentration was broken when the internal fifty-yard alarms bit at his ears. Suddenly, two scorpion moles standing shoulder to shoulder filled the tunnel, stingers high and tight above their heads, prepared to strike. Hungry for the kill.

Blackjack quickly bagged the bones together in the leather bag.

I need to take these bones to Roko. The intervention of Roko, the Master Recipe Maker of blood- smoke, will be able to conjure up a blood-tobacco mix enabling him to journey to the spirit-soul world to talk to the owners of the bones.

Chapter 7: About Arune

Kula perched on her castle launching deck that doubled for a high-altitude observation point of the Darkan Territory. At 22,000 feet, Kula slowly looked up and down the valley floor.

She closed her eyes and focused on her internal senses; sniffing the wind blowing through the valley floor, she didn't detect any alien smells.

Tilting her head, she listened for any foreign sounds that could cause her or the inhabitants of Darkan Territory any harm. So far, no sound or smell seemed to be around to warn her of approaching danger.

She placed both hands on the side of the stone cliffs connecting her domain down to the valley floor beneath, anticipating that any vibrations of larger than usual movement through the stone canyon walls would produce tremors that bit at her feet and underbelly.

No such tremors today. The only things she did hear were footsteps coming up from behind. "Kula, my Queen," said Slaughter. "You sent for me." Bowing, he added, "What is your task of me?"

"General Slaughter. Please come forward."

Slaughter moved closer to Kula, still remaining behind her in respect.

"Slaughter, my general. I need you to have your best fighter dragoon perform a full internal perimeter search of the immediate territory today."

"I will send Graper to perform that task. Are you traveling today? Possibly to Grimmbell?"

"I have been invited to Grimmbell by the high council. I need you to take the reins until I return."

"I would be honored," said Slaughter.

"If for some reason I don't return by the third moon midnight, you must take control for me. Full power of Darkan Territory, Valley of the Tomb Sleepers."

"My Queen, I'm sure I will see you by tonight. I do not believe any creature, human or otherwise would have the courage to battle you. An unrealistic undertaking, only to end up dead."

"That could be true; however, if there were a large pack of intruders, that could be a different story."

"An unrealistic mission for any number of invaders. Dead again. You are too wise and strong to have anything bad happen to you."

"You could be right, General. In any case, yes, I will be stopping along the way to talk to some of the tobacco kings."

Slaughter tilted his head with tight eyes. "Are we looking for anything in particular?"

"Maybe," said Kula, looking over the edge of the launching pad. "I want to know if someone has been seen roaming the valley."

"We are talking about Arune," said Slaughter. "I want to know about this unknown dark intruder."

Kula nodded. "Oh definitely. This entity had multiple life coins. Very rare too."

Slaughter stepped up to the edge alongside Kula. "My Queen and friend. I would prefer Graper to assist you in your travels."

"General, you know I can take care of myself."

"I know that." Lifting his head high, he added, "And I know you put me in charge of security. So, I insist."

Kula raised her head eye level to Slaughter. "I suppose you are right."

"I'm always right. And if you stay overnight, Grimmbell would be the ideal stop over."

"Are you trying to get rid of me?"

"Absolutely not. You know the King of Souls and the high council thrive on your visits to Grimmbell."

"Very well. I will be leaving in an hour."

Slaughter turned abruptly toward the hallway. "While you are absent, I will have my fighter dragons fly high and low throughout the valley today and tomorrow. Anything moving in the air or on the valley floor that shouldn't, the fighter dragoons will capture and report to me."

"Good," said Kula. "I want to know if Arune has any buddies who could be planning some type of harm against us."

Slaughter was halfway to the corridor when he

stopped. Kula looked at Slaughter. "Did we forget something?"

Slaughter spun around. "No, nothing to do with the travel plans, but when you said Arune was maybe having help… and the attack on Ella. Well, it made me question."

"Question what?" said Kula.

"As you know, I have caught a number of thieves just in the last couple of months, trying to smuggle tobacco out of the valley. *Bundles* of tobacco."

"Yes, I remember you reporting those events to me. I am not sure why people would put their lives on the line to smuggle out something as mundane as tobacco."

"As you know, my Queen, selling tobacco outside the territory can bring a very handsome profit for anyone. Someone on the cusp of hard times…or filthy greed…may find it an irresistible temptation."

"I suppose. I can see the lure of riches. If one could get away with it, anyway. There are other treasures throughout the valley, not to mention Grimmbell and the territorial battlefield and cemetery."

"The ones I have captured in the past told me they were only going to smuggle once or twice, to get enough profit the first few times and then quit. But they get greedy and want more; it is like alcohol or gambling or visiting a den of vice. What really bothers me, my Queen, is when I find dragoon skin hidden underneath a pile of tobacco leaves. These individuals are presently guests at the cemetery prison."

"Guests?" said Kula. "That's an understatement. It bothers me too, that someone would be willing to take such a risk to smuggle tobacco and dragoon skins, not to mention the harsh penalty that can be imposed by the high council court."

"The high council court imposes penalties matching the crime. Don't you agree, my Queen?"

"Yes, I do, Slaughter. Did you do a follow-up exchange with the smugglers?"

"No, not yet, my Queen. As you know, I am tough on these individuals who illegally take a dragoon skin. I would have a hard time not roughing up one of these thieves. Or any thief stealing from the valley, for that matter."

Kula nodded. "I dare say, Slaughter, but even you are not as tough as the high council court will be if the thieves are found guilty. I should hate to be in their shoes."

"I take it that your travel to Grimmbell Cemetery would involve talking to the high council?"

"Yes, I will be talking to them about the issue of smugglers. Slaughter, in what form was this individual?"

"It was an ox wizard about one month ago, traveling on the two-faced river trail. In his possession, I found small patches of dragoon skin."

"Mmm," said Kula. "Small patches of dragon skin? Did he find these by way of scavenger hunting or stealing?"

"The dragoon skin patches that I found in his bag were battle-worn pieces from past years' conflicts."

"Unsurprising," said Kula. "Pieces of dragoon skin can still be found today on the valley floor."

"Almost anywhere in the Valley of the Tomb Sleepers," said Slaughter. "If you know where to look and look hard enough, you will find plenty of skins. So that wasn't a big deal."

"What *was* the big deal, if any?" said Kula.

"He had a bag of bones with him. I don't remember everything that was in that bag, but I do remember a scorpion mole stinger tip, human skulls, and dragoon skin. There was a smaller leather bag full of tiny bones. I would say a hundred small bones anywhere from two to three inches long."

"Anything else?"

"Yes, there was, my Queen."

"What else did this ox wizard have?"

"This is where things got a little ugly, my Queen."

"Please continue. I want to know everything."

"This is the moment in which the ox wizard was getting a little unruly with me."

"You do remember, General, that an ox wizard is a troubled wizard, a wizard who has not proven himself? They have difficulties with completing the proper sequence in spoken word and incantations but yet still have wizard powers."

"Yes, my Queen, I do remember that. I did take that into consideration. Therefore, I demanded to know what else he had in his bag. He told me that he didn't have anything illegal, and I did not have the right to harass him, that he was in the protection of the Ten-crypt Alliance."

Kula turned her gaze to Slaughter.

"That's what he said. So, I grabbed the bag with my teeth and accidentally tore his arm off along with the bag." Shrugging, Slaughter added, "He can grow another arm. He's a wizard."

"What happened next?" Kula asked.

"He said, and I quote, 'I am the great wizard Novelland, and I will return for revenge'."

Kula's eyes narrowed. "Novelland. I will have to research that name. This matter is interesting and yet a little worrisome at the same time. Did you confirm that the Ox Wizard was just wandering around on his scavenger hunt, or was he working toward an objective of some kind?"

"I figured he was just wandering around looking for some type of magical artifacts to make a wizard's brew of some sort or other. But when he was so protective of the bag, from that point on, I knew he was on some type of a mission. Either for himself or the Ten-crypt Alliance."

Kula whipped her tail back and forth with force. "Or possibly, he is working for a single hunter. A hunter such as Arune."

"It certainly makes sense. You did say that the dark force Arune was going to pay Ella in life coins."

"Sounds to me as though this ox wizard could be working with Arune. If you see him in the valley again, you will bring him to me, do you understand? I wonder what he is working on."

Chapter 8: Battle in the Tunnel

Blackjack tied the new-found leather bag of bones to the levitating dark bundle that followed his every move. He proceeded down the tunnel toward the two scorpion moles blocking his path, stopping twenty feet in front of them. "I'm Blackjack, Royal Messenger for Kula, Queen of Darkan Territory and the Valley of the Tomb Sleepers."

"Blackjack," said the bigger mole, looking at his smaller partner. "I don't know of any royal messenger in this valley. Why are you in the scorpion tunnels?"

"I mean you no harm," said Blackjack. "But I have an urgent package to deliver to Grimmbell Cemetery. So, I need to pass."

The bigger scorpion mole took a big step forward toward Blackjack. "And what do you have wrapped in that bundle?" he asked, nodding toward the dark package in its tight wrapping.

Blackjack slowly moved backwards two steps, placing his right hand on the bundle itself. "It's a package I need to deliver. Its contents are of no concern of yours."

"Well," said the larger mole. "Since you are using our tunnel, we think it is of a concern of ours.

Everything that happens inside our tunnel is something we are concerned about. And rightly so."

"Look here, Mr. Whoever-You-Are, what are your names?"

"Why do you need our names, runner of the kingdom?"

"Because Mr. No-Names, I can tell by your posture and the height and direction of your stingers that you mean me harm."

"No, I don't mean you any harm, not if you provide something worthy in exchange for using our tunnel. A fair deal, wouldn't you say?"

"Something worthy," said Blackjack, poking his right titanium claw into the dark bundle, a surge of pain stinging. He bit his lip to subside the pain, pulling his claw free.

Maybe that wasn't a good idea, he thought, turning his attention back to the two moles.

"I have given you something quite valuable. Now put your stingers down. I mean you no harm, but I warn you, I will protect myself."

Thug, the larger of the two moles, shook with a concession of deep breaths. "What? You have given nothing to us."

He looked about, waving his arms as if to say, *see! Nothing whatsoever!*

Blackjack planted his right foot tight on the tunnel floor, his titanium claws still stinging from touching the unknown dark package.

Hunching with claws extended, he prepared himself for an attack from the moles. The two moles looked at each other and nodded.

Okay, here we go, thought Blackjack.

Suddenly, a mole stinger zipped over Blackjack's shoulder, making contact with the leather bag of bones, ripping a hole in its outer.

"Damn," said Blackjack. "Those tail bone stingers move very fast."

Blackjack could see the trajectory of a second stinger launching itself, navigating right for a direct chest hit. He leaped to the right himself, slamming into the tunnel wall. The second stinger missed his chest, striking the black bundle and causing a bright and loud spark.

"What the hell was that?" questioned Blackjack.

Sug, the smaller of the two moles, was leaping around like a crazy thing. "It's burning!" he yelped. "Something's stuck to the tip of my tail! Oww!"

His stinger smoked while he flicked his tail, thrashing its tip against the tunnel wall in a desperate attempt to extinguish the burning sensation. "And a pain's jabbing me in the back of my neck," he shouted, stomping his feet. "My feet feel numb! Oww!"

Thug pushed the smaller scorpion mole out of the way, hunching down, digging his feet into the tunnel floor. He held his own stinger cocked high and reloaded, hidden behind his body.

The plan was to launch a sneaky full-body strike against Blackjack.

Partly blinded by Sug's slashing at the tunnel wall, Blackjack waved his hand in front of his face, trying to fan away dirt and dust; the plumes of choking smoke were triggering him to hit the ground, stretching his body flat, hugging the dirt floor and coughing up his guts.

But he had a battle to fight, and slog it out he would.

So, he got himself together and pulled the Penetrator bundle toward him, then aligned it.

With one almighty shove, he pushed the heavy bale right into the charging belly line of Thug, hitting him with a humongous thud. Thug fell to the ground gasping for air, clutching at his stomach.

Sug, on the other hand, looked as if he'd finally got his stinger back to working order, but his small beady eyes didn't resemble those of a normal scorpion mole.

These were wide open and glowing, along with his stinger tail.

I do believe Sug's system has somehow been possessed by the power of the Dark Penetrator Arune. This can't be good for me or him.

The three glowing spots of light coming from Sug's eyes, and his stinger tail were blasting into Blackjack's vision at high speed.

Thug had finally caught his breath and turned his focus back to Blackjack.

Blackjack maneuvered to a squatting position, propelling all his strength into his legs, projecting him at super speed so that Sug could not counter.

Next, Blackjack slid underneath Sug's belly, his claws ripping him open, spilling all kinds of nasty mole guts onto the tunnel floor.

Sug lost his momentum, dropping onto the tunnel floor like a bucket of shit hitting the ground. Blackjack didn't have to look back at his first attacker. He squatted again.

Now, he was waiting for another attack from Thug.

Thug raced past Blackjack with no intent of revenge and running through the pile of mole guts, he looked down at his scorpion mole brother in arms. He poked at the motionless body, leaning forward, sniffing. Thug continued to lean over the deathly corpse and calmly stepped to the stinger end of Sug, grabbing his tail. He cut the stinger off, wrapping it in leather, tucking the wrap under his arm.

Blackjack opened his messenger's bag, pulling out a rag and proceeding to wipe the bright blood from his face, shoulder, and claws. "I really didn't want to do that. But I had no choice."

Thug approached Blackjack, his stinger tail down in the neutral position. "Why did you have to kill my friend? He was my *only* friend."

That sounded just so horribly plaintive and sad. Blackjack was almost moved to tears. Almost. "I'm sorry," said Blackjack. "Honestly, I didn't want this to happen. I wanted nothing of the sort.

But I have a package to deliver, an order from Queen Kula. And nothing will stop me from doing that."

Thug kneeled down next to his fallen friend. "I'm not sure what happened to Sug, why he made that sudden attack on you. It was like some hidden force was pushing him toward that bundle that you have."

"I'm not sure either," said Blackjack. "But I'm beginning to understand my package here, and I don't like it."

"I don't like it either," said Thug. "A voice jumped in my head, telling me I had to cut the rope to your bundle and tie you up tight. It made me aggressive, even evil toward you. I don't understand that."

"I understand those peculiar feelings," said Blackjack. "Ever since I picked up this package, a lot of strange thoughts have been filling my head. You, having those unusual aggressive thoughts toward me; I understand that. I mean it makes a lot of sense."

He was saying he understood far too often. But other words seemed to fail him in the moment.

Thug continued looking at the gutted scorpion mole lying on the ground. "I have seen many insides before in battle, but still not very pretty, is it?"

"No, it isn't," said Blackjack. "I'm sorry. Like I say, I didn't want this to happen, and that's why my journey was…is…so important. That's why I chose the tunnels, to keep this black bundle away from everyone until it can be secured by the earthers at Grimmbell."

Thug nodded. "Yes. Please get that thing out of my tunnels."

Blackjack watched as Thug dragged Sug out of sight down a side tunnel that he hadn't noticed before. Retracting his titanium claws, Blackjack looked down at the pile of intestines strung along the tunnel floor. "I didn't want to hurt him. I had no choice," Blackjack said as if repeating it would somehow make it so much better. He began checking Kula's dragoon rope. No problems; all was secure.

He continued for another hour through the scorpion mole tunnels until his internal alarm system notified him that there was a presence behind him.

Backing against the tunnel wall, Blackjack activated his titanium claws. He looked both ways in the tunnel but didn't see anything with his infrared sight.

"Must be a false alarm. Being so deep, it could be sensing a regular burrowing animal." Blackjack continued through the tunnel with his body tense, goosebumps activated and claws out.

He could see his first glimpse of light from the exit up ahead. "Finally. I'm ready to get out of here." A grip on the back of his shoulder spun him around so fast that he fell on the ground.

"Son of a… What the hell was that?"

Popping up in a heartbeat to a fighting stance, his head jerked to each side of his shoulders. Again, he didn't see anything. He shrugged. *I must be imagining things.*

Chapter 9: Spotting Tower 8

Kula launched herself into the air as she set her internal compass to Spotting Tower 8. There'd been some strange events taking place these past few days and tower 8 was the perfect spot to start asking questions. But first she needed food, so tipped her wings just enough to maneuver her body five feet above the two-faced river; it moved in opposite directions at the same time, making this meandering water a very popular mode of transportation throughout the valley floor.

With her superior dragoon eye vision, she noticed a pocket of muddy golds swimming close to the surface. These were whitefish, each one weighing up to a hundred pounds, a favorite food for Kula. The only downfall was the nasty spines protruding out of the tops of their backs.

Kula submerged herself into the river, going submarine for at least two hundred feet, scooping up a mouthful of the fish, then taking to the air in a precise movement to enjoy the feast with a modicum of delicate tongue maneuvering before spitting the wretched thorns out.

Kula gained altitude and circled the first tower, the first of eight spotting towers eventually leading to number one, located the closest to Grimmbell. She completed the second circle of the tower, making sure the approach was clear before making her final touchdown on the landing pad atop the stone pillar.

As she spiraled down to one hundred feet above the landing pad, she noticed a ghostly sight. Flying around the top of the tower was a horde of black birds and magpies, crowding the landing zone. She hovered at a hundred feet, looking in all directions for any possible threats or attacks from the sky. Not seeing any flying threats, she maneuvered her wings from full-length out to quarter-length, softly touching down on the landing platform.

The array of avaricious scavenger birds scattered,

flying off in a myriad of directions. She approached what the birds were picking at. A leather bag. She sniffed it.

"Death." She sniffed again. "Smells like death. Flesh. Flesh and bone, but it's old." She kicked at the bag. "Sounds like bones to me as well."

Thump, thump, thump. She could hear footsteps thumping their way up the stone steps to the only door that led to the top of the tower. *Definitely someone in a hurry.*

Needing to prepare, she inhaled a quarter-breath, ready to burn the shit out of anything that came out from behind that door, anything that she didn't deem safe. *Is this a trap? Who or what can that be?*

A small hairy hand presented itself through the crack in the door, waving a white flag to and from. "Queen Kula. Queen Kula. It's me, Rasp. My Queen, I'm so sorry I wasn't here to greet you when you landed. It was a last-minute decision to come out to tower eight when the earther diggers found this unique burial ground of bones, two hundred yards from the tower. I hurried over here as fast as I could. I didn't have time to inform you of my arrival. My apologies. I hope you can forgive me, my Queen."

Kula swallowed her fiery mix.

"Rasp. It must be important if I find you at Spotting Tower 8, way out here at the farthest end of the Darkan Territory. And alone on the top of the tower. This is unusual, correct?"

"Yes, it is, my Queen, I assure you. I was informed by the tower dragoons that you would be flying over today, so I was hoping you would take these skeletal remains to Grimmbell for proper identification, cataloging, and burial."

"What you got going on here?" asked Kula, picking at the bag. "You had a battle of some kind?"

"No. No battle here. Now, maybe a few years ago, but not recently. No, not at all."

"Where did you come up with all these bones? Does Roko know you are here?"

"No, my Queen. Roko doesn't know I'm here. That's another story altogether."

"You don't usually bring the remains to the top of a tower, do you? So why now?"

"Kula, my Queen, may I approach? I have something to tell you. Something…of importance."

Kula tilted her head with an eerie stare. "Come forward and tell me. You have my interest." She lowered her head so Rasp could speak into her ear.

Rasp approached Kula and gently touched the side of her head with his hand.

"Kula, my Queen, this was an interesting find. The bones of this particular burial site that my earthers were digging are unusual. The bones…or, I should say the skulls…that we found in this pocket of the dig site had engravings on them."

"What kinds of engravings?" Kula asked. "Like a tattoo?"

"Yes," said Rasp. "Like a tattoo but with all the symbols carved into the skull. Now one of the mysteries that we don't understand is when were the inscriptions put on the skulls and why?"

"I don't know the answer to that," said Kula. "But I have a feeling you are trying to figure that out."

"Of course, I am. Was it after they died? I doubt that. Or before they died? I doubt that theory too. So, they must have been engraved, tattooed, say, at birth. We're not sure at this moment, so I thought in the best interest of everyone, we need to take these remains to Grimmbell as soon as possible. That's why I'm here today."

"I understand," said Kula. "But what makes these remains so different to so many of the other digs that the earthers have done in the territory?"

"I'm glad you asked," said Rasp, retrieving a skull from the leather bag. "When we were doing a skull authenticity test, we found these skulls to be quite unusual. They had these markings on them, but also, when we did the candlelight search inside the skull…"

"Wait a minute," Kula interrupted. "Remind me again what a candlelight search is?"

"Of course, my Queen, forgive me. When we check for the authenticity of a skull, we will set the skull over a lighted black coal candle, which gives us the thickness, strength, and viscosity of it, all the unique characteristics. Thus, of course, my Queen, you know we use the best skulls to make the blood bricks in the ceremonial blood brick drop."

"Please continue," said Kula.

"Okay," said Rasp. "So, when we lit the candles, the skulls would levitate two inches and spin counterclockwise. Thus, the markings on this skull came to light, and it produced symbols moving in a specific order, showing a story of some kind. It was amazing."

Kula tightened her eyes. "Hmm, that's interesting. So, what you could be saying is that you are able to…or the skull is possibly able to tell you its whole life story?"

"That is correct, my Queen. It is exactly like that."

Kula softly nodded. "It's possible that the skull or skulls are telling you the inner thoughts, or what once were its inner thoughts, or maybe its whole life was being portrayed via those cranium markings."

"Yes," said Rasp. "I mean, that's a possibility. I don't know for sure what it means, but I've never seen anything like this before, and I've been digging and cataloging every magical creature for a little over two hundred years, so this is a first for me."

Kula nodded. "There could be hundreds of years of history here within these skulls."

"Exactly what I had been thinking," said Rasp. "I wanted to get these remains to Roko and have him engineer a batch of the death grip tobacco so we could find out more about these skulls," he said, tying the bag tight. "Would you please deliver this to Grimmbell?"

"I can do that," said Kula. "I need to talk to the King of the Soul Tree. Put them in my pack, and I'll deliver them to him."

"Thank you, my Queen."

"You are welcome, and this is intriguing," said Kula. "It's a little worrisome to a point with so many events that have come up recently, but yes. And you want the skulls to be delivered to Roko?"

"If you would, my Queen," said Rasp. "Please deliver to Roko at the Grand Hall of the Tomb Sleepers at Grimmbell."

"I can do that."

"My Queen," said Rasp with a hand raised. "What is it now, Rasp?"

"There is one more little issue that came up in the last week. It has to do with Spotting Tower Number 7."

"Spotting Tower 7?" said Kula. "That tower reminds me of the battle I had with a few of the black spirit riders. It caused a lot of uncertainty between dragoons and the spirit horse riders."

"I received a message from the King of the Soul Tree, concerning Roko."

Kula's head jerked back. "Really? You got a message from the King of the Soul Tree? The King himself?"

"Yes," said Rasp. "I was given a message from the king, delivered by his spirit messenger Messiah. I couldn't believe it myself either. I was quite stunned."

"What did he want to know about Roko?" asked Kula. She was leaning in, her eyes wide.

"The message asked for Roko the master tobacco-ologist to prepare a tobacco-herb mixture to talk to a particular wizard buried in Grimmbell Cemetery. But we were unable to locate Roko."

"Rasp, wait a minute."

"What is it, my Queen?"

"You said a little while ago that you were given a message from the King of Souls."

"Yes, I was totally startled. I thought it was a prank."

"Because Roko was unavailable at that time?"

"That is correct, my Queen. He couldn't be located."
"What did you mean by unavailable?"

"Well," said Rasp. "He could not be found."

"That sounds strange to me."

"It is, and at this point in time, it's a mystery. I'm really not supposed to say anything, but he could not be located. That's all I know on the subject."

"Really?" said Kula. "So Roko just disappeared?"

Rasp nodded. "Yes, my Queen. That's as I understand it."

"That's really odd. Did you search for him? Did you talk to the diggers? Maybe he was at one of the old battle sites.”

“Yes,” said Rasp. “We sent messages to all the gravediggers, and they checked the most recent dig sites. He could not be found.”

“That’s rather unusual,” said Kula. “Of all the years that I’ve known Roko, he has never just disappeared.”

“I wonder if there’s any foul play?” suggested Rasp.

“Why yes,” said Kula. “That’s exactly what I was thinking. Because Roko does not just go missing; he is not the type.”

“The Arune dark bundle.”

“The only thing that we did hear,” said Rasp, “was one of the diggers was sure he overheard Roko saying he was actually going outside Grimmbell to deliver a package.”

“Roko going on a trip?” said Kula. “That is odd. Not impossible. But most uncharacteristic. Did he say where was he going?”

“He said he was meeting up with Bradicus to take him an engineered two-pound bundle of tobacco.”

“Really?” said Kula. “So, he did leave the grand tomb to meet up with Bradicus?”

“That’s the rumor, but I wasn’t supposed to say anything because I didn’t have all the facts about the matter. But that’s what I heard.”

Kula watched Rasp measure the particular skeletal bones, inserting them into the leather bag.

“Rasp, since you know a few things about our history, perhaps you can shed some light… Has Roko talked about past battles recently?”

Holding onto the leather bag, Rasp stood from his kneeling position and eyed Kula.

“I think he’s been acting strange, but please don’t quote me on that statement because I could get in trouble with the king.”

“No,” said Kula. “You speak the truth; nothing will happen to you.”

“Okay,” said Rasp, taking a deep breath. “Then I’ve noticed Roko roaming through a lot of the older dig sites, the sites we haven’t been around in three to four hundred years, maybe longer.”

"Go on," said Kula.

"I traveled with him to a battlefield dig site I had never seen before."

Kula gazed out over the retaining wall of the tower. "Can you describe how you got there?"

"Well, I was told later, we went to the Three Kings Battlefield."

"The Three Kings Battlefield?" said Kula. "That would be closer to five hundred years ago."

"But of course, my Queen, if the King is aware of you coming to Grimmbell, he might want to talk to you about Roko's past weeks' activities."

"I'm sure he will," said Kula. "Although I'm assuming Roko could be missing in action to find a specific artifact for a spell. A spirit spell to control one of the lingering, lost spirits causing problems and unable to be secured by the normal agenda. So, they will have to use a different procedure to regulate this spirit. Which according to my past knowledge, probably has something to do with a spirit being taken or possibly killed in the upper world by a black spirit horse rider. That's my thought anyway."

"A black spirit rider?" said Rasp. "Do you think Roko might be able to answer that question, or that he's the only one who *can* answer it?"

Kula tilted her head to the right. "Well, Roko is the earther who developed the mixes to talk to the other side and dimensional spirits, along with setting up a trusted relationship with the souls of Grimmbell. He does have an advantage."

"Why is it after all of these years," said Rasp, "we can't control the black spirit riders going from dimension to dimension? Isn't there a way we can control the dimension better? They have too much free movement."

"Those are all good questions," said Kula. "Which leads me to think that the symbols engraved on these skulls could portray a specific story of finding that secret out."

"Really," said Rasp. "I mean, that's quite interesting. How did you come to determine that?"

"Well, if you remember, Rasp, back in the conflict with the black spirit riders, I dealt with three of them, quite a fierce battle. I was young at governing the territory at that time. I battled the three, and then later on toward the end of the battle there were four, but the three main ones, I managed to burn one to its bones. And to my surprise, when I looked over the remains, there were some markings on some of the bones. I don't know if they were on the skull, but there were markings on the remains anyway. I recorded that in my conclusions and then documented it within the dragoon wing wrap. So that history is engraved on my second set of wings, preserved in the Hanging Wings Library."

"Yes, my Queen, I do remember that story being told to me when I was coming up through the ranks, and with all due respect, my Queen, I do believe that you were scolded for battling three black spirit horse riders by yourself."

"Yes, you are right, Rasp. I'm guessing Roko has been telling you stories again late at night. In any case, I was scolded by the King of the Soul Tree, but I think he was more worried about my enthusiasm to challenge the riders, while not having the knowledge to battle four black spirit horse riders at the same time. As you might guess, it takes a great deal of magical power and focus."

"Kula, my Queen, with your permission, could I go to the Hanging Wings Library and read the history of this particular conflict? If you don't mind, I would like to help you look into this further. I would be at your service forever."

"I see no problem with that," said Kula. "You have my permission to go to the archive of the wings' library. Go to section 168 to 178; I believe that will take you to the history of that particular conflict. It was a six-to-eight-hour skirmish that particular day. Just make sure that you check with the curator, and you will have to leave an imprint of your life coin in the records book."

"An imprint of my life coin?" asked Rasp.

"Yes. Once you acquire the history, you could be called upon to relinquish that information. And may I remind you, Rasp, with that information, you could also be called upon to answer questions by members of the living kin related to the battle, and to answer to the underground court of earthers and All Verse laws pertaining to future battles."

Rasp stroked his chin and rubbed his eyes. "Wow,

that's a lot of responsibility to take on."

"There're numerous situations that could come up because you're privy to that information. You understand knowing this type of information could cost you both your life and your life coin?"

"I think so," said Rasp.

"Are you willing to sacrifice that if necessary?"

"Wow, I didn't know it could lead to such bad things for me. I'm not too sure now."

"Well, let me reassure you. It probably won't go that far to where you could lose your life, but it is possible, so I want to let you know before you move forward. This is a daunting and dangerous quest to learn more about the elusive black spirit horse riders."

"No problem," said Rasp, considering everything and weighing it up. "I'm all in and willing to take on the responsibilities. I want to explore this further. This could be a huge find, and if I may say so, my Queen, it could be connected to the tattooed skulls and what really makes them tick…and what the King of the Soul Tree is looking for."

"Yes," said Kula. "I'm starting to gather some of the pieces. An interview with a deceased soul from the past to deal with a black spirit rider. That's a smart move on the part of the Soul King, but it is not the whole truth. There is something wrong. Something missing. That worries me."

Chapter 10: Has Anyone Seen Roko?

Blackjack stopped ten feet before exiting the tunnel, turning to look down it, no images appearing in his infrared vision. He sniffed the outside air. Nothing out of the ordinary. He listened, hearing some bird chatter and wind movement, but again finding nothing to alarm him.

He slowly poked his head out of the tunnel and into the daylight, preparing for any additional attacks that the power of his dark package might have conjured up. No attacks at the moment.

He quickly exited the tunnel and ducked into the thick cover of the undergrowth of blue sage brush. Once amongst it, he picked up some tracks inside the brush undergrowth that appeared to be made from some smaller animals. He stayed on the beaten path until the tracks of the small furry animals changed into one track of single horse prints. He searched for more, but there was only one set, making him curious and a little worried. Studying the ground further, he hoped for multiple tracks.

Again, only one hoofprint every six feet or so.

Damn! he thought, his hair spiked on end. *My day isn't getting any better.*

A single horse print usually meant that a black spirit horse had come this way and—double worse— the horse was looking for a new rider. *Does my unknown dark cargo know the cause of this search for a new rider? And what happened to the previous one?*

He recalled Brazel had said earlier about Kula not telling him everything he needed to know about this journey. "She must have her reasons. A black spirit rider," he muttered, shaking his head. "They are always looking for something for a specific reason, usually not a good one either. And the riders are always trying to break into Grimmbell Cemetery."

He picked up the pace, veering off the path to a more direct route to Grimmbell.

He pushed on for another two hundred yards, then caught a glimpse through the blue bush of something moving parallel to him, step for step.

What kind of curse was I taking on when I said I'd deliver this dark power to Grimmbell?

Sniffing the air, he caught a scent that burned his nose hairs. He wiggled his nose, squatting down to the ground. Now, he saw four black horse legs stomping the ground in one spot.

"Oh, this isn't good. If this is a black spirit horse, that's one problem but if it's a black spirit rider off his horse, then that makes the problem twice as bad. Why would the rider dismount when they rarely ever get off their horses—especially not in the middle of nowhere?" Blackjack paused, trying to work out the situation. "I will do a quick rebounding shock spell to see if I can get an indication if the rider is hiding in the blue sage brush," he whispered.

He pushed outward, away from his chest with palms facing out.

At the end of the movement, a thin line of energy released from the center of his palms, moving like the wind in all directions.

Immediately, the shockwave bounced back to him, indicating to Blackjack no negative energy with no unusual clusters of dark energy.

I wonder what happened to the black spirit rider. It could be a trap. The rider could still somehow be watching me.

Blackjack approached closer, watching the dark horse stomping its hoofs in the same spot over and over, snorting.

It's as though the horse is marching in place.

Catching movement again, Blackjack ducked down below the low cluster of bushes to see a middle- aged man somewhat resembling the one he was supposed to meet up with…a tobacco farmer dealing specifically with the earthers. Blackjack had plans to pick up two pounds of Brown Leaf Barrel No. 5, a particular blend of tobacco engineered for one purpose, and that was to communicate with the black bundle once he transported it to Grimmbell

Cemetery. When Blackjack watched the unattended black spirit's horse creating such a disturbance, he noticed another problem.

The black spirit horse was setting a trap for a new owner. The new unknowing victim-rider would assume he must have found the horse lost in the wild. But once the unexpected person sat in the mount, and the horse accepted the new rider, the transmutation would take over.

Once the two joined together, the new black spirit rider would be on a bloody head-chopping rampage to capture the needed spirits to cement the bonding between horse and rider. It would be a black horse tornado ripping through the valley, stealing spirits. *This is not good.*

A closer look at the delivery man showed a face of a different being, not of the farmer but that of an old friend, Roko, master tobacco-ologist of Grimmbell.

This is extremely unusual for Roko to be outside the Grand Hall of Grimmbell Cemetery.

Blackjack exited the blue sage, brushing off the small twigs that had found a home on his shoulders.

Waving his hand, he gathered his composure and hurried to meet with Roko. "Hello Roko, how are you doing? And what are you doing out here?"

"Blackjack, my friend," said Roko. "I haven't seen you in what… it's been a while," he added, pushing his hand out. "Actually, thinking about it… it was last summer when we met in the Candy Cornfield."

"Yes," said Blackjack, "I think you're right. Anyway, what brings you here today?"

"Can't I take time off to see an old friend?"

"Of course, you can," said Blackjack. "It's just that you usually don't go outside the walls of Grimmbell, and rarely come out this far, so what's going on?"

Roko nodded in agreement. "Yes, you have a point; right to the crux of the matter as always."

"I'm just concerned," said Blackjack. "You know I've been working with Queen Kula on tightening security for Grimmbell and the Valley of the Earthers."

"Of course, I do," said Roko. "I'm one of the earthers on the Grimmbell high council who asked Kula to have you selected for heightened security of the territory.

You are one of the few who can and does travel all over it. Plus, the fact that your magic seems intertwined throughout the valley."

"Thank you," said Blackjack. "Thank you for your vote of confidence. I have a great respect for you.

Your master craft skill of blending and growing death-grip tobacco is legendary."

"Smoking tobacco is not the only crop our earthers grow, you know."

"Of course, I do," said Blackjack. "Which leads me to the question again; how come you are out here today? I was not expecting to meet with you."

"Fair enough," said Roko. "This specific batch of read-only spirit tobacco could be dangerous to use."

"More dangerous than usual?" said Blackjack. "Please explain."

Pulling the two-pound bag out of his backpack, he handed it to Blackjack. "It will take you to the destination you want to go, and you'll be able to converse with anybody you want, providing you ask the correct questions."

"What's the catch?" said Blackjack.

Tapping his finger on the tobacco bag, Roko answered, "This mix was made by an earther. Me of course, no humans, and this is the most important part…"

"Go on," said Blackjack.

"The reality is going to have an allure to it."

"Allure? What sort of allure?"

"It's going to try to put you into that world. Like the unknown world of your cargo, without you knowing it. Very powerful, very sneaky. If you go into that domain, you might have to engage your third power of Brazel to pull you out."

"Hmm," said Blackjack. "That's a new one on me. I'm not sure I understand what you speak of. If I need Brazel, my magic ally, he is controlled by my mind, and more by my subconscious mind. I have constant communication, so it shouldn't be a problem."

Suddenly, Blackjack noticed a shadow moving toward them. "What is that?" He spun around in time to see a shadow of the black rider's horse moving across the ground as if the sun was setting five hours ahead of schedule. The silhouette of the horse reared up and struck Roko, knocking him to the earth.

Blackjack reached down, grabbing Roko by the wrist and pulling him away.

"Blackjack! Blackjack, where are you? I can't see you! Help me!" Roko shouted.

"I *am* helping you! You need to get to your feet. We need to get the hell out of here!" The forward movement suddenly stopped. "Roko, I can't move you. You're stuck to the ground. Roko, can you hear me? Get up! Run!"

Suddenly, there was a large eruption of bright light blinding Blackjack and sending him reeling. "Son of a bitch!" said Blackjack, shaking his head.

He cradled his hand against his chest, looking down at his fingers running with blood. Rubbing his eyes with his good hand and trying to get a visual of what the hell had just happened, he could smell burnt blood and hair. "Roko, can you hear me? Are you there?" There was no answer.

His vision caught a grueling sight of the black spirit horse shadow, dragging Roko into the blue sage brush and out of sight. Blackjack charged through the brush to see his friend lying on the ground in front of him, his body mummified in black tar.

He reached down and poked at the motionless lump.

"Ouch! Damn!" said Blackjack, jerking his hand away. "It burned me."

Catching movement again, he turned to witness the black horse rear up, charging at him so fast that the last thing he saw was a flick of black horsehair.

Chapter 11: Who is Digging?

Kula leaped headfirst off Spotting Tower 8. Halfway to splattering on the ground, she flared her wings full out, floating within a hundred feet of touching down.

One flap of her powerful wings jetted her three hundred feet above the tower. Tilting her body just a smidge to the right, she had her internal bearings locked onto the next spotting tower.

I need to stop at the other towers leading up to Grimmbell Cemetery. Not sure what I'm going to find at Spotting Tower 7, if anything? Maybe I'm wasting my time checking out that old battlefield?

Kula glided in the morning breeze, her superior vision covering miles at a time.

Dipping down, she caught a morning belly rub on the top of brown ball trees. Swooping upwards, she continued watching the valley floor. Then she hunkered down, utilizing the best body position to gain optimum speed to cover the next hundred miles to Spotting Tower 7, strategically located directly south of the Wizard's Canyon and east of Grimmbell.

Kula approached Spotting Tower 7. Within one mile out and an altitude of one thousand feet, she could see Jinnamon gliding to a full stop on the top of the tower.

Jinnamon folded her fire orange wings next to her body, hanging her head over the landing barrier wall. She was assigned to watch everything that moved on the valley floor and in the air within her arena of duty, which included the protection and preservation of the death grip blend of tobacco and the farmers growing and harvesting the crop near Tower 7.

Kula maneuvered her wings into landing position as she approached the top of the tower, gracefully sitting down in the middle of the landing area.

Jinnamon hugged the outer barrier wall with her backside, bowing deeply to Kula. "Kula, my Queen.

Welcome. I have been expecting you.”

“Jinna. How did you know I would be here today?”

“I have seen six of your fighter dragoons flying across the skies at high and half-mast. I knew something was up. Either something bad had happened or you could be visiting my tower today. I am glad to find that it is the latter of the two.”

“Of course,” said Kula. “That’s why I put you in this particular tower. At least for now, nothing bad has happened to you, but I have my suspicions.”

“Are your suspicions looking for someone or are you looking for something? Can I help you out in any way?”

Kula poked her head over the barrier wall, looking down at the valley below, then quickly moved her line of sight to the Wizard’s Canyon.

“Are you still doing the flybys every two hours in the Wizard’s Canyon?”

“Yes, my Queen. I just got back from finishing the perimeter check only a few minutes ago.”

“Did you see anything out of the norm?”

Jinnamon looked into the distance at the Wizard’s Canyon. “No. I didn’t.”

Kula nodded. “Have you seen anything strange in the past couple of months?”

“With all due respect, my Queen, what kind of *strange* do you mean?”

“Yes,” said Kula. “That’s a good point. Have you seen anybody wandering around any of the old battleground sites near this tower?”

“No, my Queen. Only the designated earther diggers.”

“And they have been digging at the past battle sites, correct?”

“That is correct,” said Jinnamon. “The battle locations.”

“Good. Make sure you’re paying attention to them. I do not want to sound paranoid, but my intuition is leading me to recent unknown developments.”

“I cannot believe my queen would think of herself as paranoid. I believe and trust your intuition.”

Jinnamon twisted her head with a heavy eye squeeze

and walking to the other side of the landing pad, stared at a specific spot.

Kula followed her look. "What is it, Jinna? What do you see that I don't?"

"It's not that I see anything right now. But when I think back to that spot, I remember something strange from a few weeks ago."

Kula made an about-face, moving next to Jinnamon. "What do you remember?"

"It's probably nothing. It had to do with the earther diggers."

"What about the earther diggers?"

Jinnamon made quick eye contact with Kula. "On that particular day, I made my flybys checking this site. I thought it was the earthers doing their thing."

"Go on," said Kula.

Jinnamon returned her stare to the dig site. "I do not know their particular work habits when they dig in these burial sites, but on one particular flyby, I noticed three… No, now that I think about it, I don't know if the two hooded individuals were earthers or not."

"Go on, Jinn. What did you see?"

"I saw two hooded earthers, I think, standing a few feet apart on the dig site. One was holding a book, shaking his hand in a forward motion. The third figure standing downrange of them was stacking bones in a specific design."

"Hmm," said Kula. "I have seen them do that before at dig sites. They reenact specific events to record what could have happened in that battle."

"Yes, I know," said Jinnamon. "I have seen that too, but this was different."

"Well, what was so different about it?"

"There was an explosion. A big ball of fire," Jinnamon attested.

"A ball of fire? Are you sure about that?" asked Kula.

"Yes, I'm sure."

"Do you remember the fire part?"

"Yeah, for the most part, but I'm not sure exactly what you mean."

"What I mean is, how long was there an actual flame, a burning period in relation to time. One minute? Five minutes? Ten? How long?"

"I would say five minutes. The third guy, the one who looked as if he was attaching the bones together, melted. I know it sounds ridiculous, but it looked as if he melted himself over the top of the bones."

"He *melted?*" Kula questioned.

"Yes. It was as though he became part of the bone structure. But I wasn't sure. And when I made another pass, they were gone. Underground."

Kula inhaled a big breath of air and released. "That's interesting. In the archives of the Wings Library, I don't remember seeing any such formula in reenacting and cataloging the battle sites."

"But that's not all," said Jinnamon. "I also landed on the burial ground."

"Excellent. What did you find?"

"I found blood."

"Blood? Whose blood?"

"From an earther, but I don't know which one. At least not without a lineup of possible candidates."

"Anything else around the blood sample?" said Kula. "Bone fragments? Maybe a piece of clothing?"

Nodding, Jinna continued, "Yes, I found bone dust, and a black sticky paste mixed with the blood, formed into a ball the size of an orange."

Kula's eyes narrowed and speaking in a lower tone, she asked, "The sticky stuff. Like black tar?"

"Yes, my Queen. That's exactly what it was like. A black tar. It was difficult to pull off my talons."

"You should have reported this to me. This needs to be recorded."

"I'm sorry, my Queen, but I did manage to put the tar sample in this leather bag," she said, handing the bag to Kula. "It has a sulfur smell to it."

Kula opened the leather bag and snorted a quick sniff. "You're right. Sulfur." She poked her finger into the bag, rolling a piece of the black tar into a ball. "Still sticky."

"I'm so sorry, my Queen, I should have reported it. Can you forgive me? It will never happen again."

"Jinnamon, I forgive you but next time, do make sure you let me know."

"Thank you, my Queen."

"One more thing," said Kula. "Any bundles of tobacco or dragoon skins reported missing or stolen?"

"No, my Queen. The total bundle weights of tobacco are recorded and given to Roko and Slaughter. If anything went missing, I would be the first to hear about it. General Slaughter demands excellence."

"Have you come by any crosstalk relating to stolen dragoon skins?"

"No, my Queen; if I came into contact with any thieves, they would be scooped up, delivered to Grimmbell and reported to General Slaughter."

"What if they resisted? What would you do then?"

"The truth?" asked Jinnamon.

"Yes, the truth. Of course, the truth!"

Jinnamon inhaled a big breath, squaring her shoulders with Kula. "Then I would kill them."

Kula gently nodded. "Good girl. Oh, that does remind me of something." Kula retrieved a leather wrap from under her wing. She unfastened the folded leather and handed the black piece to Jinnamon. "With your aroma scents so specialized, have you ever smelled this scent before?"

Jinnamon rubbed her head hard against her torso and sniffed the dark matter in her claw. Her eyes clouded with worry. "Where did you get this?"

"Let's say I got it from an unknown dark entity. Not very long ago. So, you have this scent recorded on your skin?"

Jinn gently nodded. "Yes, I do. It has some of the same scent as the sample," she said, nodding, "at the battle site, just below us."

Kula handed Jinnamon a piece of clothing. "And was there any scent from this at the dig site?" Jinnamon dragged her head along her torso, smelling the cloth. "It's Ella. The medicine woman."

"Yes, it is," said Kula.

"No, I didn't have her scent at that dig site. What does all this mean?"

"That's the problem. I don't know yet."

Chapter 12: Roko is Gone

Blackjack picked himself up off the ground, frantically looking in all directions. "Damn, that horse is fast. Where did that black bastard go?"

A cloud of dark smoke moved swiftly, engulfing Roko, forming a circle of darkness blocking any chance to rescue Roko or to notice any charging black spirit horse.

Blackjack moved back from the screen of darkness long enough to retrieve a *pop-bang,* a white wax ball the size of a golf ball. He lit the fuse and threw it into the swirling mist. *Bang!*

The black haze started to rotate in the opposite direction, changing the shape of the oval mist into a small tornado with the bottom of the funnel being quickly absorbed into the wax ball.

The blackness opened up to a view of rider and horse.

"Holy heaven and ugly hell," said Blackjack. "The black spirit horse has a new rider, planted right in the saddle."

Blackjack studied the new rider sitting on the red-eyed, tar-dripping black spirit horse.

It's a larger version of Roko transformed into part human form and still part earther. But it's an all- black spirit rider. The new Roko smiled at Blackjack. *Does this mean he likes me?*

Blackjack didn't smile back.

The figure kept smiling at Blackjack as though they had been frozen in time, suspended.

Blackjack waved his arms in the air, calling out to the new Roko, "Roko, is that really you? Can you hear me? What the hell do you think you are doing?"

Roko closed a nostril with a finger and blew snot out of the open nasal orifice. "Man, this feels great up here."

He dug into his vest pocket, opening a small leather tobacco bag. Thrusting two fingers deep in the bag, he shoved a big wad of tobacco into his mouth. "The power ripping through my body, it's fricking amazing. I think my fat one's so hard, a cat couldn't scratch it," Roko said, spitting on the ground. "I can see so much more on my horse, quite fascinating. You need to try it. The many dimensions that I sense before me as a black spirit rider, it's unbelievable. I can choose so many dimensions in front of me right now, at least twenty."

Looking over at Blackjack, he continued, "This is amazing. I don't know how it happened, but I see now, my friend, that I can travel into diverse worlds. F**** *ye-haw.*"

Blackjack stood, mouth open, in awe as his longtime earther friend and master creator of specialized tobacco mixes was now a number one enemy of himself, Kula, and everyone in the Darkan Territory.

"Roko, if that's who you are, you need to get the hell down off that horse. Before it's too late."

Roko spit on the ground again. "Are you kidding yourself, Blackjack? It's already too late. Are you ready for this? I am Roko the Dark. The Dark Spirit Rider."

Blackjack nodded. "Okay, so now you're Roko the Dark. Same problem as before: you must dismount that horse or you are going to end up in some cold, dark, ugly underground world."

Roko smiled, showing a strong set of yellowed teeth. "I have much bigger plans than that. Come on, Blackjack, you know me better than that."

"I know Roko the Earther, my friend, not Roko the Dark, a shithead spirit-stealing, horse-humping rider. And when did he get the yellow teeth? Look, I need to ask you a question."

Roko replied, "Sure. At this moment in time, you can ask questions. They are free today, but if we should ever meet again, which I'm looking forward to, it will cost you a steep price."

Blackjack shook his head in disbelief. "I can't believe this is happening," he said, stepping closer to Roko and his tar-dripping horse. "Roko, is someone else controlling you?"

The smile of the yellow teeth disappeared and

leaning off his horse, Roko replied, "Nonsense! I do what I please." Spit peppered Blackjack's face.

Blackjack backed up until he could feel the blue brush branches pushing against his back. *Okay, this is not Roko, my earther friend. This thing is Roko the new asswipe dark spirit rider*, Blackjack thought, dipping down and looking underneath the belly of the horse. *There are no synchs holding the saddle on. Could I knock him off that horse? Maybe I can throw a dragoon rope around Roko and drag him off?*

Blackjack knew he had but a few seconds to attempt to dismount Roko from the horse. He had to try something right now. Squatting, he launched himself full speed at Roko's midsection in hopes of knocking him off the horse but before he could make contact with a punch to the midsection, the man and horse were united as one; Roko dipped his head down and rolled his shoulders to the left. The horse's head, neck, and shoulders shadowed Roko, knocking Blackjack to the ground.

"Come on, Blackjack. You can do better than that. I want a challenge here. I can't take your head without a good fight. I need blood, guts, and someone screaming in pain. Damn."

Roko and the black spirit horse stomped a path toward Blackjack.

Blackjack rolled, dipped, jumped and flipped like a grasshopper in a hot frying pan, managing to escape injury as Roko continued to guide his stomping stallion at him.

Blackjack leaped into the undergrowth of the blue sage brush, scurrying as fast as he could on his hands and knees.

His powers are growing. I don't know if I can battle Roko in combination with the power of a black spirit horse. At least not at this time.

He managed to circle behind Roko and his stomping horse, concealing himself in the underbrush of the blue sage.

He watched Roko plow his big black tar horse through the blue sagebrush, in the opposite direction, calling out to him, "Blackjack, Blackjack. Come out and play. I won't hurt you."

He watched until he couldn't see or hear Roko anymore, shaking his head in disgust. "Damn. I lost him to a black spirit horse. I never thought that would happen in a thousand years. Shit." He knew that the longer Roko was on the black spirit horse, the less chance he would be able to get his friend back.

"I need to check on my package." Blackjack retreated the same way he'd come into the thick blue sagebrush to check on his Dark Penetrator bundle that he still needed to take to Grimmbell Cemetery.

When Blackjack arrived at the spot where he'd tied the levitating bundle down to roots of the thick blue sagebrush, it was gone. A deep ripping, gouging pain stabbed into his stomach, his heart screaming with fear, performing an internal suicide dive to his crotch.

"Oh, son of a bitch. What happened to the dark bundle? Was I followed? Was this planned? I'm so screwed. Kula is going to roast me alive. And use a wild pig bone to pick her teeth clean."

He studied the immediate area. *I don't see any tracks, broken sagebrush or tree branches. Nothing.*

Blackjack walked back down the trail fifty yards, looking for an answer; here, he saw a leather bag and Kula's magic dragoon rope hanging on a blue sagebrush branch thirty feet off the main trail.

Sprinting up to the blue sage, he held his breath while he removed the rope and bag from the bush.

Why did they leave the rope? This doesn't make sense.

He quickly wrapped the rope around his waist, holding the leather bag tight to his chest as he walked back to the main trail. Sitting down on the opposite and high side of the trail, he slowly opened the leather bag, peeking inside. There was one article at the bottom.

He retrieved the item from the bag, holding it in his hand. It was a ten coin. A Life Coin. As he viewed both sides of the coin, he could see initials on the back. It was Roko's, and it had his credentials on the front of the coin. Master Blood B, Tobacco Mixer. *Why would Roko leave his ten coin? Unless the power of the black spirit horse couldn't assimilate it.*

He was starting to put two and two together. *I'm transporting the Arune unknown dark entity to Grimmbell. Roko shows up where he wasn't supposed to be. The black spirit horse has a new rider. The black bundle is gone.* It was all starting to add up and he didn't like it.

He spit on the ground. "Damn it. The first time I have failed Kula. Failed to deliver my package, failed to hold up my promise as a royal guardian and messenger for the Darkan Territory."

Blackjack rubbed the coin, flipping it from one side to the other. He put the ten coin in a small pocket inside his carrier bag. Then came the most horrendous scream.

He jumped up, looking in all directions.

"What the hell?" he said, rubbing the goosebumps down on his arms. "Roko. That son of a bitch VIM-ed this dimension." He sighed. "How am I going to explain this to Kula?"

Blackjack pulled his sword, spinning like a top, wondering if the scream was some kind of a battle cry. Staring into the blue sage, he could still see dust floating in the air where Roko had tried to stomp him into jelly. He stood guard until he realized: for now, Roko was long gone.

Digging into his chest pocket, he found his smoking pipe.

"I think I need a break," Blackjack said, and changing to human form, he sat down on a nearby log. "Damn," said Bradicus, looking at his hand and noticing blood on his pipe and that two of his fingers were cut. He wiped the blood off everything with his shirt.

"I'm not sure which one is more of a threat, the horse, or the rider?"

"Bradicus. This is Brazel. Are you okay? I sense an elevated heart rate, fear, anxiety and pain coming from my internal sensors."

"Brazel, I was wondering when you were going to jump into my thoughts."

"I was mind locked and couldn't talk to you when the black spirit horse was trying to stomp you into a fine wine."

"That's for sure. I really had to use my best moves to stay ahead of his damn horse."

"Let's not forget that Roko had the reins in his hands. I wasn't sure if you were going to transform into human form right there."

"I definitely thought about it. But I would lose a couple of seconds if I did. Could have been bad."

"Maybe you would've had more of an advantage, maybe not. In any case, I was ready to help you transform."

"In my human form, I'm taller. I could use my sword better. I wanted to stab that horse right in the neck and get it over with."

"Yes, I could sense that coming from you. Do you realize that a black spirit horse is actually different than the one riding the horse?"

"Not exactly," said Bradicus. "I know that the horse has to be compatible with the rider to be able to function and VIM the way a black spirit rider does."

"Yes, you're correct in that sense of it. The connection between the horse and rider, to some extent, is the saddle. For a black spirit horse to set his trap to lure a rider, the horse chooses their rider traits that will mix well with his own powers."

"I saw that happen," said Bradicus. "Saw it right in front of me. If I had transformed into a human during that battle, could I have killed the black spirit horse with my sword?"

"No, I don't think so," said Brazel, "but now that that black spirit horse has added the new rider traits, i.e., the knowledge and spirit essence of Roko, the horse and rider have taken on new powers. We do not know how that will turn out or what he can do with these new skills. Roko the Dark is the new breed of a black spirit rider."

Bradicus dug deep inside his tobacco pouch, retrieving a full pipe. Cupping it in the palm of his hands, he gently blew on the loaded end. It glowed back at him as he inhaled deeply, holding his breath for a full fifteen seconds before exhaling.

"Oh yeah, that feels good. That's a special blend. A tracking blend. I made it myself."

"You made that mix by yourself?" asked Brazel.

"Okay, so I had some help from Roko. Do you think he would have allowed the horse to kill me?"

"I'm not sure," said Brazel, "and I don't want to find out. But like I said, the Roko we knew is gone.

He…or they, I should say…are now a black spirit rider."

Bradicus inhaled the special mix. He closed his eyes in the next step of the process so his magic ally Brazel could enhance the tracking route of Roko the Dark.

The magic ally voice of Brazel came booming into Bradicus' subconscious. "It's ready for you."

"Thank you," said Bradicus. "What would I do without you?"

"I should be thanking you because without you, I would not exist. You saved my life, my family, and for that, I gave you my spirit and life coin."

"We have been over this before," said Bradicus, placing the pipe in his pocket. "No need to thank me. I did what I did. And I would do it again. I think I should be the one thanking you. I have a guardian angel to watch over me. We need to be tracking that black spirit horse. Don't you agree?"

"Yes," said Brazel. "Good hunting."

With the special blend enhancing Bradicus' mental and physical abilities, he levitated to a height of fifty feet and scanning the terrain around him, his vision showing him objects of interest in blue and horse tracks in red. A blue object appeared close to the stomping grounds of the black horse incident.

It also showed tracks in red, indicating the black spirit rider headed north until it reached Creature Creek. Then the tracks disappeared.

Bradicus walked the short distance to the blue object.

"Well, look at this. Mr. Roko dropped his recipe book. Never thought I'd ever see this in my hands, let alone so far outside the Great Hall of The Tomb Sleepers. Makes me wonder if he dropped it on purpose or maybe he lost it when the dark horse had him trapped and rolled up into that tar bar."

Bradicus thumbed through the front pages, acknowledging some keywords and phrases.

But as he skimmed through the next few chapters, the words and phrasing had developed into a language he couldn't read.

"Brazel. What are your thoughts on this writing?"

"Can you turn to the next page, please?"

Bradicus turned the page. "You can read this?"

"I can only make out a few words here and there. I do believe the book has to be read by a specific being."

"What kind of specific being?"

"I don't know yet."

"It's not only a recipe book for blending fine tobacco to speak to the dead and beyond, but also, this book takes on a whole different spectrum of talking to the spirit world, with a new heightened type of multiverse teachings and language. I'm wondering if Roko achieved a level of all-verse knowledge that was too dangerous to handle?"

Rubbing his neck, Bradicus lifted his chin. "I don't know the answer to that, but I'm wondering if that's why the horse and the Arune power bundle wanted to take Roko? I mean, come on, both dark powers in the same place, more or less at the same time. I think I need to secure Roko's recipe book."

"I agree with you," said Brazel. "Secure the book. Hell, maybe it should go to Luxen to hang onto; he could put it in one of the Tri-Eight holding cells."

Bradicus unraveled a thin string of Kula's dragoon rope, tying it around the cover of the recipe book vertically and horizontally with a knot sitting dead center on the book's front jacket.

Staring at the ground, he kneeled and inspected a red highlighted hoofprint left by the black spirit horse. "Yes, it's still fresh and sticky. I'll use some of the black tar and secure this knot. It's going to take somebody pretty clever to open this book without being blinded and having Kula's dragoon rope beat their ass beet red."

Bradicus tightly packed the new wonder book into his messenger bag.

At the same time, he removed the small leather bag containing Roko's ten coin, hanging it around his neck, stuffing the coin under his shirt and out of sight.

Is it worth the price of a person's ten coin to ride on the back of a black spirit horse?

"How do you capture an unknown power like Roko

the Black, traveling through unidentified dimensions?
Brazel, let's find out what happened to Roko's horse
tracks."

Chapter 13: Battle of Creek Crossing

Bradicus plunged into the blue sagebrush, following the red hoof outlines of Roko's spirit horse. He could still see the stride of the hoofprints, indicating Roko and the black spirit horse were moving fast.

He followed the tracks for three miles.

Now, he began noticing the tracks were dropping off to one hoofprint every thirty yards as the tracking smoke mix had started to wear off. Bradicus followed the reddish prints until the tracks disappeared into the water of a creek. He kneeled at the last hoofprint before it.

"Just as I expected. Hardly a print showing. Very little tar is visible, and it's grown hard to the touch.

Could be where Roko the Dark jumped into another dimension."

Bradicus sat at the edge of Whiskey Dick Creek and, measuring the width of the creek by eyesight, he pondered the question, *do the black spirit riders need water or maybe some type of geographical bookmark to activate and enter another dimension?*

Bradicus studied the landscape, looking for anything out of the norm.

He noticed a small pile of green dirt stacked on the other side of the creek and spotting a low water crossing marked by rocks, crossed over to the bank's opposite side.

Kneeling, he picked at the pyramid-shaped mound of green dirt. Noticing black particles mixed in with the green dust, he poked, sniffed, and rubbed it between his fingers.

Something's been burned. This is strange. Never seen anything like this before. I need to take a sample to the earthers. Maybe they'll know? He scooped the green dust into a cloth bag with a tie, placing the unknown sample into a secure pocket in his messenger bag.

"Excuse me, sir!" came a voice behind him.

Bradicus stood with sword in hand, spinning around to face the voice.

"Whoa! Whoa!" the man exclaimed, raising his hands. "I'm looking for my friend. I mean no harm to you. I noticed you a few minutes ago down here by the water. Did you see anyone?"

"No, I haven't seen anyone near the creek, but I've only been here a short time. How long has your friend been missing?"

The man looked up at the sun.

"I suppose it's been a couple of hours now. He came down to the creek to do some fishing."

Keeping his hand on the handle, Bradicus holstered his sword. "I noticed you are carrying a backpack."

"Yes," said the man, looking at the object.

"And a shovel? What are you doing with that?"

"I was going to dig for worms."

Bradicus pulled his sword to chest height.

"Wait a minute," said the shovel man.

"No," said Bradicus, pointing the sword at the man's chest. "Who are you?"

The shovel man's arms tensed as he raised his shovel to his waist. "I live just over the hill there," the man said, pointing with a head nod in the general direction.

"You are a tobacco grower?" said Bradicus.

"Yes I am."

"I see behind you there's a tobacco field," Bradicus said, stretching his neck and chin up. "And I do believe that tobacco crop is a brown leaf barrel number five, correct?"

The shovel man turned around and looked in the same direction. "Yes, it is. You have a good eye. You must know your tobacco."

Bradicus gripped the sword tightly with both hands, his breathing quickening.

"That's strange, because brown leaf barrel number five has much smaller leaves." With a head nod toward the field, he added, "That tobacco crop up there is brown leaf barrel number seven, the most common tobacco grown in this valley. So, shall we try again? Who are you?"

"My name hardly matters. But what's really important is that bag of green dust you have in your carry bag." The shovel man smiled, showing his crooked yellow teeth. His eyes made a clicking noise, dilating into full black then red, and back to black. "I will be needing that dust."

Standing on the balls of his feet, Bradicus positioned his legs wider than his shoulders.

Yellow teeth, just like Roko had. And what's with his eyes changing colors? This thing is either Roko in a different form or some counterpart of his.

"I will warn you now. I am the royal messenger of Queen Kula and a guardian for the Darkan Territory." Bradicus raised his sword. "The dust you want. I don't think so, you pond scum, pig butt licker."

"Pond scum what? That's not a very nice thing to say, Bradicus."

"How do you know my name?" he replied, pointing his sword at the man's neck.

"Let's just say an old friend told me."

Bradicus drew an X in the air in front of his face with his sword. "An old friend like Roko? You are not getting the dust. No way, no how."

"Maybe I underestimated you," said yellow teeth. "How did you know I was lying about being a tobacco farmer?"

"That was an easy one," said Bradicus. "Look at your boots."

The man with the yellow teeth looked down at his shoes then back at Bradicus. "I have black tar on my boots. Aren't you a smart one?"

Bradicus swung at the shovel, knocking it out of his hands. "You are a black horse spirit rider." The man stepped backwards, grinning with his bent yellow teeth.

"Wow. You are damn fast with that sword."

Bradicus stepped up the bank with his sword raised. "I'm losing my patience. Where is Roko?"

"I don't know. But I am not Roko."

Bradicus spit on the ground. "I am looking for a friend of mine who was kidnapped by a black spirit horse just hours ago."

"I don't know where your friend is. But maybe for a small fee, I might be able to direct you to his general whereabouts."

"What kind of fee?"

"Oh… let's say a bag of green dust," yellow teeth said, nodding at the bag.

"That's not going to happen, chicken lips."

"Bradicus, you don't know what you're up against."

Bradicus shook his head. "Listen here, moose breath, *you* don't know what *you're* up against. If you think I'm going to give you the dust, you can smooch my big white butt."

"Roko said you would be a handful, fighting courageously in many previous Darkan wars."

"That's great," said Bradicus. "Do I win a cigar?"

"I have orders not to kill you, but can't guarantee that I won't," he said licking his lips. "You would be quite a crowning card for me."

Bradicus relaxed his shoulders but still held the sword chest high. "I'm not giving you the green dust. It will end up where I'm going, to the Grand Hall of the Earthers."

"You are a fool," said the rider, rushing Bradicus with incredible speed, knocking him off his feet and onto his back. Huge bony hands gripped around his throat, choking off most of his air supply.

Bradicus punched a solid right hand into the man's throat, causing him to cough and spit in Bradicus' face. Bradicus pushed with both hands on the man's chin, trying to force him off, but old yellow teeth kept his grip.

Yellow teeth started to bounce on his throat. "Give me the bag of dust and I might let you go."

Bradicus couldn't answer. His vision started to blur, and he pushed with all his strength on the rider's chin. *It's like he's anchored to the ground. I can't move him.*

With a free hand, he locked onto his six-inch pocket dagger, ramming the full six inches into the right eye socket of yellow teeth, hammering on the butt of the dagger with the palm of his hand.

"I have to stop this spirit rider forever."

Yellow teeth released his grip long enough for Bradicus to throw a smashing fist into the enemy's throat. Grabbing him around the neck, yellow teeth gasped hard, rolling off Bradicus.

Leaping and grabbing the sword, Bradicus turned, ready to slash the rider when a sharp pain exploded in his left ankle. "Son of a bitch!"

Looking down, he saw his dagger piercing the ball joint of his ankle. Going nowhere, Bradicus cried out, clawing at the ground.

"Now I have you where I want you," said yellow teeth. "And I will take what I want."

Yellow teeth grabbed Bradicus' sword, sprinkling the steel with green dust from his pocket, the blade bursting into green flames. He waved the sword in a circular motion above his head and the green flames grew higher, stopping long enough to point the blade straight into the sky. That's when the sword screamed, a horrifying high-pitched screech of pain ripping through the air.

Bradicus hunched his shoulders and covered his ears.

What the hell's next? His screams are the exact same as the flaming sword.

The red-eyed rider turned his stare toward Bradicus and, smiling, positioned the flaming sword at his eyebrows, pulling it across his nose to his chin. Then, he proceeded to do the same with the right side of his face, a bloodied, burned X mark covering his features.

"Now I will take the dust. Your spirit. Your power. Everything."

Bradicus limped back to the edge of the creek. *I could escape in the creek. Fight another day.* That's when he remembered what Kula taught him.

Sometimes, the only way to win a losing battle is to use a magic different than your own.

He kneeled. "Wait! Wait! There's no need for that. I will give you what you want."

The rider approached. "You are smarter than I thought. Kind of a pity. I would have enjoyed the opportunity to battle you to the end."

Bradicus opened the messenger bag, dropping the leather bone bag he had acquired into the scorpion mole tunnel at his feet.

"Kick it over to me."

Bradicus kicked the bag past the rider to his left, and yellow teeth pounced on it.

Bradicus untied the slip knot on Kula's dragoon rope, releasing the rope from his waist. The rope immediately started whipping the black spirit rider, forcing him away from the bag.

The rider swung wildly at Kula's dragoon rope, but it had a mind of its own.

"I knew you wouldn't give up that easily. I changed my mind; I am going to kill you, Bradicus and take your power."

Bradicus nodded to the rope. It dove into the leather bag of bones, emerging like a cobra snake with the head of a scorpion mole stinger bone.

The rope and stinger bone levitated, waiting for his command.

"Attack," said Bradicus. The sharp serrated scorpion stinger bone pierced the chest of the rider while the rope circled around and around until just his head was visible.

"What kind of magic do you have?" said the rider. "This is impossible. I can hardly breathe."

Bradicus pulled the dagger out of his ankle. "Son of a bitch, that hurts." He limped over to the bound spirit rider. The scorpion stinger bone levitated above the man's head. Bradicus looked down at the black rider. "Who sent you? And where is Roko?"

"Let's just say I could be an ancestral spirit of a fallen black spirit rider. Besides, your buddy Roko is not an earther anymore. He is busy constructing his own power to become an official black spirit rider as we speak. Your rope will not contain me for long. As you can see, it's starting to smoke."

The rider was right. Kula's rope would hold for a while, but not long enough.

It was starting to get dark. Bradicus needed to get to Grimmbell, heal his wounds and talk to Kula and the high council. He nodded to Kula's rope. The serrated triangle-shaped scorpion stinger tail bone penetrated the man's neck, cutting off his head.

Chapter 14: Kula Gets Detoured

Sitting quietly, Kula continued her stare from Spotting Tower 7, directing her attention at the burial site that Jinnamon had described about the unusual digging habit of a set of earthers.

From the height of the tower, she formulated in her mind the past battles and less important conflicts previously fought around it.

Kula looked to the south at the impressive opening to the Wizard's Canyon. *I wonder if there are any connections with the peculiar earther diggers and the Wizard's Canyon?*

"Kula, my Queen," said Jinnamon. "Are you okay?"

"I was just thinking."

"Can I assist you in any way?"

"Yes, you can."

"What can I do for you, my Queen?"

"Do you still have your specialized aromatic pores in working order?"

"Yes, I do, but I haven't used them for a few years. Remember, my Queen, I was told to use them sparingly."

"You were given orders to use your talents in the heat of war, not for general entertainment. We are not at war, that is true, but I have decided to give you permission to utilize all of your skills when needed. Is that understood?"

"Yes, my Queen. Thank you."

"I need you to go to the mouth of the Wizard's Canyon."

"I have been banned from the wizard's territory. You know that I was one of Killamore's cloak-and- dagger twenty-six, a box dragon, before I became a dragoon. He still hunts me today, you know."

"I know of Killamore. I know of his box dragons and last time I talked to him, he had only twenty-three."

"Twenty-three?" said Jinn. "Last time *I* battled him,

he had eighteen. Twenty-three box dragons can do a lot of damage."

"Not if I have anything to do with it."

"Kula, my Queen, do I have your permission to engage with Killamore if I have to?"

"Only as a last resort and if it gets ugly, contact General Slaughter. I know in the great war of the dragoon skins, Killamore sent four of his box dragons to defeat Slaughter, but it didn't happen. After that battle, Slaughter became General Slaughter, but for right now, I'm getting off the topic."

"Maybe another time," said Jinn. "I understand. What is it that you want me to do?"

"Go to the mouth of the canyon, talk to the workers who work the crops across the river from the mouth of the canyon and ask them if they have seen anything unusual. Check if anyone has seen a lone wolf type of person moving up or down the valley. Find out how many dragons have been flying in and out of the mouth of the canyon and report to me within the next couple of days. Right now, I need to go to Grimmbell to talk to the Soul King."

"I will not fail you, my Queen."

Kula free-fell halfway down the tower wall before flaring her wings to slow the descent and with one powerful flap, she left Tower 7 behind. Kula pumped her wings, guiding her body into a nice glide pattern at one thousand feet above the valley floor. Catching a tailwind, Kula had Tower 6 in her line of sight and dropped her altitude to two hundred feet off the valley floor. At this low elevation, she could get a good look at any activities taking place on the ground. She completed her third and final circle pattern around the tower looking for any blue sage smoke—the smoke signal notifying that her services were needed once again on the ground. She was happy not to see any smoke.

She had one more thing to check which would be the double-V victory pattern performed by the two fighter dragoons assigned to the Spotting Tower 6. These patterns required each fighter dragoon to position their wings into a V shape while they faced each other.

The V would be seen from the sky, denoting everything was in proper order.

With the V sign in plain sight, Kula performed a left-wing dip and head nod in approval, quickly positioning her wings and laser sights on Tower 5.

Within three miles of it, Kula saw blue sage smoke high in the sky and within a mile of the tower, she watched a large object circling around the spotting tower.

This isn't right. I know of only two flying dragoon bodies that are that large. One is General Slaughter—and I know his services are focused on Ella at the moment—and the other has been banished from ever flying in Darkan Territory airspace. And it looks as if he's circling.

Kula searched the valley floor. Her heart skipped a beat and her talons ripped through the air as she noticed a dragoon down, belly up even, at the bottom of the spotting tower. *That's what it's circling.*

Within five hundred yards of the tower, Kula showed her teeth, inhaling and spitting fire napalm, lighting up the sky all the way to the ground. Her talons had changed from the normal *Jack the Ripper* black to the extended silver-tipped, nitrate *kill and shred everything that moves* mode.

She went into a low glide around the tower.

Where has that son of a bitch gone? There's just no way this can be the dragoon I'm thinking of.

From the corner of her eye, Kula spotted the large dragoon circling three hundred feet above her. *Is he smiling? I swear to the King of the Soul Tree I'm going rip his heart out and shit in his mouth.*

Kula hunched down and flapped her enormous wings to gain altitude. "I need to stop this bastard."

As she broke over the top of the tower, she looked right, noticing the big dragoon had dropped to the ground, ripping at the wings of his kill.

What's he doing? We don't eat our own. Talons out, mouth dripping liquid fire, razor-sharp teeth grinding and wanting flesh, Kula stiffened her body like a surfboard and divebombed at the killer.

Seconds before sinking her eighteen-inch silver nitrate talons into the back of the killer's neck, she was bodychecked by a black silhouette, forcing her to miss her target.

Kula performed a barrel roll which left her flying

upside down but with a full view of the black silhouette that had just ambushed her.

I'll be damned, it's a smoke dragon.

They're of metaphysical form which makes them sneaky bastards. I haven't seen one of these since they tried to attack me when I was carrying a freshly minted pack of blood bricks. I remember that day well, the one when I'd dropped one of the blood bricks near Ella's little medicine hut.

The smoke dragon dived, twisting and turning into a black funnel cloud, engulfing both dragoons on the ground.

Of course, thought Kula. *It's setting up a smokescreen for that dragoon killer to finish his nasty act of betrayal. Not if I can help it.*

She stretched her neck out and pulled up, gaining altitude so fast her body left a dragoon stream, producing an aftershock that blew the feathers off a dozen crack-winged vultures.

A sneak attack? That's how they want to play. Bring it on. I'm ready. For every killer rogue dragoon heart that I take, I am queen for another three hundred years, with enhanced strength, speed, and All-Verse classification.

Kula circled sharply, leaning her head against the left side of her body, simultaneously performing swimming motions with her arms and flogging her tail like a whip, facilitating an even faster divebomb technique to kill the intruder.

"This time, I'm going to rip your throat out and eat it with pickled berry jam," Kula said, talons fully open, dripping 10,000°F sticky napalm, front shoulders hunched for initial front-force impact.

Hundred feet to impact; fifty, ten. *Boom!* Her body rammed, talons ripped, mouth tore.

Within the smoke cloud, she ripped at the neck while the napalm burned through the armor skin of the dragoon, her claws digging deep into the intruder's body, hurting her talons to squeeze any tighter.

With limited movement coming from the invader, Kula positioned her bodyweight over the downed dragoon to keep the dragoon from attacking.

When the smoke had cleared and Kula caught her

breath, she opened her eyes to see the throat she had ripped out and spit on the ground was not from the intruder flying dragoon.

It was one of her own. A fighter dragoon posted at Spotting Tower 5.

Kula searched the skies for the killer dragoon and its sneaky smoke shadow. They had somehow escaped under the cloak of the smoke dragon's black tar smoke.

Kula stood over the dead dragoon.

Tasting dragoon flesh, she took three steps back, spitting flesh and shaking her head in disgust. "I'm sorry, my brother. I assure you; your family will be taken care of and you'll be buried at Grimmbell, your name engraved on the top row of the blocks in Tower 5."

She studied the body of the fallen dragoon, especially the fatal wound located in the abdomen. By the shape and size of the hole, it was from a dragoon horn. This particular wound was large and shaped like a five-pointed star. An attack from the underside. *I know who it is.* The killer dragoon shadowed his kill from below and then powered upwards for the fatal attack. Only an older dragoon with this type of non-typical five-star-shaped horn, strength, and sophisticated battle skills could have done this.

Kula studied the ground, noticing the depth of the killer's footprint. He was big and heavy. She sniffed the ground. *I know that smell.*

She licked the ground for any clue to the killer's blood.

"Damn it," she said, spitting, the mix of flavors confusing her. Black tar licorice. Bloodstone brick, and wizard's blood.

Kula circled the dead body, feeling the jagged edge endings of where the wings used to connect. *This big boy had incredible strength to rip the wings off.* Kula reached under the slain dragoon, rolling it onto its side. She studied the ground, raking her foot back and forth in the loose dirt. One of her talons snagged a rock, pulling it to the surface. She kicked at it a few more times.

"Hmm. This rock is heavy." Picking it up, she brushed the dirt off. "This is no rock." She sniffed it. "This smells of old dragoon." She spit on the object, wiping it clean and noticed an old but familiar pattern. Kula spit on it again. Wiping it off, she studied the object closely.

"It's body armor. Very dense. Over seven hundred years thick." The dragoon armor revealed a burnt orange-colored outlined in white agate. "It's actually quite beautiful and quite deadly." She put it under her tongue for safekeeping. "I need to make sure this is the real thing."

Birds of prey were landing near the dead dragoon.

Kula shot out a stream of napalm, sending them all on their way at least for a little while. *I need to take care of the body now.* Kula inhaled a brewed mix of her very unique fire napalm, positioned herself like a cannon and shot a fireball high in the sky. It hovered and then exploded into an array of colored explosions, symbols, and numbers, releasing a shockwave shaking the very ground she stood on.

Kula stood over her fallen fighter dragoon.

I failed as his queen. I let him die on my watch, and not in battle. I hope I will be forgiven by the Grimmbell calibrators. Will they allow me to calculate the correct vibration to take his spirit to the quantum fields of realities?

Now, she would have to wait for Cremator to arrive and begin the releasing ceremony, a number of rituals necessary to properly dispose of a fighter dragoon in the Darkan Territory.

Kula floated directly over the top of the fallen dragoon. She bit her wrist, dropping blood onto the belly of the dragoon. The droplets burned through the armor of the young dragoon warrior. Shortly, a thin piece of rope-like material climbed upwards twenty feet above its belly, branching off into four directions, perfecting a web-like structure surrounding the body of the fallen dragoon.

"Your spirits and souls are protected now," said Kula. "Protection from anything above or below the ground. Nothing will be able to penetrate my dragoon blood barrier."

Kula flapped her wings one stroke and softly landed on top of Tower 5.

"Now I will wait for the necessary personnel to

perform the proper rituals. My death star explosion would have announced to everyone in the valley what was going to take place. It will be a great day. My fallen blood brother will now guard the entities living in the battlefield cemetery. There, my brother will rise up again to fight and protect spirits, souls, and the King of the Soul Tree."

Kula rolled the piece of armor around and around in her mouth then holding it in her hand, she studied the piece of breastplate.

One of the very first tests to check for the authenticity of dragoon armor was the fire test. *With the reflection of the sun shining through the piece of armor, I should be able to start anything on fire or melt any type of material. I have a hunch this fire test will be true, but I will test it anyway.*

Kula spotted a rodent digging in the cracks on the tower landing arena.

She positioned the armor with the sun and tagged the rodent with the beam of light.

Poof! The rodent burst into flames, then exploded.

"Fast and painless," said Kula. "I can only hope that's the way I go."

Kula studied the valley floor from the top of the tower, watching and waiting for everyone to arrive for the releasing ceremony. She spotted the first group of contributors two miles out, five transparent figures walking toward the tower to start the task at hand.

"Ah yes. The spirit guards will be arriving soon."

Kula watched as the spirit guards each acquired their positions, one guard for each of the four All- Verse directions. North-south, south-north, east-west, and west-east.

The fifth and final spirit guard floated above center of the downed dragoon.

Positioning its arms out to the side to form a T pattern with its body, a blue light emitted from the center spirit, connecting it to each of the corner spirits.

The floating spirit clapped its hands, dissolving Kula's protective rope cage.

The body of the fallen dragoon warrior had officially become the property of Grimmbell Cemetery. Now in the protection of the five spirits, the spirit guards immediately illuminated together into a bright penetrating blue, white light.

Kula scanned three hundred and sixty degrees, noticing a flight pattern of large dark objects coming in from the northeast horizon. She crouched down and immediately lifted her wings ready for lift.

Something is coming.

"I will kill them all."

Kula took flight immediately, ready for revenge. She climbed to altitude until she reached three-thousand feet and pushing her body downward, gained implausible speed while churning napalm in her chest cavity.

"Oh, this is a good batch. It's extra sticky. It will burn nasty. I'm going to take all the hides I kill today and make a nice throw rug for my launching deck."

Kula leveled out, her speed at a blistering pace, maneuvering her napalm from the holding cavity of her chest to just the back of her throat, ready to spray a wide path of sticky hot death.

Small tailings of napalm flowed out the side of her mouth, leaving burning ribbons of smoke and napalm syrup falling to the ground. She stretched her body outwards into surfboard mode.

"Fifteen seconds and counting." Kula saw a huge tactical advantage, a massive fluffy white cloud.

She flew into it and hovered. Waiting patiently, she watched the first four dragoons fly by. "They are my dragoons, part of the Elite 100."

Suddenly, a huge blast of air rubbed over her from behind, followed by the very tip of a dragoon's tail. "It's General Slaughter." She bolted out of the cloud bank after him. "He's a tricky one."

General Slaughter slowed and waited for Kula to catch up, then dipped twenty feet below. "Greetings, my Queen. I see that you are okay."

"Yes, I am fine, General Slaughter. I was expecting you to come in from the northeast not the southeast."

"Yes, my Queen, you are partly correct. I had twenty-one of the elites come with me and another twenty-one come in from the northeast, to have a backup plan if need be."

"Of course, that's why I made you my general."

"Thank you, my Queen. I saw the death star fireball but had to finish up with Ella first. Then I caught up with the twenty-one fighter dragoons and headed this way." Nodding his fighters off, he said, "Go to the site and be ready for the ceremony."

The twenty-one fighter dragoons dropped in unison to the left and disappeared. "The death star fireball?" said Slaughter. "Who and how many went down?"

"One. Killed by another dragoon. A big and powerful dragoon too."

"Another dragoon? Are you sure about that?"

"It was a big one. When I spotted him on the ground, I thought I saw him rip the wings off of this fighter dragoon with very little effort."

"I haven't seen another dragoon attack its own kind since the dragoon skin wars. That's two hundred years ago, so why now?"

"That's a good question," said Kula. "I don't know. And why tear the wings off?"

"Is this dragoon a scavenger, possibly gathering ingredients for something bigger?"

Kula nodded. "That's very possible, but I have a piece of his armor. I think you might shit little rubber nickels when you see the color of it. I hope I am wrong, but don't think I am."

Slaughter looked over his shoulder toward the ground. "Spirit guards are here. Let's get on the ground. I want to take a look at our fighter dragoon and that piece of dragoon armor."

"Yes, the spirit guards were first on scene. I'll let you identify and mark the fallen dragoon, of course."

"Must've been Tower 5?" said Slaughter.

"That is correct, General."

Slaughter slightly nodded. "Yeah, that's a young one. Three, maybe four years old," he said, looking over at Kula. "It's Graper, and his wings were torn off."

"Graper?" said Kula. "Wasn't he one you had chosen for The Elite 100?"

"Yes, he was."

"Do you think someone is targeting them?"

Slaughter studied the shattered wing bones poking out of the body. "I don't know, my Queen."

"He didn't lose them in the fight?"

"I don't think so. When I spotted the killer dragoon, our fighter dragoon was already on the ground.

Attacking the big dragoon, I was ambushed by a smoke bandit dragon."

"A smoke dragon? I can't believe this shit."

"Believe it," said Kula. "By the time I got to the ground, the big dragoon had already ripped his wings off."

"What about his heart? Did he take that?"

"No! Nobody took the heart."

"It's very logical that he was going to take the heart, but you stopped him."

"I thought about that too. Unknown possibilities right now. I can see him wanting this particular dragoon heart. But the wings are for himself. No. The wings are for the highest bidder in the covert underground circuit."

"Who do you think it is?" said Slaughter.

Kula picked the piece of armor out of her mouth. "Take a look at this."

Slaughter studied the piece. He sniffed it, licked it, and blew a flame over the top. Suddenly, the armor plate turned an orange-yellow color.

"Damn," said Slaughter, shaking his head. "Orange plates with a yellowish center. Shit, there's only one dragoon with this design of armor coating."

"I'm pretty sure it's Tarragon," said Kula.

"It is a piece of Tarragon's armor," said Slaughter.

"General Slaughter, you know that Cremator will find out for sure who killed our fighter dragoon."

"Yes, I do. Unless… "

"Unless what?" Kula asked.

"I'm wondering if the smoke dragon robbed Graper's thoughts before the attack, using a neuron detachment activity sequence prior to being attacked by Tarragon."

"I guess I never thought of that until now," said Kula. "Although, I don't think the smoke bandit had enough time. You know they have limited power and time when they are created."

Looking around, Slaughter nodded. "Well, is it possible that the smoke head had what? Six to eight minutes? I do believe that is in their range."

"Yeah," said Kula. "Give or take a minute or two depending on how much they were programed for flying and fighting time. Usually, there are three or four working together because of their limited time."

"But you said you saw only one?"

"Yes," said Kula. "I only saw one, but that doesn't mean there wasn't more than one."

"My Queen," said Slaughter. "I had a thought when I was working with Ella right before I saw the Death Alert Signal."

"What was the thought?"

"It's strange. Well, I mean it's strange that I never thought of it until I was with Ella. She passed the blood brick bath test, which should unlock visions for her and for us, for dragoons?"

"Yes and no. There are other reasons too, but we need to focus on what's at hand."

"Wait a minute, my Queen, I just received a message from my fighter squad. They have landed and are in position."

"Good," said Kula. "Let's take our positions on the spotting tower and you can share your thoughts with me. I want to hear what you have to say. I might have missed something."

Slaughter was the first to glide down, circling the tower one time and landing. Kula followed, sitting down next to Slaughter.

Chapter 15: The Rolling Head

Standing over the headless body, Bradicus looked at the decapitated head with its eyes wide open, looking back at him, those ugly yellow teeth still displaying a feeling of danger.

Suddenly, the head spun face down into the dirt.

"Damn! Shit, and what the hell! Is this thing still alive?" Bradicus raised his sword shoulder high, thrusting it into the chest cavity of the headless rider. Kneeling, he reached for the head.

"Damn! It burned my fingers." Pulling away, he noticed Kula's dragoon rope had untied itself, moving away in a snake-like fashion from the headless rider, the scorpion stinger tail bone following.

Bradicus took a step back. "I think I better keep the head with me."

What the hell can I put the head in? I have to have something to cover up that ugly face. The earthers can make this head talk. First, they will have to boil it down to a bare skull. Second, breathe the brown barrel number five death-grip tobacco smoke into the nostrils. And third, we will be able to ask the skull questions, find out what the hell this thing is. Maybe find out about this green dust?

Bradicus grabbed the leather bag containing the bones from the scorpion tunnels. "I think I should have enough room to put the head in the bag. Well, I'll make room." Kneeling with his hands buried deep into the leather bag, he noticed a round object rolling toward him.

He spun on his knees to face the object.

To his surprise, it was the head of the black spirit rider rolling straight at him but this time, the eyes were closed, and the mouth moving as if it was speaking but no words were coming out. The ugly yellow teeth were biting down hard, making a clicking noise.

"Okay, I've had enough of this nonsense." Pointing a finger at the head, he said, "You're going in the bag, then

I'm going to boil you. What do you think of that?"

The head opened its eyes, rolling backwards toward its beheaded body.

Bradicus stood and followed the head with the leather bag in his hands. *This thing is evil. I'm not sure I'm even doing the right thing. Maybe I should bury it and come back later?*

Bradicus pulled the sword out of the chest cavity of the rider, ready to harpoon the head when yellow teeth rolled next to its body and bit its own hand, ripping two fingers off. The body of the rider deflated and kept shrinking to where it looked like a black tarp lying on the ground.

The head turned, tilting back, looking up at Bradicus.

"You will never catch me."

"We'll see about that," said Bradicus, leaping at the decapitated head, only to catch a clutch of dirt.

Yellow teeth started rolling away, gaining speed very quickly. Bradicus looked up to see the head rolling out of sight toward the nearby tobacco field.

"Bradicus, this is Brazel. The only way you're going to catch that thing is to transform to Blackjack.

In that form, you will have the speed you need."

"Brazel, what type of magic does that rolling head have?"

"Feels old," said Brazel. "It's complex. There's more than one source of magic in this entity. Right at this moment, I can't put my finger on it. Go now; you need to if you're going to catch yellow ugly teeth."

Blackjack stopped along the edge of the tobacco field and sniffed the ground.

"It entered here," he said, entering the first three rows and noticing a path of tobacco plants had been squashed and lay on the ground.

Moving further in through the center of the field, he knew he was now hunting an enemy smaller than himself. *I need to stay close to the ground to find old yellow ugly teeth. It will be easier to spot the head since I'm closer to the ground. And the fact that the head will be looking for a man hunting him, not a magically engineered magicjack, may give me a slight advantage.*

Continuing farther into the field, he stopped. Seated quietly and turning his body to the opposite side of the field, he rotated his sensitive ears, hoping to catch movement within the tobacco fields. "Something's moving. Just creeping along. Quick stop and go movements. No! That's not yellow teeth. I know that movement. It's a smaller rodent. Maybe a packrat. Damn!"

Suddenly, Blackjack felt a soft vibration through the ground. Something bigger was moving and he listened intently.

"No, there's more than one thing moving. Sounds like footsteps. Two varying strides, one heavier than the other."

Standing on his back legs, he stretched up to scan the field, his head pivoting back and forth. That's when he noticed one man chasing another. Considering he was carrying a sickle; a chunky man was surprisingly gaining ground on the skinny man. Blackjack sprinted to the center of the field, giving him a higher elevation gain to determine why the heavier sickle man was chasing the skinny guy.

"Oh shit!" said Blackjack. Skinny tripped and fell to the ground, and immediately, the heavier guy attacked him like a fat kid on a cupcake. "That doesn't look good."

"What does the fat guy want with the skinny guy?" asked Brazel.

"I'm not sure. To eat him, I think, looking at the size of him," said Blackjack. "That sickle that the big man has, if I'm seeing that correctly, is glowing green. That means the rolling head somehow took over another person's body. It's the same head I cut off, just on another body. It's still a black spirit rider. What the hell?"

"If that rider is really yellow teeth reincarnated," said Brazel, "then I would suggest the next time you cut off his head, don't forget to poke his eyes out. That should disconnect its power."

"Good advice. I'll take it."

"Good luck. Let me know if you need to transform."

Blackjack sprinted toward the two men. Within ten yards, he retrieved his dagger, biting down on the blade. "I'm going to stab his eyes, then I'll have the advantage," he said, leaping directly for a head shot.

Too late.

In one fluid motion, the black horse spirit rider sliced the skinny man's head off and caught Blackjack in his meticulously designed, shoulder-mounted, steel-fanged animal trap. He chuckled.

Blackjack screamed. Bones crunched and blood flowed, the dagger tumbling to the ground.

The man with the sickle immediately walked up to the headless skinny guy, picking up the severed head and staring at the facial features. "This is perfect. The man was scared, screaming for his life just before I cut his head off. That only amplifies the purity of the screamer's dust. This skull is textbook for making the VIM dust." Sitting the serrated human head down on the ground and turning his attention to Blackjack, he released his shoulder trap, flopping Blackjack onto the ground.

"So, we have someone's pet here, some type of tracker. It's… it's muscular, the fur very shiny. And the four-color variants of the hide in a coordinated pattern... I want to keep this animal for myself."

The spirit rider sat his sickle on the chest cavity of the skinny dead man and quickly picked up Blackjack's dagger. He kicked at Blackjack lying on the ground, stepping on his head. Still nothing.

"Wow, this is quite a find. Much bigger than any animal I've ever seen before in this particular form.

The color and shine of its fur is truly remarkable. And look at those claws," he said, tapping on them with the blade of the dagger. "They're hard as steel. This is a magical animal."

Gripping the dagger by the handle, he flipped it in the air and caught it.

"Oh my! The balance of this blade is perfect. I'll be able to kill the enemy's powerful tracker with its own weapon, then the blade will belong to me, delivering a mystic bond to this animal. Then, I'll be able to exploit some of its power. This gets better all the time," he said, dancing around Blackjack lying on the ground. "Plus, I should have enough Blackjack pelt here for a shiny new screamer dust bag." The black spirit rider straddled Blackjack with dagger in hand.

He leaned down, grabbing Blackjack's belly fur.

***

When Blackjack opened his eyes, his neck and ankle were on fire. "What the hell's going on?"

He heard Rasp's voice. "Blackjack! Are you okay?"

Blackjack jerked to attention, sitting up and looking around to see Rasp sitting on the chest cavity of yellow teeth himself.

"What happened?"

"Not to worry, my friend," said Rasp, slapping his hand hard against the black rider carcass. "Hard as a rock. Nothing to worry about."

"What happened to the head?"

"Not to worry again, my friend." Looking up, he added, "Here she comes now."

Blackjack looked up to see a deep red-colored dragoon spreading her wings wide, floating down to the ground. "Jinnamon."

"Yes," said Rasp. "Jinnamon swooped upon your unknown intruder here, just as it was looking to cut your belly wide open in the middle of the creek with your own knife."

Blackjack reached for his side. "My dagger?"

"Don't worry, I have it right here," Rasp said, handing it to Blackjack.

"The head," said Blackjack. "We need the head. Actually, the skull. But yes, the head."

"Jinnamon stuffed the black spirit rider headfirst into the ground, then she dug him up." Blackjack squinted with a frown. "How did you know I was here?"

Rasp tapped on his temple with a finger. "Your subconscious friend Brazel sent an alarm to Kula. The rest is history."

"I didn't know he could do that, or the fact that Kula could receive spirit splinters from Brazel?" Rasp stood, pulling Blackjack to his feet. "Kula received a subconscious message from you for help. She sent us to assist you."

"My ankle," said Blackjack, swinging it in a small circle. "It's fixed."

Rasp held his hands out and shrugged. "Of course,

it's fixed. I'm not just a pretty face, you know."

"Thank you," said Blackjack. "How did you fix it?"

"Hey, we all have our secrets, right?"

"Fair enough," said Blackjack.

"Blackjack, I have been thinking about this Roko thing."

"What are you thinking?"

"What if Roko for some weird unknown reason wanted to meet up with you the other day?"

"Why would you say that?" said Blackjack.

"You know me and my analytical mind, and I think it would be to lure you into the black spirit rider trap. I'm wondering if the ploy was initially set for you, not Roko."

"Wow! You *have* been thinking. Go on."

"When you first came across the riderless spirit horse, were you alone?"

"Yes, I was."

"And how long was it before Roko showed up?"
"About fifteen minutes."

"There you go," said Rasp, nodding. "Plenty of time for the black spirit horse to lure you into its trap, or possibly with the help of Roko if the first attempt failed."

Blackjack nodded. "An interesting story. Scary, but interesting. But I don't think he would do something like that."

"What if he had to?" said Rasp. "Maybe he'd been promised some grand prize."

"What kind of a grand prize?" said Blackjack.

"Maybe he was promised a piece of the power change. It's possible, right?"

"Anything is possible."

"That's right, but they failed to capture you, so the black spirit horse took Roko instead."

"It does make sense," said Blackjack. "But that still doesn't make it true."

"It's a theory I know, but I wonder if this Arune is looking for a Signiant type of power force, and Arune could be the boss of the black spirit riders? He still wants you and Roko's the man they could send after you."

"That's a scary thought."

"It's a clever thought. If they could capture you,

super bonus, if not, they still have Roko—he knows you better than most, right?"

Blackjack leaned into Rasp. "Are you sure you're not part of this plan, because what you are telling me sounds both logical and terrifying. Sounds like you have some insight."

"It's just a theory. I'm thinking aloud here. I would never do anything to help a black spirit rider."

"I understand what you're saying, and it's a very feasible theory, but let's hope you're wrong."

Rasp kicked the hardened black spirit rider carcass. "Blackjack, someone out there wants your power. They want you as one of them or an ally, or both, but they want your juice to enhance some dark, dirty deed."

Blackjack caressed his mouth and chin. "That's a question I've been asking myself."

"What is that?" asked Rasp.

"I was supposed to meet with Cremator the day Roko was taken by the black spirit horse to pick up a fresh mix of tobacco."

"What kind of mix was it to be used for?"

"I don't know," said Blackjack. "Some sort of a smoke mix ordered by the queen."

"A special order," said Rasp. "Do you remember if the mixture was more of a dark blend or a light blend combination?"

"I don't know anything about the type of blend. The letter I delivered to Roko a couple of weeks before had a list of ten tobaccos. At least that's what he told me. The day I met up with him, I know one thing for sure—that I could smell a unique aroma coming from the packages."

"Could you describe the aroma to me?"

Blackjack closed his eyes, inhaling deeply. Then exhaling, he said, "It was only for a couple of seconds, but I could smell walnut, rolled damp dirt, coffee, and something sweet. Can't really describe the sweet part, but it was definitely sweet smelling."

Rasp nodded. "When Roko handed you the packages, do you remember how they felt?"

"They felt like bags."

"No, I mean when you received the bags, were they

stiff or soft?" Blackjack folded his arms across his chest. "You would ask me that. Both."

"Did any have a rattle?"

"Well now that you mention it, yes, the bags on the very top rattled a little."

"Do you remember how many of the bags rattled?" asked Rasp.

"No, I'm not really sure, but I think it was the two on the very top."

"Were these the same size or smaller than the others?"

"You're lucky I can remember details so well, Rasp," said Blackjack. "How many more questions do you have? Well, the two bags on top were half the size."

"That's interesting," said Rasp. "Why is that?" said Blackjack.

"Usually, a smoke mix in a smaller bag would be a higher concentrate. Finer grained and more powerful."

"Do you have an idea of what the blend could be used for?"

"Not exactly," said Rasp. "It would be a lot easier if we had his master's recipe book. That would cut it down to a hundred possible matches or so. You didn't see any book, I suppose?"

Blackjack looked at the ground. "I didn't see any book with him."

"Let's hope not," said Rasp. "The law of the King of Souls states that the book must never leave the Grand Hall."

"That doesn't do us a lot of good," said Blackjack. "Not considering the fact that he could've hidden the book, or someone could have taken it from him."

"If someone other than Roko has the book, it really doesn't matter because they'll not be able to read it."

"Why not?"

"For one thing, it's been written in earther dialect."

"I can read a fair amount of earther dialect myself. What I mean is, I've spent many nights with Roko mixing smoke, learning the language. How many others can too?"

"Then there's something else you should know."

"I'm listening," said Blackjack.

"It has to do with reading the book."

"I'm all ears."

"Like I said before, you have to be able to read earther dialect, not to mention the understanding and performing the mixing rituals. You see, that's the secret. That's the key."

"I'm not sure if I'm following you. Could you explain a little further?"

"Certainly," said Rasp. "You have to have the book; that's obvious. And you have to be able to read the dialect. That's obvious times two. And you have to understand the ingredients. Times three. And then you have to be able to perform the mixing procedure, that's times four. The last ingredient, which is the most important of them all," Rasp said, nodding with a smile, "is you have to have the hands of a master tobacco spirit mixer. So, without any one of the key elements, the book's entirely useless."

"Of course," said Blackjack. "I can understand that."

"No," said Rasp. "You don't quite get it. What I mean is you have to have the hands of a master tobaccologist."

"Okay, Rasp, you got me on this one. I don't understand what you mean."

"It's okay. So, once you have the book, understand the language, gather the ingredients, perform the mix, you still have to actually have 'the hands' of the master."

Blackjack squinted with a beep brow. "So, what you're telling me is that you need to actually have a specific set of hands to read the book."

"That's correct. Pretty tricky, isn't it?" Blackjack nodded with a sigh. "Very clever."

"That's what I thought too. *Literally*, it's a process called 'changing of the hands.'"

"That would be an all-out commitment on someone's part," said Blackjack. "How do you know about all this?"

"I've been reading the wings," answered Rasp. "You mean the dragoon wings?"

"Yes," said Rasp.

"The *actual* dragoon wings?" said Blackjack.

"Yes, actual dragoon wings at the Hanging Wings Depository."

"There's only one way to get into the wings' history. It involves both permission from Kula and leasing your life coin."

Looking down, Rasp sighed. "You got it; I had to give up my life coin."

"What better person to lease your coin to than the queen herself?"

"It definitely makes a statement," said Rasp.

"Leasing your coin to Kula is noble. However, to receive your coin back, you can't wander too far off the chosen path, correct?"

"Don't I know it?" said Rasp. "The queen informed me about many things, including about the possibility of losing my life."

Blackjack kicked at the ground. "Speaking of other things. At first, I didn't want to believe your theory about Roko and the black spirit rider. But now, I feel something bad's brewing."

"I'm pretty sure of that myself," said Rasp.

Blackjack flicked his wrists, producing his titanium claws. "If Roko and his goons do want me, then they're going to have to come and get me. They better pack a lunch, that's all I can say."

Chapter 16: Wing Wrap

Jinnamon unwrapped her wing halfway to get a good look at Blackjack. "Cremator, are you sure this temporary wing wrap will be able to heal him to full power?"

"Sure, it will. Before Rasp was ordered elsewhere to another part of the territory, he said Blackjack was feeling okay, but he couldn't interface with Brazel. He's not quite himself, so that's why I brought some herbs from Ella for a temporary wing wrap."

"How does he look?" asked Cremator. "Bring him down to my level. I just want to take a peek."

Jinnamon lowered her wing to eye level with Cremator.

"Hmm, sleeping like a baby hogasaurus." Standing on his tippy toes, he said, "I would say he is healing comfortably, not to mention sucking on his thumb."

Jinnamon lifted her wing back to her line of vision. "No, he's not. Wait a minute. You're right, he is.

Do we tell him later? I really think we should."

"You'd be surprised by how many bodies I have seen sucking their thumbs while waiting for the precise moment when the body heals itself or switches over into spirit, something I haven't been able to figure out for a long time."

Jinnamon leaned down eye level with Cremator.

"Maybe it's that moment of truth where a life force is born and lost at the same time. A neutral position. Total post-body relax. Hence, sucking their thumb."

"Maybe," said Cremator. "Maybe the thumb sucking's the key for the transformation to spirit mode."

"Or it could be that moment of truth where their life source is changing over from the death of the body to the life of a spirit. Kind of like you said."

"That's one of my theories anyway, and you've taken the words right out of my mouth. Well said, but I haven't been able to prove it works like that."

"Personally, I think it means Blackjack at this very moment is obtaining healing at one - hundred percent optimum dragoon wing power after the battle with the black horse rider."

"I agree," said Cremator. "I think hand-to-hand combat with the power of a rider causes danger to the body more than we know."

Cremator planted his shovel into the ground next to the rider's buried head. Twenty-two shovel loads later, he kneeled, picking up the pieces of the smashed skull.

"So, what other theories have you come up with?" asked Jinnamon.

"How did we come up with this topic? One minute, we're rocking Blackjack to sleep and the next minute, we are leaping into a missing Death Time dimension between death and spirit."

Jinnamon's eyes narrowed. "A missing dimension? Is that a theory, or do you have proof of that?" His bushy eyebrows seemed to glue together. "Why the interest in Death Time dimensions?"

"I didn't even know there was such a thing."

"Yes, that concept I've never spoken of before, it just happened to pop out of my mouth." "Is that another theory?" said Jinnamon.

"I'm not sure yet. Maybe we should just focus on Blackjack."

Jinnamon lifted her wing even with her eyes. "He's still sucking his thumb. Must be good."

"In my Death Time dimension, which I haven't proven, I believe that is the most vulnerable time for one's life force to be stolen."

"So, it's true, a spirit can be stolen?"

"Yes, the spirit can be stolen. During one phase of the releasing ceremony, if a spirit doesn't want to release from the post body, then you have problems."

"What kind of problems?"

Cremator fumbled with the broken skull. "This is messy. Hand me a rag please. Two problems can happen when you don't have a clean release. The spirit can be stolen by other entities, or you have to pull it out of the post body. That can take other spirits to help in that process and even the soul chaser offers a hand to help in the transformation."

"But I thought you were there during the process?" said Jinnamon. "So, that would not happen to a spirit. It being stolen, I mean."

"How are we going to glue this skull back together?"

Jinnamon breathed on a small pile of wood lying nearby. It burst into flames. "We'll probably need a little heat when he wakes up, so how do you keep the spirits from being stolen?"

Cremator turned his head away, quietly looking at the ground.

"I'm sorry, did I bring up bad memories?" Jinnamon said, lowering her wing to ground level, unwrapping it and laying Blackjack gently on the ground near the fire.

"You go in with your armor on."

"You mean, literally armor?" Jinnamon asked.

"No, not entirely. I mean, there have been a few times where I actually did wear armor. Spirit armor. In one particular situation, the life force of body transforming over had a very violent past, so there were violent entities wanting his spirit for payment." Cremator shook his head no. "I shouldn't be talking about this stuff. In some ways, it's confidential. Actually, it's classified in a lot of ways, written in words only to be found in the Great Hall's recipe book."

"Did someone say recipe book?" came Blackjack's voice. "Blackjack?" said Cremator. "How are you doing?"

"I'm doing better now. What happened to Rasp?"

"Nothing to worry about. Queen Kula had him go to the archives of the wings. Research."

"Of course," said Blackjack. "When the boss calls."

"Blackjack, what do you remember?"

"I was in the water trying to contact Brazel but couldn't link with him. My concentration was weak, and my muscles burned on the inside. I could barely move. And then, you guys showed up."

Cremator finished crawling on his hands and knees, picking up one last piece. "I think I've found all the pieces to his skull."

"You have all the pieces?" asked Blackjack, his expression sliding into worry. "So, it's possible that we can talk to the skull, right now?"

"Yes, with the proper smoking mix." Holding the skull at eye level, Cremator said, "I don't have the ingredients here to make the proper mix. Especially with this skull."

"Why? What's so different about this one?"

"It could have properties in it that would cause it to burn a green flame."

"Like this sword. It burned green like that."

"How did the sword burn green?" asked Cremator.

"He put screamer's dust on it, then held it over the fire."

"Screamer's dust?" he asked, rubbing his chin. "What's screamer's dust?"

"Oh yeah, that's right, you guys weren't there for that. Actually, it's a long story. But for now, I'll try to keep it short. Number one, I think I know whose skull that is."

"You know whose skull this is?" said Cremator. "Really? Care to elaborate?"

"Hang on," said Blackjack. "When I tracked Roko to this creek, I heard a nasty howling scream. I figured he must have jumped into another dimension, crossing to the other side of the water. But then I found the green dust. He wanted to kill me for it and damn near did."

Cremator pinched some dust from the leather bag. "When they found you lying in the creek, face down mind you, you were covered with a thin coating of this stuff."

Blackjack nodded. "Yeah, that stuff really locked my joints tight. Thanks for saving my ass."

"Thank her," said Cremator, pointing at Jinnamon. "She smashed the dark rider into the creek bank." "Rasp told me she crushed the rider. My theory is that this screamer's dust is one piece of the puzzle

in which a black spirit rider transports to another dimension. And"—he stared at his two-person audience—"I think the spirit riders make the dust by killing any creatures that are screamers when they're hunted."

Jinnamon was the first one to speak. "Because of this dust?" "They scream?" Cremator said.

Bradicus shrugged. "That's my theory. Well, that's *our* theory. I had additional input." Pointing to the broken skull, he added, "Roko here, I mean old yellow teeth…"

"Wait a minute," said Cremator. "Roko? Why would you think it was Roko? He's on our side. He's the one who taught me," he said, shaking his head. "Where did you come up with that idea?"

"Look, I know what you're thinking. Roko's my friend too." Blackjack sighed. "I wasn't going to tell anyone until I had enough proof."

Jinnamon leaned down. "Are you sure you've made the transformation back to human form appropriately?"

"Jinn, what the hell does that mean?"

"I know. I know. I thought maybe the green flame might be talking; you did say it burned from the inside out. Could be some kickass spell. Maybe old yellow teeth's still talking through you."

"No. No, and no."

"Can you prove it?" said Jinnamon. "I just want to make sure. When I was flying over here, I saw a figure with a big-ass sickle, chasing two men in human form. I figure two of those four skulls Cremator fished out of the creek were the two humans running."

"What's got you spooked? Jinn, look at me. What do you see? I'm Blackjack. I could change into Bradicus right here, in front of you. That would prove to you I am who I am."

"That would be a start, I guess."

Shaking his head with a sigh, Blackjack said. "Better yet, Miss Jinnamon, do you remember when you got released from Killamore?"

"Of course I remember. Why do you bring that up?" asked Jinnamon.

"Because you're making me bring it up, that's why. You're the one who started this. And I'm going to be the one to finish it."

"Make your point if you can?" Jinnamon sounded short-fused.

"You know, Jinn, you're starting to piss me off. We need to figure out who or what Roko and his goons are going to do next. Yet we're messing around with events that happened a long time ago. But let's get to the point; when you got released from Killamore, there was a price paid for your release to Kula, right?"

"How did you know about that?"

"I deliver all messages from and to Kula. All confidential and super-secret. When you got released from Killamore, there was an exchange. A fee. A trade. An agreement."

"Okay," said Cremator. "You two are getting out of control here. I know how to make this skull talk."

"What's got you spooked?" asked Blackjack.

"I don't know for sure," said Jinnamon. "Kula got me thinking about the past the last time I talked to her. What was the cost for me to be released?"

"Four," said Blackjack, holding up four fingers.

"Four what?" asked Jinnamon with a heavy twitch in her tail. "Four fighter dragoons."

"Shit. How did you know that? Only two other people knew that. Kula and Killamore."

"No, there were three. I delivered the message to Killamore."

"You are Bradicus-Blackjack, so I should never have doubted you. I'm truly sorry. You think we can keep that transaction quiet?"

"Keep what quiet?" said Blackjack.

"Thank you," said Jinnamon, looking at Cremator. "How do we make the skull talk?"

Chapter 17: Group Strategy

Cremator stood next to the campfire, studying the skull pieces by the firelight. Maneuvering the sections of skull right side up, upside down, and left to right, his brow heightened with a mellow grin.

"I think… No, I know how to talk to this skull."

Shrugging, Blackjack looked at Jinnamon. "Do you think that's a good idea? I mean

out here? The Great Hall's a long way off. Don't you need some special mixing bags or tools?"

"I think the real tool needed here is guts," said Cremator. "I'm not sure about reading the skull of a black spirit rider… But nothing ventured, nothing gained."

Blackjack moved next to Cremator, looking at the portions of skull in his hand. "We've come this far, so I don't think we can stop now, right?"

"Yeah, you are correct, although the last time I had anything to do with a black spirit skull, Roko and I were creating a mixture to speak to the skull when a green flame burned my hands and my beard—and six skulls were missing from the Great Hall."

"Six skulls," said Blackjack. "These skulls went missing?"

"Yes," said Cremator, nodding. "By the time I'd put my beard out and my hands had been

medicated, only then did we noticed the skulls had vanished. I didn't get the chance to perform the black candle check."

Blackjack frowned. "Do you recall if the six skulls came in as a group? Or were they individual skulls that came in at different times?"

Cremator cocked his head. "That's an unusual question to ask. What are you getting at?"

Blackjack pointed his index finger up. "Let me explain. When I was battling Roko—sorry, I mean when I was battling yellow teeth, he told me—"

"Wait a minute. Time out," said Cremator, gritting his teeth for control. "Here you are again, telling me that this skull in my hand could be Roko. Now I'm seeing why Jinnamon questioned you earlier."

"Look, I know it's hard to believe and I don't want to believe it either, but Roko for whatever reason met me yesterday, or two days ago, and I was supposed to meet up with you. But it was Roko, and he fell prey to a black spirit rider trap. It's got him. It turned him, and he tried to stomp me with his black spirit horse." Blackjack rested his hands on his hips, glaring at his friends. "Why would I lie about something like this?" Pulling his leather carry bag to his chest, he opened it, withdrawing an envelope.

"I can't believe you two. You're paranoid," Blackjack said, stuffing the letter into Cremator's chest. Jinnamon looked over his shoulder. "It has the Queen's Seal on it."

"The Queen's Seal?" said Cremator.

"It's okay," said Blackjack. "You have my approval, and only with my approval can you open that leather envelope. Go ahead and open it; that way, we'll get this nonsense over and go back to work."

Cremator looked at Jinnamon with lifted eyebrows, then focused back on Blackjack. "Are you sure about opening this?" said Cremator.

"Open the fricking wrap."

"Look, I'm sorry; maybe I overreacted."

"That's okay," said Blackjack. "I think with all the unusual events that have been going on lately, we're all a little tense. At least for me, bad stuffs happened that I couldn't stop. I had no control over the black spirit rider trap. I escaped. Roko didn't. Cremator, open the envelope."

Cremator carefully opened the envelope, breaking the seal, his eyes moving quickly left to right, over and over until he reached the letter's end.

"Wow! Okay, I'm Captain Dumbass here at the moment. An unknown entity, some type of a Penetrator that you are transporting to Grimmbell?"

"That's where I was going when I ran into Roko. And then bad things happened. That's all I'm going to say about it." With a nod toward Jinnamon, Blackjack added,

"Let Jinn read it."

Cremator handed the message across to Jinnamon. She blinked once at the letter.

"That's why the Queen was uneasy when I spoke to her at the spotting tower," she announced. "Why, what did she say?" asked Cremator.

"She wanted to be notified of any unusual movement of individuals or large groups. Actually, she was very persistent that anything strange be reported to her at once."

"I will inform her immediately," said Blackjack, patting the rope hanging over his shoulder and across his chest. "But as you are aware of her intuitive antenna-tool like her dragoon rope, she has a general idea of what's happened since I started this journey."

"Okay," said Cremator. "I think I have an idea of how I can talk to this skull."

"You have my attention," said Blackjack.

"Mine too," said Jinn.

Cremator stood in front of the duo. "Right, if anything goes bad, I need you to promise me that you'll keep my skull safe, and out of the hands of the black spirit rider."

"What are you talking about?" Jinnamon asked.

"If something goes bad with me and you need to stop me, as in kill me, then don't destroy my skull, okay? *Don't destroy my skull.*"

"What are you not telling us?"

"Look, I'm going where no earther's gone before, and don't know for sure what'll happen. It's very possible that Roko the Dark and his red-eyed pupils could take my body spirit and use it as their own."

"If that's the case, why didn't Roko take my body when I was lying in the creek unconscious?"

"I'm only speculating here," countered Cremator. "But I believe he couldn't control both of your personalities, Blackjack and Bradicus, at the same time."

"What does that mean?" said Blackjack.

"It means he couldn't pull two separate magical entities like yours together, for one thing."

"Do you think he tried?"

"Oh, hell yes, he tried. But like I said, you're

unique," Cremator insisted. "Because I have Brazel too, right?"

"Yes, because you are Bradicus in human form, Blackjack in animal form, and your third being and power, Brazel, your very intelligent subconscious."

"Wait a minute," said Blackjack. "How do you know I have a third being?"

"Because I talked to it, of course."

"You *talked* to it?"

"Yes, I did. Well, sort of. You spoke to me when I fished you out of the creek."

"What did I say?"

"You told me not to destroy this skull."

Jinnamon lowered her head into the huddle. "That means we are on the right path, gentlemen.

Cremator needs to talk to the skull, so let us not delay any longer."

"Yes, indeed, let's get this show on the road," said Blackjack. "Jinnamon, can you get that campfire any bigger?"

"Are you kidding?" she said, spitting a small fireball into the fire.

"Blackjack, could you and Brazel create a temporary portal that functions inside the fire?

"I don't know. I've never created a temporary portal. Portals take an enormous amount of energy.

And if I'm successful, I have no idea where this portal will take you."

"I have a hunch," said Cremator. "With the screamer's dust, the rider's skull as the mixing

ingredients and the energy of the fire, I should be able to combine the rider's dimension and this present one for a short time. Once I walk through the fire into the temporary portal, I will end up right here where I am standing now. Except..."

"Except what?" said Blackjack.

"Damn, I'm not sure if this skull in my hand here will actually take the place of *my* skull and allow me to talk to you or vice versa, or if I can just talk to the skull by holding it like I am now. I don't know for sure. I suppose it might not let me do either one."

"Do we really have to kill you if it all goes to shit?" asked Blackjack. "Don't you think that's a little extreme?"

"No, I don't," said Cremator. "Just remember to keep my head. Whatever you do, don't let the spirit rider take it with him. One more thing. If it gets ugly and you have to kill me, put my head into a leather bag, face down. This is important. Don't stare at my head if my eyes are open because it's possible that I could take your body and spirit to make more screamer's dust. Just be on the lookout for that, okay?"

Jinnamon and Blackjack hesitated, staring at each other, but nodded in agreement.

***

Cremator walked up to the fire, kicking at the wood and sending sparks up into the air.

"That's good, the sparks are floating up," he observed. "Doesn't appear to be any crosswind blowing them off course." Turning, he looked at Blackjack. "What instructions did Brazel give you on making a temporary portal?"

"Brazel said we were messing with black lash multiverse magic. He also said the best way to create this particular portal in anticipation of opening and connecting with the skull of the black spirit rider would be to acquire these items."

"What are the items?" Jinnamon asked.

"I'm glad you asked," said Blackjack, counting on his fingers. "We need the cauldron he used for boiling the other skulls. A yellow tooth from the rider's skull; we have that. A one-foot-square piece of clothing he wore. The head-chopping sickle blade, and a pound of beeswax. Oh, and wait a minute, the most important part. The screamer's dust."

"Okay," said Cremator. "Beeswax?"

Jinnamon looked over her shoulder to the crest of the hill behind her. "I have a good idea where that sickle was lying."

"I have the screamer's dust," said Blackjack. "We have the boiled skulls lying on the robe." He pointed at it.

"We have all the ingredients except the beeswax," said Cremator.

Blackjack squeezed his eyes closed. "Beeswax? Where can we get some beeswax?"

"I know where we're going to get that," said Jinnamon. "Three miles back when we were flying to your rescue, I noticed a tobacco farm that had a separate building with bees. They have to have a kettle to make the golden-eyed honey spider jam. I can smell it a mile away. I have a thing about that sweet stuff. What would you guys do without me, eh?"

She lifted off and out of sight with one flap of her wings.

"How do we make this portal work?" said Cremator.

"It shouldn't be that difficult," said Blackjack. "You do it all the time. It's a recipe. Just follow the directions."

"Well, what are the directions, my friend?"

"The first thing we need to do is set the kettle on the fire and add water from the creek. When the water's boiling, put the skulls into the kettle for fifteen minutes. Remove the skulls and chop them into pieces with the sickle blade. Pull one tooth from the rider's skull and cut a one-foot-square piece of clothing from the left arm of the shirt to wrap the tooth, the pieces of the boiled skulls, and one handful of screamer's dust into a ball. Once all those ingredients are together in the robe bag, tie the top of the bag firmly together with a leather strap. Heat the beeswax to liquid form, them submerge the entire bag into the beeswax. Remove the bag from the hot wax and let it cool for one minute."

"I hope you wrote that down," said Cremator, "because I didn't remember everything you said."

"Don't worry, I have it memorized. And look at that," Blackjack said, looking up. "Here comes Jinnamon. Perfect timing."

Jinnamon landed softly, smacking her lips and bearing a handful of beeswax. "This is a very good year," she remarked.

Blackjack explained the directions to Jinnamon, and she got the kettle on the fire with the skulls boiling. Cremator had the cloth bag cut out and ready with the tie.

Blackjack added the screamer's dust with pieces of skull and with all the ingredients added, he secured the bag.

They now placed the bag in the palm of Jinnamon's hand, together with the wax. It melted instantly. Once the bag was coated with the beeswax, Blackjack held it by the strap to cool.

"Now comes the tricky part," said Blackjack, dangling the waxed bag in front of everyone. "Here's what we have to do. With the fire burning as hot as hell—I leave that to Jinn, of course, since the sickle was the weapon of choice for the black spirit rider—Cremator will hold the sickle in the fire and once the blade's red hot, you need to swing it in a circular motion counterclockwise until a red ring forms.

That's going to be the start of the portal opening. Once the rings are in full view, I'll throw the waxed bag into the center of it. That should open and transform the fire ring into the portal to let you enter… and exit, I hope. All right, everybody get into position."

Cremator took his position over the fire with the sickle, nodding to Jinnamon. She blew into the fire, making it dance like a drunk monkey at a barbecue.

Cremator held the blade in the fire until it was glowing red. "Start the counterclockwise rotation," barked Blackjack.

Swinging the sickle in a circular motion faster and faster, Cremator called out, "You better hope this works because I'm getting tired. I don't want to let go of this sickle and send it flying either."

"You are doing great," said Blackjack.

With the portal ring glowing a bright red, Blackjack threw the bag into the center of the hole. The portal burst into a dazzling bright red, sucking Cremator right out of his furry little boots and into the portal without touching the ground.

"Wow," said Blackjack, looking at Jinnamon. "I guess he didn't have to jump."

Chapter 18: Cremator and the Portal

"Wow," said Jinnamon. "Did you feel the pressure pushing out from the opening?"

"Yes, I did. I tried to take a step forward toward the opening and couldn't. I walked into an invisible wall."

"It appears the portal is selective in who or what can enter. Don't you think?"

"That's the impression I'm getting too," said Blackjack. "That's interesting. That would make sense that a black spirit rider would be the only one who can enter its portal."

"Or *exit* the portal," said Jinnamon.

"Yes," Blackjack replied, biting the inside of his lip. "I wonder if all portals work that way? A portal—or at least *this* portal—had to have the suitable ingredients for Cremator to enter. Could it be that easy?" He was looking at Jinnamon.

"I don't know about it being easy. Sure, the actual making of this portal wax ball was easy, but how often are we going to have the key element of screamer's dust?"

"Even if that *is* the key element," said Blackjack. "We don't know that it is for sure. Maybe the dust is the igniter and one of other elements the key ingredient?"

"Do you still have some dust left over?"

Blackjack quickly grabbed his mail sack, stuffing his hand deep inside and pulling a small bag out, holding it at chest level. "I have the good stuff right here. I got this at the creek crossing; in fact, I found it on the far side of the bank, right after Roko made the jump."

"You are sure it's Roko we're after?" said Jinnamon.

"My visual paint tracker displayed the hoofprints of the black spirit horse, the very same steed that our friend Roko was riding when he jumped dimensions at the creek. And the very same horse and rider that tried to stomp me to death."

"Blackjack. Brazel here. You need to pay attention

to the fire."

Blackjack leaned away from Jinnamon to get a better look. Small fire sparks were ejecting out of the center of the portal and the sparks were growing larger.

"Um, Jinn. I believe we're being called to action," Blackjack said, pulling his sword from the sheath. Jinnamon nodded as she flared her wings horizontal to her body, leaning in toward the portal,

positioning for quick action if needed. Suddenly, a charcoal-colored canvas bag flew out of the portal, skipping across the ground and ripping open.

"Look at that," said Blackjack, pointing to one of the closer objects from the bag. "It's shiny.

Watch the opening while I take a look."

"Don't worry, I'm watching."

Blackjack quickly approached the object. Kneeling, he picked it up and turned toward Jinnamon. "It's a skull of some kind, I think."

"Quick, bring it over to me."

Blackjack ran over to Jinnamon but not before he was shotgun blasted by exploding fire sparks hurling from the portal.

"Dammit, these fire sparks stick and burn." Blackjack handed the skull to Jinnamon. "Blackjack, did you see that something's moving in that bag? Shouldn't we check it out?" Blackjack crept up to the bag with sword in hand. It stopped moving.

He looked back at Jinnamon.

"Go on, check it out," said Jinnamon. "I have you covered."

Blackjack held his sword tip inches from the bag. "Oh shit." Blackjack swung his blade, knocking a skull-sized fireball to the ground and yelled out to Jinnamon, "Did you see that one?"

"Yes, I did. What's in the bag?"

"Let's find out. Dammit!" Blackjack cut the full length of the bag with his sword tip. "It's a furry little foot with no boot." He latched onto the furry foot, dragging out whatever was attached. "It's Cremator."

"Are you sure?" Jinnamon asked.

"As I say, it's Cremator." "Is he alive?"

"I don't know, but he doesn't have any hands."

"What?" Jinnamon said, lowering her head to get a better look. "I said his hands are gone," said Blackjack.

"They're gone? Are they in the bag? Have they become detached?"

Blackjack leaned over, digging deeper inside the bag. A huge torrent of blue-green light vaulted out of the portal, pinning him to the ground.

A dark figure with red eyes vaulted out too, sitting on a black tar spirit horse, flaunting his hands at chest level.

"No, they're not in the bag. And you can't have them back." Jinnamon raised her head in snakelike fashion, ready to strike. She inhaled deeply, inflating a large glow in her throat.

"If you burn me to the ground, dragon woman, these hands will burn too. Then how is your precious Cremator going to be any use to you if he can't mix the smoke to talk to the spirits?"

Blackjack stood, grabbing his sword with both hands and approaching the dark figure. "How do you know his name?"

"I know lots of things. I know that your human name is Bradicus. And you have magical names too."

"Roko, is that you? What are you trying to do here? Don't you realize you were lured, trapped and consumed by the black spirit rider? You will die in the end."

The rider turned his glare toward Jinnamon. "You might tell your dragon woman to back off." Blackjack pushed his hand toward the ground. "Jinn, at ease, but stay hot."

Jinnamon relaxed her head and shoulders, but the glow in her throat didn't dissipate.

Blackjack stepped closer, raising his sword. "What if I were to stab your horse in the heart, rip you off that saddle and cut your freaking head off?" Blackjack smiled. "Then I'll cut your hands off and give them back to their owner. What do you think of that, pissant red eyes?"

"Roko said that you were a valiant fighter and wouldn't give up at any cost. He was right. Although he never told me you had a colorful vocabulary."

"Really?" said Blackjack. "I have another idea,

Mister pond-scum-sucking butthole sniffer."

The dark figure retrieved a pipe from his jacket. Lighting it, he inhaled deeply, releasing the smoke via his nose. "I would like to hear your idea."

"Sure. After I stab your nasty tar-dripping horse, I'll rip you out of that saddle, cut your head off and boil it into my own version of screamer's dust. I think I will call it Brazel dust."

Leaning down from the horse, the rider said, "You are fearless, my friend. Can I give you a hand?"

"That's right," said Jinnamon. "With the screamer's dust, we can follow you. And when I catch you, I will eat you with a jar of honey. Yummy."

Blackjack stepped back from the animal, but close enough to keep the tip of his sword on the dark figure. He pointed to Jinnamon. "Fire up the stove."

Jinnamon reared her head back, the glow in her throat increasing tenfold.

"Roko," said Blackjack. "Give yourself up. We can go to the King of Souls. He might be able to help you get back to your earther self."

The horse's head, butted Blackjack in the chest, knocking the sword out of his hands as he stumbled, dropping on his back.

"I am not Roko."

Guiding the horse back, Blackjack said, "I will let him know you want to talk to him." He looked again to the portal. "Here he comes now; you can talk to him yourself."

Jinnamon reached out with catlike reflexes, scooping Blackjack up in her mouth. Retracting her reach back to the starting position, she released him on the ground next to her.

"Get ready, my friend. I'm going to incinerate pissant red eyes to a puff of ash."

"Wait!" said Blackjack. "I need to get Cremator's body. At least his head."

The portal closed momentarily, then reopened to a thousand hooves stomping on the ground.

"Holy shit, I think the portal's going to explode. I have to get Cremator," said Blackjack, rushing over to the lifeless Cremator, grabbing his leg and pulling him back until he tripped on Jinnamon's tail.

Looking up at Jinnamon and with a quick nod toward *red eyes*, he said, "Light him up." Jinnamon executed a cobra head strike, vomiting a ball of fire, engulfing *red eyes*.

"Is that all you have?" Red eyes reined his horse to the left, continuing the act until he'd transformed himself into a spinning black ball, propelling masses of the super sticky hot black tar in every direction.

"Look out for that spirit horse tar," yelled Jinnamon. "It will burn right through you. Stand behind me."

A horrific scream pierced the air, followed by the echo of a thousand hooves pounding the ground.

Blackjack hunched behind Jinnamon, trying to block out the horrible sound.

A larger dark figure riding a much bigger black spirit horse emerged from the portal. The dark rider pulled back on the reins, bringing the horse to a momentary stop. "Sometimes, you have to do the dirty deed yourself."

Jinnamon poked Blackjack with her tail. "Is that Roko?"

"Brazel, this is Blackjack. Can you close the portal?"

"No, I can't. It will remain open for eighteen minutes, then close." "How long has it been?"

"Seven minutes."

"Can you sense Cremator?"

"I can. I can feel everyone," said Brazel. "You can sense everybody here?" "Yes," confirmed Brazel.

"The big dark figure is that Roko?" asked Blackjack.

"It's Roko's body, but his mind and actions could be controlled by someone else."

"Do you know who?" asked Blackjack.

"I'm not sure. There's interference. Appears to be a grab bag of magic participants."

"Is Cremator alive?"

"In what mode? Real-time, spirit, or soul?" Brazel questioned. "Real-time."

"Yes, he's alive in real-time. Although when he does wake up, he will be in a lot of mental pain. He's coated with a continuous stone stun spell. Say that three times real fast and see how you get on. The portal's closing."

"I guess that's both good and bad. Brazel, could you open it again?"

"Blackjack! What are you doing?" said Jinnamon. "Red eyes is talking to the bigger horse rider." "I'm here, Jinn. I was talking to Brazel."

"Brazel, can you—"

"Yes, I can," Brazel said.

Red eyes marched his horse next to Roko. Handing him a bag, Roko opened it, pulling out one of the amputated hands, clenched into a fist, pallid and stiffened by now.

"Ah yes, a hand I can read with." Reaching into the bag a second time, he retrieved the other hand.

Holding both now, he nodded. "His hands will work for now, but my master wanted *your* hands, Blackjack. You are his favorite, but Cremator had more knowledge than I assumed. Fantastic! This gets better all the time."

"Umm, why does it get better all the time?" asked Blackjack. "With my newly acquired powers, you know."

"No, I don't know, Roko. You will have to tell me. Fill me in on what I'm missing."

"Well, you see, with my growing powers as a superior black horse spirit rider, I cannot read my own book; that would not achieve anything. Because of security reasons in my past life, I initiated a spell on the master recipe book. Only the hands of a master earther can read the Great Hall's master recipe book, reading by their fingertips and not their eyes, in a process called *smoke oil braille*. So, I needed to acquire Cremator's hands, which I now have in my possession, to read the master recipe book."

Roko tied the hands together with a string of leather, stuffing them back into a bag and slinging the carrier into the waiting arms of the red-eyed rider. "Keep them safe while I deal with these two."

Without taking her eyes off the two intruders, Jinnamon positioned herself to strike, poking Blackjack again with her tail but this time, a lot harder. "Are we waiting for them to make the first move?"

"Hang on here, Jinn." Blackjack lowered his shield. "Jinn, be ready to send another one of those fire blob balls."

"I'm ready right now," said Jinnamon.

"Not yet, I want to talk to Roko," Blackjack shot back. "Are you sure that's who it is?"

"Keep an eye on Cremator," answered Blackjack.

"Be smart, I will be ready to strike in a heartbeat," confirmed Jinnamon. "Copy that, dragon woman," Blackjack said, winking.

Walking up to the larger horse, Blackjack lowered his shield, although keeping his sword chest high. "If you try anything stupid like trying to stomp me again, I will have Jinnamon the dragoon woman modify her burning technique and this time, we will burn a black spirit rider into a lump of tar." Leaning on the saddle horn, the dark hairy figure grinned.

"Blackjack, my friend, I wouldn't do that to you again, I would do something much more stimulating."

Blackjack raised his hand. "Yes, I was counting on that." Immediately, Jinnamon inhaled, pulling her head back ready to strike.

"Have Mister Pissant Red Eyes back his horse over by the brush." Roko pointed at *red eyes*.

Grinning, the red-eyed horse rider pulled the reins back, guiding his horse thirty feet backwards to the brush, resting his sword on the saddle horn.

"Since you know so much about me," said Blackjack. "Why don't you tell me who you are?"

"You do know me, Blackjack the transporter of secrets, the personal message dealer for Queen Kula. I'm Roko the night horse rider. I ride by the light of the moon and the stars. And tonight, the moon is full and bright. Best for chopping heads."

"What about Roko the Earther, my friend, the mixing tobacco wizard from this valley? Where is he at? Is he still alive? Maybe inside of you somewhere?"

"Your friend is here somewhere." Looking down at the saddle, he added, "Maybe sitting on this very horse. Your other friend there, the one without the hands, he entered my portal without a scream."

"Amazing. I want to know how he did that, but let's back up a little bit."

"When I found your friend in the portal, he was mixing a batch of tobacco to be able to read one of our skulls. Well, I couldn't let that happen. The knowledge to open a portal which, by the way, you won't be able to duplicate, was pure magic luck."

"We will see about that, Roko. You don't know my true powers."

Roko stared at Blackjack. "That's why I look forward to battling you. And your portal infiltrator trying to read a rider's skull; not good. Can't let that happen. According to your friend, Roko the smoke wizard"—he looked at the moon—"you are much more. Do you remember the last time you asked me questions?"

"Yes, I do," said Blackjack. "You said the next time we met, it would cost me to ask you questions."

"That's right, I did. If you can defeat my student, or the one you call *red eyes,* I might answer a question tonight."

"Sounds to me as if you are the one needing to ask a question tonight. Remember? How did Cremator open the portal?"

"Yes, that would be a worthy question, but it wasn't *me* wondering that."

"Someone you work for?" asked Blackjack.

"A black spirit rider does not work for any one form."

"I see, so you are a freelance spirit hunter?"

"The individual who's really curious about the portal opening is your friend from the medicine herb shop."

"You mean Arune, the unknown dark entity who can filter his magic into the living?"

"I don't know this dark power you speak of, but I've felt its presence in this dimension. I look forward to seeing what it wants to penetrate."

"Blackjack! Brazel here. This is a trap."

"Brazel, what are you talking about?"

"Red eyes is twitching over there. Too many coffee beans or chocolate-covered skulls. I think he was the one Jinnamon saw two weeks ago at the dig site by Tower 7. He's going to make a move."

"Not if I can help it," said Blackjack. "We need to take Cremator's hands." Lifting the necklace out of hiding, he dangled the ten coin side to side. "I want to speak to Roko the Earther, not the rider. Look what I have here."

"A life coin will not save you tonight," said Roko. "This is not a life coin."

"Then why are you showing it to me?"

"This is taking too long," said Jinnamon, spitting a fire ball dead center at Roko, rolling the dark rider and horse to the ground.

"The heat is melting them into a tar ball," said Blackjack. "That should keep him tied up for a while."

"Not long enough. This rider knows us all too well."

A shower of sparks blasted out of a hole, forming twenty feet above them. "Brazel, I didn't order a portal."

"I'm not the one opening it."

"They're making a run for it," said Blackjack.

Red eyes reared up on his horse, charging Blackjack with a silver spear aimed for his head.

Blackjack yelled at Jinn. "Where did he get the spear?"

"Throw me as hard as you can at red eyes." Jinnamon flicked her tail, transporting Blackjack supersonic toward the charging red-eyed one.

Blackjack tucked his head low, arms straight out, claws extended, fists tight. "Brazel, I'm going to rip straight through his chest cavity if I can."

Jinnamon had taken to the sky, circling the top of the open portal for enhanced speed, nosediving at Cremator.

"Blackjack. This is Brazel. Nobody has ever done this before, I mean, charging into a black spirit rider. If you hit red eyes head on, you could literally get trapped inside the rider and in an unknown portal, or both, forever. Do you know something I don't?"

"I'm going…" said Blackjack.

Roko managed to free his chest from the tar ball mess, gaining control of his posture. "Your dragoon woman cannot defeat me with sticky fire balls."

Jinnamon snagged Cremator with one talon, lifting him off the ground and into her mouth, and she swallowed. "I need a little honey please."

Roko stared at Jinnamon with a blank look. "Well, kick me in the ass, she ate him. Maybe I should recruit her. The first ever dragoon spirit rider. Wow, that's a damn good idea. I need a bigger portal hole."

Jinnamon charged skyward for two hundred feet then quickly banked left, her sights set on Roko. Roko positioned himself to battle with the dragoon woman.

Raising his sword, it flared with green flame.

"Red eyes, kill the furball and get their bag of dust. The portal closes in two minutes. If you're not in the opening, we lose the spirits and the hands of powder."

Jinnamon was leveling out for a frontal attack with Roko when she noticed Blackjack had knocked the red-eyed rider off his horse with the saddle attached. The horse continued running at Blackjack, lunging its tar-dripping hooves for a fatal throat kill.

The rider jumped up quickly with the spear held high, running behind the horse.

"Blackjack," said Brazel. "Cut its head off. Cut its head off. What are you waiting for?"

"Whose head?" said Blackjack. "Whose head? The horse's or the rider's?"

Blackjack kissed the ground, causing the black spirit horse to miss its mark, the red-eyed rider stopping in front of Blackjack. "Look, it's my old friend from the creek crossing. You cut my head off once before, and you still couldn't defeat me. What makes you think you can beat me now? I want your power source, Kula runner."

"I don't think so, swine breath. Neither you nor Roko will ever get close to my power source." The red-eyed rider laughed. "I don't understand. I already have your friend's hands."

"Cut the horse's head off!" yelled Jinnamon as she flew over Blackjack.

Regaining her focus on Roko, she charged him with a blowtorch velocity of fire and a massive chest bump, forcing Roko into the opening of the portal.

"Come on, giant rabbit man, let's dance," red eyes said, swinging wildly at Blackjack.

Blackjack threw his dagger at red eyes, sinking the entire nine-inch blade into his throat. The rider plunged forward to his knees, dropping his silver spear, grabbing his throat with both hands.

Blackjack caught the black tar horse lowering its

head, charging him again. "I know how to defeat you, horse breath." Blackjack lifted his sword over the rider's head. He stood like a statue, keeping most of his attention on the black tar horse.

"Cut his head off!" screamed Jinnamon.

Shifting his weight toward the horse and swinging with every ounce of power he and Bradicus could articulate in one unitized motion, he sliced into the neckline of the tar horse. The blade penetrated, stopping halfway. The horse fell to its knees with a horrific bright blue-violet beam of light and burning sparks causing Blackjack to lose his grip on the sword.

"Brazel, I'm on fire. What the hell is going on?"

"Grab that sword and start swinging. Don't stop now or we'll both die. Start swinging. Do it now! Do it now!"

"No," cried red eyes. "Don't kill my horse."

Blackjack managed to pull the sword out, slamming it deep into the open cut again, and again. "Don't stop. Don't stop," said Brazel.

With sparks of blue light stuck to his face, Blackjack said, "Goddamn, these blue bugs are like the green flame, burning through my cheeks into my tongue."

"Keep swinging," said Brazel. "Oh damn. Look out for shithead; he's about to harpoon you with that spear."

Blackjack shouldered to the right, meeting red eyes head on, but it was too late. The steel of evil punched inside his chest cavity, swelling his lungs with cold hard iron.

Blackjack folded forward. "I-I can't breathe."

"You can't stop now," growled Brazel. "Lift your fricking head up and kill this asshole." Blackjack swung his blade at the rider, slinging blood in a circular wave of cast-off gunge, connecting with the neckline and dropping the rider's head at his feet.

Lifting the sword one more time, he thrust down, cutting through the remaining section of the horse's neck, the weight of the sword falling loose from his hands and landing on top of the severed horse head. Backing away from the fresh kills, he fell to the ground.

The spear is still in me. Where in the hell is Jinn?

Laying his head back, he stared at the moon.

Chapter 19: Wounded

Looking down at Blackjack, a large dark shadow blocked the view of the moon. "Can you heal yourself, or do you need some help?"

"The blue lighted sparks," said Blackjack. "The blue light that exploded from the cut in the horse's neck peppered me with these little rocks. Made me feel sick and dizzy." Maneuvering his tongue, he gathered the small pieces of the blue rock, spitting them onto the ground.

"Jinnamon, what happened to Roko? Don't let him take the skull of red eyes or Cremator's hands."

"Roko is gone," said Jinnamon.

"That rider is not the Roko we once knew," said Blackjack. "No fricking way. That Roko is evil. He is correct in saying he's Roko the Dark, because I could sense his thoughts, feelings, emotions and intentions."

"What kind of intentions?" asked Jinnamon.

"Bad intentions. Nothing in order of importance. To create an imbalance of power. But I still don't know what his master plan is."

"I guess we'll have to wait and see," said Jinnamon. "Where did he go? I need to take chase after him." "Disappeared through the portal."

"You let him escape?"

"No, I didn't. Once I shoved him into the portal— you're welcome, by the way—and when you made the last cut through the neck of the black spirit horse, the portal went ballistic, producing a nasty hurricane force of suction into the portal."

"That's interesting," said Blackjack. "I wonder what that means?"

"I don't know, but it pulled him in. I couldn't stop him. I was digging into the dirt, trying to save my own ass from being pulled into an unknown portal of unknown destination."

"Blackjack. This is Brazel. You need to pull that spear out of your shoulder. You can talk later." Blackjack grabbed the spear. "Jinnamon, my partner is telling me to pull the spear out.”

“I was going to ask you how long you were going to leave that elongated dagger in there, but it looked as if you were in no pain, right? Or you liked it being there, right?”

“Ha! Definitely not that. Call it a momentary lapse of brainpower and of course, I had my pain threshold modified before the fight. But yes, I do need to take care of this problem.”

“I would hope so. How are you going to heal that wound? An injury inflicted by an evil unknown entity? I could fly you to Grimmbell.”

“You could but I have an idea.”

“An idea. Are you serious? Just an idea?”

Pointing to the bag hanging on the rider’s belt, he said, “Grab that bag of screamer’s dust.”

“You don’t even know if that will work,” said Jinnamon. “It could take your power. It might kill your subconscious friend.”

Blackjack nodded in agreement. “Maybe. Pull this spear out and pour the screamer’s dust on the wound, then throw some fire on it. Got it?”

“Yes sir,” said Jinn. “It’s your funeral.”

“One more thing,” said Blackjack.

“Seriously.”

“When you pull the spear out, use it to secure the skull in the ground. I don’t want it rolling off again.”

Jinnamon performed the task as directed, throwing down a whisper of flame on the nasty cut, sticking the rider’s skull with the spear and handing it to Blackjack. “Here is your rider kebab.”

“How did you know that would work?” Jinnamon asked, watching the gash from hell heal. “I took a chance,” said Blackjack.

“You took a chance? I don’t believe you. How did you know it wouldn’t hurt you?”

“I didn’t know for sure, but figured if they’re using the screamer’s dust to separate and open a portal and then turn around to close the portal, I figured it would have the same reaction to my injury.”

“You mean because your wound was like an open portal, it would close just like the portal—the wound, that is?"

"That is correct." He rubbed the side of his chest. "It's like it never happened," he said, pulling up his shirt. "And look at this. No scar or mark of any kind."

Jinnamon twisted her head to the right and left, slowly nodding.

"I'm amazed that you figured that out. I would have never thought of that. You must know more about portals than you're letting on."

"It was a hunch from my internal Brazel side."

"I would like to know more about these portals. To use in battle. To escape. Stuff like that. Would you be willing to teach me?"

"As you know, portal philosophy and technology are governed by Kula and a select few, and even those individuals don't have all the answers. The event that took place tonight is information that they need to know about. These black spirit riders must have the knowledge to transmute energy into an energy form they can utilize. This energy, if it could be harvested, controlled, packaged—"

"You mean like having a power drink during a battle?" said Jinnamon. "Need a little kick-ass juice. Activate your powerpack. That type of thing?"

"Yes, that type of thing, but used in a much broader spectrum."

Blackjack gripped the spear shaft of the rider kebab, touching nose to nose with the skull. "We need to find out what this skull can tell us."

He looked away from the skull, eyeballing Jinnamon with a troubling look. "You ate Cremator? Did I really witness that or was that a Fig Newton of my imagination, by any chance?"

"You witnessed it. It's the only way I could save him and battle Roko at the same time. But I didn't chew, I only swallowed him. Didn't have the heart to chew him up."

"Trust me, Jinnamon, I'm not complaining. I'm grateful for your help. Although I didn't know that you were a belly-drop dragoon. I knew there was a belly drop positioned at one of the spotting towers, but I didn't know which one."

"That isn't a problem, is it?"

"No. No problem, whatsoever. Having a belly drop in our collection of tools is a good thing, although"—he rubbed his neck—"how do we get him out of your holding pod?"

"I would like to show you how, but don't actually know," said Jinnamon. "You have never used your belly drop before?"

"I've been used to transport specific products before, but the actual process of removing the product from my secret compartment… Belly drop, I don't remember. I do recall going into some type of a dream state and when I woke up, my compartment was empty, and I don't remember anything apart from that. It's quite confusing and scary."

"That's interesting," said Blackjack. "When they put you to sleep, are you totally out of it or do you remember anything about it?"

"I remember some type of a mind tap. I would hear someone talking to me when they did the procedure. Which, by the way, intrigued and scared me when I knew you had that ability to read minds."

"Ah, yes. Is that why you were cautious?"

"To a point. I thought maybe you might have been part of the team of shamanistic mind-benders who'd created a method of removing goodies from belly drop dragons."

"I understand," said Blackjack. "And you thought I showed up the other night to have you transport what I had, and then what I'd been chasing?"

"It crossed my mind a few hundred times."

"Yes, I can appreciate that. I don't think I would want you to transport Roko and his horse or anything to do with a black spirit rider."

"Bradicus, this is Brazel. Is it possible that someone wanted Jinnamon to swallow a black spirit rider? Maybe Killamore?"

"You have been reading my mind."

"Of course, I have. That's what I do," offered Brazel.

"I was thinking of that too," said Blackjack. "And if that was the case, she would've had an opportunity to eat Roko when she was pushing him into the portal."

"That is a likely possibility," said Brazel. "But I believe that the portal had too much suction and she didn't want to get pulled in. Just an observation."

"But I thought you had all the answers."

"Don't forget that some of my electrified thinking is part of you."

"I will talk to you later. Thanks for the update."

"Goodbye."

"But aren't we forgetting something?" asked Jinnamon, holding her hands out, flexing her talons. "Cremator's hands," said Blackjack. "I haven't forgotten. We need to reattach them. We need to get

Cremator out of your belly drop and reattach his hands, because right now, with Roko on the dark side, and Rasp, I don't know if he has the experience to go under like Cremator. So, as of right now, the only man who can perform this task is Cremator. Oh shit, I need to get the bag containing Cremator's hands from the saddle."

"Don't worry, I already did it," said Jinnamon, handing the bag to Blackjack. "It was my pleasure. Although, I had the super bright-blue rocks blast into my armor." Blackjack looked at Jinnamon with an interested gaze. "The sparks come from his hands?"

"No, the sparks came from old Black Beauty, the tar horse you slayed."

"Really? The sparks came from the horse?"

"Yes, they came out of the horse and attacked me too."

Blackjack kicked at the fallen tar horse. "Blue sparks. Super-hot energy. A lot of energy. Screamer's dust. Portals."

"What are you talking about?" said Jinnamon.

Blackjack paced back and forth in front of Jinnamon. "Is it possible that the riders are producing the screamer's dust by using what's inside the human skull, and not the skull itself?"

"Or both," said Jinnamon.

Blackjack continued his pacing. "Are the riders matching the energy from our dimension—or at least from our bodies—in our own dimension and mixing it with outside spirit energy to open another portal in a different dimension? Does that sound plausible to you?"

He wasn't waiting for an answer to his question.

"Jinnamon," said Blackjack, making eye contact again. "I don't suppose we still have some of those exploding blue rocks that burned my face and your armor?"

"Yes, we do. I have some pieces right here, stuck in my armor." She showed her wrists. "They couldn't burn through. They just kind of welded to it like exquisite jewelry."

"Then I can pull them out for you. I'd like to keep the samples for Cremator to look at."

"Of course," said Jinnamon, lowering her arms within reach of Blackjack. "It would be easier for you to pull them out than for me to try and do it."

And so, that was what they did. It took but a few moments for Blackjack to focus on the task and get it done. He tweezed each one out as if it was a pimple that needed popping.

"Finished," said Blackjack, holding the last one between his fingers. "I pulled about fifty of these burning little rock sparks out of your armor."

"Thank you," said Jinnamon. "I could feel the rocks grinding between my armor plates. Nothing major but it does feel better without them. You could have been a skilled surgeon, you know."

"Well, I can't say I'm sure about that, but thanks for the compliment. Always nice to hear good words spoken about oneself. Especially from such a dear friend, one who knows me better than—"

"Though you do realize it was a joke," quipped Jinnamon, waving her arms to enjoy the new-found feeling of lightness now the metal adhesions had been surgically excised from her body armor.

Blackjack grinned, then dropped the last of the tar horse energy rocks into a small leather bag, stuffing it into his larger messenger bag. "This thing gets heavier with every mile of my journey."

"How much energy is still trapped in the spirit horse? It's too dangerous to leave it here."

"Brazel. I need you to check our inventory list."

"What is it that you need?"

"I need some type of container to hold an unknown energy form."

"Is this container going to be located on the ground in a cave, underwater, or what?"

"I'd like to keep it off the ground, but in the air," said Blackjack. "Well, I suppose off the ground and in the air are one and the same, kind of. But you get what I meant."

"Do you want some type of a sky marker, so you don't forget where it's located?"

"A marker? I am assuming this marker could only be seen by me?"

"That's correct, unless you choose otherwise, in which case that would be an entirely different process. But yes, for now, you would be the only one able to see it."

"What do you have for me?"

"I have an energy kite suppression container."

"Please send it now."

"I did," said Brazel.

"I still don't see it."

"Of course, you don't. It's invisible. You have to use your night mode vision. I'm assuming you are not alone."

"That's correct. What would I do without you?"

"I don't know, but let's not hurry to find out." "Ah yes, there it is," said Blackjack with a nod.

"There what is?" asked Jinnamon, looking in the same direction. "Jinnamon, I need your assistance for a few minutes."

"Okay, what do I have to do?"

Blackjack walked over to the black tar horse. With the tip of his sword, he drew a ten-foot circle in the dirt surrounding the fallen steed.

"Do you see this circle that I have drawn in the dirt?" he asked as if he believed she needed fitting with glasses.

"Of course, I do. How can I not see that?"

"Well, what I mean is I'll need your superiority in guarding it."

"My *superiority?* You're correct, of course, but you mean my *security* skills. That's my specialty.

Security," said Jinnamon.

"I know. And very good. Don't let anything step inside this circle for the next twenty minutes." Jinnamon nodded. "Twenty minutes. No problem." She gave a salute.

Blackjack stepped inside, outlining the circle in dirt with Kula's dragoon rope, positioning his arms horizontal with his palms up into a T formation. Raising his arms in unison and clapping his hands together above his head, he disappeared into the circle.

"Blackjack, where did you go? How in the hell did you do that?" He had disappeared with the rider's horse. "How can you disappear with that huge beast? A dead horse!"

Jinnamon looked at the circle drawn in the dirt. Had he opened a portal? "That son of a hairy furball, he used the energy of the horse to open the portal, leaving me here. Well, I'll be—"

Jinnamon backed up, inhaling and smothering the circle of ground with a torrent of fire.

The flames stuck to the structure, outlining the shape of a tent or a dome. The heat caused Jinnamon to back away from the fire with a shrill shriek.

"Jinnamon," said Blackjack. "What the hell were you doing? I asked you to guard me, not try to cook me for dinner. An act like that could get your hands slapped by Kula."

"I'm sorry. I wasn't sure where you went. For all I knew, you'd been kidnapped. Call it a battlefield type of reaction. Autopilot kind of thing. *When in doubt, burn it out,* is my motto. Where did you go?"

"Actually, I didn't go anywhere; I was inside an invisible dome. I had to have total concentration in dealing with this energy horse, had to talk to dead Beauty. I needed information."

"You can actually talk to a horse?"

"Yes, I can. And more than that, I did."

"Wow. What did you find out?"

"Some of its memories had been erased when it transformed into a spirit horse. From what I could understand, her memory would erase a little bit each time they traveled in and out of a portal into a certain dimension. It was quite interesting. But not very pleasant. The horse itself had been trapped into becoming a black spirit rider horse, pretty much against its will or instinct."

"So, what did you do with the horse?"

"I let it go. Gave it its freedom, of course; it was a magnificent beast, and it's just a shame it got itself sucked into all this. Horses are innately good… but anyway…"

"What about the energy? The blue rocks, all that stuff. What happened to it? Are we not going to have to report that to Kula?"

Blackjack nodded in agreement. "Yes, we will have to report this to Kula." Raising his hand, he paused. "Hold that thought. Incoming message."

"Bradicus. This is Brazel. I encountered a really weird mixture of thoughts and feelings, and they weren't coming from you when you were inside the energy container."

"I'm assuming they were emanating from the spirit horse? I do take it they seemed equine?" There came no answer to that.

Brazel continued, "And I also had a hard time staying connected with you. There was a very powerful interference of energy blocking our connection. It's interesting though. When there was a certain temperature increase, I picked up the crosstalk between you and the horse with more clarity."

"That would be Jinnamon, and her heatwave fit. What else were you able to pick up?"

"Well, just listen to this! I picked up around seven ancient languages," mused Brazel. "Not new languages or ones still in use today, but ones that haven't been used for quite a while. As in millennia."

"I'm sure you are going in a specific direction with this info," said Blackjack. "I hope so."

"These languages haven't been spoken in nine hundred years, maybe more. Although there was one dialect, I was not familiar with. One being of under-verse type of Grimmblical proportions."

"*Grimmblical* proportions?" inquired Blackjack.

"Yes, at least from what I could interpret, it has some form of possible Grimmblical reference, something about a dark superior being and the sacrifice of a mixed bag of millions of souls."

"Millions of souls, huh?" Blackjack pondered on it for a few moments, his mind whirring. "Then I wonder if this unknown entity is the type of a superior being, using this energy from these completed souls to form itself? It's quite feasible, wouldn't you say?"

"Well, I don't know," answered Brazel. "I don't honestly possess sufficient information to make that sort of conclusion. Like I said, there was a lot of distortion. So, I'm not one hundred percent on that specific topic. It's something we'll need to check out at a later date."

"This mystery Arune power source is really fricking things up," Blackjack observed. "We can talk about that later. Is the energy sealed inside the suppression container?"

"Yes, it was a successful transfer and sealing process." "Good, I feel a lot better about that because—"

He was rudely cut off.

"Although there was some energy that did escape, but it was also captured at the same time. Were you aware of this?"

Thankfully, he was.

"I am aware of that. I transferred that energy into a ten coin."

"Oh, really? And the ten coin was able to capture and hold the power?"

"Yes, it did because it's hanging around my neck as we speak. And it feels so *goooood.*"

"Bradicus, is this your personal ten coin?"

"No, it's Roko's. At least it was before he turned into Roko the Dark. He lost it back in the blue sagebrush when he tried to stomp on me with the spirit horse."

"Are you sure it was even Roko's to begin with? Was it hanging around his neck, or did you find it on the ground? *How* did you find it exactly?"

"I found the coin hanging on a tree branch. It has his initials on the back. It was definitely his."

"Well, that may be so, but I don't think you should be wearing that coin of power. We don't know what would happen if the power of a ten coin happened to mix with the energy of the spirit horse."

"Brazel, wouldn't the end product of mixing these two energies be determined by the owner of the ten coin itself?"

"It's a possibility that the power would be determined good or bad depending on the person who created the ten coin. That's an unknown specific energy, an energy created by ten diverse entities in ten worlds. It could affect you in a thousand diverse ways, and it would be totally impossible to know what would happen if you mixed the energies and more importantly, the energy could be world destroying. And how would you destroy the coin if you needed to? Bad mojo here, Bradicus. Doesn't feel right."

"Yeah, that's what I was speculating too. The ten coin did absorb the blue energy, but I'm not wearing it. I'm just messing with you."

Brazel heaved a sigh.

"Bradicus, I sense the dragoon Jinnamon is getting impatient."

"Yes, I know. Most of your fighter dragoons are inpatient, but they make great allies. One more thing before you go," said Blackjack.

"What is that?"

"If you have any unusual sensations concerning the screamer's dust, blue energy, rider's blood or whatever you want to call it, please warn me. You will be the first one to know."

"Got it. Will do."

Blackjack was finally able to turn his attention back to Jinnamon.

"Okay Jinnamon, so sorry about that. I had information coming in that I needed to address."

"Was it Kula?"

"No, we don't have a mind-melt connection this far apart."

Jinnamon handed Kula's dragoon rope to Blackjack. "Thought you might want this back."

"Yes, I do. Thank you."

"What happened to the energy from the horse, and what about the rider himself?" she asked next. "I have the energy stored in a container."

"A container?" Jinnamon questioned.

"Yes, a container. Actually, it's more like an energy vault. As far as the rider himself, I'm not sure how much energy he carried, then the black spirit horse absorbed his power when I destroyed him. The important thing is that we still have his head. I believe red eyes must have been controlled by Roko, a puppet on a string. The real energy for the rider was all coming from the horse."

"And you will be able to read the skull?" said Jinnamon.

"*I* can't read the skull. But Cremator will be able to read red eye's skull."

"Cremator," she said, touching her belly.

"Roko wanted Cremator's hands. We need to get Cremator out of your belly drop and reattach his hands, then maybe we can find out what the hell Roko is going to do next." Blackjack rubbed his chin. "This is only one piece of the puzzle, and I know there's more to come. I'm just kidding myself wanting to believe that Roko will come to his senses, but we know better, don't we?"

"I do believe we'd be fooling ourselves if we assumed that," said Jinnamon.

Blackjack stared at Jinnamon as she sniffed the area where the portal had collapsed in on Roko. "How are we going to open her belly drop?"

Chapter 20: The Releasing Ceremony

Kula sat quietly on top of Tower 5, watching Slaughter dance a fifty-foot wave of blue fire over the heads of the distinguished crowd of earthers, humans, and ore trolls, the many varieties of the Darkan Territory residents living in the Valley of the Tomb Sleepers.

They had assembled near the fallen dragoon warrior in anticipation of the releasing ceremony.

He circled around the spotting tower, making another low-altitude flyover, this time, propelling sixteen rock jaw firebombs into the air. They hovered above the crowd then one by one, exploded into a variety of burning colors, each depicting a distinguished feat the dragon accomplished before his death.

The heads of the high council were present, performing their specialty in the releasing ceremony, each one deciding how to release the spirit of the fallen warrior depending on the color history of the rock jaws. The spirit guards were first to perform their part of the release.

The head spirit governor Theanine floated directly above the dragoon, viewing the color history at the same time. Satisfied with what he saw, he ordered each of the four spirit guards on the ground to release their hold on the dragoon's spirit. Then, Theanine lowered himself onto the ground with a blue and white semi-transparent rope in his hands. It separated into four smaller lines, each line attaching to the dragoon.

The four spirit guards elevated to a height just above the dragoon, located at their respective positions, two at the top of the dragoon and two at the bottom. Pulling on the rope, Theanine nodded to the spirit guards, and they immediately plunged inside the belly of the downed warrior.

Theanine turned around, hoisting the rope over his shoulder, leaning forward and pulling on the rope. Kula watched the spirit guides, turning her head toward

Slaughter. "Will they get his spirit?"

"I don't see why not," said Slaughter. "He was a respected fighter and in his last Order of Confidence hearing, he stated that he wanted his spirit to be taken to Grimmbell." The first spirit guard emerged from the belly to be absorbed by Theanine.

He pulled harder, then the remaining spirit guards emerged from the inside of the dragoon and were also absorbed by Theanine in exactly the same manner. He turned, facing the dragoon, tugging on the rope. Suddenly, there was slack in it, and Theanine fell to the ground.

The dragoon spirit had released from his body and was now floating above the ceremony crowd.

Theanine gathered up the rope's slack, dropping it to the earth and quickly stepping on it with his foot. He looked up at the high council. "The soul shaper will take control from here."

The soul shaper stepped down from the high council platform and moving quickly, took the rope in his hand, absorbing Theanine and pulling the dragoon spirit down to stand next to him.

"May I have your soul? Will you let me place you at Grimmbell?" "Yes, I am ready to go home," replied the dragoon spirit.

The soul shaper gave a slow head nod to Slaughter to get permission for placement in Grimmbell. Slaughter looked down from the tower, nodding to the soul shaper. "Please take my brother home."

The soul shaper started his journey back to Grimmbell Cemetery with the virgin spirit of Graper floating just above his head. "I will transform his spirit into a warrior soul, and it could come to happen that his soul placement be on the soul tree. I will need permission from the high council to use some of his dragoon skin for the making of his soul bag to hang on the branches."

Kula leaned in toward Slaughter. "Send two fighter dragoons with them. His color history was outstanding. Make sure they get to Grimmbell without any problems along the way."

"My pleasure. Thank you, my Queen."

"We are getting closer," said Kula. "The next step is

the wishbone pulling of the bone, and who will receive the wealth of the skull, skeletal bones, organs, and the dragoon armor skin."

"And then another important part of the releasing process," said Rasp, closing the tower door leading to the floor of the landing arena. "Then follows the releasing of the most treasured magical organ in the valley, the heart of a fighter dragoon."

"Greetings Kula, Queen of the Dragoon Clan," said Rasp, then turned to Slaughter. "Welcome, General Slaughter, decorated warrior of the Earthers' Valley. I do hope you are both enjoying the curriculum expertise of the ceremony?"

"Yes," said Kula. "Speaking for myself, I have greatly enjoyed the proficiency of each step so far." Rasp removed his hand from his pocket.

"I am very sorry to see that it is one of your own that has fallen," he said in a suitably somber tone. "Thank you; that is kind of you. I am saddened too," said Kula. "More than you can imagine. Death

will arrive on swift wings to the one who is responsible for Graper's death."

"Although," said Slaughter, "I am anticipating that when you conduct the smoke process, you will have some information to share with us about his demise."

"Oh, of course, General. You and the queen will be the first ones to find out what happened to your fighter dragoon. I do hope that we have earned your approval so far in representing the Queen's Warrior with the doctrines of this ceremony."

"I was pleased with Theanine, the spirit guards and the soul keeper in how well they performed," said Kula. "I say this especially considering that I've seen some failed attempts when removing the spirit soul from deceased creatures; they didn't go as planned, especially the spirits that did not want to leave their body. Then you have to send in the nasty spirits to force that one out. Truly, it's not a pretty sight."

Clasping his hairy little paws together, Rasp said, "Ah, you mean the hell rippers, I take it."

"Yes, we keep the rippers on hand in case of a

situation just like that. They are effective but it's still not an enjoyable affair. But we didn't have to do it today, so I'm pleased with the outcome. Fine, enough said. I need to return to the ceremony as the next step in the releasing process is starting very soon."

"Of course," said Kula. "Rasp, one more thing before you go. Is the wishbone tug-of-war consisting of visitors versus family? Or is it going to be family versus family this time?"

Rasp spun around in front of the tower door. "I think it's going to be family versus family, although I did see a few human names and an earther on each side. Looks like a balanced team either way. Should be a good battle. I'm so sorry but I have to go," Rasp said, closing the door behind him.

Kula shrugged.

"Did you notice that Rasp didn't seem to be stressed about the presenting of the heart?" she asked.

Slaughter nodded in agreement. "I noticed that, but I suppose he could've been focusing on reading the rules for the bone-breaking stage. The rules can get complicated."

"Yes, I suppose you are right."

Slaughter nodded. "Although having said that, the aftermath of presenting the heart could be the most stressful stage of the ceremony. As you know, the heart is awarded to someone that many wouldn't agree deserves it, then that individual ends up dead, the heart missing. Presenting the heart, I can only say it's a killer in more ways than one."

"Yes, it can get horribly violent and unspeakably bloody to say the least," said Kula. "I do remember one particular time when there was some spirit tampering during the cut and removal process of the heart; that created a mess. Is that male spirit responsible for that still in the holding cells at Grimmbell?"

"No, he is not," said Slaughter.

"They let him out? Why wasn't I informed of that? That's utterly preposterous!"

"Oh, no, no! He was not let out, my Queen. As you rightly say, that would have been an absolute travesty and an injustice. He has been destroyed."

"Destroyed by what?" said Kula.

"My information conveys to me that the spirit was assassinated by an unknown soul from the tree of death. I am at least convinced of it, though it was not given to me in so many words."

"If there is truth in your statement about the tree of death being utilized, then we both know it was carried out by a hell ripper or at least another form of that type of spirit."

"It could have been arranged by a virgin spirit that wanted to keep its heart, but that's another story."

Slaughter's head whipped around from his gazing into the crowd below. "That reminds me. I need to talk to Luxen, guardian of the holding cells. He reported to me that he's investigating that particular incident, and he promised he would let me know the outcome as soon as possible."

"Good," said Kula, looking down at the ceremonial crowd. "Let me know what you find out. It looks as if Rasp is starting the next step of the ceremony."

Rasp stood at the table of the high council, announcing the splitting of the wishbone tug-of-war would start in five minutes. He leaned over, retrieving two life coins from a leather bag. With a coin in each hand, he set them down on the table for the members of the high council to examine.

The members duly passed them back and forth and when the whispering and secret talk had been completed with their approval; the coins were placed in a dragoon skin bag.

And there it sat on the high council's table. Salamare, a high council member, rose to his feet.

"Rasp, you may begin the splitting of the wishbone," he said.

Rasp bowed to the high council. "Thank you for your approval. I will begin," he said and waved to each team to gather at the head of the fallen dragoon.

He watched as all twenty-two members, eleven on each team, approached the dragoon's head. "I'm beginning to believe that this stage today might have more tension and heartbreak than the presentation of the heart."

With all members standing in front of him, he read the rules aloud.

"As you know, there are eleven members on each team. One member from each team has provided their life coin to legally acquire the riches from the dragoon's body, excluding the heart.

"The two hardback wishbones have been removed from the dragoon, and as you can see, each one is being held up by a fellow fighter dragoon."

He pointed north of the fallen dragoon's head. "There will be no talking to either fighter dragoon. If you are caught talking to either dragoon for assistance or advice, your disqualification will result.

"When the signal is given, you start pulling. When the wish bone breaks, the team with the majority of the bone will be the winner of that pull. Should one team take both breaks, they will be the automatic winner. If each team wins one breakaway pull, then the winner will be decided by the heavier weight of their wishbone. Are you ready to begin?"

The team leaders nodded in agreement. Rasp huddled with the leaders of each team.

"You do understand that one of you will lose your life coin, and the really brutal part, the losing team leader will forfeit their life after the event is completed. Do you understand and agree?"

Both parties nodded their heads in agreement.

"Now comes the tricky part," Rasp said, looking directly into their eyes. "The losing team leader will be stabbed eleven times precisely. Ten times by ten members of his losing team and one time by a member of the winning team until pronounced dead. Do you understand and agree to these terms?"

"Yes," said the two. "We do understand and agree to these terms. We have given the high council our life coins to participate in this ceremony and we are one hundred percent aware of the outcome. One of us will be dead. We wish to continue. Please, can we just get on with it?"

"Very well," said Rasp. "As you know, your life coins were accepted." He pointed to the high council table. "They have been placed in the dragoon bag. Right, let the games begin."

Kula bumped a shoulder into Slaughter. "Did you notice that team A has four Plowgond humans in their lineup, whereas team B has two miniature ore trolls on their side? They have been known to weigh up to five hundred pounds each. Could be a weight dispute here. It looks uneven at best."

"I see that," said Slaughter. "But team A has a few granite rockbusters, and let's not forget these creatures are freakishly strong. Damn mean to be quite honest. But then you come right back with team B having a Horgsdale, a beefy horse with extraordinarily sure footing."

"Wait a minute," said Kula, pointing, "I didn't see those two there on team B. Looks like two tomb carvers. This type of earthers is low to the ground at only three feet high and they have the most impressive pulling ability with an extra-wide chest and rib cage."

"That's indeed a nice touch," said Slaughter, nodding assuredly. "And don't forget those tomb carvers have double strength in their mighty chests, backs, and leg muscles along with some added features such as two hearts and the third lung for oxygen gathering and advanced air capacity. Wow. The team leaders have put some thought into these two groups."

"It's a harsh reality," said Kula. "Anytime you give up your life coin along with death… These two team leaders have definitely gone the extra mile to ensure their team wins."

Slaughter nodded. "It's a steep price to pay for the wealth of a fighter dragoon."

"So very true," said Kula. "The wealth of the remains of a fighter dragon could satisfy the wants and needs of an individual and their family for two lifetimes. Which leads me to question where the team leader found the two miniature ore trolls on team A. I haven't seen many ore trolls since the last big battle. The last one I saw was working maintenance detail on the cemetery wall. They usually work at night or underground. When was the last time you saw ore trolls?"

"I do believe there are three, my Queen."

"Three?"

"Yes," said Slaughter, giving a hand signal to a fighter dragoon to fly a little bit higher. "The two who are here today, and Smelly, the crematory ore troll."

Kula turned her view to Slaughter. "They still have an ore troll to burn the bodies? I haven't seen any debris from the smokestacks. I figured we were done with all that long ago."

"On occasions, they will ignite the burners in the crematory but not during a war. Right now, it's been burning the bodies caused by natural everyday events. Old age, work accidents, mishaps in the wilderness, that kind of thing. An occasional sanctioned dual which led to a death. All everyday events, and of course, the special burns, the purifying of the selected skulls used for making the blood bricks.

"Ah, there it is," said Slaughter. "Rasp has signaled to us that they are ready to proceed with the *splitting of the wishbone* stage."

"Yes, I saw that, General. Rasp is always waiting on me. Go ahead and give him the signal to start."

Slaughter inhaled, enlarging his chest, spitting out a spiraling tunnel of flames one hundred and fifty yards long, sending the long plume ripping above the crowd below.

Eyeing the crowd, Rasp motioned to the earthers who were holding up a bushel basket of glossy red apples. They scurried in front of the assembled onlookers, setting their basket down.

"This should be noteworthy," said Rasp, directing his attention to the crowd. "These red apples are the customary apples grown and altered by our very own royal medicine woman, Ella. The apples will give everyone a boost of outrageous power for just one minute flat. We will see who uses that minute to their best advantage."

The crowd cheered and began their customary red apple toss, flipping them at the twenty-two contestants. The contenders frantically gobbled the apples down to their core, some even eating that as well. The ore trolls quickly tied a rope to the top of their side of the bone and leaned way back, digging knee-deep into the ground as the bone bent with a loud cracking sound.

"Look at that," said Slaughter. "Those ore trolls didn't waste any time. They could break it right now, ending in a very quick victory."

"Not so fast, my friend," said Kula. "The four

Plowgonds are standing on each other's shoulders, grabbing the top of their wishbone, performing some type of catapult maneuver. It's lifting the entire side of the wishbone."

"Wait a minute, my Queen. The Horgsdale Horse has a tomb earther rider. It looks as though the little guy has a dark-blood tobacco root rope tied to the foot of the bottom man of the Rockbusters. He's going to try to pull that manmade ladder to the ground."

Kula's eyes widened. "Where did our earther friend get that kind of rope? That's comparable to my personal dragoon rope."

***

"Wait a minute," said Slaughter. "Hang on, something's not right." Slaughter stirred, quickly leaning over the landing pad wall and spitting two fireballs at his fighter dragoons. "All ground forces alert. Ground forces alert. Move now," Slaughter ordered, rearing his head back and spitting three bright orange fireballs into the air. The fireballs exploded, sending a shock wave along the ground and inciting a strong vibration all the way to the top of the tower.

Kula reared up, talons digging into the granite barrier wall.

"*Ground alert?* Why are you calling ground alert?" he demanded to know. "What's wrong?"

"Just look at the competitor's feet," said Slaughter.

"Why would I look at their feet? You think I am interested in feet?"

"No, no—not like that! I say it because their feet are turning into blocks of stone. They can't move. It looks as if they're turning into stone statues, frozen solid right where they stand."

"Oh, hell," said Kula. "Look at the rockbuster's ladder. The man on the bottom just got crushed by the weight of the men on top of him. We need to get into the air."

Slaughter pumped his wings as hard as he could.

"Look," he said. "You can see I'm trying to lift off, but I can't. Look at my feet! Look at *your* feet." His voice was trembling as hard as the jitters passing through his pointless wings.

Kula looked down. "My feet are sinking into the granite blocks as if I'm in quicksand. We are being absorbed and transformed into the Earther's Valley's largest spotting tower statue," Kula said, desperately flapping her wings too. "I can't get out. What the hell is going on here, Slaughter?"

"It's somebody's magic. I'm going to try to free our feet by using a lift-off igniter. I should be able to blast us free from the spotting tower." Slaughter reached to the center of his chest, removing a square of armor by rotating the top layer to the left then back to the right.

Ripping an opening between the granite blocks that cemented Kula's feet on top of the landing pod, he inserted the lift-off igniter into the gap.

"It will send this landing pad into a pile of rubble at the bottom of the tower. Count to three, then start grabbing for air. We should be free. One, two, three." *Boom!*

Kula and Slaughter flapped hard in unison. "Keep flapping! Keep flapping!" shouted Slaughter, lifting them all up and mobilizing them way beyond the cloud of dust molded at the top of the tower.

"Get up another five hundred feet," barked Kula.

"Do not worry, my Queen, my dragoons already circle us. Nothing can touch us at this altitude."

"I'm not worried about us; I'm worried about the ones on the ground. Do you see any type of a threat moving toward the ceremony crowd?"

"No, I don't," said Slaughter, dipping down two hundred feet. "I see the ceremony crowd has left the grandstands and they're quickly moving away from the spotting tower. Some of the competitors are still frozen in place. Wait a minute! The four men who made it up the rockbuster's ladder are frozen in stone, an exact replica of the men turned into a solid rock statue, even showing their facial expressions."

"Nothing's happening above the ground," said Kula. "At least from what I can see and I'm not seeing anything out of the ordinary. Have the fighter dragoons circle at a hundred feet."

"Circle at one hundred feet?" questioned Slaughter. "That's rather low. Do you know who the attacker is?"

"I don't know who the attacker is, but I know what they want."

"Of course," said Slaughter. "They want the ceremonial bag of life coins at the table. They won't get it. I have four fighter dragoons guarding the high council as we speak."

"I thought about that too, but now I think about it, I can't help believing the stage we were to complete next in the ceremonies is the real reason of this attack."

Slaughter gritted his teeth. "They want our dragoon. That's what they want."

"Yes and no," said Kula. "No, they don't want the entire dragoon. Yes, they want the dragoon's heart. That's exactly why they're here, whoever it is." Kula continued scanning the ground. "How many dragoons would it take to lift Graper, do you think?"

Slaughter dropped down to twenty feet above Graper's body, then he quickly nodded.

"At least three. Graper is heavier than the others. Look at that, my Queen, do you see? Rasp is flying.

He's riding on top of the spirit of Graper! How remarkable. I didn't even know he could do that."

"Oh yes, they can do that. Rasp's taken immediate action, flying the virgin spirit back to Grimmbell instead of risking the feet of stone incident. But he takes a huge chance because it's a virgin spirit, and a virgin spirit is like a wild horse, very unpredictable and prone to sudden erratic movements, not to mention a dogged stubbornness. That spirit could just take off and end up in No Man's Land or another dimension, never to be found again. And even worse, an evil entity could be controlling that spirit.

"The black spirit riders would love to get their hands on a virgin spirit," Kula finished. Rasp rolled to the left gliding between Kula and Slaughter.

"Kula, my Queen. General Slaughter. I need to tell you something."

"Yes, we know," said Kula. "You are going to ride the virgin dragoon spirit to Grimmbell instead of walking there. I don't have a problem with that. Do it now. Do it fast."

"That's not what I wanted to talk about," said Rasp.
"What *do* you want talk about?" asked Kula.

"Your fighter dragoon; it's heavier than normal."

"Yes, I am aware of that. We were thinking it would
take three dragoons to carry Graper to the cemetery."

"No," said Rasp. "Graper is heavier but not in the
way you think." "What are you talking about?" said Kula.

"When I was talking to his spirit, he told me his heart
weighed beyond the normal dragoon's heart."

"How much more?" Kula asked.

"The spirit didn't say," replied Rasp. "His spirit told
me Graper's heart is also thicker than a normal dragoon
heart."

"Heaver *and* thicker," said Kula, staring at Slaughter.
"Did *you* know his heart weighed more than normal?"

"No, I didn't know that at all," commented
Slaughter, his eyes wide. "That's both amazing and
worrisome at the same time. If his heart weighs more than a
normal one, then it's obvious this invisible attack that took
place or is possibly still in effect, is what they're here for.
They came for the heart. We have to get him out of here
right now. Either we take the body or cut the heart out and
take it with us."

"Bigger, thicker heart," said Kula, shaking her head,
brow furrowing as if she couldn't get her head around this.
"Slaughter, did you say Graper came from our stock or was
he created by someone else?"

"Do you mean created by someone else and sold to
us by Killamore?"

"It's possible," Kula replied. "We have received a
few specialty dragons from him that turned out to be
excellent fighter dragoons."

"That is true, my Queen, at least after extensive
mental and physical training. As far as I know, he came
from our stock."

"Kula, my Queen," said Rasp. "If we can't fly him to
the cemetery, then we need to have the heart cut out here.
But that leads us to another problem."

"What's that?" said Kula.

"That not just anyone can cut that heart out. Plus, it

would be out of sequence which could nullify the authenticity of the releasing ceremony. And if the cutting process isn't precise, you could lose the power within the heart. That would be a huge tragedy. And that's not the worst thing that could happen."

"What could be worse than that?" Kula asked.

"I don't know if I can tell you that, my Queen. Please forgive me. The ceremonial ritual has been performed by earthers to prevent outsiders…anyone, the enemy…from stealing the heart. A guarded secret for many earther generations."

"I am your queen. Who are you protecting in this *guarded secret of many generations* statement?"

"The Queen of the Darkan Territory, Valley of the Tomb Sleepers."

"Then I don't understand since that would be me. *I* am the Queen of Darkan Territory."

"Yes, my Queen, that is why we keep it a secret. Let me explain…"

"Was I not shoulder to shoulder with the earthers in one of the bloodiest battles we had against the scorpion moles?"

"Yes, my Queen. Of course, I remember that particular war. We lost almost half of our population. It is impossible to forget something as terrible as that."

"Yes indeed," said Kula. "And when we joined forces, what happened then?"

"When we joined forces, we defeated the scorpion moles."

"Yes, we did," said Kula, spitting a red-hot blob of sizzling napalm onto the ground. "If you cannot trust me now, then who will you trust? We are running out of time. Someone or something is still very close, waiting to attack again."

"You are right, my Queen. I panicked. Forgive me; I'm such a fool. Let's go."

"They probably have us exactly where they want us, stalled out, hovering in midair, trying to figure what to do. Confusion and hesitation will get us all killed, then the enemy would have something to cheer about. They would have my heart and the rein of all the tomb sleeper's valley.

We need to do something now. And I do mean right now, no more stalling. It is imperative."

General Slaughter looked toward the western horizon. "I *am* doing something now, my Queen. I have the Queen's Elite 100 coming to us right at this moment," Slaughter said, pointing a long harp red talon toward the horizon. "There they are, The 100."

"Outstanding," said Kula, spitting a napalm fire ball into the air. "General Slaughter, you will meet up with your hundred and find out what's going on here. You have my authorization to kill anything and everything that does not belong to us. Take prisoners only if you think they will benefit us. No questions asked. Do you understand?"

"Damn right I do," he said, beating his chest as if fired up for a brawl at an inn rather than a battle. "Long live Kula. Queen of the Dragoons! We shall kill everyone and everything!"

"I will stay here with Rasp," Kula added in a calm tone, as though she had not just observed Rasp's peculiar display. "We shall protect the high council and all who attended today until you get back."

"Yes, my Queen. I will be in the circular 10-2 fight pattern. Fifty of my dragoons will be flying the two o'clock pattern and fifty will be flying the ten o'clock pattern. Nothing will escape us, and you still have the six fighter dragoons positioned on the ground."

Kula and Cremator were pushed downward by the downdraft made by Slaughter's immense and powerful wings lifting him into battle position.

Kula looked to the western horizon again.

"I do believe there's some kind of an attack going on through the air though I can't make out the enemy force from here." She was spellbound, squinting toward the sky and watching the circular 10-2 fighting pattern perfected by Slaughter and his 100-fighter dragoon unit. "They are a well-groomed fighting machine. I'm so glad the 100 are on my side."

Rasp pushed against the side of her leg. "Kula, my Queen. Look at your fighter dragoons guarding Graper's body. They are stuck to the ground just like the wishbone team. They're flapping their wings as hard as they can, and still, they can't get off the ground. What's wrong with them that they cannot get airborne? They look like newly fledged chicks, trying to launch themselves for the first time."

Kula looked down at the area making up the ceremony grounds, then checked the six positions. Two dragoons in the middle, and one dragoon at each corner of the ceremony pad.

Who or what can hold down six fighter dragoons in six locations at the same time?

"Strong fricking magic. Rasp, we need to get the high council members and all spectators out of here. *Everyone* if we can. Go now, and get them to huddle close in a group, no stragglers. Have them lock their arms together really tight as though their lives depend on it, because they do. I will swoop down to pick everyone up at one time. We have only this one chance to get it right."

Kula executed one full circle of the spectators, strategizing the best pickup position.

She floated in position long enough to see Rasp hovering on the virgin spirit dragoon ten feet up, frantically waving his arms as if directing some invisible orchestra.

"That's my cue." Arching her chest outwards, Kula accumulated a mouth of napalm, keeping her wings vertical. Maneuvering her body into a nosedive position, her wings tight against her body, she dropped from the sky like a bowling ball.

Within fifty feet of smashing into the ground, she spread her wings out as far as they would go, slowing down long enough for her to spread a circle of fiery, red-hot napalm around the high council members and all the arm-locked individuals. "That should keep the intruders out long enough for me to gather everyone and take them to safety," Kula said, holding her position twenty feet above the ground.

Rasp had done a great job gathering everyone within the circle and had them wrapped up in one huge ball. Kula delicately inserted her talons into the center of the ball of flesh and blood and with two flaps of her wings, she skyrocketed to a safe altitude, leaving the circle of fire behind her.

Rasp tucked in behind Kula, using her draft to help

him keep up.

Kula slowed and hovered at fifteen hundred feet, waiting for Rasp to catch up to her.

"Kula, my Queen, could you set them down on Tower 4? That spotting tower has the biggest landing platform so it will hold everyone. They can travel the tower tunnels back to Grimmbell."

Kula nodded. "Can you keep up?"

"Graper and I can keep up," he said, patting the side of the virgin spirit. "I will make sure everyone gets back to Grimmbell and their homes."

"Let's get going." Kula leaned to the right, dropping five hundred feet to gain impressive speed then pulling back up to fifteen hundred feet, heading for tower four. Drifting over the top of Spotting Tower 4, she gently sat her cargo on the landing pad. Without even taking a breath, she was already gaining altitude, navigating a sharp left-hand turn and setting her sights on the rescue of her fighter dragoons.

"I don't know if they'll still be alive or not. I do know one thing for sure. The heart of Graper offers a high possibility of being what they were after, whoever the hell they are. Who would dare attack me, Kula Queen of the Dragons in the middle of the releasing ceremony?"

Kula stared at the western horizon. This time, the picture looked very different. She could see tiny winged dots circling, diving, bobbing up and down, twisting, turning, rolling in every direction possible. Then there were the winged black dots tangling with another winged dot.

Seconds later, one of the tangled flying dots went plummeting to the ground.

How convenient, thought Kula. *A battle of diversion. Someone planned that sky attack, pulling Slaughter and myself away from the ceremonies, then attacked* the fighter dragoons on the ground with a clock of dark cloud cover. *Graper's heart. I left it there. Shit.*

What the hell was I thinking? I'll lose my crown now, for sure.

How has everything ended up in such a mess, when only a few days ago, I was going to visit the King of Souls to receive the Wreath of Darkan? What a turn-about, to receive the wreath one minute, and now I'm meeting the possibility of losing my crown the next minute. I can't let that happen.

Kula steered supersonic, returning to the scene of the crime. "Have to check things out first. I can't land into that dragoon trap," she said, swooping back and forth over the ring of fire.

The fog of dirt and dust concealing the fate of the six ground dragoons an hour ago had reared its ugly head. *How can this be?* Kula shook her head in disgust. Five of the six dragoons lay motionless at their assigned posts, their wings torn off, except for one set still flailing in the wind like a butterfly trapped in the claw of tree sap. *What happened to my dragoons?*

Kula snarled, a huge blast of propelled napalm covering the ground below.

I'm going to kill whoever is responsible for this. This is an act of war.

She thrust up two hundred feet to get a better view. "I must be missing something."

Kula studied the ground below. "There he is. I see movement. My sixth dragoon, and he has something pinned to the ground not far from Graper's body. That must be our attacker." Kula circled the ring of fire one more time, landing quietly behind the lone moving fighter dragoon, her wings held high for immediate liftoff if necessary. She recognized the fighter dragoon right away. "It's Banner."

There were very few dragoons marked like Banner. A very distinct strip of light brown beige two feet wide darted from his tail section to his front foot. Not unseen, but rare in the male dragoons.

She froze, eyes wide, struggling to understand.

"Banner, what *are* you doing? This is Queen Kula." There was no answer, so Kula stepped closer. "Banner, I command you to answer me." Still no answer.

Kula stretched her neck out to get a view around the left side of his body. She couldn't believe it. Banner's head was gone or at least had been buried in the dirt and sand. An erratic, tugging motion pulling at the neckline where it disappeared underneath the dirt. "Did something pull his head into the ground, or was he trying to rip an intruder out of it? This is pissing me off."

Kula charged up to Banner's neck area, rubbing against his body as she approached. Her jaw clenched. She rammed her right shoulder against his.

"Banner, what's going on here? Can you hear me? Pull your head out!"

No answer from Banner. His neckline kept jerking, slowly being pulled inch by inch into the dirt. "What the hell is going on here? That odor. I know those scents." Kula inhaled deeply, held it and released. "Roko, Arune's snake, and the black spirit horse. Well, I'll be damned."

She started digging, ripping at the ground, tearing free huge clumps of dirt to land two hundred feet behind her tail. She continued digging, knowing she was getting close to Banner's head when she uncovered a head horn. "This is not good."

She kept digging.

Suddenly, the tension of his neck went limp, the weight of Banner's body slumping backwards, ejecting his severed neckline into the air, a wave of blood painting Kula's face.

His chest cavity fell limp, lifeless on top of his front feet.

She stood over Banner's decapitated body. "Two fighter dragoons in one day. This can't be happening." But it was indeed occurring, and his bright blood dripped off her face onto the ground.

Ripping at the earth with her powerful talons, and with a horrendous roar, she shouted, "Come on, attack me! Come and get me, you cowards! Afraid to face the Queen of all the dragoons, are you? Queen of the Darkan Territory… I'm going to bleed you all dry."

Next, she climbed on top of Banner's back, ripping his hide with her razor-sharp talons. She could hear the blood rushing through her head.

Nostrils flared and boiling with fury, she ground her teeth and clenched her jaw so tight it hurt, and she spat the words through gritted teeth. "Come one, come all. I will find the creature and their magic that did this," she said, spitting fireballs into the air. "And when I do, I'm going to roast you alive. Eat you. Use your bones as toothpicks. I will go hunting for every being that you've come in contact with. Grind all their bodies together at one time to use as sprinkles for my dessert."

Kula stared at the remains of Graper. Hopping down from the back of Banner, Kula walked up to Graper's body, her overwhelming anger almost blinding her to the unexpected display of weirdness.

She detected right away that an emergency heart shield alarm had been activated.

Unbeknown to her and everyone at the ceremonies, two individuals had apparently burrowed underneath Graper's body in an attempt to steal his heart.

"Somehow, they managed to break the spirit barrier initially set up to protect the remains of the fallen dragoon."

Kula walked around Graper's body, studying the site thoroughly and thinking the events through. The thieves got close enough to cut around the body armor and remove the armor plate covering the heart, and when they started to cut the skin, the electromagnetic heart shield was activated.

The thieves were dragged out of their leather sandals with their flesh melted onto the ground, their bones fused to one of Graper's rib bones that had been exposed for the breaking of the wishbone pull; it had killed them ever so very slowly. "Serves them right."

Kula studied the bone statue of the dynamic duo, tilting her head back and forth, trying to picture how this had happened. She could see a partial eyeball, three teeth and some rib bones welded higher up on the rib bone of Graper.

"These could be bones from an ore troll or possibly a skull skinner or both. The wedges of flesh resemble the features to match an ore troll *and* a skull skinner."

Following Graper's rib bone down, a foot appeared, two toes, melted together with a partial hand.

"Look at that. A skinning knife clutched in the hand bone. That's not a foot with toes; it's a foot with fingers."

Kula tapped the bone statue with her talon. "Hard as a rock. This is real. Is it a tongue? Okay, that's enough. It appears the dynamic duo got what they came for, to live for eternity as a bone statue."

"That was actually a pretty good duo to team up with. The two little buggers were sneaky and clever to do it this way. The ore troll is skilled in tunneling and the skull skinner is a multipurpose skull harvester skilled in cutlery. He would have been the one to do the precise cutting to retrieve the heart. Interesting. I wonder what they were promised if they retrieved Graper's heart, and who put this twosome together? Sounds like an inside job to me. Maybe Arune teamed up with Roko's magic?"

***

Kula looked to the western horizon in hopes of a sighting of Slaughter, but the afternoon sun blocked the view in that direction. Looking down to regain her focus, she suddenly noticed shadows outlining the ground on which she stood. She jumped next to the rib cage of Graper. Positioning herself like a cannon and tilting her head toward the sky, she inhaled deeply, ready to send a whiplash of volcanic sticky napalm onto any intruder who dared try to pull her head underground.

She studied the shadows on the ground, keeping her head low. Backing up against Graper for cover, she studied the sky, realizing that the shadows were from a group of fighter dragoons consisting of The Elite 100, circling in the two familiar fighter dragoons' fight patterns, the 10-2 circular drift.

Kula relaxed her shoulders, spitting the fireball to the ground.

A wave of cold air pierced her backbone as she caught a microscopic glimpse of Slaughter's tail flashing by her head. "Wow, his speed and unity of maneuvering power never cease to amaze me. He's one mean-ass killing machine."

Slaughter maneuvered the sharp left-hand turn with ease as he landed in front of Kula, simultaneously roaring orders to the dragoons in the sky.

"Kula, my Queen. What happened here?" Slaughter asked.

Kula's head nodded to the dynamic dual statue and tapped on the bone one. "We had some thieves who thought they could steal pieces of Graper. But as you can see, they decided to stick around."

173

"Were you injured?"

"No."

"Did anyone try to attack you?" Slaughter inquired next.

"No. Not yet anyway."

"Why do you say that?"

"Because obviously, the attackers could still be here. From what I've seen, I suspect they came from underneath the ground." She pointed toward Banner. "Look at our warrior there. He has no head. His feet were pulled down, encased in the ground. So, they could take advantage of him. Why would they take only his head, when all of his body parts would be extremely valuable?"

"I don't think the killers had time to take any other body parts at that time. Like we'd suspected, they were only after the heart of Graper."

"Yes, I suppose you are right," said Kula. "Then why did they take the wings from the other fighter dragoons and nothing else?"

"I have a pretty good idea why we were attacked," said Slaughter.

"Yes," said Kula. "Because of Graper's enlarged heart. The high council, spirits, souls, me, you and let's not forget the King of the Soul Tree was in route. A lot of important cogs of what makes Grimmbell and the Darkan Territory function were here today. And maybe in the future, not a good idea. Look at this mess."

"Gutter dragons," said Slaughter.

"Gutter dragons?" asked Kula. "Do you think they're smart enough to make an attack like this?"

"Not by themselves. It wasn't really an attack. I think it was more of a diversion."

"That's exactly what I thought. They wanted to pull you away from the ceremony." Slaughter looked up into the sky and roared.

Kula's eyes followed, watching one of the fighter dragoons drop out of formation, nose-diving at a tremendous speed, stopping just short of the ground and touching down gently.

He bowed in front of Kula and Slaughter.

Slaughter nodded. "Approach, Grandar. Show our

queen what you have."

The dragoon warrior stepped in front of Kula and bowed his head reminding Kula of the superiority of these battle-driven dragoon warriors. Grandar proudly inflated his chest to show off his badge of the past one thousand plus kills.

These warriors had body armor reinforcement interlaced with extinct giant battle rock tortoise shells, infused with just a twist of blood brick dust, producing an armor that couldn't be penetrated by fire, arrow, axe, sword or hammer spells of any kind. Their retractable wings were used for a shield movable to any position due to a small rail track running the full length of their backs.

Interchangeable wings and positioning enhanced battle maneuverability and speed for both high and low altitude, but these were not available on all models.

The dark green giant moved with grace.

Each step was precise, quick and agile movements controlling the flow of his body with a tight and directive path of energy even though this big boy, weighing in at sixteen tons.

"Kula, my Queen. I am honored to stand before you today," Grandar said, setting a large canvas bag at her feet. "My Queen, the enemy in the sky has been defeated. I have proof of their attack. These items are my trophies I took in battle." Grandar stepped lightly on the canvas bag and bowed his head. "I present these skulls to you, my Queen, for the honor to be recognized under the direction of General Slaughter, the 100 Warrior."

Touching his forehead with her hand, Kula said, "Grandar, raise your head high. I see these wonderful gifts that you've brought me today. I am flattered and acknowledge the fact that you have fought in the skies today and I honor you for the victory."

"I have more, my Queen."

"More gifts? Please show me."

Grandar reached under his wing and presented a silver crown, handing it to Kula.

"What do you have here?" Kula studied the crown. "It has inscriptions on the inside of the band." Tipping her head at an angle, she read the inscriptions. "I can't make out all the words, but I am pretty sure these inscriptions are written in chalk talk."

"Chalk talk?" said Slaughter. "That makes sense."

"Yes, it does," said Kula. "When you told me they were gutter dragons, I knew they had to be controlled by someone else. That species is troubled, not by their own making but unfortunately, they just turned out that way and are often used to do someone else's dirty work. Most of their missions are ones of suicide, and whether the task is completed or not, the crown will fall from the operator's head. In this case, I'm assuming one of the gutter dragons had been wearing the crown?"

"My Queen, the gutter dragon wearing this crown was killed by me. I wounded him in the air and forced him into the ground and only then did the crown actually appear."

"Was he alive after he hit the ground?" she asked.

"Yes, but only for a short time."

"Did you interrogate him?"

"I asked him about the attack and who'd initiated it," responded Slaughter.

"What did he say?"

"He told me that he didn't want to go to battle against Kula and her dragoons, but he'd been promised a gift that would enhance his life and the life of many others of his clan."

"Did he describe this gift to you?"

"He told me of an ancient magic. A warrior's tonic that could be produced with this silver crown."

Rolling it in her hand, Kula studied the crown.

"I have heard of such a crown, but until this day, I have never seen it before. Controlling so many dragons or any large number of moving bodies at one time would take a gigantic amount of control; mental control." Kula held up the crown. "This is the Mental Seven Crown, or as some of the elders call it, the Suffering Crown," she said, kicking the canvas bag.

"These gutter dragons were sent to us to create a diversion, controlled by someone else. The last person to wear the crown would have to be the seventh to wear it."

"To control the crown, all tasks not completed by all

the kings before the seventh individual, would have to be completed by the seventh king before he or she could control the power of the crown."

"I suspect those tasks of years gone by were not fulfilled. Somehow, this leader of the gutter dragons, even if only for a short time, figured out a way to enlist the power of the crown to facilitate this attack. The Suffering Crown is the perfect match with the gutter dragons. The Suffering Crown was created by an unknown entity. It was a conglomeration of several kings wanting greatness by way of evil. Each king embarked on a quest to dominate their domain but failed, then suffered mentally for their loss. So, the last king standing somehow managed to combine all the mental capacity of the other six kings and merged all of their suffering into this crown, the Suffering Crown. The mental crown is cursed. It has great power if you can understand the chalk talk. It's a reusable type of power that has virtually no ownership and cannot be traced back to the one who initiated the course of action. It's almost the perfect weapon. Activate it, throw it into a ring of fire and walk away. Mission accomplished." Worry lined her forehead. "Something here doesn't make sense though."

"Kula, my Queen, I need to send Grandar to assess this battle and provide me with a full report. Are we finished with him for now?"

"Yes, General, I do believe we are finished, although I do have one more thing for Grandar."

"Of course, my Queen."

Kula exhaled a slow-rolling fire on her right-hand talons, causing them to glow red hot. "Grandar, please step forward."

Grandar stepped forward, bowing his head.

"Grandar, raise your head in recognition. I have counted the tokens you have brought to me. There are one hundred sixty-one. Today is a great day for the 100. Today, I'm going to give you your first badge of the Queen's Seal."

"Thank you, my Queen. I would die for you."

"Thank you Grandar. I know you would." Kula approached Grandar, carving her Queen's Seal one plate below the symbol of The Elite 100 on his chest. She cut her wrist and smeared blood into the seal, the blood drying quickly with a bright orange glow.

"Thank you, my Queen. May I go now? I have battle duties to fulfill?" he said, looking at Slaughter with anticipation.

"I want a full report." His head dipped a quick nod.

Grandar leaped forty feet into the air and within two wing flaps had surpassed five hundred feet altitude, bolting toward the western horizon.

Kula's forehead creased with concern, focusing on a distinctive spot behind Graper's body. "Did you see that?"

"See what, my Queen?" Slaughter asked, looking in the general direction.

"Do you feel the air being pulled away from us?"

Slaughter kicked dirt into the air. The drift of dirt particles didn't fall to the ground but floated away from them, toward the direction Kula had been looking.

"You are correct, my Queen. The dirt is being pulled away from us."

"If I'm not mistaken, I believe there could be some type of a portal breach right over there," she said, pointing with her long sharp talon. "Follow the dirt."

"Wait a minute, my Queen," he answered, blocking her path with his shoulder. "Please let me get a look at this portal first. It could be a trap."

Kula nodded her head in agreement, and Slaughter approached the suspected portal area.

"You were right, my Queen, there is something strange here. I can see the dirt being sucked into a circle of rippling air waves." Picking up a large sand rock, he threw it in the general direction of the heaving air waves. The rock hit its mark with a loud thud and fell to the ground.

Kula arched her eyebrows with an intense stare toward Slaughter. "Arune transformed his powers with the black spirit riders, do you think?"

Slaughter glared back. "You really think so? What about the Suffering Crown? Does Arune have its power in that too?"

"I believe so, and that's not all. I can smell a strong scent of Roko and the black spirit horse. I smelt the same scents at the ceremony field with the dead fighter dragoon

Banner. I have a bad feeling about this. I need to talk to Blackjack."

Chapter 21: Roko's New Power

Blackjack held his paws, palms out, in front of him, feeling the energy waves still coming off the closed portal through which Roko escaped. "I can still smell his horse. I can feel his energy and its rigidity on my stomach. Weird." Then, an echoing scream ripped through him, causing his sphincter muscles to squeeze tight.

"Did you hear that scream? Roko jumped another dimension. I'm going after him."

"What scream?" said Jinnamon. "I didn't hear a scream, and you don't even know where Roko is at, do you?"

"Not at the moment, but I will figure it out."

Blackjack stomped his way toward the top of a nearby hill. "I have this gut feeling he's not too far away. He wants to stay close, to try to figure out my next move."

"That makes sense," said Jinnamon.

"Jinnamon, you need to make contact with Kula, let her know I am going after Roko the Dark. And get ahold of Rasp."

"Why Rasp?"

"Because he's the only one who can make the smoke. We have to get our friend out of your belly."

Blackjack heard another scream. This time, he felt the scream biting into his back, trying to rip his spine out, followed by a huge burst of brilliant green light with a surge of dust billowing above his head. He bent over, clawing at the point of pain, but with no relief. "It looks like a green rain cloud."

Pushing forward to the crest of the hill, Blackjack saw a black spirit rider mounted on his horse in the bottom of a valley, nestled within a bundle of trees.

"Is that Roko? Maybe the new version of Roko the Dark?"

Another scream with a blast of green dust blossomed in the sky. "I can taste that scream, and it doesn't taste good."

Looking closely, another black spirit horse rider emerged from behind the same cluster of trees, stopping in front of Roko.

"I need to get a look at these creatures, find out what the hell makes them tick." Blackjack enhanced his internal vision ability. Lying on his stomach, he zoomed in on the face of the dark rider. "Damn it." Squinting and blinking, he couldn't get a clear picture of the face.

"Brazel. What's the problem? I can't get a visual on these shit birds."

"You're not going to either."

"Why not?"

"I don't know for sure, but my enhanced sensory antenna tells me they have some type of camouflaged energy blocking your view up close."

"Yet I can see a fly on their horse's butt. How does that work?"

"They don't care if you see a horse's butt," said Brazel. "And maybe I have an answer, or at least a theory. Would you have time to hear it?"

"I don't think they know I'm here. Tell me your thoughts, or are they still *our* thoughts? Just kidding. I'm listening."

"Okay, here goes," said Brazel. "In my personal research with black spirit horse riders, each time they leap from one VIM Zone to another, it takes a mixture of some type of electrically charged dust."

"VIM?" said Blackjack.

"Yes, VIM is my own creation of words. It stands for Volatile Interdimensional Movement."

"I think I'm still following you. You mean, like right after Roko was taken by the horse and then disappeared at the creek crossing?"

"Yes, that's a good example."

"What about this electrically charged dust?"

"It's not like dust on the back of a plow horse. This dust is electrified and entirely different, way more advanced than any other type of electrical particles I have seen before."

"How many types of dust *have* you seen?" asked

Blackjack.

"I have seen several varieties of electrical dust, but I must emphasize that this green dust is not really dust but particles, ones that can vibrate incredibly fast, so they cannot be seen by our eyes. This green dust is something I haven't seen before."

"Could this electrical charged dust be the same as the screamer's dust?" Blackjack asked. "The green-colored stuff at the creek crossing."

"That would be a safe bet," said Brazel.

"Why is it we hear that terrible scream?"

"Sadly," said Brazel, "I believe that the illegally taken spirit is activated, burned to release the stored energy in the spirit to cause some type of ripping effect in a particular space to open it."

"A portal as such. When the spirit dust is triggered, the owner of that spirit actually feels the pain and screams out through the burned dust particles."

"Is the scream the actual voice of the creature it was stolen from?"

"That I don't know yet, but I think it is," said Brazel. "The only way to find out would be to do actual testing, but I don't think we want to do that, right?"

"No, we don't," said Blackjack. "Maybe in a battle scenario, but not right now. Anyway, what are they doing with this dust?"

"My thought here is the riders use actual raw screamer's spirit dust, a sophisticated filter-finished product."

"How do they filter a spirit?"

"Not sure on that procedure either," said Brazel. "Maybe you can find that out at some point. So, back to the powder."

"Of course, my ever so talented third voice. Please continue."

"Thank you," said Brazel. "This powder appears to be used for opening gateways and portals for the spirit horse riders."

"The ripping effects? The scream, right?"

"In my opinion, yes. When the riders are threatened and need to escape, they activate the screamer's dust, the portal opens, and they disappear. Or maybe that's where they hide out all the time, in an internal space and dimension. This could be how they travel unseen when they want."

"What about the scream; that would give away their location, right?"

"Not entirely," said Brazel.

"Can you explain?"

"You are one of the very few individuals who can actually hear the scream."

"Why do I hear it though?" asked Blackjack.

"That's an easy one. Because you are not any ordinary ninety-pound, four-colored, titanium-clawed, super-powered jackrabbit."

"Don't forget about my *unbreakable* titanium claws."

"I haven't forgotten it," said Brazel. "You really think I'd forget that? And don't you forget about your third soul, that's me, that grows in you every day."

Blackjack nodded. "My third power or article; we haven't completed any type of mind taps into that section of my being. How come?"

"That will come with time, my friend."

"How much time?"

"It will appear to you when you are ready for it and when you can handle that type of power."

"Are you saying my powers are unknown even to me until I use them, or when I need to develop them?"

"Yes, that's what I'm saying. If you were to gather all my information at one time, you would develop bleeding in the brain and possibly die."

"Really?"

"It's a possibility," said Brazel, "but I won't let that happen. Now give me an update on what's happening down the hill with your friend Roko."

"Okay, so, what is going on down there… Is that rider a superior, or what?"

"I do believe so," said Brazel. "That rider is higher up on the black spirit power chain."

"How can you tell? They all look the same?"

"Much higher," said Brazel. "It wears silver gloves

and carries an impressive sword. Don't you see that rather long sword the rider is carrying?"

"Oh yeah, you're right, I missed it. The sheath hangs to the horse's knee. Damn, that sword's long." Suddenly, a heavy scream followed by a loud *boom* forced Blackjack to hit the ground on his belly.

"Holy green shit balls of smoke and dirt. Look at the size of that dust cloud."

"Was that another scream?" Brazel enquired.

"Yes," said Blackjack, maneuvering to a sitting position. "Damn, that one hurt my ears. I'm not sure about that scream. It wasn't a typical scream I've ever heard before, but it definitely informs the world that something is taking place. Hold on! Something else is coming out of the dust cloud."

"Is Roko making the leap into a portal?" asked Brazel.

"No, an object is emerging from the dust cloud. Can't see if it's coming out of a portal or not." "What is it? I want details," said Brazel. "I want to record it on mental video."

"Whatever it is, it's noisy. Obviously, they're not worried about being heard." "Like I said before, maybe you're one of the very few who can hear them."

"Oh yeah, that's right," said Blackjack, stretching his head higher to see. "Well, I'll be damned."

"What is it?"

"It's a chariot."

"A chariot? Are you kidding me?" Brazel said.

"Nope, not kidding this time. It's a chariot, with four big white horses pulling it."

"White horses. Really?"

"White horses, with some type of creature driving the chariot. Looks like a zebra type of creature."

"A zebra creature. Give me more details."

"I can't see a face but do know it's wearing a long robe with a hood. Wait a minute, I'm able to zoom in a little bit closer. Oh, the creature is wearing a black and white robe with two red lines circling the bottom few inches."

"What else can you see?" asked Brazel. "Tell me

more."

"I'm still partially blocked. I can't zoom close enough so there's only one thing to do."

"Don't do anything stupid here," said Brazel.

"I'm going down for a closer look. I want to find out what's in that big-ass brass pot on the back of the chariot."

"You didn't say anything about any big-ass pot."

"I'm guessing that's what it is but I'm not sure, so that's why I need a closer look."

Blackjack sank low to the ground, carefully choosing each step. Approaching a rocky area, he found an opening at the base of one of the numerous large rocks.

He poked his head inside until his shoulders touched either side of the hole. "Could be a tunnel leading to a closer view. I think I'll check it out."

Dropping inside the hole, it quickly curved to the right, forming a space where he could stand. His eyes automatically switched to infrared mode.

Along the way, he had to widen two choke points within the passageway. *No problem*. Digging through a tight spot was easy when you had titanium claws.

"One hundred seventy-five. One hundred seventy-six. Ahh," he said, spotting a faint light ahead of him. "That could be a way out and put me one hundred eighty yards closer to the spirit riders."

Edging at the end of the tunnel, he could hear a faint dialogue of voices.

Slowing poking his head out of the tunnel little by little, he exited, crawling to the base of a boulder directly in front of him. Pushing his chest tight against the rock, inhaling deeply and exhaling quietly, he gripped the granite boulder with his titanium claws.

His ears lying flat, he pulled his head above the top of the rock, just enough to see two black figures crawling out the top of the big-ass brass pot, the wind blowing a thick black wave of dust off their backs.

Dropping to the ground, the medium dog-sized creatures scurried to sit one on each side of the silver gloved spirit rider. Roko maneuvered his horse to stand alongside silver gloves.

The rider immediately handed him his long sword.

Roko rode his horse next to the zebra man standing next to the brass pot. The zebra-cloaked figure took the sword from Roko, thrusting it into the big-ass pot. Taking a step back, he pulled his hood off to reveal an oversized skull burning a bright green flame, its green fire dancing in height, the massive flames extending three feet above the king-size-skulled creature.

The fiery green skull opened its bony jaw and ripped out a scream that carried away into the nearby trees, scorching the leaves and burning the nearby blue sage brush to ash.

Blackjack swallowed hard. "D-Did you see that? What the hell is that entity used for?"

"I don't know," said Brazel. "But it doesn't look friendly."

Laughing and then kissing the top of the tin vessel, the fire head continued its weird ritual with a flurry of head banging, *boom, boom, boom* on the side of the brass pot, ripping the sword out of the big- ass pot, holding the steel high in the air.

The long blade jumped alive with green clusters of flames expelling balls of fire into the air and dripping liquid green fire onto the ground. The burning skull of a man grabbed Roko by the arm.

"Give this to Silver Glove. Soon Roko, you will become Roko the Darkan Rider, a black horse spirit rider till the end of fricking time."

Roko clutched the sword with his hand, his arm becoming engulfed in green fire. "Holy shit balls, Roko is on fire. How do they do that?"

"I don't know," said Brazel. "But it's pretty damn amazing."

The green skull of fire pointed to the silver-gloved rider. "Give the blade to him. Quickly."

Roko handed the sword to the silver-gloved rider who took it from Roko. Drawing the blade of fire backwards past his shoulder at waist level, he thrust it forward into Roko's chest.

"Damn," said Blackjack. "They stabbed him."

"No way. Is that's part of this ritual?"

Not letting go of the sword, Silver Glove plunged his

free hand into a leather bag attached at his waistline. Clutching a fistful of dust, he flung it over Roko and his horse.

Whoof. Roko and horse burst into flames from top to bottom.

"What the hell?" said Blackjack. "Roko and horse ignited into flames."

"This is some good stuff," said Brazel.

"How can you say this is good stuff?"

"Because, my hairy little friend, I don't think it has been witnessed by any outsider before.

Understand?"

"Of course," said Blackjack. "I was just making sure you were paying attention."

Roko spurred on the horse with everything he had. They bolted past the silver-gloved rider engulfed in an inferno of flames, the sword bouncing inside his chest cavity with every stride of the horse.

Roko, at full ballistic bullet speed gallop, pulled the sword out of his chest and with both hands, drove the blade deep into the mane of his power connected horse.

The powerful horse bolted to the right, sending Roko summersaulting on the ground over and over, but he quickly gained his posture as he watched his lone stallion split into eight flaming horses, sprinting at great speeds for one hundred yards side by side.

Running in a circular pattern, four of the steeds swung to the left and four to the right, not showing any signs of slowing down. Each group of four was on course for a head-to-head collision but right at the moment of impact, a large flash occurred, and they all disappeared.

Another large flash and all eight horses re-appeared running side by side, blending into each other until only one big black spirit horse stopped in front of him, pawing at the ground.

Roko approached the horse. Hugging the animal, the flames went out and he mounted the stallion and raced back to the silver-gloved rider handing him the sword.

"Welcome, Roko the Darkan. Welcome to the brotherhood of the black horse spirit riders."

"Blackjack, what's going on? For some reason, I

can't see what you see at the moment, but I sense your heart struggling to pump blood as if it were thick as mud. Blackjack, can you hear me?"

"Brazel. Can one kill a black horse spirit rider?"

"If you're talking about the one with the long sword, I don't know, and if you *were* lucky enough to kill him, then you have the chariot zebra-man to deal with. I don't know his full function or power."

"I can see Roko."

"You already said that."

"No, I mean I see Roko in his natural form. As a three-foot-high earther being dragged by the new spirit rider Roko."

"What are they doing with him?" asked Brazel.

"Oh, this doesn't look good. Damn."

"What doesn't look good?"

"The new Darkan Roko is dragging the old Roko by a rope tied around his neck toward the zebra man."

"That's a haunting thought," said Brazel.

"Holly shit balls, the rider's drawn his long sword, and Roko is holding something in his hands. They're all huddled around him."

"Is it his master recipe book, the book he uses to talk to spirits and souls?"

"I'm not sure," said Blackjack. "Can't see inside the circle."

"Can you hear what they are talking about?"

"I can hear some of the words."

"What words are you picking up on?"

"Activate the dust. The scream. More effective. Powerful. Screamer's dust. Stealing something.

Grimmbell. Blood, brick, skull. Ripper's dust."

"Ripper's dust?" said Brazel. "Sounds to me like the gruesome threesome are working on a new improved screamer's dust mixture. And what better person to have in making advanced improvements on your supply of screamer's dust? A twist of Roko the Earther with his brilliant means to talk to advanced levels of spirits and control, or in this case, to steal the energy of spirits and souls along with the unharnessed control of a black spirit horse. Wow, it doesn't take a genius to figure out they have been hunting for someone like Roko.”

“Wait a minute. Oh shit,” said Blackjack.

“Oh shit, what?” said Brazel.

“The rider’s raised his sword above his head.”

“Blackjack, I sense extreme danger. What’s happening?”

“I’m not sure. I can see… well, I’m not sure.”

“Spit it out.”

“I see Earther Roko. He appears in a transparent outline, blue and white. They’ve taken him behind the chariot. The zebra guy hopped up on the back of the chariot next to the big-ass pot and lifted the lid. The sword came down…”

“The sword came down?”

“I can’t see what happened. They are hiding behind the chariot to do their nasty deed. Brazel, do something; I can’t just sit here with my finger up my butt.”

“What exactly do you want me to do?”

“We have to find out… Oh shit, I can’t believe it. They cut off a head. They cut off a head!”

“Whose head? Whose head?” Brazel asked.

“The bald-headed skeleton dude is holding a head. Now he’s cradling it like a baby. Talking to it, licking it. Can you believe that? Licking it. He put the head in the pot. It’s in the pot! Oh, my Queen Kula, where are you when I need you the most? The sons of bitches. Brazel, I’m going in. I need to find out whose head they put in that powder pot. I’m going to kill them all.”

“You can’t kill them all,” said Brazel. “They are too strong together.”

Blackjack stood up. Pulling his sword, and with a twist of the wrist, the titanium claws were fully extended. He jumped down from the boulder when a huge explosion ripped through the air, sending a thirty-foot wall of green dust hurling toward Blackjack, knocking him flat on his back, pinning him to the ground and covering him with a thick coat of dust.

“Brazel. I can’t breathe. I can’t move. Help me.”

Chapter 22: Tamerrick Attack

"Blackjack. Calm down. Just breathe."

"Brazel. What happened?"

"A huge wave of green dust just kicked your ass. You need to get up." Blackjack felt stiff and sore. "Damn. This stuff is like hardened wax."

"You got the wind knocked right out of you."

Blackjack kicked his feet, breaking free. "What the hell?" He broke free to sit up and pull big chunks of green wax of his chest. "It smells of death. What is this stuff?"

"I don't know for sure, but I do know you need to get your ass moving because Roko the 'new and improved' is charging up the hill."

"No way. He knows we are here? Is it just him?"

"Blackjack, we need to move."

Blackjack jumped to his feet, pulling out his sword.

"Don't worry about that," said Brazel "Let's hide! Fight another day."

Blackjack ran for the tree line. Within jumping distance, he activated his titanium claws, sinking them deep into the trunk of the tree. He powered up the tree trunk twenty-five feet, looking down as the new Rodark-Roko frantically stomped the ground below him on his mighty black stallion spirit horse.

Rodark raced back and forth under the trees. "Blackjack. Where art thou? Why won't you come out and play? Blackjack, I know you're watching me from somewhere. Take a look at this."

Rodark kicked his feet out of the stirrups, jumping on top of the saddle and quickly performing a handstand. "Blackjack. What do you think? Wait a minute, I can do this with one hand."

He posed upside down with one hand on the saddle horn. "Come on, I know you want your own black spirit horse. I can make that happen. We can work in the spirit world together."

Shaking his head in disbelief, Blackjack watched the new creation of Roko perform his acrobatic moves. "I don't know what the hell he's doing. One minute he wants to kill me, the next, he's performing like a clown. He's lost his marbles."

Rodark lowered himself back into the saddle. Holding his arms out wide with a big smile, he quickly popped on top of the saddle, standing with a hand on each hip bone.

"He's definitely trying to lure me in. But he must know I'm not that gullible."

Blackjack continued to watch Rodark balance himself on the saddle, cringing as he witnessed Rodark pull his pants down, grabbing his crotch.

"Now what the hell is he going to do? Not sure I want to watch this." Rodark started swaying side to side.

"Oh, shit. I don't believe it. He's stood pissing off the horse, trying to write his name in the dirt?"

Rodark finished his duty and pulled his pants up. "Blackjack, I feel so free, where anything is possible. It's a great feeling." He quickly sat in the saddle, inserting his feet into the stirrups and grabbing the reins. "Well, I've marked my spot. This will always be my spot. But I have to go. I have this intense urge to kill for skulls."

Horse and rider were underway, heading north away from Blackjack. Rodark looked back over his shoulder. "I'm getting hungry, and I want to feed."

Blackjack heard a loud and terrifying scream, the black spirit rider vanishing into thin air.

"Blackjack, I think we have a big problem."

Blackjack sighed. "Brazel. Emphasis on big."

Rodark reappeared at the base of one of the many flat-topped buttes populating the valley floor.

Choosing the highest of the closest three, he rode his horse up the switchbacks to the top, studying his surroundings below, checking the wind direction for dust clouds.

If there were any, it could mean a caravan of travelers going to or from Grimmbell.

"Ah, there we go. Grimmbell in the distance. My old stomping grounds. I want to get into that for sure. It can't be more than ten or eleven miles. I shouldn't have any trouble getting past the spirit barrier. I'll use some of my magic just in case."

Inserting his hand into the dust bag attached to his waistline, his fingers found the bottom.

Pulling his hand out, he leaned over the bag to get a closer look. "Well. Double shit. I don't have enough dust to VIM." He licked the screamer's dust on his right hand, sucking his fingers like a baby sucking its thumb. "That tastes *gooood.* I need some more of that."

He looked at Grimmbell in the distance again. "Shit, there's no way I'm going to have enough dust to VIM through the spirit barrier. I'm going to have to find some food closer."

An hour passed before he caught sight of a dust cloud, feeling his internal energy getting low. He felt sluggish and slow. Rodark sat on his horse, looking over each shoulder, wondering where he was getting all these instructions rushing into his head.

"I'm not sure why I'm feeling this way but for some reason, I have this overpowering urge to acquire skulls. All kinds of skulls. Oh, and a dragon skull. That would make a super sweet treat. Any way I think about it, I need skulls. Boil them clean, grinding them into a fine dust. The grinding process has to be gentle, to acquire a fine smooth dust. Then baked and sprinkled with an essence of spirit."

Rodark continued watching the dust cloud two buttes over. "I think I'll swing by and see what's cooking."

When he rounded the second butte which put him directly in front of the mostly settled dust cloud, he couldn't believe what he was seeing. Sitting in a wagon pulled by two horses were six earthers, one shaman, three diggers and two inventory recorders.

It appeared they were having a food break, comparing notes about uncovering and recording an area where there had been a small conflict fought many years ago.

The skeletal remains of this battle were partially uncovered and scattered in an area behind the wagon but still embedded into the ground.

The shaman earther jerked to attention, quickly standing with a bone dagger in his right hand, and his left hand squeezed the shoulder of the nearest earther still sitting down.

Three diggers jumped out of the wagon and rushed to where they had sunk their shovel heads in the dig site. The two recording earthers quickly ran to the front of the wagon behind the driver's seat, digging deep into a wooden box.

The diggers returned with shovels and had strategically placed themselves one at the front and back of the wagon while the third one guarded the horses.

Standing up in his stirrups, Rodark lifted his chin to get a better view over the wagon and onto the burial ground. He presented a huge smile.

"From what I can see… there must be at least… twenty skulls waiting to be picked up, correct? But I'm in need of fresh skulls too, especially the six fresh skulls looking back at me at this very moment," he whispered.

"I am Tamerrick, member of the high council and personal shaman of Grimmbell."

Rodark focused on the shaman. "Hello Tamerrick. I'm glad to eat you. I mean, I'm glad to meet you."

Tamerrick stepped to the edge of the wagon closest to Rodark. "You don't have any authority or authorization to be here at this dig site."

"Funny you should say that. I have been told that before," said Rodark. "But I didn't listen to them either." He winked at the earther holding the horse's reins. "Yummy."

Tamerrick pointed his dagger at Rodark.

"Leave now, and I might forget to report you to the Soul King," he said.

"I find it hard to believe that a member of the high council, a shaman, would be willing to forget to report a free radical such as me. A supercharged, hungry, killing, black spirit horse rider. I think not. No matter what happens in the next fifteen minutes, someone will make a report."

Tamerrick's eyes narrowed as his eyebrows pulled together. "You look somewhat familiar. But that can't be. You're a black spirit rider."

Rodark bobbed his head up and down in enjoyment. "You might know a friend of mine. His name is Cremator."

"Cremator? I know Cremator. He is a member of the high council, but I don't think he would consider *you* a friend now." Tamerrick leaned out over the edge of the wagon, inhaling deeply. "You smell of fresh-burned free radical waste, and tar. You have been in a battle recently, mentally as well as physically. Who did you try to take?"

"You shamans," said Rodark, jerking at the reins. "Sometimes, you know too much too soon. It can get you killed; you know?"

Tamerrick leaned back to normal standing position in the wagon. "If you do anything stupid here today, you will have to answer to the Soul King as well as Kula, Queen of the Dragoons. Do you think you can handle that, mister? I smell of sticky black tar stuck in the crack of my ass."

"I didn't know shamans had a sense of humor."

"I don't," said Tamerrick.

"You are one of the smartest shamans I've ever crossed. How did you know of my masterplan, to have an encounter with the Soul King and Kula that you speak of, plus another one?"

"Another one, you say?" said Tamerrick.

"Yes, another one," said Rodark, grinning. "A very powerful one. He—or should I say they—go by the name of Bradicus Blackjack."

"Blackjack the royal messenger, the personal messenger to Queen Kula?"

Nodding, he said, "Yes, that would be the one. Or should I say that would be the two. Could be more than two. I don't know, but I'm going to find out."

Tamerrick tensed his shoulders, his pulse pounding in his throat. "Who are you?"

He grinned wide. "I used to be Roko. But now I'm Rodark, the greatest black horse spirit rider ever created. And my soul is hungry for virgin spirits."

"Roko, the master tobaccologist, highchair monarch in the Great Hall of Grimmbell? I can't believe that to be true."

"Oh, trust me, Shamey, it's true," Rodark said, spitting a big wad of tobacco juice on the ground. Tamerrick stared at Roko. "I can feel your energy. And it doesn't appear that you are lying to me."

"Well, there you go, Shamey, you're smarter than you look. Now it's time to eat."

Tamerrick retrieved a second bone dagger from his

left pocket. With one in each hand, he nodded at the two earthers sitting at the front of the wagon. They nodded back.

Rodark guided his black horse forward, pushing up against the side of the wagon. "I don't know what you're up to, but do you really think you can defeat me?"

Tamerrick tapped his bone dagger on the side of the wagon. The three diggers immediately turned, running as fast as they could away from the wagon.

"This is perfect," said Rodark. "I love a good chase."

Tamerrick licked each bone dagger, and with precise accuracy, propelled the razor-sharp daggers into the chest of each of the two earthers in the wagon, the earthers collapsing onto each other.

Rodark sat up in the saddle. "You kill your own kind? Maybe the black spirit horse should have recruited you instead of me?"

"I didn't kill them, tar face, I put them to sleep under my power. As long as they are spellbound under my control, you can't get to their spirits. You are not as smart as you think you are."

Rodark unleashed his sword and spitting on the blade, it burst into a green flame burning the full length of the steel.

Tamerrick jumped back from Rodark.

Rodark thrashed at the side of the wagon, each powerful blow ripping out chunks of wood and setting the wagon on fire. "Even if you burn, shaman earther, I will still take your spirit and soul."

Tamerrick leaped to the driver's seat and whipped the reins, and the wagon shot off. Rodark charged after the wagon then quickly peeled off toward the three diggers that had fled earlier.

Tamerrick looked over his left shoulder and saw Rodark almost on his friends. "Shit, I was hoping he'd chase after me. I can't go back, Rodark has too much power. I can't defeat him while I keep the spell bound on the other two."

Tamerrick whipped the reins harder, looking back at Rodark one more time.

"Damn, those riders are brutal." He watched as the

black spirit rider ran the last earther down into the dirt, cutting his head off and stuffing the bleeding stump of fur into his saddle bag. He whipped the reins harder. "Dammit, I killed my diggers. Please forgive me. I will try to find you in the spirit world. Maybe I can bring you back to Grimmbell."

Tamerrick studied his surroundings.

"There must be a dust-off butte close by. If I can make it to the top of that, I can signal Kula. She can stop this dickhead black spirit rider, then we can be transported back to Grimmbell."

Tamerrick spotted the magical stone markers positioned at the base of the dust-off butte. "I knew there was one close. Probably three hundred yards until we start to make the accent up the butte."

Tamerrick looked over his shoulder for any signs of the dark rider. Rodark was not pursuing him, although he could see the black horse rider back at the battleground. "Why didn't the dark rider come after me? Is it going to take all the skulls buried within the dig site? Does it just take the skulls?"

Suddenly, a set of fingers hooked on the top of Tamerrick's collar, pulling him back. Tamerrick turned around to see Zip and Zap had been viciously awakened from their safety nap.

"You stabbed us," said Zap, pulling the dagger out.

"I'm sorry my friends, I had no choice. And you are still alive."

Zip yanked on Tamerrick's sleeve. "Tamerrick, our wagon is on fire."

"Good thing I set your spells for only fifteen minutes, otherwise, you could have been burned alive."

Tamerrick could see the ground rushing by where the floor of the wagon used to be, and the wheels were looking thin and transparent. "This ride isn't going to last much longer."

"What are we going to do?" said Zap. "The black spirit rider is going to catch up to us and eat us alive, spitting our eyeballs out on the ground to rot."

"He's not going to come after us," said Tamerrick. "He has three fresh skulls to tend to. But we need to take action. This is what we need to do. Position yourself to where you can walk out on the tongue and jump on one of the horses. I will be right behind you."

Zip and Zap stared at Tamerrick with a hollow look.

"Do it now," said Tamerrick with a heavy head nod toward the horses.

Zip and Zap jumped into the front seat with Tamerrick, leaning forward to look down at the wagon tongue connecting to the horses.

"Holy moly," said Tamerrick. "The wheels won't last much longer. We need a leap of faith now."

Zip and Zap didn't waste any time, speedwalking across the wagon hitch and jumping on the horse to the right.

Tamerrick could smell his hair burning and the intense heat on his back. He hurdled the wagon hitch, landing on the unmounted horse on the left. With his bone dagger, he cut all connections to the burning wagon, watching it slowly roll to a stop and shrivel to the ground in a cloud of fire and smoke.

Tamerrick grabbed the mane of the opposing horse, slowing them to a stop, still giving quick looks over his shoulder.

Zip and Zap noticed the quick jerky head turns. "We're still in danger, aren't we?" said Zip.

Tamerrick took a deep breath and exhaled. "You'll be fine. Go to the top of the butte. I'll stay here to make sure Rodark doesn't show up. Go now!"

Zip and Zap turned away, nudging the horse toward the climb up the butte.

Tamerrick spun his horse around, ready to defend himself from the dark rider. He closed his eyes and anchored his attention on his breathing and within a couple of minutes, he released his spirit from his body to be carried with the wind currents blowing toward Rodark and the decapitation site of his three friends. When his spirit arrived at the dig site, Rodark was gone. The three headless bodies of the diggers were all lying on their bellies, their hands staked into the ground. "He wanted them to be scared to death, literally, before he cut the heads off. But why?"

Tamerrick viewed the dig site further. It looked like a piece of Swiss cheese, a hole remaining where each skull had been removed. He felt his chest and stomach aching. It was time to bring his spirit back. He counted back from fifty-seven and opened his eyes, puking onto the neck of his horse.

He wiped his mouth on his shirt sleeve and breathing in through his nose and out of the mouth, he settled down his internal spirit enough to set back on the horse and somewhat relax.

"Rodark. That bastard means business."

Chapter 23: The Reading Chamber

Awaiting the arrival of Bradicus and Rasp, Kula rested comfortably in her chambers nestled in the Maroot Mountains, the 1040-mile range bordering the Valley of the Tomb Sleepers to both sides.

Rasp would be performing his first official smoke mix for the queen later in the day but first, Kula and Bradicus needed to exchange a reading of their mind maps, a proven method of transferring information between each other without speaking, for security reasons.

It was a chance to compare notes on what had happened in the past few days.

Kula heard the third and final barrier bell sound off, notifying her that Slaughter was outside her chamber door.

Slither and Slank, positioned on each side of the wooden door opened their eyelids, showing off matching bright yellow eyes.

Raising charcoal-colored heads, they looked toward Kula, purring with a low hideous hiss. "Okay boys, settle down. It's probably General Slaughter at the door."

The crushed glass-covered hides of the cobra dogs reflected a thousand tiny lights from the glow of the fireplace as they positioned themselves into a hunched down attack mode.

Kula turned her attention to the doorway. "Enter."

Slaughter pushed the agatized wood doors open, poking his head past the doorway. Slither and Slank hissed again, sitting themselves in front of Kula.

"Don't worry, Slaughter, you know how the boys are. They like to hiss at you." Satisfied by the entrance of Slaughter, Slither and Slank lay down at Kula's feet.

"Kula, my Queen. Bradicus and Rasp have arrived."

"Bradicus?" said the queen.

"It looks that way, my Queen. They're waiting for you."

"Please escort Bradicus to the reading chambers.

Take Rasp and show him where the observation area is located. Have him set up there."

Slaughter bowed his head. "Yes, my Queen."

"Wait. Before you go…"

"What is bothering you?"

"Don't forget to double the guards around the observation room."

"Already done. I have four blunt-force dragons stationed at the entrance to the hallway. Only one way in and one way out. That area is secure. My Queen, do you want the 100 on standby?"

"Yes, I would. As a matter of fact, I would like an additional two fighter dragoons at each spotting tower. Six at the Grimmbell Cemetery, and three at each of the two entry points into the valley."

"I will send out orders immediately." He motioned with a head nod to the dragoon door guard. "I'm on my way to the reading room; it will be ready in one minute for you and Bradicus."

"Very good," said Kula. "I will use the drop hallway to enter the reading room. Bring Bradicus in right away."

Slaughter closed the door behind him and walking down the hallway to the central duct entryway, a solid wind blew into his face.

"This wind condition is perfect." Jumping out into thin air, he flared his wings to gracefully drop four hundred feet, enabling him to swoop into one of the lower hallways.

This led him to the open arena of the reading chamber.

The hallway's natural light dimmed as Slaughter made his way through the stone fortress to where Bradicus and Rasp were waiting.

"General Slaughter," said Rasp. "We are here to see the queen."

"The queen is waiting for Bradicus in the reading room. Rasp, I will escort you down to the observation room."

"The observation room?" said Rasp. "But I need to mix the essence of smoke. It helps with the mind mapping. I'm the official travel agent if you know what I mean."

"Yes, I do. You can mix your spirit smoke from the

observation area. It's a multi-function chamber, allowing you to send your brew to many areas of the castle."

"That's perfect. As long as I have an area to work in."

"It's the same area where Roko performed his magic. I'm sure it will work for you." Slaughter turned his attention to Bradicus.

"You may enter the reading room, the queen is waiting for you."

"Thank you, General. I wanted to make sure she was ready for me. Do you know if the spirit runner has delivered a blood brick to the autopsy um, I mean observation room?"

"A blood brick?" said Rasp. "We have a blood brick here?"

Bradicus stepped next to Rasp. "Not to worry, my friend, we needed a blood brick for the observation room investigation and Able is to deliver the brick directly to Kula."

Spinning to face Slaughter, Bradicus said, "General Slaughter, may I have a few minutes with Rasp."

"As you wish. I will be right down this hall. But don't keep the queen waiting."

"It will take two minutes," said Bradicus.

"With all due respect," said Rasp, "can we trust Able to deliver? If you remember, it was Roko who created Able."

"I am fully aware of that," said Bradicus.

"Maybe Roko might try to enlist his services for himself to get inside the reading room or observation room today. Do you understand what I'm saying?"

"I know what you're saying," said Bradicus, gripping his shoulder. "I thought of that too. But there's a number of things you don't understand about this particular blood brick."

"Is this something I need to take notes on?"

"I guess it wouldn't hurt," said Bradicus. "It's totally up to you."

"Bradicus, I never thought I would say this, but there's a lot of pressure taking over from Roko and Cremator."

"Have you been thinking late into the night again?"

"Maybe, and now that Roko is gone, and Cremator temporarily gone, I have been able to go through some of Roko's notes. The creation of Able. That one is kind of weird. When you said Able was going to deliver the blood brick, I got a little worried, yeah."

"That's good," said Bradicus with a hard head nod. "That's good?" Rasp questioned.

"You should be worried, to a point at least. If you're not apprehensive about some of the details that come to your doorstep, then maybe you're not taking this seriously."

"Oh, believe me, Bradicus, I'm taking it seriously."

"I know you are, that's why Kula put you in charge of the spirit smoke. Because you know as well as I do, a lot of aspects can go wrong."

"Yes, I do know that," said Rasp, digging in his shoulder bag. "On any given day, we can be killed by details being mislabeled or mishandled, among other things, so welcome to the real world."

"No problem," said Bradicus with a head jerk to the left. "Now let's continue, shall we?"

"Let's do this," said Rasp.

Bradicus walked down the hall toward Slaughter.

"The blood brick is being brought in by Able, a spirit runner, which… You know these spirit warriors are super tough and relentless if attacked. Woodford will shadow Able through the mole tunnels, also he will be followed by an ox wizard in the daylight and not last but least, if the blood brick senses great danger, it will self-destruct and kill all of us. Slaughter is waving; we need to get started."

"Bradicus. This is Brazel."

"Brazel, is there something wrong?"

"No, not necessarily, but did Rasp bring any sweets with him?"

"Oh yeah, that's right, I totally forgot about that. I will ask him. Thank you."

"No problem, that's why I'm here."

Bradicus grabbed Rasp by the sleeve. "Did you remember to bring any sweets or candy with you?"

"Yes, I did. I have the triple honeybee wraps with

me. Two dozen."

"That's perfect," said Bradicus. "You might need them."

"Who are they for, the queen?"

Bradicus chuckled. "That's funny. You could give them to the queen and I'm sure she would appreciate that, but they are for the blood spirits associated with the blood brick. Sometimes, you have to entertain and bribe them when you bring them out of the brick. They can get a little unpleasant."

"Roko never told me anything about candy to feed to the blood brick spirits."

"Well, maybe he forgot. In any case, if you have trouble with one or two of them, offer them the candy. Go now, before Slaughter comes up here and drags your ass back there."

"I'm leaving now," said Rasp.

Bradicus turned away from Rasp and, walking to the reading room door, he pressed the palm of his hand flat against the door and waited. "These door spells. I wonder how long it will take?" The spells systematically changed every fifteen seconds, depending on your handprint.

The door clicked open, revealing Kula sitting comfortably with an array of food and drink presented on the table.

"Welcome Bradicus, Blackjack, and Brazel."

"Kula, my Queen, it's good to see you again. Why the reading room? We could have met up in the field somewhere?"

"Please, sit down. Have something to eat and drink."

Bradicus walked up to the table. "Wow, this is quite a spread. All of this for little old me."

"I know you've been running hard and fast for the past number of days. Besides, can't the queen offer her friend some food and drink?"

"Kula, you know I didn't mean any disrespect."

"I know that. Just relax and to answer your question, yes, we could have met out in the field, that is true, but I wanted privacy. In this reading room, nothing can penetrate the blood brick stone walls, nor can anything escape. So, our friend Roko the Dark cannot enter as a spirit and listen to what we have to say."

"You are right," said Bradicus. "I forget that Roko is not on our side anymore, or at least whatever he's up to is very skeptical."

"And the fact," said Kula, helping herself to a handful of roasted oxen, "I had limited information coming to me from my magic rope didn't help matters. Sometimes, I knew where you were and what you were doing to a point and other times, I had no idea. I didn't know you didn't make it to Grimmbell with the package until it was too late to help."

"I'm sorry about that blunder. I failed you, my Queen. What is my punishment?"

"It wasn't your fault."

"It wasn't?" said Bradicus.

"No, I should've known my dragoon rope would not hold that much energy for an extended period."

"Why do you say that? It's your rope. Your rope is not the average dragoon rope carried by the fighter dragoons."

"Maybe," said Kula. "But still, not powerful enough to contain the broken circle entity for that length of time. I underestimated the power of this particular enemy. This Penetrator Arune figure was engineered a totally different way than I have seen before."

"What was so different about it?" Bradicus asked, adding a large spoon of gravy to his slow-baked cow loaf.

"Once I received information about what happened to Roko, poor soul, I figured the black Penetrator box you were transporting was a spell inside of its own spell."

Bradicus stopped eating and looked at Kula. "It sounds like a self-igniting… timed-reversal spell.

We have dealt with those before, haven't we?"

"Yes, I suppose we have somewhere in the past. In a battle. But this particular energy was smart. It recognized my rope spell, the linear foot time spell pattern holding my rope together. When I burned one form of the Penetrator to ash, the ashes from the fire transformed into another energy force. You do remember the tattoo on the Penetrator after the burning?"

"Yes, I remember," said Bradicus, motioning with his fork. "It was the broken circle by an axe."

"That's right, a symbol I haven't seen in this arrangement before."

"But your dragoon rope is a time-lock spell, so it could only break at exactly the time that you wanted it to be broken, couldn't it?"

"It's hard to believe," said Kula. "Time-lock spells are virtually impossible to break. You have to know the exact time the spell will open, and only I knew what time it would be. So that one has me stumped."

"It was as if like somebody could read your mind," said Bradicus. "And when it found out your specific time of that spell, it manipulated it to its advantage."

Shaking her head and spitting a bone into the garbage, Kula said, "It appears that way."

"The Broken Circle Axe Entity, aka Arune, released itself at the precise moment to attach itself to the black spirit horse to trap Roko."

Bradicus placed his hand over his mouth, nodding. "What?"

"I'm thinking Rasp is smarter than he looks or possibly smarter than he's letting on."

"What do you mean by that?"

"He made the comment to me just the other day, about how the black spirit horse trap was actually designed to catch me, not Roko, because I have this all-knowing third power."

"Don't you think we're jumping to conclusions?"

"Maybe, but I'll admit I'm looking at all possible connections. I have no proof; it's just a theory."

"Nothing wrong with looking at situations in a different light."

"I'm still looking. When the trap didn't catch me, the Penetrator, Arune, took Roko and tried to kill me; well, that's not entirely true."

"The entity *didn't* try to kill you?"

"The new rider who I call Roko the Dark tried to make a deal with me first."

"That's interesting. What kind of deal did he offer?"

"He said he would share all of the information in the Great Hall recipe book with me."

Kula blinked her eyes, exhaling a small burst of

flame out of her nose. "Hmm. If I'd been in Roko's position at that particular time, I think I'd have offered you the same deal."

"How do you figure that?" said Bradicus, filling his mouth with a bite of buttered bread.

"Are you kidding me? What better ally to have than the three of you? How many people know of your unconscious third entity?"

Bradicus stabbed a potato with his fork, watching the gravy ooze out. "I believe the real question here is whether the Penetrator had knowledge of my third soul."

"That's exactly what I mean."

"I see where you're going with this. You're right."

Kula picked out a pig bone wedged between her teeth. "Not a lot of the people in the valley know you can transform between human and animal form. But the third power source, that's a big deal. Roko the Dark would try anything to get absorbed into your third source."

"You're right. Could he use a blood brick for that process?"

"I believe he could, which points a finger to the events that have taken place the past week and other incidents from a couple of months ago that could be tied into the present."

"What else have you heard or seen?"

"Slaughter told me he saw an ox wizard walking along the river two months ago. When's the last time you saw an ox wizard roaming so close to our boundary?"

"It's been a number of years since one has been caught," said Bradicus.

"Then a few days later, after the initial sighting of this ox wizard, Slaughter caught him with a backpack of boiled skulls."

"Screamer's dust?" said Bradicus.

"That's what I was wondering. I read that from your mind map."

"That's interesting. Did Slaughter kill him?"

"No, he ripped his arm off when the wizard tried to hide his backpack from him. But the point I'm trying to make is that I feel a huge negative shift in the energy field protecting the valley."

"A shift in the energy field? I never thought of it that way. I'm conditioned to being attacked by an evil force that I can see coming right at me, an army of creatures of some kind."

"That's what makes it so unpredictable," said Kula. "I still think it'll be some type of attack but it's not going to be head-on. Probably a sneak attack of some kind, someone we don't see coming. Something of that nature. Does that make sense?"

"It makes total sense, but it also makes me wonder when you use the word *someone*. That scares me even more. We've had many attempts of humans and creatures making an attempt to control this valley, but this concept of someone wanting to harness another energy, that's downright spooky."

"Yes," said Kula. "It should scare us a little bit more, or at least make us more aware of our surroundings. Like I told Slaughter, let me know who, what and how many of anything is moving in and around the valley. That's one of the main reasons I was going to talk to the King of Souls about this Arune unknown energy."

"Not only that, but also, because of my mistake in not being able to deliver the Penetrator, we didn't have the opportunity to interrogate that someone or thing. That has set us back too."

"Again, Bradicus, not necessarily your fault. Even if you would have arrived at Grimmbell with the package, it doesn't mean the earthers would have acquired any answers from the Penetrator even with the right smoke mix."

"Why do you say that?"

"Because I think the Penetrator energy source is smart enough that it would self-destruct or even take on a shape we would be unaware of."

Bradicus cleared his throat. "Or even worse than that."

"Even worse how?"

"What if the dark force wanted to be taken to Grimmbell, to get inside the wall, then explode its energy over every spirit? What kind of power would it yield then?"

Bradicus exited the reading room, following Kula as she gracefully maneuvered through the hallways of her fortress.

"Watch your step here." Kula circled around an open wind shaft in the middle of the hallway floor.

"I don't know how you don't get lost in here, my Queen. It's a total maze. Every hallway looks the same, and all of these open shaft ways in the middle of the floor."

"It definitely tests my memory in the middle of the night."

Sliding his hand against the wall, Bradicus said, "These walls are so smooth. Even with my keen night vision, I would need a lantern to avoid falling into one of these wind tunnels."

"The openings of the wind shafts in the floors have been engineered not to be seen. So, the extreme wind velocity churning out through the tunnels is a sure sign to watch your step. One wrong move without wings or some type of flying magic, and you would probably die. There have been a few such deaths over the years," said Kula, looking down into one of the shafts. "They were not paying attention and fell to their demise. Serves the enemy right."

"Does the wind blow up from the bottom of the valley floor, or is it a suction type of thing?"

"Some do both and some don't."

"You must have quite the mental mapping of this castle."

"Well, that's one of the secrets of this fortress."

Bradicus looked up at Kula. "Is that a secret you're willing to share?"

"The fact is this particular rock castle is comparable to Chameleon mud. It will reflect your thought process. Most particularly, your memory receptors will be unable to store any castle data in your brain."

"No way," said Bradicus. "It throws your thoughts back at you?"

"In reality, the rock will ingest your thoughts."

"It will eat my brain waves?"

"Precisely. Therefore, you cannot remember or store anything you want to remember, so no mind mapping."

Blackjack walked around another wind shaft. "Must have taken you a while to find your way?"

"Yes, it took me a while to get familiar with the

layout. 322 levels. Each level three hundred yards high and roughly 303 rooms per floor. Give or take a few rooms."

"Why so many rooms?"

Kula twisted her head looking down at Bradicus. "You haven't ever been on these upper floors, have you?"

"No, I haven't. When I pick up the royal messages, I think that's on the sixth floor."

"Actually, it's the seventh, but close enough. When we have more time, I'll show you around."

"Kula, my Queen, with all due respect, I'm getting the feeling you don't allow too many visitors in your home."

"I can't afford to let just anybody in here. Security reasons, you understand."

"Yes, I do very much understand, and it makes sense. Today would be a prime example. How many other individuals would be very pleased to have the opportunity to follow you to the observation room?"

"Some would like that a lot, but their motives would perhaps be quite a bit darker than what we want to do today."

They rounded a corner that opened up into a larger hallway. Bradicus stared down the hallway then looked up at Kula.

"Kula, this particular hallway looks as though it doesn't have an end."

"It doesn't. It's a trap hallway."

"Then why are we going this way?"

"Security reasons," said Kula. "Just in case some type of spellbuster got lucky enough to get inside to follow us."

"What if they did get inside?"

"I'm glad you asked. Any intruder gaining access will end up in this hallway. The hallway of doom."

"What happens to them then?"

"Depends on the electrical mapping of their personal magic grid."

"I have heard of something like that in my travels. Like an I.S.D.?"

"An I.S.D.?"

"Yeah. Internal Source Detector," said Bradicus.

"That's what I call it, anyway."

"We *can* call it that, depending on how complex it is to open their I.S.D. grid."

"You mean how advanced their energy grid is and what it will produce?"

"Yes, whatever type of energy is sealed within their bodies will determine what happens to them.

Some become flushed out through the bottom of the castle, prohibited to be within a hundred miles of it. They are forever marked. The others will be destroyed."

"What about the magic grid itself? What happens to that?"

"The energy of the captured source will be filtered through the blood brick and if the filtered essence is useable, it will be absorbed into the castle or maybe into another blood brick. That's what makes each blood brick unique."

Bradicus followed Kula into the observation chambers. He peeked around her to see Jinnamon lying on the large circular viewing stone. It was her being transported by Molehol.

"Damn, when did all this happen?"

Kula looked at Bradicus nodding her head, releasing a heavy sigh. "You did see Molehol flying near Spotting Tower 5. Correct?"

"Yes, I did, but I didn't know who it was."

"It was Jinnamon," said Kula.

"My Queen, we need to get Cremator out of her belly drop. We have to find out what happened when he was in the portal with Roko."

"I'm surprised we've waited this long to talk about that."

"I wasn't sure how to bring it up," said Bradicus.

"I understand. I should have addressed this right away, but I also knew from the information I received that she did help in defeating Roko the other night."

"I know where you're headed with this," said Bradicus. "Yes, she did help in defeating Roko. And when we go even further back, I delivered the paperwork that allowed us in the trading of Jinnamon with Killamore. You thought I had a soft spot for her?"

"I was trying to figure out a way to break the news in

a professional manner.”

“So, she’s the one I saw being transported by Molehol?”

“I’m afraid so.”

Turning away from Kula, Bradicus stared off into space.

“When I was at the tower, I was surprised to see Molehol fulfilling the rituals of circling the tower twice for a dragoon warrior when in fact, I was almost certain he was not transporting a fighter dragoon. That made me wonder what was really going on,” he remarked.

Kula enlightened him.

“I had approved Molehol to follow the traditional warrior ritual of circling each tower twice before going to Grimmbell. But as you know by now, she was never taken to Grimmbell.”

“No, she wasn’t. She’s waiting for us in the observation chamber,” he replied.

“She is?” asked Kula. “Another reason why you and Rasp are here today.”

“You want Rasp to make up a spirit mix to talk to Jinnamon’s spirit?” Bradicus wanted to know.

“Yes, of course,” said Kula. “To see if Rasp can open her belly drop.”

“To find out if Cremator is still alive or not,” said Bradicus.

“You would agree, right? We have to know the outcome.”

“Yes, of course, my Queen. Did she die a quick death?” asked Bradicus.

“Yes, she did,” said Kula.

“How did she die?”

“She was given the warrior’s choice.” Kula was nodding as if expecting Bradicus to understand.

“Really? Normally, the choice isn’t given to any non-warrior dragoon,” Bradicus said, slowly nodding his head.

“So, you showed her mercy.”

“I did and I didn’t.”

“What do you mean by that?” he inquired.

“General Slaughter actually requested she be given a

choice, so I approved the request. That's all."

Tilting his head, he answered, *"Slaughter* made that request? I find that hard to believe."

"I did too at the time, but when I arrived, let me just say it was not an appealing sight."

"Why? What happened?" he asked pointedly.

"Are you sure you want to hear the details?"

"Yes, I do."

"Well, then I sent Slaughter to find you, he was flying a high post pattern. He saw Jinnamon at a lower altitude level and circled around to make contact with Jinnamon to find out where you and Cremator were located. He followed Jinnamon for about a mile to make sure no one was using her for bait. A trap, if you know what I mean."

"Yes, I do," said Bradicus. "With Roko and his black spirit riders being able to do some amazing feats. I understand."

"Slaughter noticed Jinnamon having trouble flying straight and true, and it looked as if she was having either a heated conversation or trying to bite an intruder's head off."

"Okay, that's good. Still fighting."

Kula looked up. "Yes, I suppose, but Slaughter reported nothing visible around her."

Bradicus pushed against the stone table. "You know as well as I do it could have been an invisible source."

"I asked the General about that."

"What did he say?" asked Bradicus.

"He flew within inches of her body. Both sides top and bottom. He didn't sense any energy bumps coming from another source."

Bradicus put a hand in his pipe pocket as his eyebrows joined together in confusion. "She was disillusioned, or could she have been scared of something?"

"I don't know for sure," said Kula.

"What happened next?"

"Slaughter forced her to the ground. Her eyes were partially glazed over." Kula stopped, lowering her head. "Slaughter said she was crying. That he saw for himself a great fear in her eyes."

"She was crying?" said Bradicus. "Maybe she just had something in her eyes?"

"Maybe, but he said she looked at him with the saddest expression he has ever seen. He was barely able to stand looking at her because of it. So of course, he asked her what was wrong."

Bradicus gripped the table. "And what did she say?"

Kula sighed. "She tried to speak."

"And?"

"She mouthed some words, but apparently, nothing was vocalized. It seemed the words were sticking in her throat, and while she was attempting to get them out, she was clawing at her neck."

Bradicus stared down at the floor, then looked at Kula.

"It's very possible that Roko somehow poisoned her when she battled him in the opening of the portal, or that the energy of the portal affected her in a negative way."

"Something affected her well-being," said Kula. "Like I said, she was having trouble flying. Her color was bad. She looked sick. Slaughter could not communicate with her. Or at least…" She shook her head. "She didn't or couldn't communicate very well with him. It appeared she might even be under some spell, being controlled by someone else."

"Where was she going?" Bradicus asked.

"From the direction she was heading, it could have been to Grimmbell or maybe Killamore Canyon."

"Killamore? That son of a bitch," said Bradicus. "When I delivered the royal message to him for the trade of her, I knew he would never really let her go. I think he wanted to transform her into human form, to be his queen, something weird like that. I thought he was kidding or just blowing smoke, but maybe he wasn't."

"Are you serious?" asked Kula. "I mean, it's possible, but it takes a huge sacrifice of multi-verse of Shaman interactions to make that type of transmutation."

"Only specific people can make that type of transition, and it usually takes two individuals working together. And one of those people is in her belly."

"You could be right," said Kula. "It just seems that

Jinnamon could have been set up to capture Cremator."

"Which she did, but at the same time, saved his life."

"I'm not entirely sold on the Killamore idea."

"Granted, it was a shot-in-the-dark thought," said Bradicus, "but I think it points mostly to Roko. He was there that night. He wanted Cremator's hands."

"His hands? I don't understand," said Kula.

"The only way Roko the Dark can read the Great Hall recipe book is with other hands than his own. Because his hands now are black spirit rider hands, the book will not let him read it, and that's why he needed Cremator."

"I think Rasp could be right with the idea of Roko wanting you more than Cremator. Is it possible that Brazel can read the Great Hall book?"

"I have given that some serious thought, but I think Cremator or Rasp are much easier targets than I am. Roko knows that."

"Why didn't he go after Rasp?"

"I don't think Rasp has enough knowledge to read the book and prepare the recipes. You know that's a dual process procedure at times. You have to summon your spirit to help. Very risky."

"You are right. That *is* a dual procedure. At this point in the game, there is a lot of speculation. Even if Jinn ingested Cremator on purpose, there's only one way to find out and that's extracting Cremator from her belly. And maybe the only way we're going to find out what is going on with Roko and the Penetrator is this process. I hope Rasp is prepared to fulfill his duties."

"Kula, one more thing before we operate."

"Of course, Bradicus. Please speak your mind."

"You said that you authorized Jinnamon to have the warrior's choice in how she died."

"Yes, I authorized that."

"What was her choice?"

"She chose close-quarter combat."

"Close quarter combat with whom, General Slaughter?"

"According to the general, when he took her to the ground, she managed to spit out a sentence or two. She wanted to be remembered for dying in battle against one of the greatest dragoon warriors in the Darkan Territory."

"Did she request an audience?"

"She asked for two others to be there."

"Who did she choose?"

"Me and you, but we couldn't locate you at that time. I will make sure her battle with Slaughter will be written into history on my wings. She will be remembered in the library of the wings forever."

"How did she die?"

"She put up a good fight against the general, and he didn't give her any breaks. When it was all said and done, Slaughter had physically knocked her unconscious, then stabbed her with the Madagator sword."

"The Madagator sword? Wow! Being killed by the Madagator sword, that maneuver gave her full ritual and burial rights as a fighter dragoon at Grimmbell."

"Yes, it did. She earned that right."

"Even if she ingested Cremator on purpose?"

"There's one way to find out. We need to get on with the process of extracting Cremator."

"You don't think it's going to be that easy, do you?"

"Let's go find out."

"The observation rooms. The last time I was in here, it wasn't very pleasant," said Bradicus.

Kula nodded. "You are right. It's usually not a pleasant experience, but something we have to do."

"Agreed."

Kula and Bradicus walked the last few feet and stood in front of Slaughter. "General Slaughter, is everything in order? Are we ready to proceed?"

"Yes, my Queen, everything is in order. Rasp has given me the okay to enter the chamber."

Rasp approached Kula and Bradicus and bowed. "My Queen."

"Master Rasp, where are we in the procedure?"

"I have already started the first step. I released my special smoke mix to set up the proper scanning of the body with a mind drift which also allows me to eliminate any hidden surface bombs on her body."

Kula nodded with respect, saying nothing and walking around the body. Bradicus walked around the body in the opposite direction, both meeting at the dragon's feet and looking at Jinnamon's belly.

"Bradicus, do we even know what type of belly drop dragoon she is?"

Rasp scooted in between Kula and Bradicus, pointing at her head. "She's of White Butte origin."

"How do you know that?" asked Kula.

"She was one of the very first pre-spirit ritual walk-throughs I did with Roko."

"When did you do that?"

"When we traded for her from Killamore."

"So, she's from the White Butte Trading Company. That does make sense," said Kula, "considering the fact Killamore did a lot of trading with White Butte."

"I didn't read a lot about the White Butte Company," said Rasp.

"I'm sorry, I should have explained this sooner. The White Butte Trading Company gathered, herded, rescued, and even captured dragons during a phase when there was an explosion of dragon reproduction, a mix of poorly orchestrated magic that was to help increase the dragon species but went overboard. That's when Killamore stepped in to facilitate the problem. And some even say that's when Killamore created his box of twenty-six for hire."

Rasp perked up.

"Are you talking about the twenty-six miniature dragons Killamore kept frozen in a box?" he asked.

"I am," said Kula. "You have been doing your research in the library?"

"Yes, my Queen. You gave me permission."

"Yes Rasp, I gave you my permission with the acceptance of your life coin."

"Just wanted to make sure I wasn't stepping on anybody's toes."

"You are not stepping on my toes," said Kula. "It's good there's someone else reading the history of Darkan Territory."

"Although, the twenty-six were not frozen, but kept in a state of being comatose."

"Sounds like one big ass sleeping spell to keep that many dragons in sleep mode," Bradicus said.

"He did become quite famous," said Rasp, "for his ability to control the twenty-six with his medicine wizard magic."

"Please continue, Rasp. Now is not the time to be modest."

"Okay, this gets even better. Part of this wizard magic is a special ingredient unmentioned in the archives, allowing the dragons to be housed in a small box collection until needed to grow to full-size dragons. And I might mention he had some other creatures too, but the main ones were the twenty-six."

"And they are still around today," said Bradicus. "Although, didn't Killamore start off renting these dragons out as a workforce, flying large loads of product throughout the valley and eventually outside the valley? Then Killamore got more ambitious, renting out his box of dragons to the highest bidder to do whatever they wanted."

"That's when I stepped in," said Kula. "But with that box of power, it was a double-edged sword. The dragons accrued skills from many cultures, making each creature very adaptable, blending in well with their surroundings. But on the other side of the coin, it equally made them vulnerable at times. Some didn't fit into some surroundings because of the multiplex of abilities, which is why I traded for Jinnamon because of those skills. But I also knew she was aggressive and could be unpredictable."

"Of course, and that's why you had her at Tower 5," said Bradicus.

"Indeed," said Kula. "She was watching the Killamore Canyon. What better dragon to have watching Killamore dragons than an ex-Killamore dragon?"

"But we're missing the point here," said Rasp.

"What is this point?" said Kula.

"The point is she's dead. That makes it more like an experiment to open the belly dump; the many cultures weaved into her makeup will make it so much harder to open her up. Each culture she learned and accepted could bring with it some type of a trap."

"What kind of a trap?" asked Bradicus.

"A failsafe spellbuster bomb is one example. An internal protection device, set to blow up in our faces if we try to open her belly dump.”

“Unless you can read her tongue tattoos,” said Bradicus.

“Tongue tattoos?” said Rasp. “How do you know of these things?”

“Roko once spoke of this process. Besides, you have to remember I am part earther too.”

“Can we read her tongue?” said Kula.

“I can mix some smoke to get her mouth open, but I don’t know about reading the tongue from my recipe book.”

“Won’t do any good,” said Bradicus.

“Why not?” said Rasp, thumbing through his recipe book.

“You can’t read a tongue tattoo with any of our tobacco grades. You would need magic with a lot more kick.”

Rasp closed his book. “I could try a few other methods. With a little luck…”

“I believe there’s another way,” Bradicus interjected. “Roko showed me this trick one night when we were drinking wine.”

“A trick?” said Rasp.

“No offense, Rasp, it’s really not a trick. He was working on a project that particular night. He was doing a lot of talking. *I* was doing a lot of listening.”

“So, what exactly happened?”

“It was after a battle. I can’t quite remember every detail, but we had a particular creature in the tomb chamber, I believe a deep-ground ore troll digger. To make a long story short, this creature had tongue graffiti. Tattoos. Roko called it stone lick graffiti.”

“That’s what he called it?” said Rasp. “Stone lick graffiti? I’ll have to write that one down.”

“In any case, you have to remove the tongue.”

“We can do that if we can get her mouth open.”
“What about using hellbuster spirits?” asked Kula.

Rasp looked at the queen, then at Bradicus. “Um… we can… these spirits should be destroyed after the process. Is everyone okay with that?”

“I’m okay with that,” said Kula. “I will have to

answer to the King of Souls, but I'm prepared for that. Continue."

"Once you do remove the tongue, then you have to have it re-attached to another creature. If you can get the creature to speak, it will tell you what the symbols mean to open the belly drop."

Rasp secured his book in his armpit. "What kind of a creature?" Rasp asked Bradicus.

"Can't be anything smaller than an adult human. At least pound for pound. And it should have four legs."

"How about a black spirit horse?" said Kula. Rasp and Bradicus looked at Kula in unity.

"Where and how are we going to get a black spirit horse?" asked Rasp.

"Actually," said Bradicus, "Brazel just informed me a black spirit horse is our only choice for the exchange of tongues."

Rasp nodded. "I am assuming Roko shared this horse tongue exchange idea with you that night?"

"Yes, he did. That's what he talked about most of the night."

"Did he comment on how to reattach the dragon tongue to a horse or vice versa?"

"No, I'm sorry, he didn't get that far. There were high casualties coming in that evening." Bradicus stared at Kula. "What about this horse, my Queen?"

"You have a black spirit horse? Wow," said Rasp.

"I have knowledge of a horse that could work for us."

Bradicus continued the stare. "And where might this horse be located?"

"I have a black spirit horse at Grimmbell Cemetery."

"Where exactly is the horse being kept?"

"Do you remember Luxen?"

"Luxen?" Bradicus asked. "Yes, I remember Luxen."

"Who is Luxen?" said Rasp. "How come I never read this in the history of the wings?"

"Because I didn't have it recorded on my wings," said Kula.

"May I ask why not?"

"Bradicus was there, in Blackjack form. He can tell

you some history of Luxen better than me."

Blackjack inhaled deeply, holding for a count of five, then released. "Luxen is the caretaker guard of the Tri-Eight at the Grimmbell prison depository."

"Who or what is the Tri-Eight?"

"That's another story you won't find in the Library of Wings archive." "I thought everything was recorded?" said Rasp.

"Everything is recorded, but not all of the recordings are detailed on Kula's wings, or in the hanging wings archive."

"Then where are they recorded?"

"The story of Luxen and the Tri-Eight. I have those recorded, but you can't read them at this time."

"Why not?"

"Ask me in a hundred years. Now, can I tell the story?"

"I will shut up now," said Rasp. "But I'm going to take notes."

"Luxen is the most decorated mortal ground battle warrior I have ever seen. I fought alongside Luxen in the battle of the Tri-Eight."

"The battle of the Tri-Eight?" said Rasp. "I would like to read about that. It sounds scary from the start."

"During one of the last battles of the war, Luxen was separated from his squad. He had run out of food and water two or three days before that. In the distance, he saw the enemy mounting another attack, and he started rummaging through the fallen bodies all around him. He found a copper cup. With the cup, he cut the dead at the jugular vein and drank their blood."

"Later that evening, a divine entity, the guardian of the cup of wells, paid a visit to Luxen. He asked Luxen where he had got the cup. Luxen guided the individual to the dead man who had it."

"The guardian of the cup got down on his hands and knees and started sniffing the man's body. He nodded in satisfaction. Standing, he told Luxen that was the man who had stolen his cup from the 10,000-year well. The guardian held his hand over the dead body of the man."

The corpse shook violently, bouncing on the ground.

Opening its eyes and emitting a yellow light, the cadaver screamed, bursting into flames and running away. The guardian tossed his rope and caught the man's legs, ripping him to the ground. The screaming continued until the flames burned out.

"The guardian approached the pile of ash. Luxen kneeled and presented his cup to the guardian. 'I didn't know you were the owner of this cup. I used it to drink blood. To stay alive. It's yours, so please take it back. I will find another drinking vessel for I fear I have many a battle ahead of me'."

"Retrieving a rag from his pocket, the unknown guardian entity gently sat down on a corpse and cleaned the cup to a shine. He held it up to inspect, then it filled with water out of thin air. He drank from the copper cup, smacking his lips, nodding in gratification."

"The guardian stood, pushing the cup back into Luxen's chest. 'You are the owner of the cup. I have a new cup to hang at the well. Your cup will provide a life for every time you need one for as many times a man has drank from the cup of wells'."

"The guardian turned, walking back to a stone church that had suddenly appeared. Once he walked through the huge wooden doors of the church, the guardian and church disappeared."

"Early the very next morning, Luxen watched as another wave of warriors prepared to launch another attack. He caught the soft voice of a woman calling out a name over and over. He tracked the woman, watching her rolling bodies over, wiping the dirt off their faces, then moving onto the next."

"Luxen approached the woman. 'What are you doing here? A battle is going to erupt soon'. The woman said she was looking for her husband and their four sons. He told the woman again that she needed to leave as an army of warriors would be here soon, and she would be killed or worse."

"She told Luxen that this was not a battle—that had stopped many days ago and had become entertainment for the kings. Luxen asked the woman what she meant by that."

"She woman replied that the eight kings were

wagering large amounts of gold, silver, and land on which one of their fighters could kill the Lost Warrior."

"This made Luxen very angry. He remembered what the guardian had said about his copper cup. Luxen convinced the woman to let him use her spirit body to enter the camp of the kings and in exchange, he would bring her husband and four sons back to life. She agreed."

"So Luxen had the woman drink from the copper cup, then he assumed the woman's form and entered the king's camp. She told the king's guards she had talked to Luxen the Lost Warrior."

"The guards took her to the eight kings sitting at a table inside the king's tent."

"Luxen, in the woman's form, told the kings they could not kill the Lost Warrior, and they'd suffer a huge loss of lives if they continued to hunt for him. The kings laughed at her, demanding she take them to talk to the Lost Warrior. She agreed. The eight kings and six thousand soldiers met face to face with Luxen who told them he was tired of the fighting and killing, that they should take their dead and go back home. The kings didn't like anyone daring to tell them what to do and told Luxen that if he could defeat the top warrior from each of the eight armies, they would leave his land."

"He agreed but advised them if he defeated all eight warriors, each king would dismount from his horse and hand him their crown. The kings couldn't figure out why he would only want their crowns when he could have asked for gold, silver, land, or even horses. They agreed."

"At the end of the day, eight warriors, one from each king, tried to kill Luxen. They all failed. At the end of each conflict, he would drink from his cup."

"The kings sent a hundred men at Luxen. Although Luxen became wounded many times, and should have died many times, he didn't, instead defeating all who came to hunt him."

"Luxen returned to the king's camp, dismounted his horse and went up to the first king in line."

"In this king's presence, he said, 'I will ask you one more time for your crown. If you refuse, I will take your crown with your head still attached to it. Do you hear me?'"

"One by one, each king dismounted and handed their crowns to Luxen, and soon, he was dangling four crowns on each arm. When he mounted his horse, there ensued a bright blast of blinding light."

Some say the sun must have exploded and a piece of it had slammed into the ground. But when the extreme brightness subsided, so had all of the king's warriors, the eight kings standing in place."

"Wait a minute," said Rasp. "You're talking about the Tri-Eight. They are the kings who were at the battlefield? They are the ones in prison at Grimmbell?"

"That is correct," said Bradicus. "The Tri-Eight are the eight kings who all tried to kill Luxen."

"So, what happened to all the warriors?"

"Nobody knows, or I should say, Luxen isn't telling. Nor are many others."

"There were others?"

"Yes, many, but I'm not going there right now."

Rasp rubbed his chin. "Has anyone tried to do a live spirit talk with Luxen?"

"Good luck with that," said Bradicus. "Roko has tried, a long time ago. Wanted to find out about the eight kings. I know Roko, he wanted to find out about the spirits of the eight kings, and rightly so. A king's spirit has much more to offer than others."

"So, he didn't find anything out?" said Rasp.

"That I don't know for sure. I never asked. He never told me. Maybe it's in his journal."

"The Great Hall recipe book," said Rasp. "He could have had a recipe made up just for that."

"Could be," said Bradicus. "Maybe he called it the spice of eight. Or possibly eight pieces of pie."

"Gentlemen, don't you think we should get back on track here?" Kula interrupted.

Bradicus nodded. "Yes, we do. I got caught up with Luxen. Sorry about that. We have a colleague stuck in that belly right there."

"Like I was saying, Luxen has a horse, a black spirit horse, and that horse will be able to recite the symbols on

Jinn's tongue."

"Actually, the black spirit horse is the only type that will work. We just have to figure out a way to trick it to read Jinn's tongue."

"How are we going to do that?" asked Rasp. "I need to go talk to a man about a horse." Kula tapped on the observation room door.

Slaughter opened it, poking his head into the room. "Is everything all right, my Queen?"

"Yes General, we are fine. Bradicus will be leaving soon for Grimmbell. Rasp will be my guest in the castle. Grant him access to this chamber and the necessary rooms for him to continue his work on Jinnamon."

General Slaughter nodded.

"Of course, my Queen. I will inform my security staff of his presence here."

"Very good. Thank you."

General Slaughter pulled the door closed. "Now for you two," said Kula.

Rasp and Blackjack stood at attention.

"Bradicus, you transform into Blackjack," said Kula.

"Yes ma'am. I figured it was time to get my game face on. I'm ready."

"Hold on," said Kula, "I've been thinking."

"What have you been thinking about?"

"The fastest way to Grimmbell would be by dragoon."

"That would be the fastest way, although I can travel fast and quiet myself. But I have a feeling you do not want me to take flight with a dragoon."

"You are right," said Kula staring into space. "I'm thinking I would like you to go by land."

"You mean you want me out in the open, without using the mole tunnels?"

"I swear to the King of Souls you can actually read my mind." Blackjack stared at Kula. "I speculate."

"Travel at a normal speed," said Kula. "Not at a slow pace but not at a fast pace either."

"Where are you going with this?"

"I have a hunch that Mr. Roko the Dark might pay you a visit along the way."

"You want me to keep this form in hopes he will want to make contact with me?"

"I do. I think Roko likes to challenge you more when you are in animal form."

"You have my curiosity. Why do you think that?"

"Because when you change from one form to the other, the transition process produces a very unique form of energy."

"I guess the process does. I haven't thought a lot about it."

"When you transition, which of the changes produces or uses more energy? Human-to-animal form or vice versa?"

"Nobody's ever asked me that before." Blackjack stared at the floor, saying nothing, then looked up at Kula. "I do believe the only way I will answer that question is when there's only two of us in the room."

"Rasp, you need to leave this room for a while. There's a dragoon outside the door that will take you to your temporary quarters. Go now."

Rasp said nothing, walking to the door and closing it behind him. "Are we good now?" said Kula.

"We are good now," said Blackjack. "The most energy produced is when I go from human form to animal form."

"I had a strong impression that Bradicus to Blackjack involved the stronger magic."

"How and why did you ever even think that? You mean the energy produced when you change?"

"Yes, the energy produced. Do you have a special sense where you can smell a number of types of energy or what?"

"I don't understand."

"I will explain here in a minute. What are your thoughts about meeting with Rodark again?"

"The idea of having Rodark show himself depends on how many goons he has with him."

"I want you to have a spirit runner in front and behind you at all times."

"Thank you, my Queen. My third entity will be able to pick up any disturbances including Rodark if he shows himself."

"I will not take no for an answer," Kula replied, glaring at Bradicus. "I will have Rasp produce at least two spirit runners for you. And I believe I'm going to have a warthog-zebra-tiger type of runner."

"The more the merrier," said Blackjack, producing a smile. "I have seen those type of runners in action before. I think it would be a good idea to have them with me."

"Good, I'm glad you agree with me on the runners. I would not want to lose you to Roco because we were not prepared."

"Plus, the fact, my Queen, I have seen Rodark in action. I believe his power is growing stronger as we speak."

"If Roko… I mean, Rodark, does show up, which I'm pretty sure he will, he wants a bite of you."

"Agreed," said Blackjack. "He wants something to do with me."

"Number one, we will at least have an opportunity to figure out what he wants. And number two, this is the part I really want to tell you about. Now, you have to remember this is only my theory."

"You have my undivided attention."

"At the presenting ceremony, General Slaughter and I came upon a portal that had been opened near the presenting floor."

"Another portal? Could it have been the same one that Jinnamon forced Rodark back into? Maybe the portals were connected?"

"I don't know for sure, but I do know this particular portal hadn't fully closed. For some reason, that specific energy that was keeping the portal open could be the same type that transforms you to a different shape."

His eyes arched. "Wow, that's hard to believe. My energy, the same as a universal portal system."

"I mean, it's only a theory."

"I'm very curious as to how you came up with this idea."

"I've been present when you've made your major change from one form to the other. And it wasn't until I was at the portal near the ceremony that I felt the same sensation when you change over. I actually thought you might have been in the portal, or at least in the area.”

“It’s possible I was in the area if the two portals were connected. It’s also possible that Rodark was going to crash the releasing ceremony. But when Brazel and Cremator produced our temporary portal, he came running to our end. That’s just my theory.”

“It was really bizarre,” said Kula. “It worried me at first. Then my mind blasted off into thousands of questions and possibilities of us being able to harness the power of the portal. It’s an unknown territory, at least it is for me.”

“That is a very intriguing concept, and like you said, scary too. But let’s say you’re right about your theory for the time being; if that’s what it takes to lure Rodark out into the open, then I should take a path to Grimmbell that would invite him to visit me.”

Kula leaned down eye level with Blackjack.

“Do you think we can capture him without destroying him?” she asked.

Blackjack turned, walking to the opening of the wind tunnel and looking down, the wind blowing hard into his face.

“You’re not thinking about jumping, are you?” Kula asked.

“No, of course not. Maybe a guided tour of the tunnels sometime in the future. That would be nice.” “I will personally give you the ride of your life,” said Kula.

Walking back toward Kula, Blackjack stopped a couple feet away. “Are we trying to capture Rodark alone, or both him and his horse?”

“That would depend on how risky it is. I don’t know how Luxen came across a black spirit horse?”

“Maybe I should talk to Luxen before we lay a trap for Rodark.”

“I thought about doing that first, but also figured that Roko is definitely going to try to battle you again and it’s probably going to happen sooner rather than later. He wants you to transform so he can

harness that energy. Along with the fact that we know he’s traveling by the portal system, if he’s figured out how to enter Grimmbell Cemetery via a portal… how many spirits would he destroy?"

"I agree with you, but I believe if he ever… and maybe this is what he's trying to do, but if he ever broke the barrier and got inside Grimmbell Cemetery, I figure he'll try to steal an elder blood brick."

Kula flared a four-foot flame out of each nostril. "I don't even want to think about that happening.

As long as we're speculating, how do we know that he would go for total control of all the spirits?"

"You mean taking control of the King of Souls himself?"

"I think we are both correct, my Queen."

"There are hundreds of scenarios that could take place. We know that one of our biggest challenges is to keep him out of the cemetery. So, I think he will make an attempt to stop you before you get to Grimmbell."

"He will definitely make contact with me, although I don't know when. But Roko the Dark will come at me head on."

Chapter 24: Leaving the Castle

Bradicus leaned against the retaining wall surrounding the front of the landing arena. He quickly noticed the three fighter dragoons perched in their own guard houses, looking down at him.

Kula emerged from the darkness of the tunnel that channeled to the landing arena. A quick glance up at the fighter dragoons produced a smirky smile. "Those are my quick-load dragoons."

"Quick-load dragoons?" said Bradicus. "Those three look as though they're just waiting to kick someone's ass. I would have them positioned there too."

"Yeah, they are smaller than most dragoons, but faster and super strong for their size, designed altogether differently than the bigger fighter dragoons. Built for quick-action fighting in tight spots, like this landing arena. They are highly effective."

Bradicus continued to stare at the elevated dragoons.

"I would almost bet you couldn't make it across the pad before one of those bad boys… oh wait a minute," said Bradicus, looking above the landing pad. "The one in the middle is a female."

"I picked her out myself."

"Does she have a name?"

"Sophia. She's a hard-hitting little bitch."

Bradicus turned his attention to Kula. "How many species of fighter dragoons are there?"

Kula focused on the three dragoons. "Hmm. Let me see…" Her head bobbed to a mental count of the species of dragoons. "Six. As of right now, anyway."

"That's interesting. I will have to keep that in my long-term memory."

"You mean you couldn't just read my mind and figure that all out by yourself?"

"I suppose I could have, but I wasn't quick enough when you started to do the mental count."

"Well then, someday, we will discuss the six species of dragoons over a dozen roasted wild pigs."

"As long as there are no Rarebrook rabbits on the menu," said Bradicus.

"There will be no rabbit on the menu."

Suddenly, Slaughter erupted from the darkness of the landing pad opening. "Kula, my Queen. Rasp has made contact with Cremator."

"How do you mean?" said Kula.

"Rasp informed me, through some type of a mind tap, he could feel that Cremator is still alive. But he's made no verbal contact with him."

"Anything else?" said Kula.

"No, my Queen. Rasp insisted I tell you this before you leave."

"Very well. Keep me informed if anything changes."

"Yes, my Queen." Slaughter turned away from Kula and disappeared into the dark opening of the mountain.

Kula leaned down to eye level with Bradicus. "You don't seem surprised."

"I am relieved, but not entirely surprised. I had a strong feeling that he could make a connection either with Jinn or Cremator, or both."

"That still leaves us with the issue of getting Cremator out of Jinnamon's belly box. How long has it been since you talked to Luxen?"

"Two years," said Bradicus.

"Did he receive you well the last time you talked to him?"

"Yes, he did. Even if we do trap him, we still need to figure out how to get him off the horse. To break the bond."

"Do you really think that Luxen is going to let you use his horse?"

"I don't know for sure."

"And another problem comes to mind," said Kula. "How are you going to control a black spirit horse once you're on it?"

"Maybe I can get lessons from Luxen."

"That's funny, when the only way I know how to control a black spirit horse is to sit in the saddle.

And when you sit in the saddle, you make that

powerful connection to the horse." Kula nudged Bradicus in the butt with her tail. "Then you could have another problem of not being able to dismount. You are trapped there forever."

Bradicus nodded, eyes locked onto Kula, but he didn't speak.

"Yes, you're thinking about that. I don't want to see an energy source such as yours connecting with the energy source of a black spirit horse. That could be a catastrophe."

"Actually, that's a great idea," said Bradicus. "Why didn't I think of that?"

"You can't be serious. You could be trapped forever."

Bradicus stared at the valley below. "What a great way to get on the same level as Roko. There must be a way to disengage from the black horse when needed."

"I don't know if I feel right letting you do this. I think maybe we're jumping ahead of ourselves. We need to back up. The first thing we need to do is talk to Luxen; maybe he'll have a better way."

"In either case, Kula, I have to talk to Luxen about his black spirit horse for two possible outcomes.

To free Cremator from Jinn's belly drop and to defeat Roko."

"Then we have a plan. You will go to Grimmbell to talk to Luxen about his horse. Meanwhile, General Slaughter and I will be investigating the attack at the ceremony presentation. Still a lot of unanswered questions that need responses."

"Do you think Rodark had something to do with it?"

"I'm not sure yet but I'm going to find out. What if Rodark makes contact with you before you get to Grimmbell? Do you have a plan?" Kula asked.

"I have a plan."

Kula hunched down, ready to thrust her body off the landing pad. "What do you say we talk about that over a feast of roast pig?"

"I look forward to that. Be careful."

Kula catapulted herself off the landing pad and into the air.

Bradicus watched her disappear into the horizon.

"Shit. Maybe I should've asked her for a ride to the valley floor. No worries. That gives me a little bit more time to think."

Chapter 25: Road Trip to Grimmbell

Bradicus traveled the single-track pass down the mountainside to the valley floor. With the sun setting low on the horizon, he settled in for the night under a small rock overhang.

Tearing off a fist-sized piece of the food ball he had received from Ella, he gazed into a medium-sized campfire. Chewing slowly, his mind wandered.

Roko… Well, now it's Rodark. What kind of a transformation process does the dark horse have to perform to mold a resistant life force into its own use? Do I really want to ride a black spirit horse? Maybe I'll sleep on it.

Bradicus woke half an hour before sunrise. Feeling no hunger, he decided traveling by horse might be the smartest mode of transportation to Grimmbell.

I don't want to transform into Blackjack at this time. Not yet, anyway. Transforming could be some type of locator device for Rodark to find me.

Kula could be right. Maybe this whole thing was set up to trap me.

My transformation energy may be similar to portal transport energy? What if I can create my own type of portal? That would be totally cool. And dangerous. I think I will keep that to myself.

He climbed on top of the rock formation that served as his house for the evening, looking at the lay of the land, showing one of the larger tobacco farms approximately thirty minutes away.

Three silver coins later, Bradicus was the owner of a healthy, dark gray and brown stud by the name of Britannica and later that afternoon, he made it to the outside walls of Grimmbell.

Approaching the spirit protection barrier, he could see the essence of spirits moving in and out of the spirit wall, the first of many checkpoints before entering Grimmbell. The spirit wall barrier had been created by the

King of the Souls himself when the first and present-day granite stone walls were erected; the same walls built around Grimmbell Cemetery on the site of the first battle in the Valley of the Tomb Sleepers.

He could feel the presence of spirits lightly bumping his shoulders and pushing at his back. One particular life-force knocked his hat off, whispering in his ear.

"Are you sure you want to enter? What is your business here?" Britannica reared, lashing out with his front hooves in the air.

"Easy, big boy. It's only the spirits testing our courage." Bradicus quickly dismounted as Britannica kicked at a passing armless horse-riding spirit standing atop his saddle, gripping the reins with his teeth while bending over, showing the full spectrum of his spiritual butt.

"Well now, I haven't seen that one before. They must send him out first for entertainment purposes."

Suddenly, the mood became darker. Bradicus saw Katmando, a double-colored spirit rider he'd been familiar with before. Katmando came trotting toward him.

Katmando was a burly, blocky, brick-shithouse-shaped bull-man figure, brown-rust in color while his horse was snow white during daylight hours. But when the light of day turned to moonlight, Katmando turned into Anamosa; a tall, slender, blue-white witch figure on a dark red rust-colored horse.

Bradicus guided his horse, quickly transforming into Blackjack. Pulling his spirit sword out of the sheath, his hairs were alert, high and tight. Flicking his wrists, the orange titanium claws flared with color and he charged Katmando on foot, yelling at the approaching spirit.

"Katmando, I am Blackjack, royal messenger of Queen Kula and I will defend myself if needed."

Galloping at top speed, Katmando dismounted his horse, touching ground level on all fours at a dead run. He lowered his head, blowing snot clouds of dark red dust out of his nostrils.

"That square bull-headed son of a cow pie is going to try to split my head in two. Fifty feet till impact."

Blackjack ran faster, lowering his head but keeping his eyes on the target. "Blackjack. This is Brazel. You can't win going head-to-head with him."

"I know that, but thanks for the warning. Got to go."

At three feet from impact, Blackjack stretched flat, sliding under Katmando and lightly slicing a two-foot cut along his belly. "Tag. You're it."

Katmando grunted, sinking his feet into the earth, coming to a sudden stop. Spinning around, he spit on the ground. "Dammit, you're much faster than last time. Have you been training?"

"I don't know if I would call it training," said Blackjack. "More like survival."

"That's the best way to train. Life or death. No bullshit. Get it?"

"I didn't know that spirits had a sense of humor."
"Some do," said Katmando.

"I found that out a few minutes ago, seeing the spirit riding his horse without his pants."

"Oh yeah, you're talking about Frank-no-pants. He's what we call a friendly free radical spirit. They're very good at distracting individuals coming up to the wall, giving us a chance to size up the sightseer, to determine if the visitor's friend or foe."

"Well, Frank-no-pants is a very good diversion because I didn't see you until the last minute. So, I guess your strategy is working."

"That's good to hear and make sure you tell the King of Souls when you see him."

"I'm not here to see the king; I need to see Luxen."

"Luxen? Are you sure about that?"

"I'm sure."

"If you are a friend of Luxen…"

"I am," said Blackjack.

"Okay, if you are a friend of Luxen, what is printed on the cup of Luxen?"

Taking his shirt off and turning his back to Katmando, Blackjack transformed to Bradicus.

Katmando kneeled in front of him. "Oh my gosh, you are familiar with the cup of Luxen. You were there. On the battlefield. With him."

"I was there. That's all I'm going to say."

"I haven't seen the cup," said Katmando, "but I have

come across spirits who have some knowledge of its enormous power."

"Have you ever spoken to Luxen yourself?" Bradicus asked.

"One time, when he first arrived here with the eight of kings."

"Are you a protector for him?"

"Let's just say we made a deal."

"I hope it was a good deal?" said Bradicus.

"He made it possible for me to get revenge for the death of my family. I look out for the King of Souls first and foremost, then Luxen, warning him if anybody is coming to see him."

"Do you need to warn him that I am here to speak to him?"

"No, I don't. So how can I assist you?"

Bradicus transmuted back to Blackjack. "Have you seen any portal activity lately in or around Grimmbell?"

"I haven't seen any activity during the daytime, but Anamosa saw strange activity during the moonlight hours."

"What kind of *strange activity?*"

"A vortex of wind pulled her toward some type of opening in the air a couple of days back. Said she heard the sound of pounding of a thousand horses."

"That's interesting," said Blackjack. "I have heard that same sound. What else?"

"She watched a black spirit rider appear."

"From the vortex opening?"

"She never said, although she did say the rider actually dismounted his horse."

"He got off his horse?" said Blackjack.

"Yes, and his horse stayed right there with him, never leaving his side."

"The horse is his connection. Then what happened?"

"She watched the dark entity walk back and forth while moving his hands from left to right, as if trying to figure out how to get around an invisible wall. Then it kneeled down, digging in the dirt, right out there," he said, pointing toward Tower 1. "I don't know what it was looking for."

"Or maybe what it was burying," said Blackjack.

"Did it know you were watching it?"

"No, it didn't."

"How do you know?"

"Because you must remember that by the light of the moon, I become Anamosa. I'm not the same form as in the daylight. Her intellect is much more powerful at night than I am in the day hours."

"Do you know if Anamosa checked it out? Did she dig anything up?"

"I won't know anything more until we change forms this evening at dusk."

"That's interesting and worrisome and the sooner I talk to Luxen the better."

"Well, wait a minute," said Kat. "Anamosa did say something about green dust on her fingers."

"Green dust?" said Blackjack, snapping to attention.

"Yes, and she collected a small sample of it in a bag."

"A sample, you say?"

"That's what she said. It made her night spell work far more effectively."

Roko the Dark is up to something, and it could have something to do with Grimmbell. Is Rodark and Arune about to make an attack on Grimmbell?

Katmando mounted his horse. "I have to go, and you are clear to pass."

Blackjack watched the boxy, bullish, manlike figure disappear into the spirit barrier wall followed by a scream when a pool of blood sprayed out of the wall onto the ground.

"I hope it wasn't anyone I knew."

***

A cobblestone walkway led to the signing ledger, a podium located halfway between the spirit wall and the 120-foot granite wall surrounding the eighty-three acres of Grimmbell Cemetery.

Each and every cobblestone was marked by one drop of blood, hand mixed and poured by a tomber. The ground earthers combed the battlefield on foot and with the assistance of earthers in the surrounding five towers obtaining a bird's eye view of the goriest fighting, they located the bloodiest site or sites of the battlefield enabling them to set up their underground living tombs to cultivate the blood dirt.

This was the blood that seeped its way into the underground tomb; here, the famed and magical blood bricks would be calculated, formed, mixed, weighed, stacked, housed, tasted, and given the stamp of approval by the same four tomb earthers who'd been working the blood brick drop work area in that crypt all their lives. The time required to make a blood brick was twenty years, making these a precious commodity over which battles had been fought. On some occasions, a battle had been purposely fought over a tomb site just to rejuvenate the blood supply. And the story went on...

When walking on the cobblestone sidewalk in route to the signing podium, some Grimmbell spirits lived and harvested the fields of candy corncobs growing parallel to the cobblestone walkway.

Occasionally, they would throw handfuls of candy pellets at passersby, along with an occasional whole ear of candy corn attached to a nasty note from a friend or relative from inside the walls of Grimmbell.

It was all an attempt to scare people away.

To the ones unsure of why they were at the entrance of Grimmbell, the candy corn ears would stick to them like shit on a shingle and burn them while their bodyweight increased to the point where they fell on the cobblestones. The candy corn spirit sprinters would then come to collect you, never to be seen again. Once you signed the Carnelian rock ledger sitting on the signing podium—and if your signature were to be accepted, then began the walk with the unknown to the ringing of the Grimmbell gate bell.

***

Blackjack walked toward the signing podium, hundreds of ears of corn bombarding the walkway like rain on a stormy day. The corncobs hissed, spun, fizzled and zipped around on the ground, exploding, sending small flumes of thick colored dust into the air.

Blackjack couldn't see in front of him, but he saw the cobblestone path at his feet. Keeping his head down, he followed the path, sensing the Grimmbell front gatekeepers all around him, hidden within the heavy dust clouds, all analyzing Blackjack while escorting him to the front gate.

Blackjack continued walking.

I've been here before on official business, so I shouldn't have any problems.

When he arrived at the signing podium, the sheet of Carnelian cut rock glowed enough for him to sign his name. With the last stroke of his name's last letter, he heard an echoing of many voices saying his name over and over and something with a firm grip grabbed his arm.

Looking at his limb, he could see a large bony hand with a tattoo on each of the seven fingers. A voice broke the silence. "Follow us, Blackjack."

Blackjack said nothing, bowing his head. The thick colored dust cloud had thinned a little bit, allowing Blackjack to see the silhouettes of his immediate ushers.

These things are tall, thick and old. They remind me of giant walking trees.

Arriving at the main gate, a dozen more corncobs smashed into the gate, followed by a hideous laugh and horse hooves pounding off in the distance.

"Must have been Frank-no-pants' crazy-ass spirit." Blackjack stopped at the front gate with his escort.

The fog had disappeared for the most part, revealing one gatekeeper at his side. The gatekeeper stood nine feet tall, no facial features able to be seen due to the overlap across its face, its brilliant red-gold- green-colored dragon-skinned robe dragging on the ground, a skeletal scorpion-tipped tail attached.

Looking at Blackjack from the other side of a very black, thick-fenced gate stood a Grimmbell earther.

"Greetings! I am Rambunctious, the earther hall walker, but understandably most call me Ram," Ram said, tilting his small furry head to one side. "You are special. The body that holds three souls." Ram glanced at Blackjack. "Your fur is quite beautiful, and I'm sure many would love to hide you in their belt pouch. Be aware, furry friend. By the way, are we related?"

Wow, that was a mouthful. "No, I don't think we are related," said Blackjack. *At least I hope not.*

Rather an odd earther, but I have been labeled odd myself.

"Would you like to see someone inside the walls of Grimmbell?"

"Yes, I would. I need to speak to Luxen, guardian of the Tri-Eight."

"Well, twist my pickle, you go right for the jugular, don't you?"

"Well, I have business with Luxen."

"Very well, keeper of the three souls, the first thing you need to do is ring the Grimmbell gate bell."

"Of course, I was just waiting for your command."

Ram nodded his head at Blackjack who then pulled the rope tied to the bell hanging at the very top of the 120-foot granite wall.

The bell's long hollow bong pulsated down the wall, echoing through the cobblestones and stinging Blackjack's feet.

"Damn, that bell has volume."

"It sounds great," said Ram with a smile. "That bell notifies every soul, spirit, essence, and life-force dead or alive that you are entering the gates of Grimmbell."

"It's nice to be announced," said Blackjack. "Makes me feel important."

The hooded gatekeeper stepped up to the black iron gate. As he extended one of his tattooed fingers into the lock box, the gate clicked and lurched forward one inch toward Blackjack. And in that instant, the gatekeeper dissolved in a cloud of colored mist and settled back into the spirit barrier wall.

Ram pushed the gate open and bowed down without losing eye contact; he extended his hand out to his left. "Shall we?"

Blackjack walked through the gate then watched Ram struggle to pull it closed. *Bang!*

"Please stay close. I wouldn't want to lose you."

"Yeah, me neither," said Blackjack. "I was inside the walls a few years ago, and came through the same gate but don't remember going this way."

"That's because the passageway changes every single day, sometimes more. Security, you understand?"

"I understand," said Blackjack. "Blood bricks."

"Yes. Do you know that this wall here…" he said, dragging his hand on the surface, "that the surrounding wall of Grimmbell was constructed by hand, no magic involved?"

"And the secret strength of the wall is a blood brick cemented into a secret position," said Blackjack. "Its location in the wall is unknown to anybody."

"Wow," said Ram. "Your history of Grimmbell appears to be quite adequate. The secret, my shiny- furred friend, is the mix of both, the blood brick being magic in how it was made, and the wall being built by non-magical hands with over eight hundred million mud bricks stacked 120 feet high, surrounding eighty-three and seven-eighths of a mile of Grimmbell. That was one impressive group effort. Do you also know the bricks were fire dried by the dragoons themselves?"

"No, I didn't know that," said Blackjack. "I'm assuming the heat from the dragoons' fire would make the mud bricks have a special seal, making them weatherproof and very strong."

"That's right, and another reason why the wall is unique," said Ram. "I don't want to bore you with history lessons but there are another five specialties interwound into the bricks."

"No, not at all. It's not boring," said Blackjack, looking up at the wall. "Although I wonder if this information is scripted on Queen Kula's wings?"

"That's a good question, but I don't have an answer. Maybe someday when we have more time, we could share information."

"I would like that. Good information is vital to survival."

"Survival is the key. I know that most of Grimmbell's history is recorded on the reigning Queen's wings, although we do keep specific events of Grimmbell history in the earthers' archives."

Blackjack looked in a 360-degree circle, noticing the

main gate hadn't disappeared from eyesight and yet he counted three right-hand and two left-hand turns in the last twenty-five minutes.

"Excuse me, Ram. I've noticed that the main gate looks like it is twenty feet behind us, but I know we have walked farther than twenty feet. Is this a trick?"

"No trick. Well, kind of a trick," said Ram. "The cobblestone pathway that we are walking on is continuously spinning counterclockwise under our feet as we walk and talk. According to my brick count, we have covered roughly one mile."

"Another security measure?" asked Blackjack.

Ram nodded his head yes. "Another security measure. Ah, here we are. Gate number 399."

Blackjack twisted his neck to see the gate behind him had disappeared. Another entrance of the same size, shape, and color of the front gate stood before him and Ram.

Ram stood smiling. "This is your gate."

Blackjack walked up to the gate and looking through the bars, could see the same cobblestone walkway twisting, turning, and splitting off into countless walkways, branching off in all directions throughout the cemetery. Some of the pathways lead to and stopped at the front door of huge burial tombs and crypts. One tomb door in particular caught his attention, hand-sculpted in a lighter colored green jade with streaks of white every five feet resembling lightning bolts.

"That one is quite beautiful. Who was it built for?"

"Yes, that's a grand structure, isn't it? You should see it in the morning sun. But I'm sorry to say I cannot help you with that question. I am the official hall walker, so I've never been inside the cemetery itself."

"How do I get inside?"

"I have notified the Queen of the Keys. She should be here…"

"There you are my sweetheart."

Blackjack turned to see a young girl with beautiful skin, robed in a green and black dress following her strawberry-colored hair and touching the ground. Her eyes changed color each time she blinked.

"This is Cryptsee. She will take you inside the

cemetery."

Smiling and extending her hand, the young girl approached Blackjack.

Blackjack pushed his hand out toward hers, but her hand didn't meet with his, instead, she quickly touched his chest with her delicate fingertips. "I hope you don't mind. Your fur is so beautiful. I can see my reflection." Lowering her hand, she stepped back with a soft smile.

"Not at all. May I ask how old you are?"

"You may. I am eleven years old." She tilted her head to one side. "At least, I was eleven when I died in human form. In this particular form…" Squeezing her eyes, she looked at Ram, who mouthed the words 'one-oh-one'. "Oh yeah, that's right, I'm one hundred and one in this life form. I had a birthday two weeks ago. I will have to send you an invitation for next year."

"Yes, maybe next year, but please let me know ahead of time and I will deliver the invitations personally."

"This is where I must leave you, Blackjack," said Ram. "Cryptsee will be your guide into the cemetery where you will find Luxen."

Cryptsee walked up to the gate, revealing a ring of keys that appeared suddenly out of the sleeve of her robe. With both hands, she brought the keys to her mouth and whispering some type of dialect, made the keys vibrate.

"I have never heard that type of tongue."

Cryptsee inserted the key into the lockbox of the gate, turning the key to the right, then to the left. The gate came alive, a large hole appearing in the center of it like a lion's mouth surrounded by black steel teeth, which would ring out *clang, clang*, each time the mouth of the gate closed.

"Don't worry," said Cryptsee, smiling in relation to the ear-piercing sound. "The buzzing only lasts for a week or so. Just one thing, when we walk through the gate, you need to hold my hand. Do not let go until we get through it, or you will die."

"Okay, I'll take your word for it. Has someone died before?" asked a concerned Blackjack. "Yes, but he didn't hold my hand. He let go to fight the magic inside the gate."

"Why did he do that?"

"Because he was a fool," said Cryptsee.

"I am no fool. I will hold your hand with pleasure."

Cryptsee smiled at Blackjack. "I like to hold your hand. Your fur is so soft." Cryptsee pulled at Blackjack's hand, guiding him through the teeth of death. The gate closed its mouth with a loud *bang*.

Jumping from the unexpected noise, Blackjack looked back at the gate. "Damn, that gate is hungry."

"It should be. It's been a long time since it's eaten a live soul. Come on, follow me."

Blackjack walked quietly behind the young girl, through the abundance of battle treasures laid upon the ground of Grimmbell where huge numbers of fallen warriors of a thousand battles had come to die.

He tried to read the names etched on some of the tombstones but there were too many.

He walked by crypts with solid gold doors protecting their dead, many still under construction by earthers and spirits alike.

"Remember, and this is essential; *do not* look into the eyes of a spirit for very long."

"Why not? What happens?"

"They'll be able to look outside the gates of Grimmbell through your eyes to find friends and family and try and talk to them, but they won't be able to communicate with the outside which will make them mad. They will want to fight you, so be aware."

"Do not fight with the spirits? I got it. How far till we meet up with Luxen?"

"Not very far now. We will go up this walkway near the soul tree, but we'll turn off to the left down the long hill. That's where the Tri-Eight are housed."

Blackjack noticed the abundance of warrior spirits housed near the soul tree, the spirits definitely watching every move he made. Blackjack touched the top of his sword.

"I know you are there, my sword of life. Don't be sleeping today." Walking backwards, Cryptsee noticed Blackjack studying the tree of souls.

"It's a beautiful sight, isn't it? My soul hangs from that tree somewhere. Don't worry, they are protecting me and many others."

Blackjack reached the crest of the hill. Looking down, he could see a two-story brick house, a barn and some type of rock formation towering out of the ground and into the sky eighty-something feet.

It appears to be some type of important land marker.

Hey everyone, look what we got in this part of the cemetery.

Inside the rock formation was a dark hole.

"This is where I leave you," said Cryptsee. "The towering, pointed rock formation is the entrance to Grimmbell Prison Depository. Luxen will meet you at the gate. I have another visitor at gate 121. Don't forget, birthday party next year."

"I won't forget," said Blackjack.

He watched Cryptsee cross the top of the hill and eventually disappear out of sight. "Okay, let's go see a man about a horse."

Blackjack descended the hill, noticing four thick rock poles strategically located at each corner of the prison property. A wood and stone one-story house with a large barn stood to the left of the prison opening. The wooden gate in front of him itself stood alone with no fence line attached to it.

Although he could feel an invisible surge of energy on either side of the entry, he walked up to the gate. Looking down, he saw a wooden bucket full of rocks and painted on each was, 'Throw at house'. "Really? Throwing rocks? Okay." He picked up one of the rocks and throwing it at the house, the rock bounced off just left of the front door.

A man emerged from the prison cave opening inside the rock formation. He stared at Blackjack. Not saying anything, he looked back toward the dark hole, making a subtle hand gesture with his fingers.

Two more men stepped out of the darkness into the daylight, the three huddling together.

With hand gestures and much rubbernecking, the three broke the huddle, two of the men sitting on a wooden bench outside the black hole entrance of the rock formation.

The leader of the pack slowly walked up the slight grade of the hill toward Blackjack.

Suddenly, the barn doors blasted open, releasing a horse so black one's eyesight would lose depth perception, plunging into an abyss of darkness and uncontrolled falling.

Blackjack became dizzy and his stomach weak. He quit the stare factor at the horse, looking away every two to three seconds to keep from participating in a barf fest.

This horse has uncontrolled power bleeding all over it. What is its purpose?

"Blackjack, is that you?" Blackjack broke his glare from the black horse, turning his attention to the man coming out of the barn. "Open the gate. Come on in. Don't worry about the horse; it won't chase you. At least I don't think it will."

"You don't think it will? That's reassuring."

Blackjack watched the black horse immediately charge after the group leader of the three prisoners, crashing him into an electrified invisible barrier between one of the four stone prison boundary markers.

An explosion of sparks catapulted the man thirty yards backwards, rolling him on the ground like a rubber ball. The black horse caught up with the fallen man, performing a strategic hoof-stomping dance all around him, then casually pissed on his face. Charging away from his stunned victim, it raced around the spiked rock like a piece of black licorice being twisted by giant hands.

The barn man approached Blackjack with a chuckle in his throat. "Must have been excited to see you?"

"Luxen, my friend, good to see you. What was that all about?"

"I'm not sure, could be the fact that you look like an eighty-five-pound, multicolored Rarebrook rabbit with devil eyes and a matching pair of titanium claws."

"Oh, I spooked him? I find that hard to believe."

"Why is that, my friend?" said Luxen.

"If I am not mistaken, which I rarely am"…he turned his view toward the horse which had made its way to the other side the barn, ripping his way through a large patch of devil's dick brush…"that horse is a black spirit horse. How in the multiverse did you get your hands on that particular breed? They are the glue that connects a black spirit rider to its horse, outlaws in the animal world. Ruthless. Spirit killers."

"It was a gift," said Luxen, looking at the horse digging at the needle brush. "A gift, if you can call it that. A present given to me at the Battle of the Eight Kings. You were there."

"Have you seen or spoken to your friend since it appeared that night at the battle?"

"No, I haven't. That particular entity was not in a talkative mood. It was after one thing only, the cup."

"You have kept the horse hidden for the past fourteen years?"

"I don't know if I really kept it hidden. Kula flies over on a regular basis, so I'm pretty darn certain she knows the horse is here"…Luxen nodded his head at the horse…"right here in this block of cemetery dirt."

Blackjack stared at the horse. "You have kept it hidden from the other black spirit riders?"

"That part could be true, or they haven't made an attempt to challenge me for the horse, but Kula knows it is here."

"That's why I'm here. Luxen, I'm here to borrow your horse. I need him to speak the graffiti tongue language in connection with a belly drop dragoon. We need to open her belly drop. And I'm assuming that a black spirit horse is the only one that can speak graffiti tongue?"

Luxen grinned. "Yes, that's the horse you want. Actually, that's the only black spirit horse that can read and speak graffiti tongue."

"Have you ever ridden the horse?" asked Blackjack. "I have done, and I do ride the horse."

"How do you ride a horse that tricks you to ride it, trapping you as its prisoner forever? How did you get away from that?"

"I have an advantage that most do not."

"You drank from 'The Cup of Wells'."

"No surprise there," said Luxen. "My gift and maybe my curse. This is what I know so far. First and foremost, your life force is taken from you and transformed to the horse's spirit and soul. And I'm not done yet. That energy is altered into other functions inside the black spirit world of which I don't know the origin of."

"Untapped power sources," said Blackjack. "That's what I've gathered in my travels, but I cannot confirm my findings. Have you had any interaction with portals inside the walls of Grimmbell?"

Luxen shook his head. "No, but I think you need to know something first."

"What is that?"

"I ride the black spirit horse bareback."

"That's how you do it? That's how you can dismount the horse? You don't have the saddle making the spirit connection?"

"I never said that," said Luxen.

"You do have a saddle?"

"I do have a saddle. Maybe I should back up a little bit."

"Please, back up and continue."

"It is true in the last days of battling the eight kings, the keeper of the cup did present himself to me. He saved my life. And much more, he gave me the ability to live thousands of lives to do what I wanted with them."

"That I remember," said Blackjack.

"The evening, before I was to go to meet the eight kings and take their crowns in victory, the keeper of the cup asked me what I was going to do with the eight kings."

"What did you tell him?"

"I told him that they should be locked up and never be able to use their power in such an insignificant way."

"What did the keeper of the cup say?"

"He told me that there would only be one place where the eight kings could be housed. To be guarded by me without them being able to use their royal blood birthright powers to govern."

"Grimmbell Prison Depository?" said Blackjack.

"That's right," said Luxen. "Not just Grimmbell itself, but yes, the prison depository. I didn't necessarily ask for that duty."

"Did he say why you have to be the one to be their curator person of the prison?"

"He said, and I quote, 'I trust you will follow and

fulfill your request. For I have given you Life'.

Kind of hard to say no to a deity."

"Exactly," said Blackjack.

"How do you say no to a god of some kind or to a god of any kind? In any case, that was the deal along with the horse."

"How did he get a black spirit horse?" asked Blackjack.

"I don't know. When I woke the next morning, there it stood, looking down at me."

"Was the saddle on the horse?"

"No, it wasn't, it was lying on the ground and inside one of the butt packs was a leather wrap with instructions inside."

"Instructions for a horse?"

"I think it was more of a contract," said Luxen. "But yes, there were instructions."

"What did the contract say?"

"I was to present the contract to the King of Souls. If he accepted the terms, the eight kings would be housed at the prison depository, and I would be their guardian until all eight kings died a natural death. They could not commit suicide or be killed by one of the other kings."

"Natural death?" said Blackjack. "That could be fifty years."

"Like I said, a blessing for the cup of life *and* a curse because I am here, all in one. Natural death is the only way that the king's spirits would be released into the Grimmbell Cemetery. In the event of their natural death, their spirits and souls would become freed to the soul master by way of transportation from the holding cells to the preparation site on the back of this black spirit horse."

"You have to watch everyone who's in the prison depository, don't you?"

"At first, I didn't have to, I only had to watch the kings. But since I had the ability to check all the holding cells with great accuracy and speed because of the black spirit horse, they gave me the full-time job."

"So, you've been here for the past seven years?"

"Yup."

"You're right. You were given a gift and a curse at

the same time." Luxen sighed. "Could've been worse."

"Have you ever had the saddle on?"

"Yes, I have."

"How in the hell did you use the saddle and not get trapped?"

"I found a secret that works for me," said Luxen.

Blackjack leaned toward Luxen. "If you have the secret of how to dismount a black spirit horse whenever you want to, then you could be the most wanted and hunted man in the Valley of the Tomb Sleepers."

"Actually, I wouldn't be the most hunted person in the multiverse."

"You wouldn't?"

"No. *We* would be the most hunted people in the multiverse, because I'm going to tell you how I did it. I might need your skills again to fight another battle with me over this information."

"I'm not sure I want to know. I'm already being hunted by Roko the Dark." Luxen frowned. "Roko? I thought he was a friend of yours."

"He is, but it's a long story," said Blackjack.

"You need my horse to fight Roko, right?"

"I need your horse to fight Rodark. I have definitely thought about going against him head-on for sure, but I definitely need your horse to free another friend from the belly of an unconscious belly drop dragoon."

"Well, my friend, if you're going to have any type of control over this horse, you are going to need to know the secret."

"What is this secret?"

"The secret for me," Luxen said, placing his hand on his chest, "is a handmade saddle blanket."

"A saddle blanket?" said Blackjack. "That's the key to not getting trapped on a black spirit horse?

What kind of a saddle blanket?"

"A special kind of saddle blanket. I found out if you block the connection between the saddle and the horse, you can control the horse and even dismount."

"It's that easy," said Blackjack.

"I don't think there is anything easy about it. There are other stipulations."

"What kind of stipulations?"

Luxen inhaled deeply and let the breath go. "Back pain, burning hands, delusions and one time, the horse bolted at such a super speed to the point where my brain couldn't focus on my surroundings, causing me to plunge off the horse and vomit."

"Super speed. Okay, I think Brazel could help me out with the super speed."

"That's when the delusional part kicked in, I found myself crawling on the ground, picking up rocks, thinking they were actually my own beating heart."

"Blackjack. I need to interrupt. This is Brazel." "Brazel, what do you have for me?"

"You cannot ride any black spirit horse."

"Why not?"

"I did some checking on your request."

"And."

"Your energy when you transform has some of the same electrical DNA as the portals."

"What does that mean?"

"It's very possible that if you were to attempt to ride the horse with or without a saddle or even bareback, your energies could open at least two portals, maybe three."

"Is that bad?"

"The portals would rip you into pieces. End of story. Lights out. Do not pass go. You're history."

"Okay, I get the point. What percentage is very possible?"

"98.7."

"Blackjack. Hello," said Luxen. "What's going on? Your lips are moving. Who are you talking to?"

"An old friend."

"You connected with a family spirit here?"

"Sort of. Luxen, do you have the final say in what happens to the kings?"

"I have the final say, except for death by natural causes. When I took their crowns, I took their lives too. All of them."

"Because you wear the four bands on each wrist, correct?"

"There is more than just one bonding element to the

control I have over the eight. The crowns are a key element to the control I possess.”

“What would you say to having the most influential king of the eight mount up on Black Beauty there and help me set a trap for Roko?”

“You need to catch this Roko guy that bad?”

“Yes, I do. I need to put an end to his madness.”

Looking at the ground, Luxen rubbed his chin. “King Rozet would be your man. He is the one who came out of the double dungeon prison entrance when you arrived.”

“What did the kings lose when they surrendered to you?”

“Everything,” said Luxen. “All the gold, silver, jewels, land, cattle, horses, castles, power, respect, and family.”

“There we go,” said Blackjack. “Family.”

“Why this particular king?” said Luxen.

“Because he has a large family,” said Blackjack.

“Yes, he does. Nine children. Seven boys and two girls, the girls being the youngest. How did you know that?”

“It’s a long story. A friend told me. How often, if at all, are the family members allowed to visit?”

“They are allowed one visit for one hour every three years.”

“That will be the deciding factor,” said Blackjack. “That will be the bond. The handshake. Being able to see his children more often. If we have to make a deal with him, can we allow him to see his family more frequently?”

“You want me to give this man special privileges? Do you remember what terrible things this man instigated at the battle?”

“I remember, but maybe a second chance to prove himself.”

“I didn’t think you were the second-chance type of man?”

“I’m not saying he’s innocent, but there were eight men making decisions concerning that battle.”

“Okay, for argument’s sake, if I let him go on this mission, we still have to get him on the horse. I can ride the horse because I have a barrier, a blanket that blocks the black horse connection."

"Yes, you told me that, but you haven't told me what the secret is?"

"In my case, it's skin."

"What kind of skin?"

"Human skin."

"You have a man rug as your saddle blanket?" asked Blackjack. "Yes, sort of."

"Sort of? Someone from the battle?"

"No."

"Should I keep asking questions or do you want me to shut up?"

Gazing into the horizon, Luxen spoke. "When I came back from the war with the eight kings, I caught my wife in bed with another man. She tried to explain to me that he was just a friend, and nothing happened between them. She was lonely, scared and needed a man to hold her at night." Luxen paused, staring at the ground. "Someone had informed her that I had been killed in battle, so I guess I don't blame her now, but back then, when I first got back from that war, I was mad at everything. Never really knowing the truth, I just couldn't control myself, so I killed both her and her friend. And after that, I skinned him and tanned his hide. Then I saw the error of what I had done."

"Wait a minute, you have the power of the cup. You could've saved them both. It was a mistake. An accident. I could see that happening."

"That's what I thought too. So, I tried to save them, but it didn't work. I killed my wife."

"Why didn't it work?" asked Blackjack.

"It took me a while to figure it out, but I noticed these tattoo symbols on her friend. I later found out that he was a shaman."

"How does that change things?" asked Blackjack.

"Another shaman told me that he had performed a protection spell to protect her. But in this case, he was actually the spell himself."

"So, this human shaman skin is a layer of enormous protection. That's why you couldn't save them, because the protection spell is still working after his death?"

"That's right," said Luxen. "I couldn't save them

even if I wanted to. I was shit out of luck."

"I'm sorry, Luxen."

"No, you can't tell me that. I deserve what I got. With great power comes great responsibility. You are the first person I've told that story to, but I don't think you've traveled all this way to hear my sob story."

"Sometimes, it's better to keep one's mouth shut and listen," said Blackjack.

"Well said, Bradicus Blackjack. We need to get back to business. Tell me more about this Roko the Dark character."

"Roko is an earther friend; well, he *was* a friend until a black spirit horse trapped him, transforming him to the dark side of the spirit world. Now the new Roko—otherwise known as Rodark—is attempting to harness and change the power source of Grimmbell, while blasting through the portals stealing spirits, killing creatures to make screamer's dust, and he has taken body parts from a tobacco spirit reader who at this moment is trapped inside the belly of a dragon."

Luxen stuffed his hands in his pockets. "You don't make things easy, do you?"

"We both know there is nothing easy to the game of life."

"So true," said Luxen. "So, how are we going to get the black spirit horse to allow Rozet to ride him, and what is his reward if he lives through this plan?"

"I have an idea how King Rozet can ride the black spirit horse."

"You do?" asked Luxen.

"Yes, it just came to me. But first, I have to check with my friend Brazel to make sure my guidance doesn't kill the king."

"And his reward?" said Luxen.

"I can't answer for that. You—and only you—have control over that decision."

"I'll figure that out," said Luxen. "If he does come back alive."

"Sounds fair to me. There is one more thing I need to make this work."

"What do you need?"

“I need total control of Rozet.”

Luxen glared at Blackjack. “I would have to give you control of the crown?”

“Only for a short time. I promise you will get it back.”

“I trust you, Blackjack. If for some reason Rozet thinks that he can escape, you can destroy him by destroying the crown. Is that understood? He runs, he dies.”

“Understood,” said Blackjack.

Chapter 26: A Ring of Gold

Luxen rolled up his shirt sleeve, revealing eight gold bands clasped around his bicep. He closed his eyes and whispered a lengthy phrase to himself. The top gold band made a popping noise and released its grip, opening a small gap within the circle of gold.

Opening his eyes and removing the inch-wide band from his arm, he pushed it into Blackjack's chest. "This is it, huh?"

"That's the connection between you and King Rozet now."

Blackjack held the circle of gold in his hands, flipping it to the front and back. "So, this is his invisible leash, so to speak," he said, carefully rolling the golden circlet between his fingers. "What kind of gems are these?" He picked at the stones with his index finger.

"They are birth stones," said Luxen.

"Birth stones for what? There must be over a hundred embedded on the outside of this crown." "I don't know," said Luxen. "I asked him once, but he never answered."

Holding the crown toward the sun, Blackjack said, "These gems are rare."

"Rare, as in the power they hold or who made them and how?"

"All of the above," said Blackjack, catching the light from the sun. "The stones are interesting. They have a delayed sparkle effect."

"A what?" said Luxen.

"Wow, wow, and wow," said Blackjack. "These gems were cut by lightning."

"Are you telling me the stones in that crown were shaped by lightning from the sky?" Luxen asked. "That's exactly what I'm saying. Unbelievable, I know, but it's an old, old technique used by…"

"Used by gods?" said Luxen.

"Yes, Gods and undergods."

"Are you sure about that?"

Holding the crown in front of Luxen, Blackjack ventured, "How does the crown work?"

"Slide it over your hand and push it right up to your bicep, but you would have to be in human form,"

Luxen explained.

"Then what?" Blackjack inquired. "It will do the rest."

"Ok" said Blackjack. Closing his eyes as he transformed into Bradicus.

Bradicus slid the crown all the way up to his forearm, then stopped. "Do you know if this crown was worn by someone before King Rozet?"

Luxen shook his head. "I don't know. Why? What do you know that I don't?"

Bradicus guided the gold ring into place. "Wow, it clamped itself around my bicep. It shrank to fit my arm. That's amazing."

"And that's precisely how it works," said Luxen.

Bradicus flexed his bicep, extending his arm out and back. "Can't even feel it's there. How do I get it off."

"You can get it off by releasing the king or if the king dies."

"You're telling me, I can release the king from Grimmbell Depository?"

"That's right. I have put Rozet in your hands. You are his regulator now."

"What if he gets killed on this mission?"

"Then he's released as well as you."

"What if I want to release him?"

"You were at the battle of the eight kings. That will be on your conscience."

"Luxen, are you telling me that if the king lives through this encounter, and I release him, you would be good with that?"

Luxen looked over at the jagged rock extending a hundred feet into the sky, signifying the entrance to Grimmbell Depository. "Did you know that every year the king has been held here is equal to twelve years? So, eight years times twelve is actually ninety-six years."

"Then how come he doesn't look that old?"

"It doesn't affect your age. The years' work on your conscious and subconscious mind. That's the stickler. The battle between these two will destroy him on the inside and outside, eventually extinguishing his entire framework of his body, mind and soul."

"Sounds to me like you're satisfied that Rozet has served his mental ninety-six years?"

"I am satisfied, but I don't think he'll live long enough to dismount from Luther to see his family during this lifetime. Anyway, time's a running, and you need to start your trip back to Kula. I have rounds to make, so Cryptsee will guide you out."

Bradicus watched as the seven kings gathered around King Rozet. Many handshakes and an occasional hug later, the king broke away from the group, walking toward Bradicus with all his worldly possessions including a leather bag hanging around his shoulder and the clothes on his back.

Bradicus turned away from the king and looked at Luxen. "I just took two of your prized possessions, and we know nothing comes for free. So, my friend, what do I owe you for the hospitality?"

"When you're finished defeating Roko the Dark and maybe saving your friend, you could do me a favor," Luxen replied.

"And what might that favor be?" said Bradicus.

"Find a replacement for me. After seeing you and realizing that there is still a world out there beyond the walls of Grimmbell, I would like to participate in that world again."

"I will find your replacement. I owe you that much. What is my timeframe?" Bradicus inquired.

Softly shaking his head left and right, Luxen said firmly, "Like I said, when you get finished with your task. It shall take as long as it takes."

"Very well, I will see you soon," stated Bradicus.

King Rozet stood at arm's length away from the two men, staring and saying nothing.

Taking a step forward, Luxen said, "King Rozet, you are no longer in my custody. This man here to my right is now your guardian. His name is Bradicus. He wears your crown as you can see."

King Rozet eyed Bradicus, staring him up and down. "Am I a free man? What about my friends?"

Luxen walked away, waving his hand in the air. "I have to leave, Bradicus." With that, he walked up to the remaining seven kings, motioning them to follow him as they all disappeared into the mouth of Grimmbell Depository.

"*Am* I a free man? You did not answer me."

Bradicus looked at the king but still didn't answer, leaning around the king, looking at the doorway to the prison depository. *Okay, I guess I do have full control here. But we never finished our discussion about how I am going to have the king ride the black spirit horse.*

"No, you are not a free man. Do you remember the battle where you killed thousands of people?"

"That was war. That's what happens when you fight in a war. People die. Such is the nature of it."

Bradicus nodded his head yes. "I realize that, but you see, I was there at the battle."

"You were *at the battle?*"

"I was. I was there for the sixteen-day fighting."

"Well, I'm sorry to inform you but the battle lasted a hell of a lot longer than sixteen days, and many of my men were slain too. I trust you are not coming to me complaining about *unfairness.* War among men is *not* fair. None of it. So come now, cease whining that *it's not fair* like a child in the playground."

Bradicus looked away, his brow furrowed, not liking the king's tone and snide remarks one bit. "And let me inform *you* that I was told the last sixteen days of that battle were more of a poker game between you and the other seven kings, where in those days, you and your king friends made bets on which team of your respective soldiers would be the first ones to kill the enemy, mainly Luxen."

"How did you know about that?"

"Like I say, I was there, at least until the last three days."

"Luxen told you about the last few days?"

"He did."

"And he took on some kind of power in those last three days that ended the battle and destroyed my life; *all of our lives*," the king said, somewhat wistful and as if he held onto regrets.

"King Rozet, I have a task for you," Bradicus said, looking at the black horse. "I'm going to put you on that horse and hopefully, it will lure in a person I need to stop from doing harm to others."

"What has he done?"

"It's rather hard to say at this time, but here's the deal. You ride the horse, we trap the bad guy. You get to go free. What do you say?"

"Will I be armed for this task?"

"Yes, you will."

"I can defend myself if need be? Must I kill this gentleman?"

"No, as I said, I want to trap him."

"If I do what you say, you will release me, and I will be free to go home to my family?"

"Yes. I have taken the liberty to draw up a contract between you and me," he said, handing a leather wrap to Rozet. "As you can see, it will bear Queen Kula's seal."

Turning his back, King Rozet took the leather wrap from Bradicus and walked a few feet away, his head bent down, eyes locked onto the leather document.

"It says here if I try to escape, you will destroy the crown."

"That is correct," said Bradicus.

"And it also states here that if I survive, I will be released immediately but the crown will have to stay in Grimmbell."

"That's the deal. Take it or you can go back to the twelve-year-for-one-year rotation nightmare." King Rozet handed the leather wrap back to Bradicus. "When do we leave?"

"As soon as I figure out how to get you on that horse."

"I will go down to the barn. Maybe I can work something out myself." Bradicus watched the man walk away toward the barn.

"Brazel, I need your help. How do we ride the black spirit horse without being trapped forever?"

"Sorry, Bradicus, I cannot help you out on this one."

"You can't help me? But I thought you knew everything. Or at least that you have the resources to find out. So now, when I need your advice, you tell me you have no counsel to offer?"

"I'm sorry, Bradicus, but to understand how a black spirit horse functions, an entity of some kind would have to go inside the horse."

"What does that mean, *go inside the horse?* And what entity exactly?"

"This is what I have gathered so far. The void inside a black spirit horse is infinite, it's like a black hole in space. You cannot connect between the walls of the black hole because it's a tunnel that goes on forever, an endless portal."

"So, you are telling me the black horse has no control of itself?"

"In the sense of a black hole, an empty void in space, yes; you could put it in that terminology."

"Brazel. I am surprised that you haven't figured this out."

"And you have?" asked Brazel.

"I think I have. I believe the black spirit horse is a wild uncontrollable outlaw type of animal that has an overpowering energy field."

"Yes, I will agree with you on that notion."

"Uncontrollable until it has a rider," said Bradicus. "And not just any rider. The horse picks a very specific individual. That's the key."

"You could have a strong point here too," answered Brazel.

"Yes, you could compare it to an energy force that has no brain until it has a rider with its own power, a power with which the black spirit horse combines to have control over its *own* power."

"Okay. You might have the upper hand this time," said Brazel. "But it still doesn't answer how we utilize the horse to trap Roko."

"I have an idea, and it involves a floater spirit."

"A floater spirit. Neutralize the energy. That's not a bad idea although there are huge risks involved for the rider."

"That's what it's going to cost if he wants his freedom. Thanks for the talk, Brazel; you were very helpful. Got to go. Talk to you later."

Bradicus walked to the top of the hill and standing on the cobblestone path, he searched the grounds of the cemetery for any sign of Cryptsee. In the distance, his eyes once again locked onto the beautiful green jade crypt-vault with white lightning bolts twisted inside the green stone.

He was turning his attention back to the crossroads of the cobblestone walkways when he saw a large male lion casually walking toward him on the cobblestone path.

I hope it's not hungry. No doubt another security measure?

Bradicus glanced back toward the barn but didn't see anyone outside, quickly turning his attention back to the lion. *Maybe it's some kind of a test.*

Suddenly, the lion hunched down, looking off to the left, then bolted at supersonic speed, leaping onto on something in a pounce, pinning it to the ground. "That's Cryptsee riding on its back. Holy shit, she's controlling that big-ass lion. Glad we got along when we did. It has something in its mouth."

Bradicus watched the lion and Cryptsee disappear behind a stone building and waited for them to reappear.

"Bradicus, are you waiting for me?"

Spinning around so fast, Bradicus lost his balance, falling to the ground.

Cryptsee dismounted the lion, running up to Bradicus. "I'm sorry, I didn't mean to frighten you," she said putting her hand out. "Let me help you up."

"Cryptsee! Wow, you are fast!"

"I'm not that fast, but Brooklyn here, he's very fast. He's my transportation and best friend, next to you, of course."

"Well, thank you," said Bradicus. "I can always use a friend, and a big furry one too."

"I've had him since he was a cub, only a bit bigger

than the size of my hand. Hard to believe that he was small at any time during his lifetime, isn't it? He's so beautiful, don't you agree?"

"Yes, he is. And big. A more magnificent beast I have ever set eyes on," conceded Bradicus.

"Yes, and I feed him a special kitty mix that will keep him growing for a while yet," Cryptsee said, enthusiasm in her tone. "Believe it or not, he still has to grow into his paws. See how huge they are!"

She clearly loved this enormous great feline, now lifting the lion's front paw and placing a flat palm against it; her hand looked minuscule. "Looks like you are ready to leave."

"Cryptsee, maybe you can help me. I need a couple of things before I go."

"What do you need?"

"I need a soul bag soaked in essence of floater spirit."

"I can do that, but I'm going to need permission from the Soul King himself."

"I figured that, and that's why I have sent a message ahead of time to get the approval from the Soul King."

"You're always thinking ahead," said Cryptsee. "Where do I need to go to get these items?"

"Two items. Two places." Cryptsee signaled with her fingers. "Our first stop will be at your favorite green-doored building where we shall pick up the soul bag. From there, we need to take an underground tunnel, putting us in the center of the cornfield. That's where Brooklyn comes in."

"Why are we taking an underground tunnel to get to the outside?"

"Because you are going to have a soul bag in your possession. Don't you realize how extremely rare a soul bag is?"

"I guess I don't. Well, I didn't until you just informed me."

"Not to worry. We have Brooklyn with us."

Bradicus nodded. "Whatever you say. You are the boss." He eyed the cat again. "Or *he* is the boss. I have no doubt of that in the slightest!"

Cryptsee chuckled.

"No, *I* am the boss," she confirmed in case of any doubt. "Brooklyn… He's just my aide. Without my command, he would do nothing but roll over and purr with his massive paws in the air. I take care of the children coming in here, and I'm the guardian for the floater spirits as you call them."

"Oh, and what do *you* call them?"

"Ghost spirits. Or some even call them free radical spirits. In any case, Brooklyn and I, we keep them under control. We have good teamwork."

"Indeed, you do, and you have a very important job here. I admire you for that."

"Thank you for your kindness," said Cryptsee. "I asked to be the guardian for the lost children and the disenfranchised souls."

Bradicus opened his mouth to speak but said nothing.

"What?" said Cryptsee. "You can ask me. I see you hesitating."

"I don't know if you can tell me this, but it does haunt me somewhat," he said after a brief pause. "Does it have to do with lost children's souls?"

"Yes, it does. In the battle of the eight kings, how many children were lost?" Brooklyn growled, clawing at the ground.

"That is a touchy subject," said Cryptsee.

"I'm sorry, I don't mean any disrespect to you or Brooklyn."

Cryptsee patted Brooklyn on his neck. "That's okay, Brook. We saved most of the children. 142 children lost their young lives during that battle and now, they reside inside the walls of Grimmbell."

"That's all I needed to know, thank you."

"Okay. I think it's time for me to escort you out. Will there be anyone else coming with us?" Bradicus spun around, looking at the barn.

"Yes, I have a man and horse that I need to take with me."

"Then you round up the man and the horse, and I will go with Brooklyn to fetch your soul bag. Meet us back here in twenty minutes."

"Bradicus. This is Brazel."

"Brazel, you must have found out some information for me?"

"As a matter of fact, my human friend, I have."

"And what did you unearth?"

"I found out that Kula's dragon rope in your possession has been partially made out of a soul bag."

"Did you talk to Kula?"

"No, I didn't, I… well, I sort of cheated."

"How did you cheat?" said Bradicus. "And more to the point, am I going to be in trouble for it?"

"I don't think so," Brazel assured. "I was mentally looking through the archives of the dragoon

wings when at the same time, I bumped into a mind tap that happened to belong to Kula."

"So, what you're telling me is that *your* mind bumped into *her* mind when she was looking through the archives at the same time as you were?"

"Yes, well stated," affirmed Brazel.

"What is the significance of the rope having been made with soul bag material?" Bradicus asked. "You might be able to use it for the reins to help control the black spirit horse."

"Does that mean we can ride it without a saddle blanket buffer pad?"

"No, but you have that already figured out, don't you?" Brazel inquired.

"I had an idea," ventured Bradicus. "I wasn't sure it was going to work, but with the information you just gave me, I feel better about my plan."

"Always glad to help. Bye for now."

Bradicus walked down the hill, stopping at the Grimmbell Depository gate. Rozet met him there. "Where is the horse now?" asked Bradicus.

With a head nod, Rozet answered, "He's in the barn. I have him locked in one of the stalls. I couldn't get a rope around him because he just kept kicking the shit out of the stall."

Bradicus pushed through the gate, jogging down to

the barn. He closed the door behind him, studying the layout of the stalls. The black stud was standing in the third stall on the right, a piercing glare from an eye staring out at Bradicus. The horse's eyes followed his every move, black and bright.

"Oh goody," said Brazel, "I get to watch a rodeo."

"Shut up, Brazel. I need to concentrate here."

Bradicus walked to the stall, standing behind the dark horse.

Black Beauty started kicking the gate with both hooves at the same time, *bang, bang, bang*, snot blowing out of his nose and dust falling from the rafters above.

"Not only are you mean, but I can also smell the nasty black tar dripping off your stinky black butt. But I know you want me. You want to use my magic to become complete. You can't do any portal runs without a true power source, can you? You need someone like me. But there is only one of me. And you would hurt me, wouldn't you? You will never be free without your own personal energy facilitator."

"The spirit horse continued pounding the wooden door with his hooves, cracking the bottom board, slinging clumps of dirt and tar against the barn wall.

"Okay, so you want to play rough? Sure, have it your way then; I can do that. You're mad because you know I'm right. You're mad because Luxen rode you like a rented mule. And you want my mojo."

"Get him, Bradicus. You tell him," said Brazel.

"Brazel. Not now, please."

Bradicus backed off two stalls to strategize, continuing to watch the horse.

Do I change to Blackjack, and jump on his back just long enough to put the rope around his neck, then jump off again? I can do that as well.

"Okay Brazel, now I need your input."

"I thought you would never ask."

"Well, I'm asking now," voiced Bradicus. "What do you want to do?" said Brazel.

"Do you remember the conversation with Kula when she talked about me having some of the same DNA energy as a portal does?"

"I do remember that conversation," confirmed Brazel. "In fact, I was very impressed with her observation of that energy comparison. Is that one of her secret hidden intuitive powers?"

"She's a complex dragoon. Seen a lot of things."

"I suppose you're right," said Brazel. "What are your thoughts about the horse?"

"Is there some technique to stun this animal for a short time? Could my energy short out the horse's own, at least for long enough for me to tie this rope around its neck?"

"Bradicus, when you transform into Blackjack or vice versa, do you have some type of process to make it happen or what exactly *does* happen?"

"I'm surprised you don't know that. You're my third person. My third entity."

"I know when you are going to change and why you want to change but during the actual real-time process, I lose a portion of the connection due to the enormous amount of energy mass traded."

"Energy mass trading?" said Bradicus. "I'm afraid I don't follow."

"Its energy transfers. A cell-to-cell thing. Millions and millions of energy reactions."

"Ah, I know what you are saying. Here's my method. When I decide to transform, I think ahead five to six body movements in time to match up with the body I'm transforming into. That way, I can adapt quickly to the situation that I will be entering, either with Bradicus' or Blackjack's form. Does that make any sense?"

"Actually, it makes a lot of sense. Then here is what you need to do."

"I'm all ears," said Bradicus. "Get it? I mean, when I change to Blackjack the rabbit man."

"I get it," said Brazel. "But it's not really the time for bad puns. Now pay attention. I do believe this will be the first time you've done this task. You need to *think* that you are going to kill the black spirit horse in your pre-set five to six body movements."

"I do?"

"Yes, you do. You need to send that five or six body

movements ahead like you always do but this time, the receiving party, the horse, will know something is going to happen. So, it will… Well, I hope it will…"

"You hope it will what?" said Bradicus.

"It will try to counter the unknown energy movements. The key here is the horse's spirit won't know what type of energy is coming at it, good or bad and it will go into full alert protocol to prepare itself."

"Full alert protocol? You keep blinding me with terminology."

"Yes, by that, I mean it will charge up all its available energy to find what is coming to attack it. Pay attention here. So now, the black spirit horse will be supercharged because it senses harm, and you will be supercharged much more than usual because you are going to *do* harm. And when the two almost identical energies merge, there will be one big fricking electrically charged explosion."

"That's a good thing, right?" Bradicus asked.

"Yes, that should knock the horse out of commission for one maybe two minutes. That's when you lasso the horse and try to take control."

"How do I know it won't knock me out as well?"

"It won't, because you are the initiating charge. You will strike first."

"Wow, that sounds good in theory. Are we sure it will work?" asked Bradicus, his eyes aglow. "It will work. Remember when you go through the advanced body-moving steps…"

"You mean when I jump, so to speak."

"When you anticipate the situation, you are going into," Brazel started, "make sure you concentrate hard on the part where you want to harm the horse. That will jack its amps way up. It will work."

"Okay, let's make it happen," said Bradicus. "If something does go wrong, would you please send a mind message to Kula, just in case?"

"Mind message to Kula. Got it."

"You did say I could control the horse with Kula's rope, right?"

"Yes, I did and yes you can. Just remember though,

you can't ride the horse with only the rope."

"Got it," Bradicus replied.

Bradicus stepped back one more stall length from the black-tarred horse and he re-focused. Another double-hooved kick to the stall door ripped it off the hinges, sending it crashing into the barn wall.

"It's now or never," said Brazel.

Bradicus jumped up, transforming into Blackjack midair and landing on the top board of the stall.

Electrical sparks of deep red and blue exploded into the ceiling of the barn.

Black Beauty jumped forward into the wall of the barn, breaking the boards of the barn wall and at the same time getting its head stuck between the rungs of wood.

Blackjack lost his balance and faceplanted on the back of the horse's mane, hunching his shoulders to counter the pain. The horse let out a scream piercing his ear drums, orange sparks erupting from the horse's eyes, burning through the barn wall and setting it on fire.

"Holy shit, Brazel, is this part of the plan?" asked Blackjack, taken back, spitting and wiping blood from his nose.

"Tie the rope around its neck, then get off the horse."

Blackjack pulled the rope off his shoulder and with both hands, he leaned over, opening the loop wide enough and biting the horse's ear, not letting go until he had the rope around the neck of the horse.

The horse jerked his head up, bashing Blackjack square in the forehead, knocking him off the back of the horse. Blackjack snagged the top rung of the stall with his left hand to lessen the fall.

"Brazel, I need help," he called out, coughing a mouthful of blood onto his chest. "There's smoke.

My arms are on fire. Blue sparks. Can't wipe them off. Getting dark in here."

"Blackjack! Transform! Transform back to human form! You have to neutralize the energy charge."

Blackjack rolled onto his belly, pawing the dirt floor to gain distance from the crazed horse, crawling until his head hit something hard. "Damn," he cried out, rubbing his scalp. "That really hurt."

***

The next thing Bradicus could remember was waking to the face of eleven-year-old Cryptsee looking back at him with a smile and tears lingering on her cheeks.

"Oooh, my head hurts," he said, pushing up on his elbows. "What about the horse? Is the horse—"

"Not to worry too much. Your naughty horse is right over there," Cryptsee said, pointing, "still kicking the stall once in a while but much calmer with the rope around his neck. Although it appears at least for the moment, that the horse is blind."

"Blind?" said Bradicus, looking up to catch a glimpse of the now roofless barn. "Oh my. Sorry about the roof. That one's on me. But how do you know the horse has turned blind?"

Luxen and King Rozet emerged from behind Brooklyn. "I would say because it doesn't have any eyeballs anymore," said Luxen.

"Bradicus. This is Brazel. Don't kid yourself. The horse is not blind. Two things took place. Number one, the exploding of the eyes is a defense mechanism. Number two, discharging of the eyes is a possible honing device for other spirit riders to find their buddy horse, and it could also be a means to lure an energy source close enough to trap them."

"Thank you, Brazel. I guess you were right about transforming back to human form to escape the black horse."

"It was a close one. When you did transform, an electric surge pushed you away and slowed the spirit horse from getting a chance to stomp your guts out. You're welcome."

Chapter 27: Follow Me

Cryptsee unhooked a leather bag from Brooklyn's collar. "I have the soul bag you requested. Brooklyn picked out the floater spirit essences himself, and they're the very same ones we soaked the bag in!" She seemed excited. "Are you going to inspect it?" Cryptsee said, handing the bag to Bradicus.

Bradicus gently took it from the young girl's hand. "Thank you. I'm quite sure it will be the purest form of essence, and it will make the perfect insulator saddle blanket. I need not inspect it, Cryptsee."

Cryptsee instructed, "But I think it would be *good* if you checked it out to make sure it will work for you. I mean, I know it has the proper mix for what you need, but just to be sure, you know?"

She was obviously seeking out compliments for her work, and went on, "Because it has *everything* in it. Dark moon death, baby blanket, wasp wax, spider bite and blood butter shade essence; they're all infused in it. Adding things is fun, you know."

Bradicus stroked the bag, pressing it to his face.

"Mmm," he said, making murmurs of approval to flatter her. "I'm sure it *is* fun. And it has a slightly sweet smell with an afterbite of soured butter and burnt wood. And an added touch for me, the bag is spongy. A little chewy, I think, Cryptsee. That should give it the exact amount of desired separation between horse and rider. I believe it will be just the right combination we need. Nice job, Cryptsee."

She chuckled, her face flushed, suddenly a little shy to receive such compliments—even after fishing for them so plainly. "Perfect. Right, then *I* think we should get to the tunnel before twilight—because there's going to be floater spirits and free radical spirits, and you know what they're like!

"And they'll all be roaming around the battlefield!" she added. "Especially when they get a whiff of that soul blanket. Don't you think so as well, Bradicus?"

"Oh, I *do* think so too, Cryptsee! I really do. Anyway, you are the boss, Cryptsee. I'm ready to go." "Right then, listen in. *Bradicus* will stay close to me," she said, grabbing his hand and looking to

King Rozet. "King Rozet, you still have enemies inside Grimmbell. Dead ones and alive ones. So, you'll need to stay close to Brooklyn. Any questions?"

Bradicus looked over at Rozet. Rozet shook his head no.

"No questions here," said Bradicus. "Sounds to me like you have the perfect plan, Cryptsee."

And so, young Cryptsee led the small caravan through the cemetery as Brooklyn chased two free radical spirits away during the thirty-minute walk to the mausoleum housing the tunnel entrance.

Cryptsee engulfed her keys in her hand. Once again, she whispered into her keys, walking up the twenty-two steps to the mausoleum door. She inserted the selected key, twisting counterclockwise six times. The door lurched forward one inch.

Looking back at the group, she said, "Come on, it's getting dark. Hurry!" Her eyes were wide, sparkling in the dusk light.

Bradicus and Rozet both climbed the many uneven steps, Brooklyn bringing up the rear. Cryptsee shouldered the door open, holding it until everyone had entered as if the mistress of a grand house.

"I don't suppose you have any source of light in here?" asked Bradicus.

"Nobody move; I will get us some light." She then yelled out, "Woodford, can you help me please?"

A small flicker of light blossomed ahead. "Ah, there he is," said Cryptsee. "Woodford will be your guide and light source in the tunnel. Now, you won't give him any grief, will you?"

She stood eyeing everyone with her head cocked to one side, now transformed into a schoolteacher who was waiting for the answer to a math question. She tapped her foot, impatient.

Ten minutes passed before Woodford, a tall skinny creature with facial features resembling a human man but with long bony alligator hands and feet, climbed the opposing steps with a four-chambered lantern in his right hand. He greeted Cryptsee with a fond hug.

"Woodford, please will you take Bradicus and his friends through the tunnel? You can bring them out at the edge of the cornfield."

Woodford nodded, saying nothing whatsoever.

Bradicus stepped next to Cryptsee. *"What* is this individual?" "Oh, he's a stretch bod."

"A *stretch bod?* Can he be trusted?" Bradicus asked.

"Not to worry, my new friend. I would not lead you astray. Don't you trust me?"

"I do! And I know that Cryptsee, but I'm not sure I trust *him* to get me through the tunnel. My infrared eyesight isn't working inside this tunnel, and it looks like Woodford has the only light source. And even more scary, I can't make contact with Brazel. I don't know why."

"Don't worry! Honestly, why do grown-ups make a big deal of *every*thing?" She sounded exasperated now, and Bradicus thought he would have to do better. But before he could speak again, she said, "Woodford will get you out. The tunnel lining's what's sucking up all your infrared, you, see?

Actually, *none* of your internal energy mechanics will work. Not here in this section of Grimmbell."

"I see. Well, thank you for your, umm, wise counsel, Miss Cryptsee. I'm very lucky to have you looking after me. If I might ask, what does the lining of this tunnel consist of?"

"Jars, of course," said Cryptsee, matter of fact as if her answer was as plain as day. "Jars? Are you serious?"

"I am. You'll see!"

"I don't understand," said Bradicus.

She sighed. "I suppose I'll try to explain the best I can."

"Please do."

"Okay, but we haven't got time. You need to get moving to the other end of the tunnel."

"Why the big hurry?"

"Because of the jars!" She heaved another gigantic sigh as if he was wearing out all her patience. She moved in toward him and whispered, "The walls are lined with thousands and thousands *and thousands* of glass jars. Like, more glass jars than you can imagine! And they're all still shut. So, inside these sealed jars, you've got spells and potions, spirits and souls, all sorts of essences, and important organ parts—bits and pieces from *hundreds* of warriors who've fought and died on the Grimmbell Battlefield."

"Oh! I…umm, I see!" But he didn't see, not really. It all sounded very peculiar, especially coming from the mouth of an eleven-year-old. "So, where does odd bod Woodford come into all of this?"

"*Stretch* bod," she corrected. "Not odd bod. Anyway, it's because…" Now, she sucked in a deep breath as if readying herself for a long and arduous monologue that would be tedious. "When the enemies of Kula and the Soul King get killed on the battlefield, the earthers enhance the smoke ritual to talk to their spirits, to find out how their magic weapons work. If the enemy spirit won't talk about their magic weapons, *that's* where Woodford will carry the spirit's remains inside his chest and belly. He'll take them over to this tunnel to work with them."

She ran out of air, stopping and taking in a massive gulp. "Taking them all for processing," Bradicus said.

"Yes, that's it. Taking them in his body."

But her long-winded description and its odd conclusion had only confused him all the more.

"*Inside his body,*" Bradicus said, almost squeaking. "He transports them in his abdominal cavity." She just stared, quizzical and anxious to get moving, now hopping foot to foot.

"In his belly, as you said," he reiterated.

"Yes! And his body will filter the information out and plonk it into the jars. It's some type of weird cooking process. Now, won't you get mov—"

Bradicus nodded, still looking astonished. "Cooking process. But how on earth does that work?"

"*Bradicus,*" she said, sounding like a headmistress now. "You do realize you don't have much time?

Like I said, you have to get a move on to the end of the tunnel! Or—"

"I know, I know. Just answer this one question for me, and then I shall be off. I promise." She grimaced. Clearly, his answer hadn't pleased her.

After she had finished contorting her face into all manner of shapes, she seemed to have conceded. "Very well, but if you're late, it's not *my* fault. So, the tunnel's like a huge *biiiig* sponge, and

Woodford collects all the vitality that's given off, a clarifying process between all the ingredients in the jars. I have been told he adds some type of his *mojo* to the jars too—you know what mojo is, right?"

Her head tilt had come back again.

"Yes, I know what mojo is," he affirmed.

And she carried on. "Well, he shakes the heck out of the jars and has them suspended in air while they go around and around, around and around."

"Rotating," he said, imagining it.

"Yes! And that process gives the spirit jar juice the illusion that they are free, so he can get lots of spiritual info from them."

"Extraction," Bradicus said.

"Do you have to repeat everything I say?" she asked, her eyes screwed up. "I don't repeat it."

"You so do!" she yelled, tapping her foot.

"No, I actually paraphrase it." He was getting argumentative. She said nothing now, just pursing her pretty lips.

"Wow," said Bradicus. "I do believe you have a very good understanding of what Woodford is capable of."

"Most of my information comes from floater spirits. I have no proof. But anyway!" Cryptsee said, pointing down the tunnel and becoming agitated. "Woodford is ahead of you. Catch up to his light."

Cryptsee mounted Brooklyn, pointing her finger at Bradicus. "Catch up with Woodford. Do it *now.*"

"Yes, don't you think we should catch up with the crocodile man?" said Rozet.

The two had forgotten Rozet was even there, so lost were they in Bradicus' endless question-and- answer session. Bradicus stared down the tunnel; Woodford's light had grown dim.

"I think that's a good idea," he said to Rozet.

"Good," said Rozet. "I don't want to be eaten by that big-ass lion."

Bradicus waved the leather wrap in front of Rozet. "Don't forget about our contract." Rozet yanked at the reins of the black tar horse.

"I will do my part. I hope you also remember to do yours."

Suddenly, Woodford's lantern went black; the mausoleum door had clanged shut. "Rozet, are you still with me?"

"Of course! Where the hell am I going to go?"

"Brazel, can you hear me? Are you there?" asked Bradicus, a hint of anxiety in his voice. A cold chill bit at Bradicus' neck.

"Yer not going to be able to talk to anyone but me inside this tunnel," came an eerie male voice. Bradicus pulled his sword. "Woodford, is that you?"

"It's a good thing that Cryptsee likes you, or I might just leave you two down here."

"I don't think Cryptsee would like that," retorted Bradicus.

Woodford relit his lantern, blinding Bradicus momentarily. "No, I suppose she wouldn't, being that she's the Soul King's daughter."

Bradicus secured his sword. "Oh! The Soul King's daughter? I didn't know that."

Woodford stared at the almost hidden entrance door. "Yeah, well, there's a lot of things you don't know. About all manner of topics, including about Grimmbell."

Bradicus arched his eyebrows. "That is true."

Woodford lowered his lantern, looking at Rozet, the horse, and back at Bradicus. "Do you think you're ready to keep up now? Or will I have to keep coming back for you?"

"We are ready."

Woodford lifted the lantern above his head, moving it the full length of the dark horse. "You have a black spirit horse?" Woodford inquired, though it was a rhetorical question.

Bradicus gave Woodford a nod. "It's the same horse that Luxen used to make his security rounds." Woodford reached up to the horse's mane.

"I don't know if I would do that," said Bradicus.

Woodford looked at Bradicus, stopping momentarily. "Why not?" Then he gently rubbed the horse's mane.

"Because not too long ago, this horse tried to dance on my head in the barn. Almost trampled me to death. I had to short circuit it to gain control."

"I see that," said Woodford, looking at the horse's head. "Something must've happened to it because its eyes appear to be hazy. Not quite in full focus."

Bradicus stepped next to Woodford. "Is the horse blind?"

"No, it's still dazed, but healthy. But this horse is very different from other black spirit horses."

"What makes it different?"

"Because it let me touch it a little too easily," said Woodford, pulling his alligator hand back. "Maybe it's still in a haze."

Woodford rubbed the palm of his hand from the top of the neck to the back quarters. "There's something else going on. I'm not sure what."

He brushed against Rozet's shoulder. "You better keep a close eye on this horse." Rozet shot a look at Bradicus. "What does that mean?"

"I'm not sure, but we are in a tunnel lined with urns of spirits."

Brazel. where are you when I need information?

"We need to get going," said Woodford, walking down the twenty-two steps to the tunnel floor.

Bradicus began down the stairs too, giving Rozet a head jerk in the same direction. "Come on, let's get to daylight."

King Rozet pulled on the reins, walking the horse down the stairs. Bradicus caught up to Woodford, matching his walking pace.

"Mister Woodford. What exactly do you do in this tunnel?" "Cryptsee didn't tell you?"

"No, not exactly. She said something about filtering the spirits," Bradicus replied.

Woodford lifted his lantern above his head, seeing it immediately casting a path of blue-white light that lit up the tunnel for a thousand yards in front of the walking trio.

"Aren't they beautiful?" he said, moving his head in a slow circular pattern. Bradicus took in the immediate scenery. His jaw fell, not saying anything.

"This place is huge," said Rozet, catching up to the pack. "What is in all those containers? There must be thousands?"

"Actually, there are hundreds of thousands," said Woodford. "Which reminds me, I will have to do my monthly inventory here in a couple of days."

Rozet pulled at the reins. "Come on, Black Beauty."

"Why are the jars a plethora of colors? What does that mean?" Bradicus noticed there were waves of rainbow colors running the length of the tunnel.

Each jar sat in its own hollowed-out shelf sitting comfortably into the tunnel's side.

"Yes, that's of my own design. Each color is for something specific. Year, month, day, time of day or night. Location on the battlefield. Which battle. How they died. Magic weapon, conventional weapon. Oh hell, the list goes on and on. Male or female. What they were wearing. Position of body. Face up or down. Everything."

Bradicus shook his head in awe. "You help the tomb earthers pick the most important and best location to cultivate the blood bricks?"

Shrugging his bony shoulders, Woodford answered, "I *have* assisted them in the past. They usually call me in around the time they need to do the labeling portion."

"You are a type of earther?"

"You could say that. I'm more of the old generation earther. A mix of earther, bone dust, and spirit.

And maybe a few other things."

"That's interesting," said Bradicus, looking at the ground. "With all due respect, where do the crocodile feet come from?"

"That's a good question," Woodford observed, perusing his own feet. "I believe it happened when I battled a free radical spirit."

"You fought a free radical?"

"Actually, I didn't have much option; it attacked me on the battlefield one day."

"Does that happen a lot?" asked Bradicus.

"It's not uncommon."

"I had an experience this morning with a free radical when I was entering Grimmbell." Woodford gave a small grin. "Ahhh! You bumped into the one with no pants?"

"How did you know?"

"That's Frank-no-pants."

"But isn't he a free radical spirit?"

"He's a harmless free radical," said Woodford.

Bradicus squeezed his eyes tight. "I'm assuming not all free rads are dangerous."

"Ninety-nine out of a hundred are. Frank is the one who isn't. The one I came across that day had been set up as a trap to whoever came across that particular body."

"What happened?" asked Bradicus.

"After the battle, I can't remember which one, but when I rolled the creature over, the free radical attacked my feet."

"You mean the spirit did, right?"

"Yes, it was a delayed spirit attack spell."

Rozet jumped between the two. "I don't understand," he said, pulling the black tar horse to keep up. "The spirit was engineered to activate once its body was moved to kill one more time. That particular spirit was a free radical spirit. A nasty one."

"So, like Bradicus asked, how come the crocodile feet?"

Woodford sighed. "That's a long story. Maybe if I see you again, I will tell you. If I see you alive, that is."

"What do you mean by that?"

"It's a feeling. I believe the next time I see you; it will be when you are in spirit form or close to it.

That's all I'm going to say about that."

Bradicus looked at Rozet. "I think we have gone far enough on that topic; wouldn't you agree?"

"Yeah, I guess so," said Rozet. "Well, maybe you can ask your friend what's with all these glowing glass containers coming up at this bend in the tunnel."

Woodford cleared his throat, his voice thicker. "Those are the free radical spirits."

"Bradicus. This is Brazel. I finally made contact with

you. Sort of. I can see what you see. Those are high-powered spirit jars. Be cautious. Don't get too close."

Woodford stopped, turning his head toward Bradicus and Rozet. "Okay, here is where we need to move quickly and quietly through this section of the tunnel." Taking two steps forward, he pointed with his finger. "The tunnel will narrow down to a choke point. This will put us close to its wall. If we make too much noise and wake them, they will see us and that could be a problem. So, let's be quick and quiet. Look straight ahead and don't touch any of the jars."

Woodford once again lifted the lantern above his head. Standing quietly, he twisted his head just a little bit to the left and a little to the right, trying to hear any sound whatsoever.

"Bradicus. This is Brazel again. I sense your heartbeat and blood flow increasing rapidly. I'm not sure what you're looking at. Something's standing in front of you. Could you take two steps, right?"

Bradicus leaned around Woodford to give Brazel a look, not wanting to move until Woodford did. Woodford took three steps forward and stopped again.

Still holding his lantern above his head, he looked and listened.

"Bradicus, I can feel a huge amount of heat coming from this horse," Rozet said, pushing the palm of his hand toward the nose. "And look, it's starting to drip that black sticky tar."

Bradicus turned around. "What are you talking about at this very moment? Dripping tar?"

"Hey, it's your friend's horse, not mine."

Bradicus walked toward Rozet with his hand in a fist. "Maybe Luxen should have disposed of you a long time ago."

Bradicus gritted his teeth, ready to throw a backlash at Rozet when he noticed the specially designed horse blanket smoking. "What the hell!"

Bradicus stepped toward the horse, but Woodford latched onto the top of his shoulder. "I don't think I would get any closer if I were you."

Rozet produced a bug-eyed bulging stare at Woodford and Bradicus, flipping the reins away from his hand but they didn't release. "What the hell is this?" He cupped his hands together and with his free one, tried to remove the reins. He pulled hard, shaking his hand violently over and over, but the reins still refused to release. His eyes flashed with anger.

"Bradicus, you and Luxen did this on purpose. You guys set this up from the start."

Bradicus waved the leather wrap in front of him. "This contract was signed under oath by me and the queen herself with her seal, so there was no foul play in planning against you. I wanted to ride the black spirit horse, but I cannot do it. My powers would kill me and the horse, so that is why I chose you."

"*Why* did you choose me? You just wanted to see me dead because of the battle. Because of the war that happened years ago. Why would you even give a shit about me?"

"I chose you because you have a family, and they are still alive."

Rozet jerked to attention. "They are alive? All of them? You saw them where? When?" Bradicus raised his hands to his chest. "Wait a minute, I never said I saw them."

"Then how do you know they are alive?"

"Luxen saw them. He told me."

Rozet shook his head. "And you believe him?"

"Yes, I do. And the only way that you could get out of Grimmbell prison to see your family again is doing this and it's a long shot, but it's the only shot you have. I wanted to give you that chance."

Woodford stepped in between the two men. "Bradicus, we need to move fast. Some of the jars are illuminating. It looks as though they are heating up."

"They are heating up from the horse, you think?"

"I don't know for certain. Most people don't know much about black spirit horses, especially this one, but we need to get through the chokepoint."

"My hand is burning," said Rozet. "What should I do?"

"Get on the horse," said Woodford.

Rozet looked at Bradicus for approval.

Bradicus gave a head nod toward the saddle. "Get on the horse. I don't think we have any choice." Rozet latched onto the saddle horn with foot in stirrup, pulling himself onto the horse. "Now what?"

"The jars are vibrating. They want to hit the floor, to break open." Woodford grabbed Bradicus by the collar of his coat. "We could be too late. Let's move now."

"What about me?" Rozet barked.

Woodford stepped next to the horse, pushing on Rozet's leg. "When we get close to the chokepoint, don't slow down; go as fast as you can."

Rozet gathered the reins up. "As fast as I can? I can do that."

Woodford ran down the tunnel toward the chokepoint. "Come on, let's go."

Running to catch up with Woodford, Bradicus could see the jars illuminating on each side of the tunnel, fifty yards before the tight spot. "Are those spirits coming alive?"

"Let's put it this way; they know we are here, and they want to ride that black spirit horse out of here," Woodford explained.

"But I thought the black spirit horse chose its own rider?"

"In most cases, yes, but I don't know about today," said Woodford. "There are way too many radical spirits here. They could combine to make one big-ass master spirit to control the horse and escape."

"Maybe we can send Rozet another way. Is there any other path around this tight spot?"

Woodford looked over his shoulder. "Go now, Rozet. Go now, and don't stop. Wait for us on the other side."

Rozet leaned forward, squeezing his legs, whipping the reins over and under. "Heeya," he shouted, and man and horse bolted down the tunnel toward the chokepoint.

"Oh, shit! Look at that," said Woodford.

"What?" Bradicus asked.

"Two jars have already been broken on the tunnel floor."

"How did they break?" asked Bradicus.

"Vibration and the energy of the imprisoned spirit. They want out. And now they can see and feel that horse, they have energy. Energy we don't understand yet. And sometimes, when they want something bad enough, they can make anything happen. Such as vibrating off the ledge and onto the rock floor."

"Yeah, well, I thought you had control of them?"

"Come on," said Woodford. "We need to get through that chokepoint. Arm yourself. Stay in the middle and don't get too close to the wall."

Bradicus retrieved his sword from its sheath. With his free hand, he dug inside the bag of screamer's dust. Quickly dusting the blade, it burst into a green flame. "Holy flamethrowers, it does work."

"What did you say?"

"Never mind," said Bradicus. "Just keep running."

Bradicus held his left arm straight out in front of him, acting as a shock absorber to Woodford's back with the blade of fire in his right hand, ready to fend off any free radical spirits.

Dead center, in the middle of the chokepoint, Bradicus ran into a stalled Woodford, knocking him to the ground. Dusting the tunnel floor with his butt, Bradicus catapulted to his knees and pointed the blade in front of him. "What the hell… Why did you stop?"

"I didn't," said Woodford. "You ran into me. We're too late."

"Too late for what?"

Woodford was picking at the ground, churning his fingers together. "There's blood."

"Blood? Whose blood? Your blood?"

"It's not my blood." He smelled his fingers and with a quick touch of his tongue, he looked at Bradicus. "It's horse blood."

"Horse blood? How can that be? Rozet and the black stallion went blasting through here like a gorilla with its hair on fire."

Woodford tasted his fingers again, lightly smacking his lips. "It's horse blood," he said, and with a head nod at the tunnel floor, added, "Look at that. There must be ten or fifteen broken jars."

Bradicus looked down at the small pile of glass, the residue of illuminating goo lying motionless on the floor. He quickly stood, assisting Woodford to his feet.

"Now what? Any chance we can catch up to them?" asked Bradicus.

"We *need* to catch up to them."

"How fast can you run?" asked Bradicus.

"I don't run. I can levitate."

"Good, because I'm going to transform."

"Transform into what?"

Bradicus brushed himself off. "I'm going to transmute into a supersonic tri-colored, titanium-clawed eighty-five-pound Rarebrook jackrabbit with lightning reflexes and an internal cellular megastructure, able to produce adenosine triphosphate at an alarming one-thousand-fold energy ratio."

"Wow! Okay! Don't think I've ever seen one of your kind before." "That's because I am one of a kind."

"Can I have your spirit blueprint?"

Bradicus squinted. "We are wasting time; we need to get going."

"If the king and the black spirit horse, along with how many unknown free radical spirits, conglomerate together and exit this tunnel out into the real world… Holy shit, I'm going to be in deep dragoon dodo poop balls."

"They cannot exit the tunnel," said Woodford. "There's an invisible spirit blocker barrier wall five hundred feet from the exit." Woodford picked up one of the broken jars and sampled the illuminated slime lingering on the side of the jar. "Damn, this one is a bad one. They called him *the Hatchet Hacker* when he was in the upper world. We're wasting time," he said, rising off the floor. "I'm ready to go, are you? Bradicus? Bradicus, where are you?"

"Not to worry, my friend, I'm right here."

"I'll be damned. I've never seen such an animal as you. Your fur is quite beautiful," Woodford said, his tall statue leaning forward. "Your claws are impressive."

"I will take that as a compliment."

Woodford danced a few feet up and down in midair. "Impressive… Come on, to the spirit barrier." Turning, he sped off.

Bradicus caught up to Woodford within seconds. "How far to the invisible barrier?" Woodford looked over and noticed Blackjack keeping pace with him. "Wow, you are fast."

"I'm just getting warmed up."

"The invisible wall barrier is roughly one mile ahead of us." "Thank goodness for security measures," said Blackjack. "It is good and bad."

"Okay, tell me the bad."

"It's true nobody will be able to exit. But on the other hand, the king, the horse, and all the radical spirits will fight it out. It could be a soupy mess." Woodford slowed his pace. "We're getting close."

"Why are we slowing down?" asked Blackjack.

"There we go," said Woodford, pointing. "A discarded spirit." Woodford and Blackjack studied the white spot on the tunnel floor.

Woodford raked his foot across the marked area. "This is where one of the spirits was destroyed."

Blackjack studied the white spot, turning his attention toward Woodford. "They actually eliminated this spirit." Inhaling, Blackjack added, "I can still smell some type of scent, a small aroma of burnt smoke."

Woodford continued to foot smear the spirit burn. "Yeah, that's what I smell too. I think the spirits, or at least some of them, teamed up and grew into a bigger, faster spirit with more energy."

"What are we looking at here, a super-free-radical spirit?" asked Blackjack.

"Yes, I believe so, since the power of these spirits hasn't been transformed into souls. The spirits tend to form together passively or forcefully. Come on, we need to find them."

Woodford and Blackjack raced through the s-curve section of the tunnel, bringing them up to an outcropping of solid rock where the path veered to the right.

Woodford stopped, looking at Blackjack. "Are you ready?" "I'm ready."

"Right around this stand of rocks, that's where everybody's going to be, but I'm not sure what we're going to find."

Blackjack nodded. "Let's find out."

Woodford and Blackjack roared out from behind the rock to find one figure standing.

Blackjack saw Rozet lying on the ground, holding his stomach with both hands, the black spirit horse standing over him with his head down.

"Oh shit, this isn't good."

Woodford immediately veered off to the left. It looked as though he was headed for a piece of ground decorated by many discarded spirits.

Blackjack was stunned on getting close enough to notice a linear cone-shaped antler of a horn sticking out of the horse's forehead. "You mean to tell me that this horse is some type of a fricking unicorn black spirit horse? Well, kiss my ass. Luxen failed to let me in on that little bit of trivia."

The horse neighed, jerking its head up and down, then took a step back. Blackjack kneeled down next to Rozet and felt the wetness on his kneecap. "What the hell happened here?"

"We were overrun by spirits. They wanted the horse really bad."

"Why didn't you just turn the horse around and come back to us?" Rozet coughed up some blood, and Blackjack wiped off his lips. "The horse bucked me off and charged after the free radical."

"Okay," said Blackjack. "Sounds like a Luther horse thing."

Blackjack pulled Rozet's hands away from the wound. "Damn, you've lost a lot of blood. So, you dismounted the horse… and then what?"

"Can you believe it?" said Rozet. "I think I'm the only human king to ever defeat a free radical spirit.

Put that in your pipe and smoke it, my furry little friend." Blackjack looked over toward Woodford.

He watched the tall skinny jar collector digging at the mini mounds of white dirt. He turned his attention back toward Rozet. "Tell me what happened here."

"The horse promised me that my spirit would be kept alive in Grimmbell if I helped him defeat the badass spirits so my family could come and visit me."

"Luther actually spoke to you?"

"Not exactly; it was more of a mental thing. Not sure, but I knew what it wanted me to do."

"Okay, you fought against a free radical spirit that was a little bit quicker with the blade than yourself."

A cocky little smirk appeared on Rozet's face. "It was the biggest and baddest of the bunch."

"Of course, it was," said Blackjack.

"Luxen's horse said to keep that one particular spirit occupied just for a minute, then it could defeat the other free radical spirits. Then we could destroy it, or at least stuff it back into a jar."

"Looking at your stomach, it didn't turn out quite the way you planned." "I had the spirit right where I wanted it."

"And then?" asked Blackjack.

"Another spirit came up from behind and bearhugged me. I couldn't move my arms and couldn't break free. The next thing I know, I'm lying on the ground"—Rozet lifted his head just enough to get a look at his stomach—"with this unwanted hole in my guts."

Woodford had completed his work on the discarded spirits and kneeled alongside Blackjack. He studied the wound for a few seconds, then looked at Blackjack.

"And the only thing that the black spirit horse could do to defeat this superior free radical spirit was to stab it in the back with its horn. But sadly, the horse stabbed you too in the process. Is that the way it happened?" said Blackjack.

"That's the way it happened," said Rozet, nodding in support. Suddenly, Rozet grabbed Blackjack by the arm, pulling him close to his mouth. "The horse said *you* can ride him."

Blackjack pulled away from Rozet, looking directly at Woodford. "What does he mean by that?"

Rozet's grip on Blackjack's arm loosened and then released, his head slowly falling away from them to the left. His body stiffened for only a moment, then relaxed.

Woodford placed his hand on Rozet's chest. Looking up toward the ceiling of the tunnel, he shook his head. "Damn, he's gone."

Blackjack turned toward Woodford and nodded. "Yeah, I figured that. Now what do we do?"

Standing, Woodford looked at the black spirit horse. "I will take care of Rozet. You need to gather your horse and get out of the tunnel."

"What about the invisible spirit wall?"

"It's already down. As soon as the last radical spirit was destroyed, the barrier disappeared."

"How far to sunlight?"

"Five hundred yards."

Blackjack looked at Rozet's body. "I was kind of hoping he would make it through this. He did have a family, although he killed a lot of families in that battle. I don't know. I guess it is what it is. People choose their own faith, right?"

Woodford had the king's body levitating four feet off the ground, quickly engulfing the body with a burlap bag and tying the opening in a knot. "We all make decisions that finally lead us to our destinations. I am not the one to judge him."

"I suppose you're right," said Blackjack, releasing a heavy sigh.

"You should probably leave as quickly as you can before we stir any more spirits up."

"Don't you mean before we break anymore jars?"

"Yes, that too. I don't want any more jars vibrating off the shelf."

"Why did they do that?"

"Do what?" Woodford asked, tying a rope around the knotted end of the burlap sack. "Vibrate. Fall off the shelf. You know—break."

"If the king is correct that the black spirit horse told him it's going to allow you to ride him, then that means all these free radical spirits had knowledge that they were only one spirit away from riding that horse themselves to freedom. That's why. But as of right now, that horse is waiting for you."

"Are you sure about that?"

Woodford tied the loose end of the rope from the burlap sack around his hand. "Yes, I am." He started his walk away from Blackjack toward the other end of the tunnel.

"Will I have any trouble with the spirits once I get to the cornfield?"

"No, you won't. You have control of the horse and all the powers that come with it. Good and bad."

"So, I don't have to worry about the spirit attacking the horse or me?"

"No, the spirits will be scared of you. When you mount that horse, you are literally a black spirit horse rider. Black spirit riders hunt spirits, so they will be scared of you. It was nice to meet you, Bradicus Blackjack."

Blackjack watched Woodford give a wave of his hand and disappear into the darkness. "Holy shit balls. I'm a black spirit rider?"

Chapter 28: Attack on Grimmbell Wall

Roko the Dark VIM-ed—that is, he used Volatile Interdimensional Movement—into a small cave neatly concealed at 22,300 feet above the valley floor in the Maroot Mountains. The cave dwelling had many extra features, making it a quality hidden hideaway. One of these was a linear rock outcropping that made the opening of the cave invisible to any overhead flying creatures, big or small.

"Roko the Dark. *Rodark.* I like the way that sounds," he said, patting the neck of his black spirit horse, Reaper. "What do you think?" The horse bobbed its head and stomped on the granite rock beneath its hooves. "Yeah, that's what I thought too."

He stared at the 120-foot granite wall surrounding Grimmbell Cemetery. "I'm not sure what I want to take from Grimmbell first." Leaning hard on the saddle horn, he said, "There are so many goodies. I could try for the most sought-after artifact made by the tomb earthers, the blood bricks. Only one or two produced per century, the most powerful artifacts fashioned by the earthers living in Grimmbell. Not to mention a piece of the soul tree, its sister being the death tree, or the hanging tree. There's a handful of specialty wizards who would offer more than gold for a wooden wand made from a medium-sized branch of just one of these three trees, but especially a mix of all three.

"Wouldn't that make the high council shit little rubber nickels, not to mention the soul king? Of course, if a blood brick were to get stolen, it could mean death sentences for their protectors."

Roko dismounted Reaper, patting his horse's butt as he walked around its other side to unhook the bag of skulls attached to the saddle horn. "Damn, the bag is heavier than I thought. And what a mess." The decapitated heads soaked the bottom of the bag with blood. "I will have to burn the bag. But first, I need to get a kettle of boiling water to clean and boil the skulls to make screamer's dust."

Rodark walked to the back of the cave to check on his assumption of what this cave had housed over the years. Artifact hunters, outlaws, drifters, not to mention many different flying creatures used the caves as a safe house for traveling through the Darkan Valley.

Rodark found what he was looking for, a granite stone chest.

"Oh yeah, I was hoping this would still be here. Good fortune is still on my side, I think."

He slid the heavy rock slab off the top of the stone box, the edge of the weighty chunk striking the floor, producing a spark that startled the black horse, causing it to kick wildly.

"Whoa! Whoa there, my black beauty of a horse. You seem a little froggy."

Rodark approached the horse, grabbing the reins. "Don't worry. We'll be out of this cave soon, and on to much bigger and better ventures."

Roko returned to the stone chest, retrieving a cooking kettle. "Perfect. A number ten kettle will hold ten skulls, and a piece of Bustnit wood to boil the water."

Inserting the Bustnit wood under the pot, the wood immediately burst into flames. Roko removed a pocket-sized leather pouch from his coat, removing a vial of essence water from it and dripping two drops of the solution into the empty pot.

"Shazam! Instant water. Two drops equal twenty gallons, more than enough to fill the pot."

After a two-hour rolling boil with rock salt and black spirit dust, Rodark removed the skulls to begin the grinding process. He retrieved a small iron mallet from his saddle bag and one by one, gently broke the skulls into palm-sized pieces.

"Now comes the tricky part."

He disentangled a feed sack from the saddle bag, placing the skull pieces into it. Hanging the feed bag over the muzzle of Reaper, he sprinkled his sword with the last little bit of screamer's dust and cut his tongue, applying a thin coating of bright blood the full length of the sword. It burst into a green- white flame and the black spirit horse stomped its front hooves.

"You know what's coming next, don't you?" Reaper violently jerked his head up and down. "Okay, here we go."

Rodark touched the sword on the back of the horse and stepped away.

Reaper burst into flames but stood in place, not experiencing any threat or pain as he slowly but thoroughly ground the pieces of the human skulls inside his feed bag.

Roko sat on the stone chest, watching the shadow of the flames dance off the cave walls. He cussed himself for losing the Grand Hall recipe book when the black entity had smothered him, and he'd ended up trapped in the saddle of the black spirit horse.

"I have a hunch Blackjack has possession of that book."

Rodark could see the flaming process coming to an end, the flames dying down to a small glow on the black spirit horse and he patted its back, extinguishing the remaining flames.

"You are no ordinary mount, are you, my four-legged chariot?"

Roko removed the feed bag from the horse. "It's heavier than I thought," he said, jerking the bag up and down. "Feels like two. Maybe two-and-a-half pounds of VIM dust, all told."

He poured the dust into the leather bag he'd secured to his waist. "Okay. It's time to go to work."

The horse pawed the stone floor, producing sparks that bounced off the cave walls. Roko mounted his stallion, grabbing a fist of dust.

Charging the opening of the cave, he threw the dust into the air and vanished, reappearing at a gallop five hundred yards in front of the walls of Grimmbell.

"Whoa! Whoa, Reaper!" he shouted, pulling back on the reins. "Slow this VIM machine down." The horse came to a stop and Rodark placed his hands one on top of the other leaning forward, bracing himself with the help of the saddle horn. He surveyed the two great walls protecting Grimmbell.

The 120-foot granite security wall stood high above

and inside the spirit wall barrier. He stroked his chin, leaning back in the saddle, musing on everything.

"I can VIM the spirit wall, but that granite wall, well that's entirely different. I don't know if that's going to happen. It's protected by an elder blood brick, one of the first ever made which means that it has even more protection power now than when it was fabricated."

Every creature that died in battle in the Darkan Territory within the Valley of the Tomb Sleepers has been fused into this solitary elder blood brick by the process of the Blood Brick Skull Drop and then secretly placed somewhere in the 183-mile-long granite wall.

An individual placed the elder brick, later to be terminated after the midnight-hour brick placement, during the black burning of the moon-sealing ceremony. There was no way to find the blood brick due to the hard fact that the location of it was unknown to anyone.

A hideous scream blasted through Rodark's ears, breaking his thought process and bringing him to full alert mode. "What the hell was that?" he muttered, jerking his head left and right.

Quickly looking over his shoulder, he found where the heinous scream must have come from.

A vortex of dust and wind materialized two hundred yards directly behind him, a black spirit horse rider appearing out of the turbulence.

Rodark spun his horse around to face the approaching stranger. The black horse rider trotted toward him, fading in and out of form.

Rodark tilted his head to the right. "Looks like that rider is having trouble staying in form when he VIMs. Probably doesn't have enough dust."

The rider's hands glowed a hint of silver as he slowed to a trot fifty yards out.

"Is that the same rider who can split horses in half at a dead run, and then join them back together?" Rodark placed his hand on his sword as he watched the rider approach, stopping in front of him. "Ah yes. You are the one who can split horses and adhere them again. Are you here to help me or to try and stop me?"

The silver-gloved rider nodded. "I am Arune, and I

am here to help you."

"How are you going to help me?"

"I will attack the spirit barrier wall at the opposite end of the front gate and when that happens, a heavy concentration of spirit guards will be transformed to that section. That should make a soft spot here, making it much easier to enter Grimmbell and steal that specific blood brick that we desire."

Rodark studied the rider.

"That's a rather simple plan, though it might work," "Thank you. I accept your help." A fake grin appeared on the silver-gloved rider's demeanor. "So glad you approve of my outline."

"Well, I approve of your plan because it will help me get what I want for now."

Arune looked Rodark up and down. "Don't forget if you do get the brick, it will help *us*. You are an extension of me. *We* would benefit."

Roko's face remained a plank of wood. "Of course, that's what I meant. But you could have avoided this business of breaking into Grimmbell which will only draw thousands of hunter spirits that want to kill us. If you would have done your job in the first place, this would never have come about."

"What are you talking about?"

"Since I am an extension of you, and you are an extension of me, I know about the peasant women at the apothecary shop. You remember Ella? You were to acquire her body that would lead you right to a rare elder's blood brick, but you failed."

Standing up in his stirrups and leaning over, Arune spit on Rodark's boot.

"Watch your tongue. I would have had her, but Kula's royal messenger attacked me. That rodent had great power and damn sharp claws. He actually tore open my power source. And the fact was I didn't have a strong enough body foundation to work through like I have now."

Rodark looked down at his marked boot. "You spit on my boot."

"I will have you know," said Arune, pointing at Rodark, "I battled Kula the Queen of the Dragoons in weakened ancient serpent form and almost defeated her."

"That is true, I suppose. If you had defeated Kula, you would have been able to defeat this all- powerful rodent and have unprecedented power in your hands, along with an elder blood brick. Did this rodent with the sharp claws have a name?"

"Yes, he has a name. Bradicus Blackjack."

Rodark howled. "My old buddy Blackjack. That's why you're so concerned about me getting into Grimmbell." Producing a grin, he added, "You want the other elder brick so you can get revenge on Bradicus Blackjack."

"Not necessarily," said Arune. "This rodent is one piece of many pieces on my list of plans. No different than when I planned for you to be tapped by a black spirit horse."

Rodark lightly gritted his teeth. "Where am I in your plan?"

"You know the familiarity of Grimmbell better than anyone. You get an elder brick, and I will let you rule Grimmbell."

"I don't know every secret about Grimmbell. I could get lost or trapped. And who says I even want to rule Grimmbell? Wherever did you get that notion?" Rodark asked, irritated.

"Your horse says so," conveyed Arune, smugly. "You can read Reaper's mind?"

"No, but I can read yours, the contents of which are transmitted through your horse to me. We are connected, remember, which leads me back to entering Grimmbell."

"I agreed on your plan," said Rodark. "What's the problem? Are you backing out?"

"No, I'm not, but you should know that there have been other black spirit riders who have entered Grimmbell and disappeared forever."

"What happened to them?" asked Rodark.

"They died a slow miserable death, many times over."

Roko secretly dipped his finger into his dust bag, then quickly licked it. "How can they die many times over? I thought death was like, once, then you're done."

"You are new to stealing spirits."

Saying nothing and spitting on the ground, Roko stared at the rider

Arune looked down at the wet spot on the ground. "If you get caught, you do realize you will be chained to the spirit pillar in front of Woodford's tunnel of free radical spirits."

"I have heard of the prison of jars holding these free radical spirits."

"I figured that much," said Arune, folding his hands on the saddle horn. "The baddest of the bad free radicals will be released long enough to stand in line, stab you the full-length of a sword and then ever so slowly, pull the blade out." Spitting on Roko's boot, he continued, "Not by any ordinary sword, mind you, but by the brother's sword, a jagged, rusty dull blade with barbs and fishhooks forged into it.

Remember now, that's a stab in and out for every spirit you've taken from a living creature so far."

"I have never seen the radical tunnel," said Roko. "Even when I was an earther, it was forbidden because of the high possibility of the free radical spirits being able to penetrate your flesh and take control of your body."

"You don't want to be in the tunnel anyway; that would mean you failed and have been stuffed into a jar, inside a lightless spirit jar prison."

"You know that firsthand?"

"Not firsthand, but a rider who managed to VIM inside the tunnel once, indulged in two or three jars of pickled spirit and shared his knowledge with me before I stole away all his power for myself."

"I'm tired of talking," said Roko. "I need to make a move. I'm behind schedule."

A silver hue flashed over Arune's gloves. "Like I said, I will draw most of the Grimmbell security to me, then you can make your move."

Arune turned away from Roko, trotting toward the opposite end of the Grimmbell wall.

Roko sat in the saddle, watching the silver-gloved rider becoming smaller and smaller until he finally—and quickly—VIM-ed into oblivion through a portal.

From what I know now, maybe I should grind up Arune and use him as screamer's dust. I wonder what kind of power cells hold him together?

Rodark turned his attention back to the task at hand, checking his bag of dust and gripping the handle of his sword for the third time in the past hour.

"If I VIM properly, then I shouldn't have any trouble passing through the two barriers, then I'll enter the great tomb of the earthers, find and open the vault of blood bricks and steal an elder blood brick.

"Hopefully once that's done, I'll VIM out of Grimmbell without being captured, imprisoned or killed by one of the tens of thousands of spirits that will feel my presence inside Grimmbell in the form of a hatred for intruders, especially black spirit horse riders."

Rodark quickly went to the earther spirit bag, retrieving a small pouch and placing it under his tongue. Once dissolved, it would enable him to see how many spirits were moving to the opposite end of Grimmbell where Arune was to perform his diversion attack.

He swallowed the juice and within a minute, could see hundreds of spirit lights flying toward the area of attack. "It's time to make my move," he said, rubbing the side of his horse's neck. "Are you ready, my black spirit rocket? Don't let us get caught."

Reaper stomped his hooves and trotted toward the spirit wall and within fifty yards, Rodark and Reaper were at a dead gallop toward the walls of Grimmbell. Gritting his teeth, Rodark grabbed a handful of dust and leaned forward. Reaper snorted, blowing steam from his nostrils.

Suddenly, out the corner of his eye, Rodark spotted Katmando, a member of the security team, the spirit sprinting towards him with a long dagger in each hand and one in its mouth.

Katmando meant business.

"Son of a bitch, that spirit is fast. I can feel the glare of his eyes burning a hole in the side of my head. He means business. If he were to capture me, I believe he would pound sand up my ass. Damn."

Rodark noticed that at his pace, Katmando would be on him in seconds. "Time to VIM." He threw the dust in front of him twenty feet before impacting into the spirit wall.

The light of the day vanished as Rodark plunged into the spirit wall with a stabbing pain in his right shoulder, the light reappearing as he plowed into the interior of Grimmbell's granite security wall.

Reaper impacted, knocking the horse backwards but Roko caught himself going over.

"Oh shit." Kicking his feet out of the stirrups, he shoved his arms toward the ground, ready for the unpleasant impact. He smacked the ground with a hollow thud, quickly digging at it with his feet and elbows to clear himself of Reaper stumbling backwards and pinning him to the ground.

"Oh, shit again." Reaper caught his balance seconds before planting his fifteen-hundred-pound body on top of his rider. "That-a-way, my black steed stud. I knew you wouldn't squash me like a grape."

Rodark looked around, noticing spirit warriors moving in for the kill, circling himself and Reaper. "Won't be long and I will have to fight through thousands of Grimmbell spirits. I need to get on my horse and VIM this wall. Where is Arune when I need him?"

He pushed with his left arm to get to his knees. "Damn." A sharp pain ripped through his right shoulder, causing an uncontrolled faceplant to the ground with a clank of metal. "What the hell is this?" Reaching to the top of his shoulder, he grabbed the ivory handle of a long dagger.

"Katmando. That son of a bitch is fast. His blade penetrated the dust cloud exactly when I VIM-ed." Reaper bunted his head against Roko's back, digging at the ground.

"Yeah, I know, we have to move or die a thousand times by the brother's sword."

Pushing himself to his knees with his good shoulder, then standing, he gathered the reins and mounted his horse, reaching for his bag of dust. "Ouch, that freaking hurts."

He quickly pulled his arm back and tucked it tight against his ribcage. Looking at his palm, he noticed small, serrated cuts.

"Every time I grab the handle, it cuts me." He

gripped the dagger with his good hand, trying to pull it out of his shoulder, but the dagger wouldn't move. "Son of a bitch, that hurts."

He relaxed his shoulder, hoping that would help to pull it out.

He grabbed the handle once again but to no avail, the cuts on his hand making the surface of the handle too slippery with blood to pull. "Dammit."

Suddenly, a kick to the back of the head, followed by a hideous laugh forced Rodark to turn around and face one of the guardian spirits.

"Roko, how dare you enter Grimmbell on a black spirit horse! You, your horse and your spirit will die here, never seeing daylight. Your horse will be skinned, and its hide cured and tanned, positioned as a windsock atop the Grimmbell wall. That windsock will always point in the direction of black spirit horse riders approaching Grimmbell. Your power cell will be imprisoned forever on the death tree."

"Not if I can help it," Rodark said, pulling his sword and swinging wildly at the spirit.

The spirit backed off only for a short time before fifteen fellow hunter spirits completed the circle around Rodark and his black stud Reaper.

He sheathed his sword, gripping the reins of his horse in his mouth, he spurred Reaper toward the wall. Clutching a handful of screamer's dust with his mobile hand, he hurled the dust at the wall.

Everything went black as he leaned forward with Reaper into the darkness, still able to hear the presence of the graveyard spirits calling for his head.

The daylight reappeared. Roko had successfully VIM-ed through the granite wall onto cemetery ground, but he took a heavy velocity of corncob thrashing to the face.

He pulled back on the reins, slowing Reaper down to a fast trot. "The cornfields. I'm in the corn. Not where I need to be. I screwed up."

He stood in the stirrups, stretching high enough just to peek over the top of the cornstalks to see the granite wall behind him.

"Shit, I went too far. I must have gone through one

corner of the wall onto Grimmbell ground, but then I kept going through the opposite corner, taking me back outside and into the cornfield that parallels the front gate. I need to get back inside Grimmbell."

He could hear the rustling spirits that inhabited the cornfields.

Roko immediately grabbed a handful of dust and leaning over, he whispered in Reaper's ear, "This isn't good. It's already too late."

He stroked the horse's neck. "The spirits that live in this cornfield are the protectors to the front gate. Be ready to get peppered with sticky ears of corn encased in a burning solution made of the sap of the death tree."

Reaper stomped his right hoof.

"Oh, by the way, did I mention the sap is powerful enough to burn through steel?" Reaper jerked his head up and down.

"I'm glad you're up for this. Although I just had a great idea. No spirit guards would ever expect a black spirit rider to charge the front gate, but that's exactly what we are going to do. The element of surprise. But this time when I VIM, I'm going to re-appear inside the tomb of the earthers, home to the blood-brick skull drop and the famous blood bricks."

Leaning over with his head just above the horse's mane, he charged the front gate.

Instantly, hundreds of ears of death corn bombarded horse and rider. Roko pressed his chin tight against the horse's mane, already pulling two burning corncobs off the side of Reaper's neck, the horse's hair sizzling with the heavy scent of burned skin.

Three more corncobs tagged Roko in the head. One bounced off his forehead. One stuck to his chin but fell off. The third hit hard and fast, sticking tight to the side of his face. It wasn't long before he could smell the scent of a different type of skin burning. His own.

"Keep running, Reaper. Fast as you can. Go for the front gate. Don't stop for anything." He ripped the corncob off his cheek. "Damn, that shit burns like hell," he said, wiping the death tree sap on his pants but it didn't help. His pants started on fire and gained volume with every stride of his horse. "Keep going, Reaper. Fifty yards and we will be through the gate."

His vision blurred by the onslaught of flying corncobs, a fog of burning horsehair seared his eyes. "I think I'm going to blow chunks," he said, frantically ripping the sticky bombs off Reaper's head and neck.

Three more soaked corncobs clung to Roko's throat. He reached for them, only to feel his fingers push through the front of his throat, touching his windpipe. "Oh no, I've been purged."

Roko could feel his life force pushing out against his hand. A stream of black smoke siphoned from his spirit form; the integrity of his power cell ruptured.

Shouts, screams, and mass cheers of victory rang out from the corn spirits lining the cornfield edge. The fire and smoke engulfed all of Roko and his sturdy horse, blinding him, and he fell forward, grabbing Reaper's mane. "Where is that fricking wall? I can't be defeated by a bunch of corn-husking spirit chucker's. Where is my dust? I'm Rodark, the black spirit rider."

Fingers burned to numbness. Eyes squinted closed. Mouth filled with ash. He fumbled around, finding his leather dust bag. He cupped what amount he could hold, throwing it up in front of his face.

Instantly, a high-pitched whooshing noise pierced his eardrums along with a violent catapulting jerk forward, plunging Roko off his horse and into an unknown darkness.

Chapter 29: Great Hall

Rodark awoke to two large nostrils pricking him with an occasional snort of hot air breathing on his face. "What the hell is…" he said as a smacking sound then a surge of wetness touched his neck. He reached up with his right hand, pushing away a hairy snout surrounded by the dampness of a tongue.

"Reaper what are you doing?" Rodark jerked up. "You're alive. *I'm* alive. Where are we?" Reaper nudged the side of his face.

"The corn spirits. Where are they?"

He surveyed his immediate surroundings. "I made it," Rodark said, blinking. "I believe I'm in a little hidden nook inside the great tomb of the earthers. I will take that."

Roko wiped his eyes clean and blinking once again, saw the blurry outline of four black sticks standing in front of him. "Reaper, is that you?" Rodark sat on the ground just until the vision of the four black posts in front of him materialized into the four legs of his horse.

Reaper lowered his head and Rodark locked his fingers together just behind the horse's ears. Reaper lifted his head up.

"That's just what I needed, a little help from my friend."

Roko brushed himself off, rubbing his throat. "The hole is gone," he said, then reached for his shoulder, shrugging up and down three times.

My shoulder… The dagger, it's gone. I wonder what happened to it?

He continued walking around Reaper, making sure he was okay, able to see patches of hair burned down to the flesh. But it was quickly growing back.

Roko paused, looking around the small skull room. "Doesn't look as though it gets used too much." He studied the horse in more detail, but his thoughts soon wandered back to the wall.

For some reason, when we VIM-ed through the wall, we were healed of all our wounds at the same time. That's interesting.

If a spirit rider is close to death and does heal after they VIM, does that make them immortal?

Roko peeked out of the storage room opening.

To his right, the hallway curved in the same direction and eventually, out of sight. "Don't think I want to go that way. I need to get much deeper into the tomb caverns."

He quickly eyed a ledge to his left, then walked the twenty-five feet to see a set of granite stone steps descending a very long way. "Not a hard choice here on which way to go," he muttered, looking back at the storage doorway. "Although, I'm not going to be able to ride my horse just now, so I'll have to leave him here. I should have enough power to move freely without Reaper. I feel supercharged since VIM-ing through the front gate, but need to move now. My time here is limited. I know I have Grimmbell's most successful hunter spirits looking for me."

Roko the Dark shot back inside the storage room. Reaper's head popped up, lightly bobbing.

"Yes, I'm glad to see you too." Rodark walked around his horse, rubbing his hand on the burned spots which had fully healed. "You're good to go. However, my friend," he said, lifting the horse's head up toward his face. "You can't go with me."

Reaper pulled away, raking his hoof across the stone floor.

"Listen to me. I will be back in an hour. Be ready to VIM when I return."

Reaper raked twice at the stone floor.

"Good boy. See you soon. Stay here and don't move out of this room."

Rodark tugged at his dust bag. "Good." Then he pulled on his sword sheath. "Good. Both waist belts are holding up."

Rodark stepped out of the storage room into the hallway, then walked down the hall that curved to the right and stopped, listening for any echoing of voices or movement.

Nothing. He looked down at the fading tunnel of steps. "Damn, it goes down a long way."

He took the first step down on the stone staircase. Stopping at each intersecting passageway that had a tunnel leading to his left and right, he listened for any movement. He finally lost count at 224 intersecting corridors, stepping on the partial remains of a skeleton before moving on to the next section of passageways. "Let's hope I don't end up like that poor bastard. Talk about a fricking maze."

He was talking to himself, of course.

One of the tomb earthers' security measures when building the Great Hall was that every intersection to the left or right had to look exactly the same, no matter which floor you're on.

Going up or down, you just get zero indication as to what story it is. And all the passageways inside the Great Hall are identical to ten-thousandths of an inch, any direction you go.

Rodark descended for another fifteen minutes, stopping at another intersection, but this time, he heard voices. He quickly and quietly retreated to the floor above.

Upon entering the passageway to the right only a few feet, spirit bumps formed on the back of his neck, running down the entire length of his spine.

He peeked around the corner, waiting for the voices to appear at the intersection of the steps. A large callus-ridden hand showed itself first by grabbing the edge of the hallway.

That's not the hand of an earther.

An arm followed by a shoulder, followed by a head. "Oh, it's an ore troller."

An ore troller was a creature standing four feet high, about a foot taller than an earther, known for their keen ability to find all types of minerals including chameleon mud deep inside the Maroot Mountains. They were known to withstand long months below the ground with very little air or water, also capable of moving tons of rock while mining inside the Maroot Mountains.

In this case, it looked as though the earthers had been using the trollers' expertise in finding the purest bloodstained soil surrounding the richest skulls for the blood brick drop.

"Quincy, stop there! Wait up for us!" Quincy took

three steps down, making room for the rest of the earthers assembled at the hallway's intersection.

"There they are. The master blood brick makers as legend has come to call them."

These were the earthers who'd designed the blood-brick skull drop, the process creating both the blood bricks and the rare elder's blood brick. They were the original earthers who had built the first Great Hall, now considered gods in the earthers' world.

That much I do remember.

However, when I did VIM into the Great Hall, some of my memory was lost.

I don't know what I will or won't remember. I certainly don't remember where the blood brick vault is located or have any idea how to open it.

The party of five started their descent of the stone steps.

Something important must be going on today. They're not usually together in one place at the same time, again for security reasons, but with the addition of the ore troller, I wonder if they're moving skulls or blood bricks in or out of a vault to another location?

Rodark waited to move until the group had descended five floors below him, quietly ducking in and out of the crossing intersections while following the earthers and troll down the steps.

The party of five continued down seven more intersecting hallways, then stopped at a small circular sitting area with benches. The troller sat while the earthers huddled together with much conversation and finger-pointing in a number of directions.

The huddle dissolved with the earthers talking to the ore troller, who nodded in agreement, turned around and disappeared into one of the hallways. The earthers watched the ore troller for a few seconds, then continued their journey down the stark stone stairway.

Rodark could hear more voices and movement with each passing hallway intersection. "I'm getting closer to the bricks. But I'm running out of time."

The earthers suddenly made a right-hand turn down the hallway and disappeared. "Oh shit, I need to catch up to them."

He counted down past five side tunnels.

"I need to take this right." Turning sharply, he entered the hallway into which the earthers had disappeared. Running the length of it, he didn't see any of them. Movement caught the last of the four, turning left down another tunnel, but that level was much lower than where he stood.

"How did they get down there so quickly? They must be using some spirit's tail dirt to move so fast and free. I can't use a spirit's tail to catch them, but I can follow them with the use of my own kind of mix. Screamer's dust." Rodark grabbed a handful of dust and threw it out in front of him.

The powder immediately took flight into the shape of a long zigzagging snake, giving him the exact passage to catch up to the earthers. "That's clever. They are using a type of illusion smokescreen to cover their tracks."

He waited as the white-gray smoke cleared and for only a couple of seconds, he could see exactly where he had to go.

I have a few tricks of my own. All I have to do is jump from here, and I'll find the bottom of these stairs. But when I do, I'll be in complete darkness until I reach the bottom.

Digging into his earther's pouch, he swallowed a small sinker's wax ball.

Pulling his sword, he leaped into the air and sank like a rock, stopping two feet from the granite floor, then gently touching down.

I hate this part. Can't even see till the sinker ball wears off.

Rodark waved his sword in front of him. "As if this is going to stop a Grimmbell guardian spirit from cutting my head off and stuffing my free radical soul into one of Woodford's jars. Or even worse, hanging it from the death tree."

Quickly, Roko could see again, and what a sight. He stood in front of a vault door built out of earther's metal. At each corner of the metal door, a jade marble carving depicted an earther's head and facial features biting on the handle of a lighted lantern. "Look like sculptures of earthers to me."

In the center of the vault door was the carving of a scorpion mole, the most feared enemy of the earthers, with its scorpion stinger tail held high ready to strike.

Rodark looked around. "It's way too quiet." He looked up to see a cathedral-type ceiling carved out of solid granite rock. "It must be three hundred feet to the crown." He made a mental note that there were four wooden doors facing him from each direction. North, south, east, and west. Each door had two thick iron rods, one at the top and one at the bottom, running through the door's width.

I wonder what's behind those doors and where they go?

He walked up to the vault door, studying it thoroughly. "Hmm. Don't see any type of handle or device to open this up."

He leaned in toward the scorpion mole carving in the center of the vault door. "I'm not sure what it's made of. Looks like carnelian, quite beautiful. In such detail." He raised his hand, then stopped. He looked around again, touching the carving of the scorpion mole. "Ouch. son of a...." he said, pulling his hand back. "That burns like hell." He rubbed thumb and forefinger together. "Still burning, dammit."

Rodark held his finger inside the dust bag, then pulled it out. "Nope. Still burning."

He dug into his earther's pouch. "I should have something in here to stop this infernal heat." He wrapped his finger with a yellow and black-striped tobacco leaf, a leopard's leaf mix.

This usually heals everything.

He stepped back from the vault door. "Them earthers. Them master earthers. They are brilliant, and when they need to be, quite deadly."

Rodark removed the leopard's leaf. "Well, I'll be a son of a bitch," he said, staring at his finger. "It burned the tip of my finger clean off. I guess that's why they don't have handles and why not just anybody can walk up to this vault door and get a brick. Duh."

Thump! Thump!

"What the hell is that?"

Thump! Thump! Thumpity-thump!

He looked behind him at the back circular wall, seeing light and shadows of figures moving up the hallways to the open arena where he stood. *Thump! Thump! Thumpity thump!*

"I can't VIM, not without my horse. Not sure I could anyway, being inside the Great Hall, too much power against the dark force."

He dug deep inside his earther's bag. Holding all of his tobacco bags in the palm of his hand, he searched for a combination that could get him out of this jam.

Thump! Thump! Thumpity-thump!

He stood looking at the two open doorways. "It's getting louder." Now, he noticed a film of smoke exiting the doorway into the grand arena. "I think they're burning a torch made from the soul tree, and with the beating on the horizon spirit barrels, it's a type of ritual to awaken all the spirits and souls that live within the blood brick wall of Grimmbell. But which ritual are they going to perform?"

Rodark attacked the nearest wooden door.

He kicked, pushed, and finally pissed on it. *Okay, maybe that was stupid.* He tried to slide the big steel pins to open it next, but nothing moved. *Thump! Thump! Thumpity-thump!*

He looked back at the open doorways. "I can smell their scents from here. Many spirits. Oh, how I want to eat all of them, and the earthers with them. With all that power, I could VIM forever.

"But let's get real. Together, they're too strong to defeat."

Roko paced in front of the vault. "I don't have enough herbs to lift myself out of this death pit. I could fight them. Maybe if I killed enough spirits, I would have the energy to get out of here. Or I would end up as a black spirit windsock on top of the Grimmbell security wall."

At this juncture, Rodark looked down at his waistline.

"What do I have on me that I can use to get me out of this mess?" He planted a hand into each of the two pouches.

"I'll mix the best of two worlds, my old earther magic with my new black spirit rider magic. Why didn't I think of this before? I'm a fricking genius, I think."

He cupped his hands together with the last of his tobacco herbs, along with some screamer dust, spilling excess onto the floor. He planted his face into his hands, inhaling, licking and chewing like a starving wild boar at a roasted corncob feast. He ate so fast that he choked just for a second, coughing and blowing screamer's dust from his nose. "Okay, dumbass, slow down and swallow your goodies."

Roko finished swallowing the mix of dust, tobacco and spell-caked wax balls.

He felt extreme pain in the stomach, as though someone was trying to tie him into a pretzel at the waistline. Falling to the floor, he closed his eyes and clutched his belly.

All I want to do is lie down and die.

When he opened his eyes, all he could see was feet. Little hairy feet, and the side of his face felt cold. *I'm lying down on the cold hard floor, with all these little hairy earther feet in front of me? My mix didn't work. They found me here and stabbed my spirit with the brother's sword.*

He reached for his chest. *But I don't feel a sword or a wound of any kind. It was painless. They took pity on me. Am I dead, or what? I can still move my hands, legs... and nobody is looking at me.*

"Hey, you hairy little rodents! Can you see me or what?" shouted Rodark. No one turned to look or made any acknowledgement toward him.

"I must be dead. They haven't yet sucked out my spirit into a jar, to place it on a shelf in Woodford's tunnel of misfits."

Sitting up against the stone wall near one of the wooden doors with the big-ass steel pins, Rodark watched the earthers unfolding a blanket inside a small two-wheeled cart.

"The cart is trickling red dust, blood dust. They are moving fresh-poured blood bricks to the vault.

It's the purifying taste-test ritual. I can't believe it. What luck! A purifying check.

"What are the odds of me breaking into Grimmbell and coming across the opening of the blood brick vault on the same day?" he whispered, shaking his head in disbelief. "I can't believe my good timing.

I've never seen it done before, even as an earther. It was solely performed by the four masters, Cremator and Serpentine, Cremator's handmade shamanic pet. All I have to do is sit back and wait.

"And when the time is right, I shall take a brick."

Rodark's attention turned to one of the open doorways, hearing the squeaking noise echoing from the hallway. He watched as the four master earthers stared at the doorway, waiting.

A resonating squeaking sound continued for another minute, then the squeaky wheeled apparatus appeared at the doorway.

"It's a set of wooden stairs. What the hell?"

The earthers pushed the mobile staircase up to the vault door, the top of the staircase touching it just under the top right jade carving of a master earther.

Pulling free his sword, Rodark waved his arms, yelling at the earthers, "Hey, you hairy little rats.

Look at me. I'm a black spirit rider. In your house. Hello! I'm going to kill you all." He grinned as no earther, or guardian spirit looked his way.

"My mix of the two magical worlds worked. I'm invisible."

Putting a hand in each leather pouch, he said, "Empty. Shit, I should have paid more attention to what I mixed together. I don't know if I can ever recreate that recipe."

He watched one of the master earthers with the longest beard walk up the staircase, placing a hand on each side of the jade carving. The carving glowed a bright green, illuminating the master earther as if he had a torch burning inside his chest.

The greenish-white light intensified from his chest onto the big wooden door to the south, the door glowing brighter and brighter until the steel bolt locks slid sideways, unlocking the door.

Rodark moved away from the door by which he'd

been sitting.

I don't know if I'll like what comes out from behind that door.

The door swung open, and a figure stepped out from the darkness, wearing a long robe with a hood concealing its face. Walking up to and standing next to the blood brick cart, the robe consisted of dragon armor and black spirit horse hide. The cuffs and collar were lined with earthers' hair, with one pocket on the lower right side. The robe sparked every few seconds, sending thin lines of lightning strikes onto the face of the vault door. "Somehow, they are connected to the vault door."

The guardian spirits rolled the other mobile set of stairs to the opposite side of the vault door and the next earther climbed the steps, placing each hand on the side of the jade carving.

He glowed a reddish white within his chest cavity, sending a jolt of red light to the north door, the light outlining it in red. Then everything inside the red outline began glowing.

The wood door started expanding further and further outwards, expanding so far out that Rodark ducked down, turning his back. "That door is going to explode, sending wood missile fragments in every direction. This ritual is unbelievable!"

He continued to hunch down but heard and felt nothing.

He peeked over his shoulder at the north door which deflated then puffed up again, and deflated again, and so it went on.

"That door is alive. It has a heartbeat."

The door continued the heartbeat rhythm…and then stopped.

The hooded individual gracefully turned toward the breathing door and nodded to the remaining two master earthers who took their positions one on each side of the door's bottom two jade carvings.

And now, the robed creature eased off his hood.

"It's an earther." Roko looked on as it reached into the cart, lifting a cloth bag into view and submerging the bag into a big-ass brass pot sitting in the blood brick cart.

"It's not heavy enough to be a blood brick."

The robed earther pulled a bag out from beneath his robe.

Dripping a red fluid on the stone floor as well as on his feet, he carried the bag to the north door and held it high above his head. The earther spoke out.

"To enter or leave. It must eat from my hands. Always, from here. In and out." The earther slid the big, rolled steel pin bolts open as if they were made of air and took two steps back.

The door swung open as the body of a scorpion mole pushed its way out the doorway, its deadly stinger tail held high above its back. The serrated tail poked at the bag with blinding speed, causing the liquid to drain out on top of the earther and the floor.

"Serpentine, you're making a mess. Now just wait a minute, and I'll get rid of the bag."

Rodark backed up to the stone wall. "It's Tamerrick under that robe." He watched in awe as the scorpion mole licked at the earther, waiting for the bag to be removed. "What the hell is in the bag?"

Tamerrick removed the cloth bag and holding a large heart above his head, he flipped it at Serpentine who snatched it out of mid-air, ripping at the heart and devouring it quickly.

The giant mole relaxed, almost lying flat on the ground. Tamerrick walked next to the scorpion mole. "It's been a while, my friend. We need to open the vault. Are you ready for that task?"

The mole straightened up. waiting for Tamerrick's command. Tamerrick nodded at the two earthers at the bottom of the vault door.

They nodded back and at the same time, pushed inward on their jade carvings. The carvings disappeared inside, the east and west big-ass wooden doors clicking open.

Out of each door stepped a *Cryptogen*, Seneca from the east door and Zeea from the west door. Cryptogens were creatures of unknown origin. They showed up one day unannounced and would usually keep to themselves, so little was known of them. The soul king said the

Cryptogens were made of dead and alive spirits, gray matter, and divine blood.

They were later found to have immense electrical grounding abilities with many types of energy associated with life and death vibrations, gathering the vibration types when they collected the dirt around any creature that had died in battle or otherwise.

Tamerrick and Serpentine moved over to the blood brick cart. Tamerrick stroked the new blood brick bars, licking his finger and dragging it the full length of the brick. Sucking on his digit, he looked up at Serpentine. "It doesn't have a metallic taste. That's the first good sign to a quality blood brick."

Seneca and Zeea floated toward each of the two master earthers stationed at the bottom of the opposing ends of the vault, each master reaching out and touching the Cryptogen.

Sparks exploded, landing on the stone floor, burning hot and bright with no smoke.

More sparks erupted out of the blood bricks lying in the cart, sending balls of blue fire bouncing off the top of the ceiling, raining down small buds of buzzing, burning hot light.

Rodark danced around all the little balls of falling death till he tripped over the hitch of the blood cart, planting his face on the cold, hard, stone floor. "Son of a bitch. Did they hear that?" he said, jumping up and drawing his sword. "They *had* to hear that."

He stood battle poised, feet shoulder width apart with an evil eye glare, gritting his teeth, gripping the sword with two hands high above his head.

No one turned around, all eyes focused on the vault door.

Rodark watched as the balls of burning death continued their descent to the floor. The more he looked at the floor, the more he observed many black burn spots. *Some spots are bigger than others. Are the bigger ones from multiple intruders or just one intruder getting hellishly fried?*

"I think I understand. This entire vault chamber is intersected magically into a gigantic shot of death by divine electricity. If the wrong person touches something, they will be fried to ashes and swept into a dark room for eternity."

Serpentine spun around, looking in Rodark's direction, his deadly stinger tail curved in strike position just above his back. Two quick strikes blasted out and back.

The momentum of the tail belched a wave of death into Roko's face.

"Damn, his tail's lightning fast. That was too close. My time is running out here."

Tamerrick looked in the direction of Serpentine's tail strikes. "What did you see, my pet? Are some of the spirits buzzing you? You know how they like to tease you."

Tamerrick reached into his waist pouch, revealing a dragoon eyeball and swallowing it. He stood still for a minute until his eyes turned a bright white, then his head swiveled back and forth over the back side of the vault chamber. "Hmm. I don't see anything dangerous. A couple of wandering spirits."

Tamerrick leaned into Serpentine's ear, whispering, "There could be a foul person among us. Wait for the vault door to open." Tamerrick stepped back.

"You are always a little jumpy when we open the vault. Me too," Serpentine replied.

Tamerrick sneaked a quick look back toward the wooden door of the west. "I think someone, or some*thing* is here in the vault room. Someone or something that shouldn't be."

Then a brain fart surged inside Tamerrick's head. He looked down at the floor.

"What if…? I hope not, but could it be Roko? He was taken by a black spirit horse?" A painful grimace painted his face; his stomach tightened, and he needed to suppress a wave of nausea.

A clap of the hands from one of the masters brought him back to the task at hand.

Tamerrick pulled the blood brick cart in front of the vault door and stopped, then the electrical connection began its magic. In the center of the vault door, just above the Carnelian carving of a scorpion mole, a five-foot circular opening started spinning counterclockwise.

Tamerrick removed a ladder from the side of the cart,

placing the top rungs at the bottom of the opening of the circular door. He reached inside his jacket, retrieving an iron bolt and handle.

He brushed the dirt away and inserted the iron screw into a one-inch hole, turning the bolt screw enough to where it stood on its own. He attached the handle to the bolt screw and spun it clockwise.

The five-foot doorway descended into the vault door and little by little, bolts of crimson light detonated out around the doorway, burning the side of Tamerrick's face.

"Damn. I'm a little too close. One more turn should do the trick."

Roko watched in awe. "So that's how they do it? It's not all about magic and secret spells that open the door; it's a combination of two worlds, magic and the simplicity of manual labor and tools. A screw and handle. Whoever would have thought it?"

Suddenly, the blood brick energy collected in the vault blasted out and into the chest cavity of Seneca and Zeea. They held their arms out wide with their hand pads up. Instantly, a crimson ball of light floated above the vault door, exploding, sending multiple shafts of light to the stone floor and creating an impenetrable cage surrounding everything in front of the vault.

Rodark looked all around the crimson cage. "Oh, this isn't good. They know something's wrong, or this is the usual practice. I think I'm screwed."

He walked within two feet of the crimson-colored security cage. Turning his head away quickly as his face started to melt, he bent over, puking up copious black soot onto the stone floor.

"Holy shit." He pulled back, holding his face and looking down, seeing yellow teeth lying in the middle of the black puke. "I'm fricking melting. They are *my* yellow teeth. Wow, I should have used some toothpaste!" He took a step, falling to the ground. "Now what?"

He reached for his foot and found a mangled ankle with a boot of mush.

Okay, I can watch this ritual another time. I need to get the brick and leave.

The circular door in the center of the vault stood

wide open, the four master earthers and the Cryptogens standing in a frozen pose as the crimson light filtered through them, enhancing the intensity of the crimson security cage.

Tamerrick handed the second-to-last blood brick to a heavy-set chunky butt earther standing in the circular vault doorway. "Only one more to go," said chunky butt.

Stepping off the ladder and pushing his waistline against the cart, Cremator noticed Serpentine's impatience. "Do you see a threat? If you see the threat, destroy it. Do you see a threat?"

Rodark forced himself up. "Only one brick left in the cart. And I have Tamerrick's giant pet scorpion mole ready to puncture me with his tail and eat my face off.

"Now is the time for me to take the advice of the silver-gloved black spirit rider. If you think you are going to die, cut open your power cell and produce a double of yourself."

He drew his sword, gripping the blade with his free hand, watching Serpentine sniff the air and scan the caged room, stopping long enough to lock his tiny eyeballs on Rodark. "He must be able to see me."

Serpentine raised his tail and moved forward toward Rodark for the kill.

Rodark pulled the blade through his closed hand, slicing it deep and within seconds, his hand spewed a pile of shining black dust equal to his height and weight, smiling back at him. He gawked at his double. "Is that what I look like? I have yellow teeth and a hairy face only a mother could love."

He dropped to the ground as Serpentine's tail struck his smiling double, yellow teeth sticking to the end of Serpentine's tail.

Serpentine spun in circles, smashing the yellow-toothed double into the bars of the powered crimson cage. Sparks flew and Rodark could feel intense heat burning his skin.

"Am I supposed to feel what my double feels, because I can feel and smell my skin burning?"

Tamerrick rushed to Serpentine's side, pulling a handful of striped wax balls from his earther's pouch, pitching them at Rodark's double. "Destroy the black rider. Kill him now." The striped balls ripped through the black rider's chest cavity.

With no one near the cart, Roko the Dark saw his chance.

Clutching his chest, he ran to the cart. "Damn. Talk about heartburn. My chest feels hard and heavy, as if I'm filling up with mud. Got to keep going."

He bent over the cart, and there it was. The last one, lying there for anyone to take. He grabbed the brick with both hands. "Wow, much heavier than I thought. It makes my fingers tingle." Rodark turned to see Serpentine pin his double of a black rider against the bars of the crimson cage. The twin black rider jerked violently, giving off a nasty hissing sound with a moldy decaying flesh smell.

Fire and exploding sparks snapped, crackled and popped, ripping through the dark double rider and onto the floor. Then the glow of the crimson cage disappeared along with the cage itself.

Tamerrick looked back at the vault door.

All participants had been released from the frozen mode into a relaxed posture. "The dark spirit rider altered the energy stream of the cage. Serpentine, detach from the dark spirit rider."

Serpentine pitched the fiery wad of black tar against the stone wall. *Splat.*

Rodark hit the steps running on his way to get Reaper. He never looked back.

Chapter 30: Spirit Horse

"Check out my new ride."

Coming to the edge of a pocket of trees tucked in the middle of Five-Star Buttes, Blackjack slowed to a walk and squatted down. With enhanced vision mode, he studied the eighty-acre plot. "I don't see any threats at this time." Standing, he looked back at the security wall of Grimmbell.

"Five miles," said Brazel.

"Five miles what?" Blackjack asked.

"You are five miles from Grimmbell. That's how far Five-Star Buttes is located from the wall." Blackjack looked at the top of the buttes. "Yeah, I figured it would be a good spot to take a break.

Check out my new ride."

"This wasn't the plan," said Brazel.

"What plan?"

"The plan that had King Rozet riding the horse."

Blackjack looked at the reins in his hand. "Plans change."

"I realize that, but do you remember what I said could happen if you try to ride a black spirit horse?"

Blackjack tied the reins to a low-hanging branch. "Yes, I do. You said something about opening unknown portals and I could explode."

"Precisely. Because of your body chemistry, the comparable energy of an open portal and your transforming procedure are similar. It could cause a huge explosion and death to both of you, or worse."

"What is worse than having your body parts hanging off a tree for the birds to eat?" said Blackjack. "Worse would be the horse could consume your almost identical vibrations of energy and fuse the

two of you together… forever. Then in the sense of it, you would be part black spirit horse, Rarebrook rabbit, human, and me."

Blackjack folded his arms across his chest. "I realize there are risks, but the tactics have changed.

Rozet is gone, and his spirit is free. Rodark has

possession of an elder blood brick."

"Roko the Dark has an elder brick?"

"Frightening, isn't it?" said Blackjack. "In his possession?"

"Correct again. He now has unknown power. We don't know what he could do with it. It's freaking scary."

"How do you know this is true?" asked Brazel.

"Katmando sent me his personal spirit messenger one hour ago. There is an enormous spirit hunt for Rodark right now."

"The strategies have changed," said Brazel. "Is it worth your life trying to ride a black spirit horse?" "Well, let's see," said Blackjack, counting on his fingers. "Roko with an elder brick. Portal surfing to the ends of the universe. Possible immortality. Destroying Grimmbell. I don't think we have a choice." "Destroy Grimmbell?" said Brazel. "Immortality. The end of Grimmbell. Is that just a theory, or do you think he would do that?"

"I don't really know what the end result could be," said Blackjack. "But I do believe to get the results they want, the black spirit riders and Arune will use the elder brick as a filtering vessel to produce the end result they want. Kula said it could be a powershift of some kind."

"We need to destroy Roko the Dark, the Penetrator, and Arune," said Brazel.

"Yes, we do because anything's possible. Roko could transform into an unknown entity-God with the elder blood brick as the filtering process… The list goes on."

"So, what is our new plan?" Brazel asked.

Blackjack nodded toward Luther. "I have the horse. Roko has the brick—" "You are talking about a duel. One on one. Battle to the death."

"Something like that," said Blackjack.

"What if he has the Penetrator with him? Have you thought of that?" "I'm counting on that. I have friends in high places too."

"So, you do have a plan," said Brazel.

Blackjack transformed into Bradicus, walking alongside the black spirit horse. "I have something that Roko might want as badly as a blood brick."

"More than a blood brick? What could that be?" said Brazel.

"And he could use this something to take out the Penetrator," said Bradicus. "You're telling me that he wants the Great Hall recipe book over a blood brick?"

"I'm pretty sure he would like to mix the brick and book."

"That would be interesting and frightening at the same time," said Brazel. "I agree," said Bradicus. "You would have a mix of—"

"You would have death," said Brazel. "A mix of Rodark, the horse, the brick, the book, and the Penetrator. I think Kula is right, a transfer of power."

"So, let's find out what happens when a Blackjack and Luther, a black spirit horse, get together." Bradicus grabbed the saddle horn with his left hand. "So far, so good."

"You're not in the saddle yet," said Brazel.

Bradicus lodged his left foot in the stirrup, pulling himself up, swinging his free leg over and planting himself squarely in the saddle. "Look, Mom, no hands."

He leaned next to the tree branch and untied the reins. "I can't believe you said that," said Brazel.

Bradicus leaned back, pulling the reins tight. "Something is happening. I'm getting taller."

"*You* are not getting taller; your horse is," said Brazel.

Bradicus leaned off the side of the horse, noticing the ground was a couple of feet farther away. "I'll be damned," said Bradicus. "Not only did my horse get taller but his legs are also thicker. Look at his mane; it's growing longer right in front of me."

"I do believe your horse just grew bigger all around by roughly thirty-five percent."

"How do you know that?"

"Because I'm smart," said Brazel. "Wait a minute."

"What now?" said Brazel. "You're getting sick?" "No, I'm buzzing."

"What do you mean, you're buzzing?"

Bradicus put his hand on the side of Luther's neck. "Wow. Very warm."

"You're warm too?"

Bradicus shook his head. "No, I'm not warm. Luther is warm, and I'm buzzing." "Make up your mind," said Brazel.

"Brazel, shut up for a minute."

Bradicus sat quietly in the saddle, looking down, and all around became very quiet. He could see branches moving with the wind but couldn't feel or hear any breeze at all. Two graybeard birds landed on a nearby branch, fighting over a small tree nut, but he could not hear them carrying on.

He snapped his fingers three times but didn't hear anything. "Okay, this is weird. What's happened to my hearing?"

Bradicus shook his head, putting a finger in each ear and twisting.

The buzzing noise continued. He caught movement in the center of the trees. It had hair and was following a path through them for a little while, then disappeared into them.

Once in a while, he could see fur passing back and forth across the open path. "Looks like a small wolf of some kind. Brazel, are you seeing what I'm seeing?"

There was no answer from Brazel.

Bradicus snapped his fingers. "Still no sound. Am I in some kind of a dream?" Suddenly, the furry animal reappeared from behind a large oak tree.

"It's an earther. It has long teeth and fingernails. The hair is longer too. Never seen that before on an earther."

It walked slowly toward Bradicus, and Bradicus grabbed the handle of his sword and pulled—but the sword wouldn't come out of the scabbard.

The unusual looking earther stopped within a couple of feet of Luther, and sat on the ground staring at Bradicus.

Bradicus stared back.

"Don't worry," said the earther, "I'm not here to harm you. I am only here to warn you."

Bradicus tried to answer but couldn't move his mouth. "What the hell is going on? Is this what happens when you are trapped by a black spirit horse? A bunch of weird shit appears in front of you, and you have no control, confusing your mind? Is this how it goes?"

The earther stepped closer to Luther, studying the horse front and back, top to bottom, gently touching the horse's leg and making eye contact with Bradicus.

She folded her hair behind her ears. "Nice looking horse. How fast can it run?" she said. "Beware the black spirit world. Beware the journey to nowhere."

Bradicus' face scrunched up in worry. "I have seen that face before," he said, a groan accompanying his clenched jaw. "It can't be, can it?" He watched the earther retreat and disappear into the trees.

Suddenly, he could feel the wind against his face, hear the birds calling about the ownership of the tree nut, and his blade moved freely from his scabbard.

"Okay, looks as if I'm back in the world again." He turned his head, studying the area of ground where the earther had exited into the trees, shaking his head in disbelief.

That earther looked just like Brazel's wife Peppersaul in the real world. I don't know what it means.

Bradicus stared at the ground in deep thought. *It's possible that the rider of this horse was the one who took Brazel's wife, the same day I inherited his superior subconscious mind. I will keep this bit of information to myself. Now is not the time.*

"Bradicus, are you there? Can you hear me?"

"I can hear you, Brazel."

"What happened? I lost connection with you."

"I don't know for sure. Everything went dead and quiet. It felt as if I was suspended in a giant spider's web where I couldn't hear or feel anything, and my body movement was limited."

"Did you see anything out of the ordinary?"

"No, it was only a short amount of time."

"That is strange," said Brazel. "I had this emotional flashback to… to when I was in your world. When I had a body. A life. My wife. I don't know what is happening. Ever since you mounted this horse, I-I can sense Peppersaul."

"You mean, ever since *we* mounted this horse, you can sense Peppersaul?"

"Yeah, that's what I meant. It feels as though she's trying to communicate with me. Maybe it was a spirit letter that got blocked, and it finally caught up to us. Don't know if I want a spirit messenger. The messengers are very exclusive and usually convey bad news at the same time."

"That's possible," said Bradicus. "You get two spirit messengers with a life coin. Have you received two spirit messengers' letters yet?"

"No, I haven't, but I had them spaced out, one every three years. And the next one won't be available for another year and a half."

"I see," said Bradicus. "Well, maybe we should focus on what will happen when I do change to Blackjack sitting on this horse."

"I agree. We have more important issues threatening our way of life and the Valley of the Tomb Sleepers, and the big one, Rodark and the Penetrator versus Bradicus-Blackjack and Luther. Although I have been evaluating some possible outcomes of you controlling the black spirit horse in battle."

"What are your calculations of us controlling the black spirit horse in battle?"

"Oh, that's an easy one," said Brazel. "Ninety-five percent of possible scenarios show us dead."

"Oh, so we have a five-percent chance of survival. Nice. I like those odds." Bradicus patted Luther.

"Come on, big boy, let's get in the middle of the trees here. I feel exposed." Bradicus rode Luther halfway into the trees.

Stopping, he dismounted, leaving the reins trailing on the ground. "What if he takes off?" said Brazel.

"I don't think he will. Besides, he has grown to like this special horse food that Woodford gave me inside the free radical tunnel."

"Are you kidding me? Woodford gave you horse feed?"

"He gave me a bag of something and told me it was for Luther, so I guess it was horse feed."

Bradicus drew a handful of the goodies from the saddle bag, and Luther perked up, pushing his muzzle into Bradicus.

He held his hand flat as the sticky horse tongue licked his palm clean, followed by a huge horse fart and some excited head bobbing.

"What the hell is in that stuff?" Brazel asked.

Bradicus held his hands up, palms out. "I don't know. Woodford said this would help keep Luther manageable until I need him to get ugly."

"What else did he tell you?"

"Wait a minute," said Bradicus, shooting a quick look to his right, squatting down to get a better look through the trees. "Something big landed over there."

"We're going to be attacked," said Brazel. "It's Rodark and Arune."

"I don't think it is, but I'm not sure *what* it is." Bradicus continued to bob around like a cork in rough waters, staring into the tree line. "Something is out there."

"Oh great, we wait half an hour, then it will kill us. Let's try VIM-ing. We haven't tried that yet."

"That's not a bad idea," said Bradicus.

"I was kidding around. You have VIM dust?"

"Why yes, I do, my subconscious friend."

"Do I want to know how you got VIM dust? No, wait, let me guess. Your buddy Woodford?"

"That's right," said Bradicus. "Told me he took it off a black spirit rider he'd trapped in the Woodford tunnel a few years back."

"You're kidding me," said Brazel. "You have actual real live VIM dust?"

Bradicus shrugged. "That's what he said. I don't see any reason why he would lie to me."

"No, I don't think he would either. Do you see anything in the trees, anything that still wants to kill us for your VIM dust?"

Bradicus drew his sword just as Kula thrust her head out of a thick cluster of brush. "Don't worry, I'm not going to kill you for your VIM dust."

Bradicus spun around, falling back into his horse. "Kula, is that you?" "Of course, it's me. Are your eyes failing you?"

Bradicus regained his posture, pushing away from Luther. "My eyes could be playing tricks on me again."

"Why do you say that? Snorting too much VIM dust?"

"No, my Queen, no VIM dust," Bradicus said, pointing at her head. "I see your head, but there is no way the rest of your body can be hidden in that small amount of brush."

Kula looked back toward the brush. "Oh that. Someone we know shared a little secret with me." Bradicus stroked his chin with his eyebrows arched. "Rasp came through for us."

"He did, with a little help from a friend."

"Cinnamon too?" asked Bradicus.

Her head dipped into a quick nod. "Yes, Cinnamon too. That's why I'm here, to fill you in."

"We could have mind melted," said Bradicus.

"Didn't want to do a mental tap at this time. Too many mind miners in the air right now."

Bradicus bobbed his head as though it was mounted on a spring. "Very true. Roko the Dark with an elder blood brick. He could steal our thoughts."

"Yes, you heard the news too," said Kula. "I'm sure he's been trying to get inside our thoughts ever since he stole the blood brick, among other nasty things."

Bradicus leaned to his right, staring at the underbrush hiding the rest of Kula. "Are you going to share your secret with me?"

"My secret?" said Kula, following his line of sight. "Oh, that. It's a gift from Cinnamon."

"And what does this gift from Cinnamon do?"

"I'm glad you asked. It allows me to shrink any part of my body, like I am doing now. Cool huh?"

"That's remarkable," said Bradicus, nodding. "What was the price to show you her secret?"

"Right to the point, Bradicus. No messing around with you."

"She's still one of Killamore's dragons, no matter how special she is."

Kula changed to full size, looking down at Bradicus. "Jinnamon was a Killamore dragon, and you said she saved your life, so it doesn't mean she's bad."

"I never said Jinnamon was bad, but I do know that

the dragons of Killamore are taught to bargain one exchange for another."

Kula lowered her head. "Yes, I had to bargain with her. I'll get to that later. Okay, here goes; try to keep up if you can."

"I'll do my best. Oh, by the way. With your permission, Brazel wants to do a verbal recording of the observation process."

"No problem," said Kula, lifting a wing. "We will be able to transfer his info to my wings at a later date, right?"

"Of course, we will. It will be stored in long-term memory."

"Great," said Kula, dropping her wing. "Rasp recorded the observation process in his master recipe book. That will give us two versions to compare."

"Sounds like a good idea, just in case we lose a version along the way."

"I hope not. I don't want any info to get lost. But first things first, this is what I know so far concerning the observation room activities," said Kula.

"Yes," said Bradicus, "I was wondering how all that turned out. Good or bad?"

"Or both," said Kula. "Good and bad. What do you want first?"

His body went limp as if all his bones had dissolved. "Just go for it."

"Okay, first and foremost, Cremator is alive. Shaky, but alive."

"He's alive?" said Bradicus. "That's great news. Cremator is alive, but shaky how, exactly?"

"In and out of consciousness and not able to stand on his own yet."

"Has he said anything?"

"Yes." Kula, nodded. "Said he was very thirsty, his eyes burned, and he couldn't feel his hands." Bradicus looked away, his eyes narrowing.

"Screamer's dust irritated his eyes inside the vortex at the same time as Roko chopped his hands off in the portal. I'm not sure what happened to them during the fight."

Kula's eyes gleamed disapproval.

"Jinnamon is dead. Rasp conjured up eight different spirit helpers in the task to save her spirit but at this moment, he's still working with her sister Cinnamon on that problem. Upon further observation, Cinnamon noticed that Jinnamon had puncture marks right through her armor."

Bradicus folded his arms over his chest. "Something stabbed her? I find it hard to believe that Jinnamon would allow anyone that close for that length of time."

"My thoughts too," said Kula, holding a bone. "Someone or something stabbed her many times, but not at random or in battle. The pattern of the holes was strategically placed. According to Cinnamon, the only thing that can penetrate her armor as well as Jinnamon's armor is a tooth from their mouth."

"A tooth? Really?" said Bradicus. "That's what you have in your hand. Her tooth?"

"Yes. When Rasp, Cinnamon, and one of his spirit colleagues figured out a way to get her mouth open, they secured it open and sure enough, a tooth was missing. This tooth was found lodged under an armor plate. It's the same tooth missing from her mouth, one of her major biting choppers."

"Somebody took a tooth out," said Bradicus. "How did they know about that?"

"I don't know for sure, but I believe someone had talked to Killamore and was informed about this tooth secret, because do you remember when Slaughter came upon Jinnamon? She wasn't herself; her flight pattern was unstable, and she was confused and scared."

"Someone had attacked her on the ground when she was at her weakest." Bradicus grit his teeth so hard his jaw ached. "Roko the Dark. That piece of garbage."

"How do you know it was Rodark?"

"I don't know for sure, but the timing matches the timeframe when I saw Molehol transporting Jinnamon in his mouth. It wasn't long after the battle that Jinnamon had with Roko."

"What if it was the silver-gloved rider?" said Kula. "The one reportedly seen with Rodark just before the attack on Grimmbell?"

"Yes, that's a strong possibility."

"The story doesn't end there," said Kula. "Cinnamon had the knowledge to open Jinnamon's belly drop."

Bradicus looked up at Kula and pointed at the horse. "I'm not giving the horse back. I will ride Luther into battle against Rodark and his power source Penetrator."

Kula exhaled. "You were long gone before Cinnamon figured out how to open her sister's belly. And the fact that we we're going to need Luxen's horse for more than just one purpose."

"Yes, I suppose you're right, you usually are."

"I am your queen, so I'm supposed to know."

"How *did* she open the belly?"

"This is where Rasp comes in. Actually, he was quite clever. Rasp invented a mix from his master recipe book that would take half of Cinnamon's spirit and injected it into Jinnamon. Once inside, Cinnamon was able to read and translate the tongue graffiti dialect to open her belly drop."

"That's interesting," said Bradicus. "He only used half of her spirit. I can remember Roko telling me that you had to use a full spirit to perform a feat like that. Never heard of a half-spirit mix."

"That's what I thought. It was quite clever keeping the other half of her spirit from being trapped inside Jinnamon and possibly losing Cinnamon in the process, luring the inside half-spirit out and rejoining them to make a full spirit again."

"That is clever," said Bradicus. "Brazel is harping on at me to find out what the tongue graffiti dialect is all about."

Kula inhaled deeply through her nose, exhaling slowly out of her mouth. "I would be happy to tell you, Bradicus. Cinnamon shared with me the story of how she and Jinnamon were made."

"You mean they weren't born?"

"Not exactly," said Kula. "When Cinnamon and Jinnamon were created, their bone structure skeletons were created first. On every inch of their skeletal frame, special worldly symbols were engraved, from many different worlds."

"How many worlds?" said Bradicus.

"I don't know. Cinnamon didn't know. Along with the special engravings, there was a tactical pattern of teeth and a tattooed tongue, enabling them to move their tattooed tongue over different teeth to activate advanced body and mind abilities. Actually, Cinnamon said she's still learning how to navigate the tongue-to-tooth dialect."

Bradicus looked at Kula with folded arms and raised eyebrows. "Let's see if I'm getting this straight.

When Cinnamon wants to do something out of the ordinary, all she has to do is glide her tongue over specific teeth in a specific pattern to activate the bone-engraved secret worldly symbols, right?"

"That's the way I'm understanding it," said Kula. "Pretty fascinating, isn't it?"

"Jinnamon is the same way, correct?"

"That's what Cinnamon said, and the fact that Rasp verified it…" Bradicus nodded in agreement. "Okay."

"Rasp followed her spirit when it went inside Jinnamon. Like you said, it was clever because now, or at least I would bet on it, Rasp has the pattern of the symbols on her skeletal form. And more importantly, the secret worldly symbols are written in his master recipe book. He's getting to be quite the stud tobacco maker."

"He's definitely learning a lot the last couple of days. I do hope that Cinnamon won't come back someday and try to kill him because of that information."

"Why would you say that?"

"Because a while back, before we were to fight Roko and some of his goons, Jinnamon questioned my loyalty to you. She wanted proof that I was who I said I was. Rather strange, I thought."

"I hope she'll not do that either," said Kula. "Because one of the things that I promised her for the exchange of her skeletal information and my special little shrinking secret is that she could take the place of her sister Jinnamon as territory guardian for Tower 7."

Chapter 31: Knock-Out

Rodark focused on connecting mind and body, particularly the lower body, to propel himself four steps at a time running up the stone stairway. "Maybe I can get five steps at a time," he said, looking back over his shoulder. "Serpentine can devour thirty at a time. Got to keep going faster. Faster. Five more levels and I will take a quick breather."

Rodark scaled the next five levels and slowing at one of the intersecting tunnel platforms, he spun off to the right, pressing his back up against the tunnel wall and holding his hand over his chest. It felt as if his heart had a sledgehammer and was trying to break its way out of his chest cavity.

"I really need to get in better shape."

He peeked around the edge of the tunnel, looking down the steps. "I don't see anybody coming after me. Wait a minute, I'm such a captain dumbass. I'm invisible, you moron."

Rodark shook his head in disgust. "I better not put this on my resume."

Taking in a few more deep breaths, he attacked the stone steps once again and continuing his concentration of mind and legs in unity, he put behind him another fifteen levels before again spinning off to rest inside one of the intersecting side tunnels.

"I have to be getting close. I never thought I would complain about having an elder brick, but this brick is fricking heavy."

Peeking down the stairway, he could still smell the burned tar of his clone. *That double of mine saved my life. I wonder if I could produce two or three of them at the same time? Wow, that would be extremely handy in battle. I couldn't lose. I better quit daydreaming and get moving.*

He climbed another ten levels when he noticed a black horse's head sticking out into the hallway. "Reaper, you big black stud, you." Reaper looked right at Roko. "I think he sees me. I'm not invisible anymore. Damn."

Rodark entered the storage room, bending over and resting his hands on his knees. "Reaper, I could have used you coming up those stairs. We have to get out of here." Reaper scraped at the stone floor.

Rodark opened a leather flap on one side of the saddlebags. He searched the bag gallantly but didn't find what he was looking for. "How am I going to get out of here without VIM dust?" He walked around to the opposite side of Reaper, digging into the other saddlebag. "No dust. Damn."

He searched his leather pouches. "I must have something between the two bags to get myself out of this mess."

Reaper dug at the floor, bobbing and shaking his head.

"You hear something, don't you? They are getting closer, aren't they?"

He creeped up to the open doorway hugging the wall, getting out just enough of his head to look around the corner. He could hear a swooshing noise, then a wave of heat slapped his face, lingering with the smell of burning dust. "I know what they're doing. A hard burn of the tunnels as they come up the stairs. They have flammable fire spirits racing through the tunnels on fire to burn the intruder out, pushing them into a trap." Roko the Dark pulled his head out of the hallway, looking at Reaper.

Reaper stomped his hooves, jerking his head in a wild trajectory.

"Don't worry, Reaper, I won't let them burn you." Reaper kicked the wall, sending an arc of sparks bouncing off the front wall of the storage room.

Rodark reengaged the open doorway and looked both ways. "Can't go down the stairs. We have to go to the left, into the curved tunnel."

He could feel the heat growing closer, along with the intensified smell of burning dust.

"Wait a minute, I'm not thinking clearly. I can make another double of myself and send the fire spirits on a hide-and-seek quest that they can't win."

He tucked himself back into the storage room, leaned against the wall and drew his sword. "Here we go, Reaper.

We will give them a black silhouette of a man they can chase."

Rodark gripped the top of his blade. Tightening his hold, he pulled down on the blade, slicing deep, a black liquid flowing down his elbow and onto the floor. "I can feel that cut a lot more than the last one. I don't feel so good." He watched the black goo bubble up in front of him.

Suddenly, a severe cramp folded him over, sucking him to the cold stone floor. Rolling to his right side and curling up into a ball, he clutched his stomach. "What the hell is this?"

The black silhouette double stopped growing. He watched as Reaper stumbled, gasping for air as snot rolled out of his nose. "It's the smoke of the burn spirits. Serpentine and the fire spirits must be getting really close. I will not let them have our spirit energy. I can figure a way to bring us back, but I need to be the one who takes our spirits out of this world, to store safely in another."

Rodark's deformed double had managed to attach itself to his hip, weighing him down, but he succeeded to stand with the help of his sword as a crutch. He shuffled next to Reaper, patting the horse's neck but Reaper still struggled for air, his eyes glazing over.

"Don't worry, my friend, I will find you in the afterworld. This won't hurt a bit." He held his sword above his head with both hands, positioning himself for a thrust into Reaper's neck.

He focused on the kill spot. "Okay Reaper. On three. One, two…"

The sword plunged into Reaper's neck, his front legs folding. Rodark quickly turned to see a hunter spirit had done the dirty deed. "The brother's sword. The spirit used the brother's sword."

The hunter stood over the lifeless horse, bearing a nasty gnarly glare.

Rodark swung at the hunter spirit with all his strength but only caught air and fell backwards, smacking his head on the floor. Three fire spirits ripped at Rodark, but he grabbed one of them only to feel another blow to his head. A blurry stare, and then his world went silent and dark.

Rodark reached for his sword, but only felt air.

"They took your sword. The soul king will have it in his chambers by now."

Rodark spit on the ground, then kicked a lump of dirt at the feet of the rider's horse. "If you are so great, then why didn't you go in and get the blood brick yourself?"

"Because I created the diversion, remember. And that's why I have you."

"I got the elder brick, remember," said Rodark. "I succeeded. You're here now because you want my blood brick."

Arune pulled back on the reins of his horse, his eyes flashing red. "It's true, you did get the blood brick, but if I hadn't VIM-ed into that storage room and pulled you out, the hunter spirits would have stabbed you with the same sword with which they stabbed Reaper. You wouldn't be here right now."

"I'm not giving you the elder brick," said Rodark. "It has so much power. And I love it. It feels good.

It talks to me and tells me things."

"What does it tell you, how you are going to die?"

"No, but it told me that when you arrived, you were going to try to steal my brick. The brick likes me, and it doesn't like you."

"What are you talking about? The brick can choose who it wants to serve? That the brick has a brain?"

"That's correct, you horse-humping piece of garbage."

Arune pulled his sword. "You don't know who you're talking to. You don't know from what world I come."

"A lot of things have come to light," said Rodark. "Ever since I acquired the elder blood brick, I have known that you can't really take full functional form in this particular world unless you can filter your present form through the brick first. But again, the brick wants me, not you."

Arune nodded with a smile. "Why are you smiling?"

"Because when I selected you, I knew I had something special. With your earther skills, the skills of the black spirit horse and an elder blood brick, well, an unstoppable weapon has evolved. A weapon that I will have total control of once I filter you into my power cell."

"You and whose army is going to filter me into your power cell?"

Arune rubbed his hands together. "I'm glad you asked. I have a friend of mine stopping by to help you find my brick."

"How do you know if I have the brick with me? I could have buried it somewhere safe."

"I know you didn't hide it, bury it or give it away. I know you filtered the brick into your own power cell with the help of Reaper."

Rodark's forehead creased with worry and his mouth turned grim.

"Did you think that Reaper was loyal to you? Reaper did what I told him to do."

"What did you tell him to do?" Rodark asked.

"Simple, take care of you and secure the elder blood brick. That's it."

Rodark picked up a rock and threw it at the rider, bouncing off the side of his leg.

Arune looked at the rock lying on the ground. "Throwing rocks, is that what it's come to? You have all this power and you're throwing rocks. You disappoint me."

"I'm glad I disappoint you. I'm getting bored. If you want the brick, come get it. It's easy."

Rodark felt a surge of warm air cover his body followed by the crackle of a large circular energy portal opening before him.

"I was hoping it wouldn't come to this," said Arune. "I had expectations that you would join my forces. But in the end, it doesn't really matter because I'm going to take my power from you."

Arune drew his sword and with an over-the-shoulder throw, harpooned Rodark in the chest, pinning him against a tree.

"Son of a bitch, that hurts." Grabbing the sword handle with both hands, he tried to pull it out, but it wouldn't budge an inch.

Suddenly, out of the portal emerged Silakon, flogging his six bull beasts with a bull's whip pulling his wooden wagon. He snapped the whip one more time, and the six bull beasts slowed to a stop.

Arune rode his horse in front of Rodark.

"Are you sure you acquired an elder blood brick, because yer not looking very strong at the moment." He was leaning off the horse. "And look there," he said, pointing. "Your power cell has been cut and your essence is leaking on the ground."

Rodark kicked at the rider's horse. "I will never give you the elder brick."

Arune dismounted his horse, holding a leather bag underneath Rodark and watching the bag fill with his granulated essence, spilling freely from where the sword exited the lower section of his back.

Arune pointed at Silakon. "Silakon, get a bigger bag; we need all of it. Do you have room in your filter pot?"

Silakon jumped out of the wagon holding a bag in the air. "Arune, my master, I have enough room in my filtering pot."

Rodark could feel his power leaving his body.

He pushed on the hood of the sword and found that the sword stood solid and strong.

Silakon positioned the bigger bag beneath Rodark, feeling the granulated essence filling the palm of his hand and spilling over into the bag. "The grains are smooth and rounded, not sticky. This is a very good mix. I hope I can get it all in my filtering pot."

"Make sure you do get it all," said Arune. "And don't forget to seize his remains." Rodark concentrated on the elder blood remaining in his veins.

His body started to buzz, and a stinging sensation pricked every inch of it. "Come on, elder blood, do your thing. Bring my double buddy back to life!"

An uncontrollable urge to vomit overtook his thinking. Whatever was crawling up from his stomach, he couldn't hold it back. He folded over and opened his mouth, the sludge burping at first then flowing down his chin, and around the blade that pinned him to the tree.

Silakon stepped back, calling out to Arune. "Something is happening."

Arune stared down from his horse. "It's his power

cell function to produce a double to repair itself.

Get the eternity vessel. Set it to entrapment mode and put it at his feet. Do it now."

Silakon returned to his wagon and pulling the trapping device from its housed box, he quickly dropped the container at Rodark's feet.

"Pull the cord," said Arune.

Silakon stepped back, stopping when the ten-foot cord went tight. Pulling the cord, the box popped open with a white light blasting into the sky. The light swirled with the velocity of a tornado turning to a heavy green light, clinging to Rodark like snot on a doorknob, pulling his feet into the box.

"What the hell is this?" barked Rodark. "You won't fight me. I have the elder brick blood pumping in my veins. You are scared of me, and you know I can stuff screamer dust up your ass. You, Arune, are a coward."

Arune sat atop his horse, laughing. "Roko the Dark, I love your fighting spirit. You have the heart of a warrior. You might have been an enhanced pick over Blackjack, and you are working out better than I thought, but at times, you don't think past your nose. Did you really think you would be able to keep the elder brick?"

"I can see past my nose quite clearly," said Rodark. "I have the brick inside of me, pumping in my veins. We are one. You can't have it."

"Look at your feet; the box by your toes is an eternity vessel. Some call it a hot box. This container will hold your remains after I absorb all of the powers inside of you. Do you get it? I will have the superior power of the elder blood brick and there's nothing you can do to stop me." Arune nodded at Silakon. "Get ready to seal the box when it's done."

Rodark could feel Arune's sword wiggle within his chest. "Ah yes, the elder's blood is starting to work."

Silakon ran back to his wagon, grabbing a five-foot long pole made out of black spirit horse tar.

Silakon stood over Rodark, poised to seal the container.

Rodark looked over at Silakon. "Seriously, you're going to use a sealing stick. Do you really think that's going to hold me?"

"Yes, it will," said Arune. "Because this isn't your ordinary sealing stick. This one is special. Made just for you."

"What makes it so special?"

"This one has a special ingredient mixed in."

"What kind of an ingredient can seal me in a box?"

"It's called tar of Reaper," said Arune.

Rodark was about to answer when he felt sharp pains in his left hip. Looking down, he noticed a huge bulge forming, watching as it started to take shape, facial features appearing first, followed by a neck, shoulders, an arm and hand. "It looks as if I'm growing another... me. Oh, this is getting good."

Glaring at Silakon, Arune dismounted his horse.

Silakon wrestled the pole underneath his armpit, grabbed his sword from his scabbard and tossed it to Arune. Arune snatched it out of the air, walking quickly toward Rodark with both hands gripping the handle. "I've had enough of this shit. Time for you to go into the box. One piece. Or many pieces."

Arune stood in front of Roko with a wide stance and swung as hard as he could, as a fully formed double figure emerged from Roko's left side. He reached out with its left hand, stopping the blade instantaneously. With its right hand, the figure pulled the blade out of the tree, and Rodark fell to the ground clutching his chest, the grains from his power cell overfilling his hands.

The box had taken Rodark's form up to his knees.

The double of Rodark now lunged, ripping Arune's sword out of his hand.

Arune quickly retreated and mounted his horse, rearing up, ready to stomp the double.

Silakon charged Rodark's double with the sealing stick, but Rodark threw his forearm out, tripping Silakon. He lunged forward, just catching the end of the sealing stick.

Silakon grabbed at the pole, but Rodark pushed him away, forcing the sharp point of the sealing stick into his chest wound two feet deep, melting into Rodark's chest and sealing it closed. Silakon reached for the pole, but it shocked him, burning his skin. He cried out, shaking his hand.

"How did you do that?"

He broke the remaining portion of the pole in half, thrusting half of the jagged end through Silakon's leg, pinning him to the ground.

Silakon cried out, curling up around the pain. "This isn't going to stop me for long," he said, pulling up on the embedded spear.

Rodark kicked the eternity box off his feet like a muddy boot. He raced over to his power cell double, ripping the swords out of his hands. "Thank you, but I need them now." He plunged Arune's sword into the clone, the black spirit rider folding over, dropping to the ground and melting in a pool of black tar. Rodark stepped in the middle of the tar pool, absorbing the pool of Reaper tar. "Oh, yeah, that feels better," he said, picking up the swords, one in each hand.

"Arune, I demand a face-off for the rights to own the elder brick."

Arune padded his horse's neck, watching as Silakon removed the splintered tar stick from his leg and limped safely back to the wagon, dragging the eternity box with him.

Arune nodded at Rodark. "Bring me the swords."

Rodark hesitated as he watched Silakon emptying his elder brick essence of the leather bag into the big-ass brass filtering pot.

The swords that Roko held in each hand automatically levitated waist high, pulling him toward Arune. "What the hell is this?" said Rodark. "I can't stop myself."

"Don't worry, Rodark, I have control of the swords."

Roko the dark locked up alongside Arune's horse as his arms raised the swords over his head. Arune sheathed his blade while he rested Silakon's edge tight against Rodark's neck.

"From what I've seen here today, you are one hell of a weapon. *My* weapon. The mix of earther, black spirit horse, and elder blood brick cannot be duplicated." He poked the blade at Rodark's neck. "But as you can see, I have control over you. Now put your arms down."

Rodark dropped his arms to his side. "I can still feel some of the elder brick inside of me."

"Yes, I know you can. That was part of the plan, but I took 99% of the elder brick that was inside you, leaving you the other 1%. That's what makes you more powerful than any other black spirit rider."

"I'm not sure what the hell you are, but you do have the upper hand. *At the moment.*"

"I'm glad to see you are coming to your senses. Maybe I'll keep you around."

"I want to rule Grimmbell," said Rodark. "Since I have had a taste of the elder brick, well, it opened up a brand-new world. I want to rule Grimmbell."

"I like the way you think," said Arune, rubbing his thumb and fingers together. "You bring me Blackjack alive and in one piece, and I will help you take control of Grimmbell."

Rodark stood motionless, looking at Arune. "Was all of this a test?"

"Something like that," said Arune.

"Did I pass your test?"

"You're still alive, aren't you."

Rodark gave a slow nod. "How do I know you won't destroy me even if I bring you Blackjack?"

"You don't," said Arune, leaning on the saddle horn. "But why would I destroy one of my greatest weapons, and the future King of Grimmbell?"

"I guess we will cross that bridge when we get there," said Roko.

"Fair enough," said Arune.

"Did Reaper really get captured by the hunter spirits? I need my horse back."

Arune grinned, giving a downward head nod to the last piece of the sealing pole lying at Rodark's feet.

"A broken tar stick. You want me to ride a stick horse; is this another test of some kind?" Arune waved to Silakon. "Silakon, bring the wagon over."

He slashed his whip at the six bull beasts and the wagon came alive, spinning a half circle in the dirt and stopping next to Rodark.

"Give him a bag of screamer dust," said Arune.

Silakon bowed his head and reached under the wagon seat, handing Roko a small bag of dust. "Use it wisely, till you can make some more."

Rodark emptied the bag into his leather pouch. "Perfect fit." Looking back at Arune, he asked, "What about my horse?"

Arune motioned another head nod to Silakon. "Wait for me at the portal opening." Silakon snapped his whip, and the wagon lunged forward.

"Gather your tar stick, build a fire and throw the stick into the flames. When the stick is fully engulfed in flame, sprinkle a pinch of dust over the fire and get out of the way."

Arune pulled on the reins, backing up the horse and spinning around. He started to ride off but stopped. Turning, he looked back, leaning on the horse's butt with a hand keeping him upright.

"Grimmbell has their best hunters looking for you. Don't forget about my Blackjack. No Blackjack, no Grimmbell."

Roko watched as Arune met up with Silakon's wagon and in a flash, they disappeared into a portal.

Chapter 32: The Ride

Blackjack untied the reins. Snatching the saddle horn with his left hand and inserting his left foot into the stirrup, he pulled himself into the saddle of Luxen's borrowed black spirit horse. With each foot inserted into a stirrup, he pulled the reins closer.

"Oh, shit. Here we go," said Brazel.

"Hang on. Don't know what's going to happen."

Luther reared up, plowing his chest into the lower-hanging tree branches, mowing the leaves and small branches to the ground, leaving only the bare stubs showing against the trunk of the tree.

"This isn't one of your better ideas," said Brazel.

Blackjack gripped the saddle horn with two hands, leaning down into the saddle. "Come on now, Luther, I thought we were friends. Don't you remember what happened in the barn?"

"Oh yeah," said Brazel. "He'll remember that as a good time. You shocked him into unconsciousness. I don't think so."

Luther's hooves hit the ground running.

"No turning back now. Let's go," said Blackjack.

Luther bolted down the animal path as fast as he could go. "Holly shit balls, this horse can gallop."

The black stallion veered from one side of the path to the other, running underneath the lowest branches possible.

Blackjack ducked the first two large low-hanging branches, but the third one caught him smack in the mouth. "Son of a bitch… he is trying to knock me off." Losing control of the reins and falling backwards off the saddle, he caught Luther's tail with a foot to spare from hitting the ground.

Luther ran faster, veering off the path and into the thickest patch of the trees he could find, Blackjack holding his arm in front of his face, blocking a falling tree branch from harpooning him in the throat.

"You need to get control," said Brazel, "before he gets to the river and drowns us." Blackjack locked onto

Luther's tail with both hands, looking underneath the belly of the horse to find out where he was going, rolling to the right and just missing the stump of a big oak tree.

"Damn, that would've been a fatal head plant." Blackjack focused to the front on the next possible obstacle heading his way. "Shit, there goes my boot. Transportation by dragging is not the way to go."

"Check out what's coming next," said Brazel.

Blackjack bobbed his head from left to right. Finally, he could see what Brazel was talking about. "Oh, this isn't good. A large patch of porcupine brush coming up fast."

"You realize that's not an ordinary sticker bush, right?" said Brazel. "These bushes are razor-sharp.

And not only that, but they are also poisonous. One prick through the skin and you will go unconscious within a minute. And from that point, you will be dragged beneath the brush by the bush rodents and stored for food."

"I don't think so," said Blackjack, and climbing hand over hand up Luther's tail, he managed to grab the butt end of the saddle, pulling himself forward to where he was seated in the saddle and clutched the reins in his hands once again.

"Okay Luther, we're going to do it the hard way." Blackjack leaned forward to where his chin touched the horse's mane, and he bit into Luther's neck.

Luther grunted, followed by a short but intense snort, kicking his hind legs into the air as Blackjack continued biting into Luther's neck.

The black stallion ran faster, forcing his body to sideswipe every tree he ran by, the tree trunks ripping at Blackjack's arms and shoulders. "Son of a bitch," Blackjack said, clinging to Luther's neck.

Luther charged out of the brush, continuing his jamming of Blackjack against the tree trunks.

Blackjack tightened his lockjaw on the stallion's neck. "Luther, I need your services. I have to fight a black spirit rider who's possessed by a darker entity called Arune the Penetrator. We need to destroy this power. When that's done, I promise I will set you free to select the rider of your choice."

Luther's powerful muscles relaxed, and he slowed down to a trot, eventually stopping underneath the branches of a large apple tree that produced giant Riddler's red apples.

Blackjack released his fanged bite of Luther's neck. "Why didn't you let me know you were hungry?" Luther neighed with a head bob.

"So, we do understand each other."

Blackjack reached up and pulled three apples from the closest branch. Dismounting Luther, he slid his hand against the horse's chest, guiding himself to the horse's muzzle, presenting the apple to Luther.

Luther took the Riddler apple in one bite, happily chomping.

"Wow," said Brazel, "I never thought I would witness a black spirit horse accepting an apple from you."

"I didn't either," said Blackjack.

"Did you see anything out of the ordinary, or any type of reaction when you changed over to Blackjack? I can't believe there wasn't some kind of negative reaction."

"I never said there wasn't any reaction."

"What happened?" Brazel asked.

"When I transformed into Blackjack, my environment speeded up immensely."

"Huh? Your environment speeded up?"

"I could cover longer distances faster without missing any details of my surroundings."

"Tell me more," said Brazel.

Blackjack fed another apple to Luther. "I rode around the eighty-acre lot of trees here twice, up to the top of each of the five buttes, and one loop around Grimmbell before we went crashing into the porcupine brush."

"Did you VIM? You're saying you used the dust?" "No, I didn't VIM. Well, yes, I did VIM…"

"I knew you had. What was that like?" said Brazel. "No, no, no," said Blackjack. "You don't understand—" "I'm listening," said Brazel.

"I never used any screamer's dust." Blackjack inhaled and released. "When I finished my rounds of the area, if you want to call it that, there were three portals open in front of me."

"I knew it," said Brazel. "Multiple portals would open."

"Yes, you were right with the *many portals open at*

the same time theory."

"That's when you used the screamer's dust, to enter the portal. Which one did you go into?"

"I went into them all without the use of any screamer's dust."

"No way. No dust, are you sure about that?" said Brazel.

"I'm sure," said Blackjack, patting the leather bag of dust he'd received from Woodford.

"That's one of your enhanced powers with Luther," said Brazel. "Your transformational DNA has connected to the horse. Wow, and shit at the same time."

"What do you mean, wow and shit?"

"It's the law of polarity or balance," said Brazel.

Blackjack nodded as he fed the last apple to Luther. "I think I know what you mean. You are telling me that riding or having control of the black spirit horse is simultaneously good and bad."

"Yes," said Brazel, "but it's Luther you are connected to, so not every spirit horse will produce the same outcome."

Blackjack gazed at Luther, grinding up his last apple. "Tell me the bad part," said Blackjack.

"One of the possible outcomes is that Luther will never let you go. To find a new rider is complicated, the process time consuming, not to mention it requires a lot of energy to convert a new rider. But wait, we're getting ahead of ourselves. What happened in the portals? What did you see?"

"Not sure this is a good idea."

"Just tell me. We'll figure it out. Remember, you are on your way to defeat Roko."

"*And* Arune the Penetrator," said Blackjack. "That too. Tell me about the portals now!"

"The first one I entered was dark. I couldn't see anything but could feel wind blowing at my face and an occasional voice, but I never saw anything in that portal. Don't know what that means."

"It sounds like an unwritten portal," said Brazel.

"Unwritten? What's that?"

"A better way to explain it would be a portal that has

not developed yet.”

“Okay,” said Blackjack. “That makes sense somewhat.”

“Number two portal,” said Brazel. “What did you see in that one?”

“My messenger bag burning. Well, let me refine that. I opened up my bag and saw a pile of ash from burned envelopes.”

“That portal could be warning you, but I’m not sure, only speculating. What about number three?”

“Remember you wanted to know about the portals.”

“Yes, I did,” said Brazel.

“In the third portal, I talked to Peppersaul.”

“You talked to Peppersaul, my wife? When she was alive?” “Yes, I did.”

“What did she say?”

“I found out that the rider of this horse did take your life. Pepper didn’t know if it had anything to do with Arune.”

“How would she know anything about Arune?”

“I don’t know. You’re the one who wanted to know about the portals, so I’m telling you.”

“Please continue,” said Brazel.

“She said there was an attack by a black spirit horse rider at the walls of Grimmbell many years ago.

That rider was defeated by Kula, but the horse survived.”

“The horse survived?” said Brazel. “I’m wondering if Luther is the same horse.”

“That’s what I was wondering,” said Blackjack. “And if he is, what does that mean to us right now?”

“I don’t know for sure, but the next time you’re in a portal, bring me a sample back if you can.”

“How?” said Blackjack.

“Remember the jar that Woodford gave you before you exited the tunnel?”

“Yes, I still have it in my bag.”

“Open the lid when you go inside the portal and close it before you leave. The jar will do the rest.”

“I can do that,” said Blackjack. “We should be getting on our way.”

“Yes, we should,” said Brazel.

“I’m still wondering about the law of balance, particularly the bad side. We don’t know what other powers I will receive.”

“Or what powers you could lose. We will have to figure them out as we go.” Blackjack leaped onto the saddle. “Let’s find out.”

Chapter 33: Sabotage Portal

Rodark glared at the lingering airwaves of the recently closed portal. He quickly cut the palm of his hand and dripping the gray-black power cell blood onto the ground, he watched as a cloudy figure grew upwards, stopping when the dark figure equaled his shape in height and weight.

"Whoa," said Rodark, taking a step back. "Look at that. This power cell double has a crimson strip from its feet to its eyes. A striped double. That's interesting. I was wondering what effect the elder brick would have on my replica power double."

The crimson-striped clone held his hand stiff in a vertical position, chest high in front of Rodark. Rodark nodded at his power cell double. "Go ahead, you know what I want to do."

The double thrust his hand into Rodark's chest, breaching his power unit. Rodark folded over, bracing himself on the arm of the dark clone.

The clone pulled his hand free of his chest, holding a purple gooey fist-sized ball in his hand.

Rodark unbuckled the belt, holding the bag of screamer's dust in front of his crimson-striped colleague.

"Put the gooey purple ball in the screamer's dust."

The dark crimson figure placed the ball into the bag, and Rodark tied the bag shut, handing it back to him and pointing at the freshly closed portal. "You have elder blood in your veins. Run as fast as you can into the remains of the portal. When you catch up to Arune, do as I tell you."

The double grinned back and charged into the lingering waves of the portal.

Whoosh. The dark figure vanished.

Rodark stared at the portal. "Wow, he was able to enter the portal smoothly. I should have twenty minutes before anyone comes along, looking to close the doorway. Twenty minutes to get my dark clone back with my elder brick inside him. If this works, I will have defeated and imprisoned Arune in an obstructed portal. The combination of the three energies coming from the soul tree, its sister tree of death and the hanging tree will disrupt the portal, trapping Arune, so no one can enter or leave. Perfect."

Suddenly, the portal opened with a suction so intense it ripped the brush out of the ground, followed by two large trees. Roko couldn't fight the suction of the vortex force. It ripped him down as if a giant Amberback troll had jumped on his back, holding his head down, dragging his face into the dirt.

He tried to lift his head out of the dirt but couldn't, feeling his entire body pulled toward the portal. "Maybe this wasn't such a good idea." He dug his fingers into the grass and dirt.

Holding himself back, his body lifted off the ground a couple of inches when the suction of the opening stopped as quickly as it started.

Rodark looked up; he could see the portal was still open.

No sign of his crimson spirit double. Pulling his fingers out of the sod, he sat up with his legs crossed, picking the dirt and grass out from under his fingernails.

"That's actually a scary sight. A portal wide open. I feel it watching me. A sensation of awareness." He stood, brushing himself off. "I need my horse back."

He remembered the directions Arune had given him to bring Reaper back to full form. He quickly assembled a fire, tossing the remaining one-foot piece of the tar stick into the flame, along with a handful of screamer's dust for good measure.

The fire's flames grew ten feet high, dancing wildly in all directions, fist-size balls erupting in the air, the fire projecting such an intense heat that Rodark had to retreat twenty feet away behind a tree.

A loud hissing filled the air, forcing him to cover his ears to stop the impelling noise from exploding his ear drums. The piercing noise continued for one minute, then stopped.

He looked around the tree to see a large jet-black horse standing where the fire used to be, scraping at the ground with his black hoof.

"Well, kiss my ass. It's Reaper, my black beauty. You look magnificent." Reaper bounced his head, stomping his right hoof.

"I will take that as a thank you. You're welcome." Rodark mounted his horse.

Sitting in the saddle again, he felt much more alive, all his senses heightened.

He could see the outside band of the portal moving slowly up and down. *It looks as if it's alive and breathing.* He could hear a small animal move in the underbrush. *Sounds like a rabbit. Rabbit? That's a pleasant thought. As soon as I'm done here, I will hunt the most elusive rabbit in Darkan Territory, Bradicus Blackjack. Oh, how sweet that will be to have a nice meal of roasted Rarebrook rabbit. Maybe I will invite Kula to join me. I can tell her it's roasted pig.*

Rodark could hear something moving toward him from inside the portal and directed his focus on that spot. The crimson double exited the portal, approaching Roko.

"I exploded the bag of screamer's dust in Silakon's wagon as you ordered. It ruptured the big-ass brass pot. All the dust was absorbed by my power cell."

Rodark drew his sword. "It's *my* power cell. What about the portal itself? What happened?"

"The portal transported Arune and Silakon to the three-tree area inside Grimmbell, then the portal opening detonated into many smaller portals, circling around the main portal hole."

"Then what happened?" asked Rodark with a grin.

With so many smaller portals circling the main opening at the same time, it caused a vortex freeze.

Like you said, the main portal opening froze closed. No one in. No one out."

"Perfect," said Rodark. "It worked just like I planned. Arune is trapped inside the frozen vortex, and the frozen vortex is entombed inside Grimmbell's blood brick walls. They're never getting out of two dungeons deep in a portal world."

The dark twin stood in front of Rodark and bowed his head. "You have served me well, but I still need my power back."

Rodark thrust his fist into the chest cavity of his double, retrieving a larger purple gooey ball. It duly exploded, covering Rodark with a thin coating of elder blood brick.

He stepped back a few feet, slicing the crimson striped clone's head off, the red and black figure falling to the ground in a pile of dust.

"There you go, Reaper, the snack you wanted. Something with a little more kick than grass."

Reaper lowered his head, munching on the pile of black dust. Roko stared at the simplicity of Reaper enjoying his super-food snack when he noticed the remaining portal waves spinning at a very high rate, the color of the portal ring turning from sky blue to a dark gray, dissolving into itself and disappearing.

"Farewell, Arune. Hello, Bradicus Blackjack."

Chapter 34: Pre-battle Talk

Blackjack looked around. "As much as I enjoy these wooded acres of the five buttes, I suppose it's time for us to move forward. I do believe I have a nasty battle awaiting me."

Kula nodded her head in agreement. "Maybe when this is all said and done, we can come back here, lie in the shade and eat pig kebabs."

"Maybe we can. I would like that." Suddenly, Blackjack perked up in the saddle, tilting his head to catch a strange noise off in the distance.

"What are you hearing?" asked Kula.

"It's not only what I can hear but also what I can feel." "Great. Tell me about both."

Luther stomped and Blackjack patted his neck. "Easy boy. Yes, let me tell you what I think is going on. I can now feel when portals open and close, at least when I'm sitting on Luther and that feeling intensifies a hundredfold. I'm sure a portal has opened."

"Where?" said Kula. "Is it Arune, or Roko the Dark, or both?" Blackjack leaned on the saddle horn with both hands.

"It's both but not exactly the way you would think."

"Not the way I'd imagine? Care to elaborate??" said Kula.

"I can feel a portal open, but the portal has been *frozen* open."

"Frozen open? In what way?"

Blackjack sighed. "I'm not totally sure but many smaller portals opened at the same time for a short while, causing a vortex freeze of the main portal."

Kula leaned down. "How do you know this?"

"My new friend here," Blackjack said, patting Luther on the butt. "Like I said, my senses have heightened tremendously in relation to the energy of portals since I've been riding this horse."

Kula squeezed her eyes. "You riding that horse, is that a good thing?"

"It is for now," said Blackjack.

"What does this frozen portal thing mean to us?" said Kula. "It's a transfer of power."

Kula raised her head, looking in the direction of Grimmbell. "A transfer of power? Grimmbell? I need to alert General Slaughter."

"Wait, my Queen, the damage has been done."

"The damage has been done? Did someone take my crown? Then I will destroy them. The exchanging of the queen has to be completed through the releasing ceremony with the earther elders."

Blackjack held his hands up, pushing them toward Kula. "Wait! Wait, this is a different transfer of power. Actually, it's a reversal power exchange. Good and bad."

"Reversal?"

"Yes, a reversal," said Blackjack. "That's tricky. That's smart, and oh my God, how did he do it?" Kula stomped her foot. "Blackjack, give me the facts."

"According to the vibes I'm gathering from Luther, Roko could have trapped Arune in a vortex portal."

"How can he be trapped in any kind of portal?" said Kula. "Arune has great power. I believe untapped power resources."

"Because Roko, aka *Roko the Dark,* is smart. He wasn't taking spirits and skulls only to make screamer dust; he was making some type of an interference portal dust. And once he stole an elder blood brick, his power intensified, which enabled him to produce this vortex freezing portal. Which led to…"

Kula snapped her head around. "Which possibly led him one step closer to some type of power transfer. Roko ended up playing Arune in the end," Kula said, shaking her head. "Of course. Damn, why didn't I see that coming?" She spit fire on a clove of underbrush. "Pig kebabs hell, we are going to have Roko kebabs. Roko is the one who's going for some type of transfer of power."

"That's not all," said Blackjack.

"Are you feeling something else?" Kula asked.

"I'm thinking he has Arune trapped in the vortex…"

"Keep going," said Kula.

"He has Arune trapped in the vortex inside Grimmbell. A double slap in the face. Not only does he have Arune trapped but he also could have the power of the broken circle by axe at his disposal."

"Of course, he's using Grimmbell grounds to stabilize the vortex in place."

"Yes," said Blackjack.

"And he will be the only one to enter, exit or destroy the vortex."

"Yes." Blackjack nodded.

"He could enter the vortex right now, take what he wants from Grimmbell. What are we waiting for? We have to stop him."

Blackjack held his hands up, flexing his fingers. "Why are you wiggling your hands at me?" said Kula. "I have Cremator's hands."

"Yes, I know that," said Kula. "They were trapped inside of Jinnamon's belly drop." Blackjack continued flexing his fingers. "No, I have his hands."

A heavy brow matured on Kula. "You have his hands?" Blackjack nodded. "Yes."

"What about Jinnamon?"

"No," said Blackjack. "I am wearing Cremator's hands."

Kula shook her head. "You are actually wearing his hands? When were you going to tell me?" "When the time was right. And now, the time is right. Roko the Dark isn't going to make any attempts inside the frozen vortex until he has Cremator's hands."

Kula grinned. "He needs the hands to read the Great Hall master recipe book to do whatever he wants inside the walls of Grimmbell."

"That is correct, my Queen. And he has the power of the elder brick too. Unstoppable combination."

"Where might the master recipe book be located?" said Kula. "The soul king had made it a rule that the master recipe book never leaves the Great Hall."

Blackjack leaned in closer to Luther's ear. "I thought she would never ask." He sat up in the saddle and grinned. "Roko's master recipe book is inside of Jinnamon."

"Inside Jinnamon? I'm not sure Rasp can open her up again," said Kula. "That's a pretty damn good idea."

"Thank you," said Blackjack. "When did you make the switch?"

"When Jinnamon and I battled Roko and his red-eyed rider goons."

"How did you know Jinnamon was going to swallow Cremator?"

"I didn't," said Blackjack. "But I figured it would be the last place Roko would look. He'd already taken his hands, so you know he searched Cremator for the book. And of course, he didn't find it. I hid the book under Cremator's shirt just before Jinnamon swallowed him. The perfect hiding place. And voilà, a super secure hiding spot. And now, since I have Luther to read Jinnamon's tattooed tongue, I can open the belly drop to retrieve the book or we could leave it there."

"Why would we want to leave it there?" said Kula.

Blackjack rolled his head and sighed. "Because we don't know the outcome of the battle between me and Rodark."

Chapter 35: Final Battle

Blackjack unbuckled his belt holding the bag of screamer dust at his waist. He looked up at Big Sky Butte, the tallest of the five buttes.

Kula studied Blackjack. "Is that where you are going to battle Rodark, on Sky Butte?"

He handed the bag of screamer's dust to Kula. "You need to take this, try it out and see what you think. I don't need it; I have Luther."

Kula sniffed the bag. "Smells of brains and bone."

"That's not all. Taste it. It's some type of simulant."

"I'll try it out, but you haven't answered me about battling on the big butte."

"No. No battle on Sky Butte. I think it will be an isolated location, but I will receive instructions to where the battle will take place *on* Sky Butte."

"How do you know that?"

"Luther," said Blackjack, turning Luther toward the butte. "If I win, I will meet you at Grimmbell sometime tomorrow."

"And if you lose?"

"I left directions with Ella. We can trust her. Goodbye, my Queen." Kula tipped her head. "I *will* see you tomorrow."

Luther trotted away but quickly opened up to a steady gallop up the trail leading to the top of Big Sky Butte. When he crested the top of the butte, a black spirit rider glistened with a flash of black armor, sitting upon his horse and holding a leather wrap.

Blackjack approached, stopping abreast the black rider. "You ride for Rodark?"

The black-armored rider handed Blackjack a red leather wrap secured by a thin leather tie. "Nice- looking horse. Something special about him."

Blackjack didn't answer. He pulled the tie, unraveling the red leather wrap and reading the script. "Dead Stone Fortress. Nice choice."

The rider pulled back on the reins, backing his horse

away from Blackjack, while grabbing a handful of dust, throwing the powder back over the butt of his horse.

A portal hole started to form, spinning wildly and then opening, producing the ear-piercing scream. The rider continued his backward movement into the portal and vanished.

Blackjack uncovered his ears with his hands. "I will never get used to that portal scream." He could feel turbulence in the air coming from the closed portal. "Not much of a talker." He studied the writing on the leather. "Dead Stone Fortress it is."

Blackjack leaned over the saddle horn, inserting his feet further into the stirrups. He synched his hands with an extra wrap of the reins. "Okay Luther. Dead Stone Fortress. We battle Rodark and his horse Reaper. If we win or if I die, my promise to you is freedom to choose your next rider. Agreed?"

Luther whinnied with a head dip and charged off the cliff side of the butte.

The wind velocity of the drop pulled Blackjack out of the saddle. Closing his eyes, he clutched the saddle horn, pulling himself back onto the saddle, his forehead bouncing off Luther's mane. Squeezing his knees tight against Luther, he shouted, "Oh shit, here we go. One, two, three, four…"

The wind stopped and he opened his eyes. "Wow, that was quick."

Blackjack stood outside the walls of Dead Stone Fortress, his eyes following the vines growing in the cracks to the top of the abandoned walls.

"Dead Stone Fortress. The very first earther settlement in the Darkan Territory. Rather symbolic." He rode alongside the wall, rubbing his hand on the rock. "This special dark stone doesn't allow any sound to penetrate in or out of the rock. It's like a giant soundproofed room. Once you are inside the walls of the fortress, nobody will hear you scream for help."

Blackjack rode to the front gate. He looked through the gateless opening just under the curved archway to see the open courtyard.

"Brazel. Are you there? I haven't heard from you in a

while. What are your thoughts of this location?" Blackjack sat quietly with his eyes closed. "Brazel. Are you still with me?"

"Blackjack, my friend, come on in and take a look around."

Blackjack opened his eyes, twisting his head toward the doorway so fast he thought he heard his neck crack. He studied Rodark sitting on his black spirit horse in the middle of the courtyard.

"There he is. Roko, once my number one friend, is now Rodark, my number one enemy."

He encouraged Blackjack to enter the fortress with a wave of the hand. "Blackjack, my friend. Come on in, we have a lot to cuss and discuss."

Blackjack patted the side of Luther's neck. "Come on, let's go in." Blackjack rode through the archway, stopping in front of Roko the Dark.

"You have been a busy rider. Killer of six fighter dragoons at the releasing ceremony. Still not sure how you pulled that off. A human tobacco farmer, three earther diggers, one tower dragon guardian, a breach of Grimmbell walls, stealing a sacred elder blood brick and destroying unknown numbers of fighter fire spirits in the efforts to get it out of Grimmbell. Anyway, I want the elder brick back."

"And I want what you stole from me," said Rodark. "I took nothing from you."

Rodark cocked his head to one side. "I beg to differ. You have the Great Hall master recipe book, right?"

"Oh yeah," said Blackjack. "That must have been about the time when you tried to stomp me in the blue sage brush with your horse."

Rodark grinned. "Stomping? I wouldn't really call that trying to stomp you. My horse was just a little froggy; something must have spooked him."

"And you dropped your book when you were trying to smash my head, remember?" Rodark smiled. "Yes, I knew where I dropped it. And I figured you had it."

"I did have it for a while, but then decided to put it in a very safe place."

"I see," said Rodark, slowly nodding. "But you did steal Cremator's hands from me, when you had Jinnamon push me into that closing portal. That was a good move by the way, but I want his hands or I'm going to take yours."

"I don't think so, moose breath," said Blackjack. "And I'm not going to kill you either."

Rodark tightened his neck muscles with a gaze. "You're not going to destroy me? How thoughtful."

"But I am going to take you back to Woodford, and he is going to bury you deep inside his tunnel of misfit free radical jars. What do you think of them black apples?"

Rodark grabbed the handle of his sword. "The only way I'm going back to Grimmbell is to rule." Turning his horse broadside, he extended his left arm straight out in front of Blackjack.

"You've seen nothing yet."

Blackjack backed away, retrieving his sword from his scabbard.

Rodark grinned with a high eyebrow flex. With his sword in his right hand, he swiftly cut his left one.

Blackjack watched as the hand lying on the courtyard started to smoke. Then the smoke began dancing and weaving upwards, forming into dark cloudy shapes.

Rodark chuckled. "You thought *one* of my red-eyed riders was a pain in the ass. Let's see how you handle *five* of them."

Blackjack watched as the cloudy shapes formed into one big cloud of smoke and suddenly, a single horse head poked through the cloud, then another and another.

He cut the reins loose from Luther, securing his grip on the saddle horn with his left hand as he raised his sword above his head.

"Okay Luther, I don't plan on dying here today. What do you say?"

Luther charged past Rodark as Blackjack bent off the saddle, leaning down stabbing the closest enemy horse in the neck. Blackjack jumped off Luther, knocking a rider off the second horse, screaming as he thrust the sword into the rider's chest.

He pulled his sword out, looking for the next victim when he took a direct kick in the back from the riderless horse, sending him on a belly skid ride for twenty feet on the courtyard stone. He looked up in time to see Luther harpoon the riderless horse in the stomach, driving the horse to the ground.

The horseless rider jerked Blackjack up off the courtyard floor, holding him in midair by the throat.

Blackjack dropped his sword using both hands to try to free his windpipe from the vice grip of the red-eyed dark rider.

He ripped at the rider's arm with his titanium claws and the dark rider howled, dropping him to the courtyard, groping for his arm from the elbow down as it dropped to the stone floor.

The dark rider screamed out in anger, raising his sword ready to engage again, when the purple unicorn horn of Luther blasted through his chest.

Luther pulled free.

Blackjack stabbed the rider in the eye, pushing his sword out the back of his head. "Two down, Luther. Three more to go."

Blackjack stared at the other three riders, waiting for them to make their move.

Rodark clapped. "Bravo! Bravo! That was pretty damn good fighting, and just where in the hell did you get a black spirit horse that can produce a unicorn horn when needed? I think I will be trading up for your horse."

Blackjack retrieved his sword and mounted Luther.

He rubbed the side of his face, feeling some fur had been ripped off, exposing his skin. "Damn, it stings like a son of a bitch and no, you can't have my horse," he said, spitting on the ground. "Come on Rodark, I'm just getting warmed up. Let's see what you got."

Rodark signaled to the remaining three riders.

"Swords, daggers, knives, maybe a spear," barked Roko. "I poke you there, you cut me here. I'm getting tired of those guys; let's do something more exciting."

The riders dissolved into a vortex of wind, spinning up to the sky and forming a low-hanging cloud above the courtyard.

"You mean like stomping on my head until it turns to jelly?" said Blackjack.

"You're still pissed about that? Get over it." Rodark leaned to the far side of his horse, revealing a burlap bag.

He laid it over the mane of Reaper, smirking at Blackjack as he stroked the bag with his hand. The bag came to life, twisting, turning, sharp punching blows outward, testing the bag's strength.

Blackjack approached Rodark, his stomach tightened, eyes amplified. He tried to swallow but couldn't find the spit to do it.

"Rodark, you piece of rodent shit; what's in that bag that shouldn't be?"

He removed his dagger from the scabbard and slowly dragged the knife along the kicking bag.

Blackjack moved even closer. "Fight me, Rodark, you lizard-butt-licking asswipe. You're a coward. You can't fight your own battles."

"Don't come any closer." Rodark cut the bag open. Dropping it onto the ground, a hand pushed through the opening in the bag, then a head and shoulders appeared.

Blackjack stared at the creature as he sat up in the saddle.

His mouth dropped open, and his beating heart plunged to his crotch. "Holy hanging big dragoon balls. It's a human. It's Ella."

"I bet you didn't see that one coming, did you?" Blackjack started to dismount.

Rodark swung his sword around. "I didn't think so. Stay right where you're at, or I'll kill her where she sits."

"You're not that fast," said Blackjack. "I can beat you."

"I don't have to be faster than you," said Rodark, nodding toward the ground where Ella sat. Blackjack leaned to his left, looking around Ella. "A snake."

"Not just any snake, my friend, look a little closer."

Blackjack sat back in the saddle, pulling on the reins. Luther stepped back. He studied the snake more carefully. "You are truly a piece of gutter trash rolled into a turd log floating on swamp water."

"You recognize it," hissed Rodark with a hard grin.

"Yes, I do," said Blackjack. "It looks like the same kind of snake that bit me at Ella's medicine shack. It's a penetrator snake. You got that from your master, Arune."

"He is not my master. I am his master, but I did

acquire his ancient snake magic from him."

"Yes, I know. You trapped him in a frozen vortex, stabilized by the spirit power of Grimmbell."

"Exactly, that's why I changed my mind," said Rodark.

"Changed your mind. Can you explain?"

Rodark jumped off his horse, standing above Ella. "Enough of this idle bullshit talk." He leaned over and vomited, covering her with a black sticky tar substance with red specks that twinkled in the sunlight. Blackjack leaped off his horse, landing on the back of Rodark, forcing him to the ground. He quickly curled his arm around Rodark's neck with the pocket of his elbow, squeezing tight against his windpipe.

Rodark pushed against Blackjack's forearm. "You are so predictable. It was nice knowing you." Blackjack squeezed tighter as he watched the red sparkly black tar goo engulf Ella, leaving only her eyes to look out in horror.

"Release her. Fight me. I am the one you want."

"Yes, you are one of many trophies I want. And I will have you shortly. Now watch the snake." Blackjack quickly turned his attention to the snake, knowing what its capabilities were. "Luther, stomp the shit out of that snake!"

Luther tap-danced around Ella, trying to stomp the snake, but the snake was too fast and was quickly at Blackjack's front door, nipping at his arm.

Blackjack released Rodark to the side, shoving him to the ground and Luther immediately charged Rodark.

Blackjack pounced on the snake, stabbing it with one of his titanium claws and wrestling the snake to his mouth, he bit its head off.

"Oh, my God. This snake is terrible," Blackjack said, holding his mouth open.

The headless snake thrashed around violently on the courtyard floor as Blackjack continued chewing on its detached head.

It burned his mouth, his tongue starting to feel numb and swell. "I'm going to puke ugly."

"Blackjack. This is Brazel."

"Where the hell have you been?"

"My thought process had been blocked."

"Blocked by what?"

"I'm assuming Rodark. Whatever you do, don't swallow any snake juice. Spit the head out now."

Blackjack didn't have too much trouble emptying his mouth as he vomited furiously on the courtyard.

"Where have… where have you been?" asked Blackjack.

"I had trouble communicating with you ever since you entered Dead Stone, and that's not even the worst part."

"What is the worst… oh God."

"Whatever is in that ball of tar with the sparkling red specks is pulling me into it. I feel as though I'm leaving your body and don't know how to stop it."

"You feel like you are leaving *my* body?" asked Blackjack. "That doesn't make a lot of sense."

"I'm leaving your body. What's in that mound of sparkling black tar?"

"It's Ella, covered in whatever gunk Rodark puked up," said Blackjack. "Ella? It can't be. We hid her from any danger, didn't we?"

"I'm sorry, my friend, but I saw her in that glob of shit."

Blackjack looked up long enough to see Luther chasing Rodark inside the courtyard. "Kill that son of a bitch, Luther."

"Blackjack, this is Brazel. Can you hear me?"

"Brazel. What are you saying? I'm missing every other word."

"Keep away…"

"Keep away from what?" asked Blackjack. "Keep away from…"

Blackjack vomited again and rolled over onto his side, holding his stomach.

"Blackjack, keep away from Ella. Her tainted power is pulling me out of you…" Suddenly, Blackjack couldn't keep his fetal position, his body stretched out like a rubber band pinned down to the courtyard.

"Brazel, help me! Are you there Brazel?"

"Brazel can't hear you no more," said Rodark.

Blackjack looked up to see Rodark sitting on Luther. "Holy shit, get off my horse, you piece of garbage."

"But I like your horse," he said with a giggling shake of his body. "How do you activate his unicorn horn?" he asked, pressing on Luther's head with his fingers.

Blackjack coughed out a nasty sticky snake tar ball onto the ground. "Damn. I've changed my mind," said Blackjack. "I'm not going to take you back to Grimmbell prison."

"You're not. Does that mean you are going to team up with me?"

"I'm not giving up, but I'm going to capture you and Arune's power, stuffing your black mix-match of a spirit remains into one of Woodford's spirit pickle jars, where you will remain on a cold dusty shelf in a dark cave for eternity."

"Of course, you are," said Rodark. "How do you plan on doing that when you are so stretched out? You're about ready to snap. Oh, wait a minute." Rodak pointed over his head. "Someone's coming."

Blackjack turned to see a smiling Ella looking down at him. "Ella, are you okay?"

"I think I am. Why am I here?"

"You're not supposed to be here," said Blackjack. "Run and hide in the catacombs. Run now."

Ella knelt next to Blackjack, gripping his hand. "Don't worry, honey. I'm here to take you back with me."

"Ella, what are you talking about?"

She closed her eyes, squeezing Blackjack's hand harder. "I didn't know you had such a forceful grip."

She leaned down, licking Blackjack's wrist. "What are you doing? Are you feeling, okay?"

Ella opened her eyes. "I'm fine, just tasting for the best spot," she said, biting into his wrist. Spasms ripped through Blackjack's muscles until it seemed as though his bones were going to snap. "Ella, stop, that hurts," he said, pulling away. "What the hell are you doing?"

"I'm in the power of the snake that's going to take Brazel away from your inner space."

"Rodark, you are always using some type of creation to steal from others. You can't use Ella to steal Brazel; it will destroy Ella and me, then you will have nothing."

Rodark stepped Luther directly over Blackjack. "I really like your horse. And yes, I can take your third power away because I am in possession of an elder blood brick."

Blackjack's body tightened even more, rising up off the courtyard stone, feeling ice cold and hard as a rock.

"Brazel, are you still with me?"

Releasing her grip, Ella fell to the ground. "No, Brazel is with me now, where he's supposed to be."

Blackjack fell with a thud on the stone courtyard next to Ella. "Uh. Damn, that hurt." He tried to sit up, but sensed his body being pulled down and dizziness kept him flat on his back, then he realized he'd changed back to human form.

Rodark backed away, looking down at Ella. "Do you have Brazel?"

"I have him," she said, hugging herself. "Right where you wanted him."

"Perfect, right where both of you belong." He leaned down picking Ella off the ground like plucking a flower from a pot of dirt. He clutched her by the neck, holding her at eye level. "I finally got you, Brazel. Now I can transform you into my power cell with the filtering process of the elder blood brick. Victory will soon be mine."

Standing, Bradicus shook off the dizziness. He retrieved the Great Hall recipe book from his shoulder bag, holding it up in the air. "Aren't you forgetting something?"

Rodark stuffed Ella into a black canvas bag, tying the top to his saddle horn. "Well now, look who showed up to the party."

"I still have your book and Cremator's hands. You will never read from this book again."

Rodark grinned, patting his canvas bag. "I have part of you right now in this bag and I'm riding your spirit horse, so you lost Bradicus."

Bradicus pulled the necklace with the life coin out from under his shirt and placed it in his mouth, then drew his dagger.

"I like your determination," said Rodark. "You never give up. Tell ya what I will do; once I take your hands, I will fix you up later and we can be black spirit riders together. Damn, we would be the baddest duo of free radical spirit chasers in the territory.”

Bradicus bit down hard on the life coin, a small explosion erupting in his mouth, causing him to gag, spitting up like a rabid dog.

“You used your life coin to save yourself; that’s not going to give you enough human power to save yourself.”

Bradicus grinned. “I didn’t use my life coin.”

“Now you are in denial. I saw you put it in your mouth.” “No, that’s where you’re wrong. I used *your* life coin.”

Rodark raised his sword and charged Bradicus. “I have room in my bag for your head.”

Bradicus ducked under Luther and jumped on Rodark’s horse, Reaper. Reaper kicked and bucked, running wildly around the courtyard.

“You can’t ride my horse, Bradicus; it has my recipes engraved on the underside of the saddle. No one can ride Reaper but me.”

Bradicus hung on for dear life, retrieving the dagger from his boot, cutting the cinch to the saddle.

He quickly grabbed the saddle horn with both hands and threw all his bodyweight off the side of Reaper. Dragging the saddle to the ground with him, he quickly gained his feet, trying to pick up the saddle.

Rodark charged at Bradicus at full speed, knocking him face down against the stone courtyard. He groaned, spitting a tooth onto the ground. “Son of a bitch.” His face ached with hot stabs of pain and rolling over on his back, he could see Rodark dismount and stand above him.

“Nice try. I thought for a minute you were going to ride Reaper.”

“I rode him long enough. I got your saddle.”

Rodark looked at his saddle lying next to Bradicus. “That was rather impressive and as I’ve said, you’re going to make a great partner someday.”

Bradicus spit at Roko’s face.

“But not today,” said Rodark. “I have a surprise for you.” He walked to the center of the courtyard. “Are you ready?” He started counting and on the count of ten, pointed up to the sky.

Bradicus looked up to see a dragoon flying two

hundred feet above the fortress wall, blocking the sunshine for just an instant before swooping down toward the courtyard wall, her tail skipping off the top of the stones. "Jinnamon."

Rodark mounted Luther, coming charging at Bradicus, stopping inches in front of him in a cloud of dust. "Now comes the prison placement for you, Bradicus, not me."

Bradicus got his knees leaning on Rodark's saddle. "What are you talking about, prison for me? You must be daydreaming again."

Jinnamon maneuvered her body low to the ground like a cat ready to pounce on its prey, Bradicus studying her every move.

Jinnamon moved toward Bradicus slowly. "Jinnamon, what are you doing?"

"What she is told," said Rodark. "She is going to swallow you, locking you away in her belly drop forever."

"I can't believe that she would agree to help you," said Bradicus. "You attacked her, stabbing her with the only thing that could penetrate her armor: her tooth."

"Oh, believe it, my friend, then I will have her fly one way into the frozen vortex with Arune where'll you'll be imprisoned for as long as I want." He nodded at Jinnamon.

Jinnamon's eyes narrowed, her mouth opening.

"Jinnamon, you don't have to do this; we can help each other," Blackjack said.

She lunged forward, snatching Bradicus in her mouth and swallowing, arching her head back then forward. She burped and looked at Rodark.

Rodark cocked his head. "Well then, that was easy, almost took the fun out of it. Now I have

everything." Dismounting Luther, he took the few steps to retrieve his saddle. Bending down, he gripped the saddle at each end and turned, stepping toward Jinnamon. "You haven't said much since you landed. You didn't chew, right? Just swallowed him, right?"

"I didn't chew him."

Rodark turned toward Luther to see a charging black spirit horse. "Damn, where did it get that cool- looking purple unicorn head horn?"

He dropped the saddle to fight the charging horse. "I can jump out of the way." He felt the horn slide through his hands, penetrating his chest and exiting via his spine.

"Holy shit, direct hit." Rodark propped himself up with the help of the horn. Looking down, he said, "This can't be happening. I'm losing my elder brick spirit-dust to the ground."

He looked at the canvas bag draped across Luther. "Shit, my elder brick. It still flows in her veins." Looking at Jinnamon, he pointed. "Help me get that bag. Quick."

Jinnamon approached, stopping ten feet short of Rodark.

"Don't stop now. Help me," he said, swinging at her. "And maybe I won't cut you up for fish bait."

Jinnamon gripped the courtyard floor with her talons, her body freezing and her eyes changing from a dazzling jade green to white.

Rodark watched as her body color changed from burnt orange to cinnamon. "You're not Jinnamon."

The cinnamon-colored dragoon tilted her head back with her mouth wide open, her belly armor plates beginning moving as if they had a mind of their own. An internal locking device had been activated.

Her dragoon armored plates zigzagged in an assortment of patterns.

Spinning clockwise and counterclockwise, the clicking clatter of the dragoon plates echoed off the fortress walls each time the armor moved, intensifying to one continuous high-pitched hum, then stopping.

The cinnamon-colored dragoon lowered her head and opened her eyes, the belly drop door opening. Stepping back, Luther jerked his horn out of Rodark's chest.

He fell to the ground and looking up, watched in disbelief as Bradicus exited the belly drop door with sword in hand. "How in the hell did you get the belly door to open? No way."

"Because this is not Jinnamon," said Bradicus. "The one you attacked and put under some kind of death spell is still in the observation chambers. This is Cinnamon, her twin sister, an ally of mine.

Surprise. I purchased her from Killamore, just a few days ago. Surprise again."

"That can't be," said Rodark. "I have control of her."

Bradicus walked up to Rodark's saddle, thrusting the brother's sword through it, pinning it securely to the stone courtyard.

"Now, that's not going anywhere, but you my dark enemy, you are certainly going somewhere."

Rodark managed to get to his knees, holding his chest. "I can't repair myself. Your horse and that damn horn. Where did you get the brother's sword?"

Bradicus didn't answer. He simply retrieved a jar from his shoulder bag, removing the seal and sitting it on the ground next to the saddle.

Rodark shook his head no. "What are you going to do with that?"

Bradicus reached into his bag and removed a small leather sack of screamer's dust, and emptying the powder on the saddle and sword, they both burst into flames.

Roko yelled out, "No, Bradicus! No, you're burning my saddle, my connection to Reaper. You will destroy our connection."

Bradicus retrieved a small object from his pocket, holding it for Rodark to see. "Do you know what this is?"

"No, but I have a feeling you're going to tell me."

"This is a death whistle. It usually hangs on a specific branch of the soul tree, deep in the heart of Grimmbell."

"What does it do?" inquired Rodark.

"It is going to make things right again. All I have to do is blow it."

"I have never heard of a death whistle. You are stalling for Kula to drop from the sky to help you." Bradicus walked up to Luther, removing the canvas bag from the saddle horn.

"That's mine," yelled Rodark. "I took Brazel. I own him. You weren't strong enough to keep him."

Bradicus untied the bag, laying it by the burning saddle. Reaching into his chest pocket, he produced a leather wrap with Kula's seal. He broke the seal and recited the command.

"Roko the Dark. You forfeit the privilege to live, work, and be prosperous in the Darkan Territory, Valley of the Tomb Sleepers, by the authority invested in me. With granted powers from the Queen of Darkan and with the support of the high council members of Grimmbell, we are in agreement that you be entombed in Woodford's tunnel of free radical spirits till we determine otherwise.

"So be it. Signed, Queen Kula."

Rodark lay on the ground, grinning. "That doesn't mean anything," he said, looking up to the sky. "Bradicus, don't do this. We were friends not that long ago."

Bradicus hesitated, holding the whistle at his lips. "I'm sorry for my real friend, Roko the earther. I know you are in there somewhere, and maybe I can set you free someday."

Bradicus blew the death whistle as hard as he could. Rodark screamed, covering his ears.

A cloud of white mist erupted from the jar, transforming into Woodford along with two burly spirit hunters.

Woodford picked up the jar, pointed to Rodark and handed it to the hunter spirits. "Take him now."

Bradicus watched as the hunter spirits leaned down in front of him, blocking his view. He heard a hissing and spitting noise, then nothing.

The hunter spirits turned around with the sealed jar, handing it to Woodford. Woodford turned toward Bradicus, holding the jar at chest level.

"He's really in there. Forever?" said Bradicus.

Woodford gave a slow nod, holding the jar against his ear. "Yes, Bradicus, they are in here."

"You mean Roko, my friend the earther, is still alive in that jar together with Roko the Dark?"

"For now, they both exist in this jar, but be aware that Roko the Dark has the advantage of Arune's power. Don't know how long your friend will survive."

Bradicus nodded. "Maybe someday, we can get him out."

"Maybe," said Woodford. "We need to go, I have to make sure the jar is placed properly in the tunnel, you understand?"

"Of course, I understand."

Woodford stepped in between the two burly hunter spirits, each spirit reaching under the armpit of Woodford, and they slowly melted into a misty essence haze and vanished.

Chapter 36: The End of it All

Bradicus watched Reaper wandering the courtyard cobblestones inside the Dark Stone Fortress and turned his attention to Luther.

"I'm shocked he hasn't bolted out the front gate. I wonder if the horse is looking for Rodark, or possibly new prey, a new rider?"

"Excuse me, Bradicus." With a tug on his hand, Bradicus jerked to attention, looking down to see Ella lightly covered in reddish tar, holding the elder blood brick.

"Ella, are you okay?"

"I'm okay. Actually, feeling years younger, recharged even. I'm assuming you want this back?" she asked, pushing the brick toward him. "Take it; it's heavy."

Bradicus took the brick from Ella, holding it against his chest. "The elder brick? How and when did you get your hands on it?"

"When you blew the whistle."

"When I blew the whistle?"

"That's right," said Ella. "When you blew the whistle, it caused some type of reaction inside my body."

"What about Brazel?"

"Never mind all this. What about us moving away from that smoking saddle?"

Bradicus gathered the reins of Luther, guiding his horse to a nearby stone pillar. Ella followed. "Will this work?" asked Bradicus.

"This will work."

He handed Ella a rag to wipe her face.

Bradicus sighed. "What happened to Brazel because he's not with me?"

"When you blew the whistle, it felt like a million pebbles of sand started to dissolve and leave my stomach. That's when I watched Brazel's soul leave me and filter into the elder blood brick."

"Of course, the elder blood brick cleaned Brazel out

of you and then filtered him into the blood brick. Oh shit," he said, pressing the brick hard against his chest. "Brazel is in the elder brick. I can feel him and don't think he wants to be inside that particular energy source."

"In the brick?" said Ella. "Can you still talk to him?"

Bradicus' shoulders slumped, his mouth falling open. "No, I can't."

"Why did he want Brazel so bad?"

"I'm not sure what the end result was going to be, but I figured he wanted Brazel's advanced understanding of magic and to incorporate me into his own power cell to help him rule Grimmbell and do whatever else he wanted with the power of the elder brick."

Ella finished wiping her face and started cleaning her arms. "This stuff doesn't come off very well and it stinks of old blood and bones."

"Yes, well, it's a very old mix of blood brick and black spirit tar that's stuck in your hair." Bradicus eyed his attention to Cinnamon who hadn't moved an inch. "Is she breathing? Is she alive? How in the hell am I going to fix her?"

Ella poked Bradicus in the butt. "Do you hear that?"

He perked up, spinning in a circle, frantically searching the courtyard with his eyes.

"There," said Bradicus, pointing at the north wall. "Something is coming through the wall." Grabbing Ella by the hand, he led her behind the stone pillar. "Stay here. Don't move," he said, handing her the elder brick. "Don't lose this." He then stormed off toward Luther.

Bradicus mounted Luther, leaning into his ear. "Luther, we won, and you have your freedom, but I need you one more time, okay?" Luther stomped his right hoof.

Bradicus pulled his sword, trotting toward the north wall.

A cloud of dust circled wildly, partly blocking the view of the wall. Bradicus sat at attention, waiting.

The cloud of dust slowly vanished, showing a whirling opening of a portal. "It must be a black spirit rider coming for Reaper, or to battle me again?"

Bradicus squeezed his legs, twisting his feet in the stirrups, gripping the reins and sword tighter. "Come out and fight to your death."

Kula's head poked out of the portal. "Ah, there you are."

Bradicus relaxed his body. "Kula, my Queen, what are you doing here?" Kula exited the portal with a rider on her back.

"Rasp convinced me to come here."

Bradicus looked up to see Rasp sitting comfortably on Kula's back, holding a bag of screamer's dust. "You used the screamer's dust?" said Bradicus.

"I thought I would try it out," said Kula.

"What did you think of it?"

Kula lowered her head to the ground as Rasp stepped onto the courtyard. "It's okay, but I would rather fly. Where are Roko the Dark and the brick?"

"Rodark is in a jar. Woodford is taking him to the tunnel."

"And the brick?"

Bradicus looked over his shoulder. "Ella has it; she's hiding behind that pillar."

Kula looked at Rasp. "Go get the brick. I believe a Grimmbell celebration is in order for your victory today."

"I'm not sure if I deserve a celebration, my Queen."

"Why is that?" She sneaked a peek at Cinnamon. "What is wrong with her?"

Bradicus turned his horse, facing Cinnamon. "I think I broke her. She hasn't moved since I exited her belly."

"What else is bothering you?"

"Brazel is gone."

"What do you mean by *he's gone?*"

"Rodark used Ella and pulled Brazel out of me via the elder brick, filtering him back into Ella. When I blew the death whistle, his energy was transformed into the elder brick. He's gone and that's not all."

"What else?" said Kula.

"I can't change to Blackjack without Brazel. I really don't know if I can be your royal messenger without him."

Ella stepped between Kula and Bradicus. "I have the elder blood brick," she said, holding the brick out in front of them. "And with the Great Hall's master recipe book and a little mix of my new variety of earther survival ball, I can return Brazel to Bradicus, I hope."

Kula leaned down to Ella. "Get on my back and keep that brick real close."

Kula sat quietly for a few seconds. "I do believe I have someone who can fix both those problems."

"Who might that be?" said Bradicus.

Kula looked over at the portal. "He should be coming out soon. He was a little behind us."

Bradicus stared at the portal. "But I don't see anyone."

"He should be…*there* he is."

"Cremator, how are you doing? You have a new set of hands."

Cremator nodded with a smile. "Yes, I'll be needing them back, but I'm alive because of you and Jinnamon."

Bradicus leaned down, scowling. "How was it being inside the belly of a dragoon?"

"That's for another time and place," said Cremator.

"Can you help me get Brazel back?"

"I don't know. We have our hands full, don't we?"

"At the moment, I do. I need to take Luther back to Luxen," said Bradicus. "However, I did promise Luther he would be released if we defeated Roko the Dark."

"That's between you and Luxen," said Kula. "And don't forget about Ella. I'm sure she wants to go back to her home. I can have a fighter dragon take her anywhere she wants to go and another dragoon to shadow Bradicus to Grimmbell."

"That would be great," said Bradicus.

Kula nodded her head. "Okay, that's what we are going to do. Bradicus rides Luther back to Grimmbell. You and Luxen figure out what you are going to do with the black spirit horse. I will have Cremator assist Cinnamon back to Grimmbell. Ella and Rasp can figure out how to pull Brazel out of the elder brick."

"That sounds like a plan," said Bradicus.

"We have unfinished business to take care of," said Kula "We will meet back at Grimmbell in three days. I need to plan an official celebration for the capture of Roko the Dark. Rasp and Ella need an elder blood brick filtering ritual to get Brazel back to Bradicus. We have to resolve

Arune frozen in a portal, stuck in the middle of Grimmbell, and I need to assemble Cremator and Grimmbell's high council to resolve the order of the releasing ceremonial ritual."

Suddenly, Bradicus cried out, dropping to his knees with his hands tightly pressed against his ears. "Bradicus, what is it?" Kula asked.

"I hear the screams of a black spirit horse rider."

Afterwords

As Frank-no-pants would say about this adventure "it is what it is."

Thank you so much for reading Grimmbell, Riders of the Black Spirit Horses. If you enjoyed my novel, I'd be grateful if you could spread the word by leaving a short review on Amazon.

Be on the lookout for book two of the series.

R.R. Duneman

www.ingramcontent.com/pod-product-compliance
Lightning Source LLC
Chambersburg PA
CBHW030742310726
48969CB00005B/1287